J. O'H. COSGRAVE II

COMPANIONS
OF THE LEFT HAND

BOOKS BY GEORGE TABORI

Beneath the Stone
Companions of the Left Hand

George Tabori

COMPANIONS
OF THE LEFT HAND

 Houghton Mifflin Company Boston 1946

The Riverside Press Cambridge

The characters in this book are ficti-
tious; any resemblance to real persons
is wholly accidental and unintentional.

The Riverside Press
CAMBRIDGE · MASSACHUSETTS
PRINTED IN THE U.S.A.

To My Father

And the companions of the right hand (how happy shall the companions of the right hand be!) shall have their abode among lote-trees free from thorns, and trees of mauz loaded regularly with their produce from top to bottom; under the extended shade, near a flowing water and midst fruit in abundance, which shall not fail, nor shall be forbidden to be gathered: and they shall repose themselves on lofty beds. . . . And the companions of the left hand (how miserable shall the companions of the left hand be!) shall dwell amidst burning winds, and scalding water, under the shade of a black smoke, neither cool nor agreeable. . . .

The Koran
The Chapter of the Inevitable

COMPANIONS
OF THE LEFT HAND

The Journey

The fly crawled north on the window-pane; the train moved south, but the fly knew nothing of north or south: there was a speck of dust it tried to move when the traveller, his face pink, his hair white, struck suddenly down with that morning's *Giornale d'Italia*, squashing the fly. Two tiny limbs remained on the window, wriggling; the rest was smeared on the top of an item about the stock exchange. The traveller looked at the window ruefully, at the rain beyond and at the newspaper; and all this made him think of death. Meanwhile, the train crossed the last viaduct before leaving the hills: now the Famous View was to appear, so familiar to him from previous journeys; the unexpected slope with the sea swimming into the framework of the forest on the left and the grey hill with the frowning mass of the Abbey on the right; after eight hours of travelling, the sea at last, peaceful and without much consequence, robbed of its eternity by the near shore of the bay. This was the spot where fathers used to rush their families to the window, raise the children high and, pointing, cry, 'Look — San Fernando!' with satisfaction that the glossy posters of the travel agents and the celebrated postcards someone had sent long ago were true to life, after all.

But the traveller, huddled on the plush seat, was thinking of death; not of the hooded skeleton with his scythe, nor of the word, empty and alien in itself, although some distant uncertainty inside him vibrated, saying, perhaps,

'Tod.' It was a feeling, vague and melancholy, of one day not being there any more; of unfinished business, of the grasping movement, the kicking of legs of someone drowning; a feeling of no more sun and warmth and cigars and cognac. It was like a vacuum; as if he had crossed a border, some imaginary line between darkness and light, waiting to leave something behind and arrive somewhere else; but there was no movement forward or back and he felt stuck between two worlds despite the steady, rattling progress of the train.

Outside, a solitary olive tree stood in the centre of a meadow, all by itself, old. The traveller remembered the tree. Last time he had passed here he had watched the tree receding. Now he leaned forward to look after it and he waved and caught himself doing so, and did not think it was funny, this waving. The feeling of death persisted. He listened to his pulse under the silk cuffs and imagined a hospital bed, a nurse, himself with sunken cheeks, bottles, pills, pain. Somewhere in a black-framed announcement there was his name, 'Stefan Farkas,' with a cross and a date, a phrase, an appreciation. In an empty room his clothes hung forlorn; on scented shelves stood silk shirts and lonely ties were stacked up in a drawer. His shoes, too, waited for relatives and servants and the dust grew thick on top of his books. From then on he would be 'late lamented': his name struck off registers, erased from files and accounts, and the postman named Coberl would come never again. In a dark flat, his crippled brother would be sitting, unable to express grief, a pale woman — Anna — crying in her bed silently, and Gizella, in smart mourning, would sniff discreetly, making pious eyes at a Madonna.

For him there would be darkness, deep and bottomless, nothing to know and feel ever again; not even nothingness for him, although he could somehow imagine himself stretched in a wooden box six feet under the modest limestone monument erected by grateful friends. There lay Stefan Farkas. Only he would be no longer Stefan nor Farkas. He composed an epitaph, 'He tickled a weary world,' and it made him sad and restless. He tried to get rid of this sudden attack of anguish and death: he touched the plush seat, breathed deeply, told himself disconnected words of magic and comfort and finally took out his wallet to see if his return ticket was there. It was.

He lowered the window and let the warm smell of rain come in. Ten years ago, he remembered, in a Karlsbad bathroom his heart had suddenly stopped for a second or so, and, as he was groping for the cold, tiled wall, he had told himself that he had started to die. That was ten years ago and he was still alive and in ten minutes' time he would arrive at his destination, San Fernando, the elderly summer resort on the Adriatic. He was going there because he felt lonely and ousted elsewhere in Europe. He was going to recover strength and self-confidence, he hoped, and get rid of disgust and fear. It was summer, and his cigar half-smoked was pulling well. The corn on his left toe hurt him no more, but the tiny blister on the tip of his tongue was still painful whenever it touched his lower front tooth. The porcelain crown, made by a dentist in Vienna, on his canine tooth was somewhat loose, and above it an old abscess throbbed and tasted sour whenever he sucked in his lips. The edge of his silk collar felt cool under his double chin, his shoulder-blades ached because of fatigue, and when he rubbed his right thumb and index finger together, they felt dry. Evidently he was alive and well despite nicotine in his lungs, glucose in his veins, the war, Gizella, impending senility, and a thousand other sources of pain. Yet for the second time that day he felt as if the train were a hearse.

Inside his breast pocket, next to the pigskin cigar case, in his wallet were a few thousand lire in cash and more in cheques; a passport which said 'aged 55,' and that he had no special marks — no scar, no mole, no missing finger; a letter from A. written in 1919 which he had kept for over twenty years as a mascot, a letter with a poem which said: 'Be he cursed who'd step into my place.' In an outside pocket he had six English pennies, for he liked to jingle with small change. In the luggage rack opposite him there were two small, elegant suitcases, covered with coloured hotel labels, some torn and battered, all reminding him of nights he had spent alone or in futile attempts to return to the womb. Inside those cases were shirts, suits, socks, brushes, the *Thoughts of Blaise Pascal,* a writing-pad, Yardley lavender, two bottles of pills, two hundred Corona cigars and somewhere, crumpled, a letter from Gizella, his mistress. 'Dear Stefan, I feel as if you were going away for good.' Outside, beyond the two tiny legs of the late lamented fly, it rained warmly, softly, over cypresses and graves, epitaphs, crosses, weedy gardens, decrepit churches, and over the sea it rained too. He flicked his cigar out of the window; it fell on wet grass and its glow died at once. The conductor, a small, dirty man, unshaven, with a gold-tooth smile, came in and said, 'San Fernando — next stop.' The traveller said nothing.

The Arrival

The station was wet and deserted when the train arrived. A few peasant boys, dark and dirty, gaped behind the gate. An old porter shuffled along the train, waiting for someone to get off. No one rushed forward with chocolate, peppermint, oranges, or peanuts as in the old days, and there were no tanned young women, slightly bulging under their print summer frocks, waiting for their men who would come from the city for the week-end. Since the war the sunny though old-fashioned gloss of San Fernando had faded. No fathers came with pale children and dishevelled wives, no young couples, hardly able to wait to get to the cool, vaulted bedrooms of the old Regina or the cream-coloured comfort of the Paradiso. 'The place has grown bald,' Farkas noticed. But Antonio was there.

He stood in front of his office on a meticulously selected spot (three yards due west of the urinal) in his smart uniform, saluting firmly, glaring at the train with stern features. His boots shone dully through the rain; he looked heroic on the deserted platform, not unlike the Roman Soldier of Pompei, a monument to duty. His moustache was thinner, Farkas thought, than when he had seen him last, seven years ago. Above him at the second-floor window sat leaning on her bony elbow his wife, Signora Clara, a small, thin woman with an enormous pile of hair set in elaborate and oily braids and waves, rather terrifying. She always sat there when the Northern Express arrived, watching Antonio taking the salute and the train emptying out the screaming, pushing mass of limbs, bags and children. People wouldn't notice her as she sat there, rather like a freak miniature, framed by two strips of lace curtains and some yellow flowers in pots. But Farkas knew her, of course, and once made up a story about her, embroidered with a triangle (station-master-wife-dining-car waiter), stressing the contrast presented by the static station and the international dash of a Wagon Restaurant. He has never written the story, but he remembered Signora Clara, and as he stepped down from the train, he looked up and slightly lifted his hat.

No one else was getting off at San Fernando, and Antonio looked increasingly heroic. Farkas told the old, apparently deaf porter that his luggage should be taken to a carriage and thence to the Hotel Paradiso. There was some argument, as the old man did not get it right and kept saying, mysteriously, 'No sun today, no sun today.' Finally the train pulled out and rumbled away in the rain, and Antonio, relaxing his heroic salute, walked over to Farkas, with dignity, to help him. He recognized Farkas at once and became agitated. 'Ah, Signor Farkas,' he said, clicked his heels and saluted. 'Welcome to San Fernando.' The last remark was accompanied by a wide gesture suggesting, 'Come to my chambers, Your Excellency,' and followed by a torrent of violent words directed at the porter, who argued back. Farkas became irritated. He hated travelling for more than three or four hours, and wanted to get to his room at the Paradiso to take a hot shower and rest before dinner. While the argument proceeded, with Antonio pointing alternately at suitcases, at Farkas, and in the vague direction of the sea, Farkas saw some empty paper bags swept by the wind along the tracks.

At last Antonio settled his argument with the old porter, who spat into his palms, lifted the suitcases, and staggered outside. Antonio politely accompanied Farkas, joining his hands behind his arched back. 'And how is the big city these days?' he inquired with interest; just as in the old days. Antonio despised cities because year after year he saw their people arriving pale, sick, and harassed, and deduced from it that San Fernando must be definitely superior. Farkas, tired and chilly, mumbled an answer and scrambled hurriedly into a carriage that stood on the square behind the station. Then they were off, and he could lean back, drawing his scarf closer around his neck, for it was getting colder as they neared the sea. The driver, who kept growling at his small, emaciated horse, wore a greasy black hat, no collar, and stank of wine.

They were driving down the old road, which at first seemed quite unchanged after seven years. This old main road curved down, from the high ground where the station stood under the vineyards, to the main square; it was lined with lime trees and some quiet villas, hidden by unkempt and lush gardens with high walls. To the left were the romantic woods with wild, dark bushes where the poorer inhabitants and the younger holiday-makers went to make love. There was no one in the street for quite a while, but later, as the carriage approached the curve where by the church the road took a sharp turn to the left, two women came walking, in large raincoats, holding umbrellas. It was very quiet, this drive: no hooting, no loud-speakers, no screaming children. It pleased Farkas, and he thought of the long rest he was going to have; he closed his eyes.

Then, amidst more growls from the driver, they turned. The gardens ended and they came to the shops and the hotels. Farkas looked out for the old Café on the right; he remembered its hot chocolate and whipped cream, the *croissants* and the little fat waitress, the concrete terrace which looked across a gap in the back yards to the sea. It was closed, he noticed, and he leaned back again, buttoning up his check travelling-coat, for they were about to arrive. There were some more people in the street.

It has become shabbier and older, San Fernando, he decided. Perhaps it was the rain; perhaps, as he explained to himself later, he too had become shabbier and older. There were cracks on the yellow limestone walls of the Regina that he felt sure were not there before. The trees looked as if they had got there by mistake and were apologizing for it. Then the sky itself, with torn clouds, bathed in gloom, was reflected by the Main Square. Farkas knew, of course, of old that it was foolish to return to a place, or a woman, after a long absence. The old emotions were gone; and what was once filled with a glow now stood an empty shell. 'Like a dish the waiter has forgotten to clear away,' he thought, and sniffed. An old man, unshaven, in pyjamas, leaned out of a window as they drove up to the Paradiso. Once he had walked under that window with Daniel, coming from the woods where they had been playing tennis.

Entry and Remembrance

Farkas never just walked into a place; he made an entry. This was inevitable; in Vienna, Prague, or Budapest he

was too well known to be ignored. 'Ah, der Farkas!' people sighed, and turned, slightly excited, as Farkas entered,
immaculately and nonchalantly dressed, his beautiful
white hair shining. He knew, of course, that he had
reached that final stage of fame when no one bothered
about his Christian name and most people recognized him.

His entry into the lounge of the Paradiso was something
of an anticlimax. He felt like Lohengrin walking on into
the wrong set — the *Merry Widow* perhaps. For one thing,
the lounge was in semi-darkness; the lights were not on
yet. There was hardly anybody sitting at the tables facing
the swing door. Farkas vaguely saw three uniformed men
in the background and an elderly woman walking upstairs.
In the centre of this gloomy emptiness stood Fritti, waiting for Farkas; he switched on the old Fritti smile, and
like a respectable sea-lion toddled towards the visitor.
'*Mon cher Signor,*' he cried, '*quel plaisir!*' He has grown
older and shabbier, too, Farkas thought; so has everybody
else.

Fritti was an enormous man; everything about him
seemed outsized: his shaggy eyebrows, his purple nose, his
hands, his voice, his belches. Farkas had a theory that
Fritti was designed by Providence to be twins, but was
eventually born, by mistake, a double portion of a man.
Farkas never felt comfortable in his presence: Fritti surrounded one with his bulk and gestures and voice, and one
felt walled in. In addition, Fritti had some rigorous ideas
about a hotel manager's proper attitude, which included
a certain baroque charm — lithe and esoteric — which did
not quite fit him. There was the smile, for instance: sweet
like that of a Biedermeier girl. He switched it on and off

smoothly and automatically, and as the years passed it grew on him like an extra limb. When he smiled, his vast face was screwed up into many double chins and little cushions of fat and looked like a lunar landscape. Then his hands: Farkas was fascinated by Fritti's hands, wrinkled and large like elephant ears.

'Happy days are here again!' Fritti chatted, flapping his large hands gracefully; then taking Farkas's elbow, led him towards the reception desk. 'San Fernando feels very honoured. Twenty-nine!' he snorted in an aside to a sleepy bell-boy who stood by in a greasy, once-white uniform. 'Your old room.' Fritti switched on the smile. 'The same old room. And the same Signor Farkas. You haven't changed a bit.'

'No?' asked Farkas.

'Not a bit.' Fritti enveloped him in a vast smile. 'You remember Enrico?'

'Good evening, Signor Farkas,' the hall-porter said. 'Welcome. '

'Good evening, Enrico,' Farkas said. 'Of course I remember him.'

Enrico, too, looked shabbier. He was a small, very bald man with tired, inflamed eyes. He could hardly have grown much balder, Farkas thought; he was so very bald seven years ago. But his neck was scraggier above the winged collar, and his eyes redder. Enrico had stood behind the desk, like this, when Farkas had come with Gizella. How they looked at each other, and both remembered Gizella. 'I must write to her,' Farkas thought, and took his key.

'Well, how is the Paradiso?' he asked as Fritti took him to the lift, gliding along.

'Oh, well,' said Fritti, and switching off the smile, said 'Second' to the lift-man, whom Farkas did not remember. 'Oh, do not ask me, *mon cher ami.*' The smile was on again, and Fritti's eyes turned towards the ceiling. 'This war will never end, it seems. It is terrible for us — we need peace. Part of my staff has gone to war, the food has gone to war, the clients have gone too. I would have closed the shop, but the Government begged me not to.' The lift made a buzzing noise. 'Ah, Signor Farkas, do you remember the old times?' He blew himself up. 'The old times, the beautiful women, the food, the lighting effects, the Prince Valona with his kidneys and the Bishop of Siena, bless him?' The lift stopped. 'Everybody who mattered came. They will come again, Maestro, won't they?'

Farkas could not let it go. 'Only they won't matter any more.'

Fritti first looked surprised; there was a vast movement of double chins and fat cushions; then, as if realizing his duty, he started to laugh. 'Yes, that's true,' he said; then, abruptly, the smile was gone. 'Here we are,' Fritti said, and opened the lift door.

Farkas told him he wanted to dine in his room. Then he was left alone, and he walked up and down for a while, looking at the large double bed, old-fashioned, brass, the little escritoire by the window, the table, the wine-red armchairs and the bulky cupboard. He went into the bathroom and switched on the light; walked to the mirror, inspecting his face. Then he returned and stepped out onto the balcony. Beneath, the square was getting dark. Above the crowns of the trees he saw the loggias of the Sanatorium, the tall chimney of the Turkish Baths, and to the right the yellow limestone walls of the old Regina. There was a man walking across the square; Farkas tried to recognize him, but couldn't. The rain had stopped, and for the first time he smelt the sea. There were some voices from below, from the covered terrace of the restaurant which sent a modest light out onto the square. The Honourable Don Teofilo might be there, playing chess with Father Giuseppe or Doctor Schmidt. Perhaps he should not have come, Farkas now thought. San Fernando looked so shabby; a sad place to be lonely in. Someone next door drew a curtain.

This was the old room, Twenty-Nine; it knew so many secrets he had half-forgotten — almost like the old flat at home. When they came for the first time, with heaps of unnecessary luggage and a governess named Julie, Father was still alive; but he couldn't remember that time except for Father slapping his face because he did not say good morning to somebody. Then, one summer, just the two brothers came, Daniel and he, superior and critical, with books and tennis rackets. The mornings felt wonderful; the clean, fresh sun and the friendly touch of white linen on their warm bodies as they went to play tennis by the sea and thence to the old-fashioned bathhouse; long, fat lunches on the cool terrace of the Paradiso with some old waiter fussing around them; the first cigarettes smoked hurriedly in the woods and the first glass of black coffee, which made Daniel sick so that he had to hold his head over the bathtub. Those were warm days. Daniel was so handsome in his white jersey and linen slacks, his fair locks unruly.

One morning they sat on the Corso, resting after tennis;

Stefan Farkas could still feel the wind that came from the vineyards. Then a woman passed, a small woman with peroxide hair and large protruding eyes, walking down the Corso. Daniel turned after her.

'That's a whore,' Stefan explained, knowing well that Daniel had no idea what the word meant.

'Ha, yes,' Daniel agreed, and blushed.

'Did you meet any in Vienna?' Stefan went on sadistically.

'Oh, well, a few,' Daniel said.

'Come on, Daniel; do you really know what whore means?'

Daniel started to spin his racket around, his gaze rigid, his ears aflame. 'Of course I do,' he said.

'Well, what does it mean?' Stefan enjoyed his triumph.

'Oh, well,' Daniel swallowed hard; then aggressively: 'What do you mean, cross-examining me? Of course I know what it means'—

'All right, what?' Stefan insisted.

'Well,' Daniel said, 'we call it differently.'

Stefan poked his ribs and laughed. 'Differently? You can't call it differently.'

'Oh, yes, you can,' Daniel was stubborn. 'We call it *walda.*'

'You call it what?' Stefan asked, suspiciously, uncertain for a moment whether Daniel was fooling him or really knew.

'*Walda,*' Daniel said triumphantly. 'Just *walda.* Of course you wouldn't know it. You haven't been in Vienna for so long.'

Later, at night, long after they put out the light and

Stefan was half-asleep, Daniel turned to him and whispered. 'Stefan,' he said, 'Stefan, I told you a lie.'

'Leave me alone,' Stefan said; 'I want to sleep.'

'No, Stefan, this is important,' Daniel said. 'Very important. There is no such word as walda and I have no idea what a whore is, Stefan. What is it?'

Then there was the However Game; they played it the following summer; or was it two summers later? Daniel was sixteen, Stefan eighteen: Daniel was even better-looking and taller, and his shyness made him popular with the girls. They were great friends that summer: they would even walk arm-in-arm, and Daniel punched the little French boy's nose for calling Stefan 'fat pig.' True, he did look rather like a pig, with his short neck and snub nose and pink face. Every afternoon at six they would elaborately dress, usually wearing the same things: white flannel trousers, and dark blue blazers, and a yachting cap, perhaps.

As they walked down from the Paradiso, with firm steps in unison, trying to look bored, cigarettes hanging from their lips, Stefan would start the However Game. He would say grimly: 'Here we are, two bronzed athletes, with extremely interesting profiles, dressed by Knize; we have come for a brief visit on our way to Monte Carlo. Our Alfa Romeos are waiting for us in the garage and our yacht is due to arrive at any moment, with Mary Pickford on board; there'll be a champagne dinner and an incredible orgy will ensue.'

Daniel started to giggle, waiting for the climax.

'And as we pass these miserable philistines,' Stefan went on, 'with elastic steps, a discreet murmur runs through

the impressed multitude. Who are those two young demi-
gods, they ask; especially the Pinelli-girls.'

He would stop, look at Daniel, and then simultaneously
they would shout 'However!' and Daniel would continue,
'However, the truth happens to be that here we are
two bow-legged, pimply-faced, thoroughly ridiculous
Rotzkerle, in miserably cut clothes that look as if we had
inherited them from a distant uncle, two insignificant
young men with bicycles instead of Alfa Romeos, a rowing
boat instead of a yacht, going for a miserably lonely walk
on the Corso while all the reasonably handsome girls are
having the time of their life in the woods. However,' he
repeated, and they laughed and slapped each other's backs,
and squinted at giggling young girls when they passed, and
spat on seeing a priest.

The Witness

*And then, standing in the dark room, almost inevitably
he remembered the night before he had left for San Fernando.* He had gone to say good-bye to Daniel and Anna.
Anna opened the door for him.

Stefan Farkas could not see her face clearly in the dim
corridor. It had always been dim, this corridor, with only
a faint light falling in through the painted windows of
the entrance door. He saw his own grey reflection in the
large mirror, and remembered how he had stood here one
day inspecting the pimple on his chin. He threw his hat
on a chair and took her arm.

'He is resting,' Anna said. 'At eight I'll take you to him. Will you have a cup of coffee?'

'No, thank you,' he said. 'I can't stay long.'

She opened the door to the study and they entered the semi-dark room. The curtains were drawn; a solitary ray of light came in through the folds, pointing to the desk that stood by the window. She stepped forward, and he heard her hand scratching on the wall; then the light was on, a pale, yellow light from the ceiling. She turned at last and Farkas saw her face clearly for the first time. She had not changed much since last time: it was the same quietly disciplined face, with the same embarrassed unhappiness she had always tried to hide from him and from everybody else. Her features were a trifle sharper and greyer. She had no make-up on this time, and the heart-shaped face was tinted with grey pallor; not an unhealthy greyness, but rather as if some years ago time had stopped one evening, and in a fine, powdery dust had settled on her face. As last time, her movements were cautious and tender; as then, now too she was sad in a beautifully tactful way.

She blushed as he inspected her, and turned her face. Her small, bony hand came up to touch her hair, self-consciously. 'Poor, dear Anna,' he thought, and she read his mind, but managed to look into his eyes at last.

'Sit down, Stefan,' she said.

As five years ago, there was the desk facing the curtains, with piles of books and typing paper, and the typewriter with the enormous keyboard he had already heard of; and as then, the small, square card-table stood in the centre of the room, covered with green baize, and with all the silly copper ash-trays Father had collected, and there were the three uncomfortable armchairs, and watching, like giants, the two tall, yellow bookcases with their glinting glass doors, cramping the room. Nothing seemed to have changed; it was the same room as when Father had died and Daniel had moved in with Anna. Father used to have his coffee here after lunch, sipping it loudly and dozing in the one comfortable easy-chair which was smuggled in between two bookcases, while he, Stefan, would sit by the desk reading a paper, and Daniel would smoke in silence. It was the same room: its colour and mood remained unchanged, with the same fine dusty gloom Anna's face showed. The light was never too good in here. Now, after five years, Farkas once more felt the unescapable resignation of the furniture that has been preserved with reverence; yet each piece looked forlorn and betrayed, and seemed to be waiting faithfully for something, perhaps for Father's resurrection. Farkas already regretted that he had come.

'How is he?' he asked.

Anna played with an ash-tray; a miniature imitation of the urinating boy of Brussels.

'Much the same,' she said vaguely. 'Much the same these last few years. When did you see him last?' she asked herself. 'Oh, yes, of course, five years, wasn't it? Or six?'

'Five,' Farkas said. 'He could hardly move then.'

'Yes,' she said, and fingered her hair again. 'He can't move at all now. He has got a new chair, and by day he sits there, his head propped up. Five years ago, you said? Let me see; he could move his head then, couldn't he; and he could speak and eat properly?'

'I didn't realize that it was as bad as that,' Farkas said.

'Bad?' She looked up. 'Yes, I suppose it must be bad. Though we have hardly noticed the change. It happened slowly, so very slowly. One by one the muscles became paralyzed; so very slowly. One morning — he could hardly speak then — he said: "Anna, my darling" (you know how polite he is), "Anna, my sweetheart, I don't think I can move my head any longer." Then, later much later, it spread to his jaw. The worst came when his tongue became affected. He loved to speak. Remember?'

'Yes, Anna,' Stefan Farkas said. I shouldn't have come, he thought. He hated nothing more than people who had the right to be pitied. Anna spoke in that quiet, vague voice that suited the room and her face. He knew she felt embarrassed at evoking pity and wanted to sound detached, as if Daniel were not her husband, but an historical event; something distant and impersonal.

'He had such a beautiful voice,' she went on. 'In the last few years he had read a good deal of poetry to me. Then it was gone. When exactly? You said you saw him five years ago — oh, I suppose it must have been a year or so later. One day he woke in bed and spoke to me with great difficulty, as if his tongue had gone numb or his throat got blocked. He could only squeeze out his words, and I called for the doctor. By evening it had got worse. The last thing he said, in a slow, painful groan was "Anna, my darling"; but he could only speak the vowels. Since then he has been silent.'

She looked quickly at him.

'Go on, dear,' he said.

'Oh, well,' she said, and her hand rose and fell. 'We had

to have this typewriter built for him. I wrote you about it, didn't I? He got used to it quickly; you know how marvellous he is, how marvellous!' Her hand came up to her eyes for a second. 'Now he just looks at a key and I press it for him. It only sounds difficult; the work goes quite quickly. We do about two hundred words a day.'

'That's quite a lot,' Farkas said, careful not to sound ironical.

She blushed again.

'For you it must sound terribly slow,' she said, raising her voice slightly. 'Didn't you write a *whole* play once in three days?'

So she remembers that, he thought.

'I suppose I did,' he replied. 'It was a terrible play too. How is Daniel's work getting on?'

She became quite agitated. 'Very well,' she said quickly. 'Very well indeed. The *Inferno* has been finished, and now he's well in the middle of the *Purgatory*. Oh, it's beautiful, Stefan, his translation, simply beautiful, much better than Babics. It's a new language, really, he makes up new words and uses old ones with a new shine; and he has that reverence and rhythm and richness that is Dante. Pauker saw the manuscript and was very excited and wanted to publish it as it is, but Daniel wouldn't let him until he had finished the whole.'

'When will he?' Farkas asked.

She answered, after a long pause, with a small laugh.

'Well, it depends,' she said. 'Five years,' she added with an uncertain gesture. 'Ten years.' She looked away from him. 'Never.'

She picked up the little Brussels boy again.

'It doesn't matter to him; or to me. He enjoys doing it, although he's often unhappy at not being able to read it aloud; and because work goes so slowly. But wasn't Beethoven deaf when he wrote the A Minor quartet? It doesn't matter. Everything moves slowly in this house; and nothing really matters now but the *Purgatory*.'

'You ought to go out sometimes,' he said. 'You look pale.'

'Oh, but I do go out,' she said quickly, and touched her hair again. 'With Pauker and other friends. I go for long walks on the Gellért Hill, and now that summer's here I go swimming.' She was lying. He knew she did not want to discuss herself.

'Is there anything special Daniel or you need?' he asked. 'I mean . . .'

She interrupted him.

'No, thank you, Stefan,' she said. 'You've been very kind — a really good brother to him. Daniel is very unhappy about your cheques. You know how he is. I wish I could do some real work, to make us less of a burden on you — but it is so difficult — I can't leave Daniel alone; also there is nothing I could really do; I'm quite useless.'

'You're the most wonderful woman in the world,' Farkas said. 'You ought to be canonized.'

'Why?' she said aggressively. 'I'm not.'

He rose and went over to her. Her face was flushed. He sat on the arm of her chair and took her cold hand.

'Yes, you are,' he said.

She drew away her hand. Her face was rigid.

'I like being married to a saint,' she said. 'I know what you're thinking. I saw you inspecting my face.' She looked up at him, sidewise. 'You think how pretty I was and how dull I am now, and you pity me. You mustn't. I'm all right. I live in comfort and I help Daniel; and he's the greatest man I know. We work together, and he is so very, very polite. Every morning when we start and his eyes begin jumping from key to key, he always makes me type first of all: "Good morning, Anna, my sweet." And he can look at me, you know; and there's nothing left to him but a loving mind and a pair of blue eyes, and when he looks at me he tells me more than Dante does. We have our private code, and his eyes can express all I want to know. And I read to him at night before going to sleep, and he closes his eyes and listens, and occasionally he looks at me. No one can look at me like that.'

No one, Farkas thought, and the old fear came back. I shouldn't have returned, he said to himself.

'But tell me about yourself,' she said abruptly. She left her hand in his. With her other hand she took from her pocket a handkerchief rolled into a ball; a small crumpled handkerchief, ancient symbol of feminine unhappiness. She dabbed her nose.

'Oh, well,' Farkas said. 'The old story, you know. Moving about. I'm on my way to Italy.'

'Italy?' she said; and it was hurting her.

'Yes, San Fernando,' he went on. 'I need a rest, and Switzerland is a greater bore than it ever was.'

'San Fernando?' she said. 'Always on the move, you are,' she added, like a reproachful mother. 'We read about the great success your new play was everywhere. I read some of the notices out to Daniel. He was very proud of you.'

Nonsense, he despises me, Farkas was thinking.

'San Fernando,' she said again, and smiled.

As he held her hand he knew she too was thinking that moment of San Fernando; of the summer they had spent there together, soon after the war; of Daniel sitting in his room with doctors pottering about him, and of the long sunny walks he and Anna had together; and the night they kissed and Anna said: 'If Daniel knew this . . .'

'Did you ever tell him?' he asked suddenly.

She wasn't surprised by his question.

'No,' she said, and made a pause. 'You must send me a postcard from San Fernando.' She drew her hand away. 'I'll go and wake him now.'

He rose and watched her get up with difficulty. Her figure hasn't changed either: the same bony, boyish Anna with modest breasts and hardly any hips. She put the handkerchief back into her pocket and touched her hair. 'He always looks me over most carefully,' she explained. 'There are cigarettes on the table, Stefan, help yourself.'

She stopped by the door.

'Oh, I must tell you,' she said. 'Don't be too light with him, or too grave either. He hates pretence. Pauker, when he came, used to burst with cheerfulness, as if Daniel had a rash, or a cold. It's of no use. He knows what the matter is.'

'Yes, I know,' Farkas said.

'Talk as much as you can,' she continued. 'He likes listening, and it gives him a rest. Talk about yourself and your plays and journeys and ask him about his work. Don't say how well he looks and that sort of thing; and please don't ask him if he needs anything.'

'I know,' Farkas said, somewhat impatiently.

'You don't mind, do you?' she said, and quickly opened the door and turned to look back at him for a second; then she was gone.

He stood hesitant for a moment, and as always when he had come here these last few years the same cramping feeling came over him as if he were small again. He resented coming here, to the old flat where they had grown up together and where life had stopped with Father's death and Daniel's terrible illness. It was like the past petrified; as if nothing had changed, nothing happened except the small, slow process of dying; as if the flat too had become lame and numb, part by part, like Daniel's body.

He walked slowly by the bookcases and occasionally leaned forward to try and read a title. The great encyclopaedia was still there and the classics bound in red; here the French books and the English; over there the German and the Spanish. Forty years ago he had stood here and reached for *Bouvard et Pécuchet* while Daniel was doing his homework; and leaning against the glass doors he had opened the book at random. He looked around: the room felt like a fossilized cross-section of the past, with samples of it swimming across his mind. Each chair and corner, the faint dust, the ash-trays, the carpet — all held a story; stories he would try to forget. There on the carpet Daniel and he used to build a stadium with Jules Verne's red volumes, with Rabelais serving as one goal and *The Penguin Island* as the other. He gazed at the carpet and saw the two of them quarrelling because he did not want to go on playing, and Daniel, so pretty and cherubic with his golden locks and large eyes, pale, but too proud to cry.

'Please, Stefan,' he would say, fingering the large black button he used for a centre-forward, 'one more game, please.'

Farkas walked on, touching the polished surface of the shelf, to inspect the many personal pictures on the wall by the tall tiled stove: the elongated photograph showing Father, grim, his head curiously distorted into an egglike shape, standing on the steps of Cologne Cathedral, with a mysterious little flag in his hand; a cartoon of Father by Kelen, depicting him half-naked, a halo around his head, fighting a duel with a hooknosed devil called 'Private Property'; portraits, of faded friends, a pilot with a big moustache and a leer whose name he couldn't remember, a demure actress with a tremendous bosom, dressed in luscious Victorian frills.

Here he had stood one morning waiting for Daniel, who was returning from the front. And then he came, in his over-sized, ill-fitting uniform, his neck thin and old, his ears standing out under the dirty forage-cap, walking heavily with the help of a cane, Father following with the kit-bag. Here by the square table Daniel had his first meal, and he observed how old Daniel had become, with his golden hair matted and dull and heavy pouches under his eyes. Daniel told him about his injury while Father listened and blinked his eyes, moved. And then the two of them had been left alone; he was standing here, under the portrait of the fat actress, near the tiled stove, conscious of his own pink, shaven face, his monocle, his silk shirt.

Daniel concentrated on his plate, cleaning it with a chunk of bread: his fingers were red and frostbitten and shaky. When he had finished, he looked up and said: 'Father told me about your new play. Sounds wonderful, a great success. What is it about?'

He answered uneasily: 'The usual triangle, you know.'

Daniel made a face as if he did not quite understand, but smiled politely and said: 'I wrote a few poems in hospital. Would you like to read them?'

'Certainly, Daniel,' he replied. 'But I must rush now — rehearsals, you know — but tonight, or tomorrow, perhaps.'

'Yes, of course,' Daniel said, and went pale as he did when asking, 'Please, one more game, Stefan.'

And there, in the one comfortable chair between the two bookcases, Daniel had sat, shrunken, frightened, just back from the first specialist, and Father stood leaning against the wall by the desk, under the dirty white bust of Beethoven, and Anna, red-eyed and so very pretty, knelt by Daniel. 'The leg will become stiff,' Father announced and there was silence. And another day Father was sitting by the desk and Daniel was resting in the bedroom, and Anna had just told him that she was going to marry Daniel. She wore a white dress, and Father listened to her quiet, embarrassed, defiant voice, his glasses glinting, and then asked, 'Stefan, what do you think?' and he looked at her. And both remembered how they had stood here once, so terribly long ago, when Daniel was still at the front and Father was in Vienna, here by the desk, naked and trembling because the room had grown cold, and how he had carried her into the bedroom. 'She will be a nurse, not a wife,' he had then answered. 'That makes no difference,' she had replied, angry and blushing.

And here, by the square table Father had talked to him shortly before his death. 'Daniel is sick and helpless, Stefan: you are rich and successful. You will help him without hurting him.' Father always stated his facts in the first sentence.

'Certainly,' Stefan had answered.

'Have you ever read his poems?' Father asked in a tired voice.

'Not yet, he hasn't shown them to me.'

Father looked at him. 'You know, Stefan,' he said, almost absent-mindedly, 'when Daniel was born, you asked me to throw him into the Danube.'

And every third month he sent Anna a cheque; each she acknowledged with a brief note. Sometimes she wrote a longer letter, an impersonal account dealing with Daniel, the weather, books she had read. Then, shortly before the war, he had arranged with his bank for the money to be sent direct. She did not write for some time; possibly she felt hurt at the new way of helping; only a coloured chit from the bank, no more cheques bearing Stefan's signature in small, pearl-like letters. And every time he passed through Budapest he would somehow pluck up courage, drink two or three double Martells and visit the old flat. It grew into a formality; they all knew it was one. Farkas would bring flowers and books or some junk he had picked up abroad for Daniel; then take his cup of coffee (he never stayed for a meal) and they would converse carefully as if afraid of spies. He tried to be funny or informative, tell them about his plays, tell an anecdote or two.

Anna enjoyed these brief visits, but Daniel just hummed and stared at him searchingly, waiting for some-

thing. It was this stare that irritated Farkas, those clear
eyes that seemed to have remained unaffected by twenty
years of pain, of the growing terror of paralysis. They
were clear, inquisitive eyes, expecting some long-sought
explanation from Farkas. Daniel would carefully inspect
his clothes, shoes, ties, and remark with irony how elegant
he was. And always there came the awkward moment
when Anna left them alone — either in the study or on the
ridiculous balcony over the courtyard; and there they sat,
the two of them, smoking and aware of the deepening
silence between them, a silence alive with some decisive
dialogue that was never spoken. They went on being impersonal; Stefan would speak of Hollywood or of his mild
diabetes; at the best he would remind Daniel of something
Father had said. Daniel would listen with his inquisitive,
slightly contemptuous eyes, talk rarely of his own work,
ask questions which would never have occurred to Stefan.
'Tell me,' Daniel would say suddenly, 'what do you think
of Mao-Tze-tung?' or 'Just had a letter from Maritain, do
you like him?' Farkas sometimes suspected his brother of
showing off, and would retort with one of his characteris-
tically vitriolic witticisms. At any rate, they had never
talked about themselves. When Stefan married his first
wife, Anna wrote a letter, very properly phrased and sin-
cere, saying that she hoped Stefan would soon bring his
wife to see them — which he never did. Caroline would
have frightened them.

One night they sat on the balcony (both Daniel's legs
were stiff now and he had his first wheel-chair); Anna had
left them, and they were silently smoking when Daniel
suddenly turned to him.

'Tell me, Stefan, do you remember the idea you once had for a book — *Grey Man,* or something of the sort?'

'Yes?' Stefan said cautiously.

'Well, why didn't you ever write it?' Daniel asked.

'Well,' Stefan said, and felt pleased, 'you know how it is. It was too *avantgardiste* — too original to sell. By the time I could afford to be original I didn't feel like it.'

'You know,' Daniel went on after a while, 'you know what's wrong with you?'

Farkas said: 'A lot. What in particular?'

'You never write about yourself,' Daniel went on, and his voice was eager and solicitous, and more intimate than it had been for a long time. 'What I mean is . . . '

But then Anna returned and said something, and the brief moment of contact was gone; it had never come back.

The last time he came on a visit, Daniel was already in a frightening condition, his face unnaturally white and smooth, his head getting bald, and his eyes so vigorous and active against the growing immobility of the body. He inquired with seemingly genuine interest about Stefan's latest play, but interrupted Farkas's account as soon as he had grasped the general theme.

'Brilliant,' he said, his eyes moving all the time as if to absorb a busy, violent scene all at once. 'But where do *you* come in?' he asked.

'I?' Stefan said suspiciously; then dismissed the question with a cynicism. 'I am the one who collects the royalties.'

Daniel ignored the remark. 'Where?' he repeated. 'That's what worries me. Are you the husband with his shallow jealousies, or the family doctor who burps wisdom and wit like a slot-machine emitting sweets, or the trembling youth — which one? I wouldn't recognize you in any of them; why the modesty? I'd like to know more about you — as the public and as a brother.' He coughed and went on: 'Also, all your characters are so well-off and so very nice; they never seem to think or go to the lavatory.'

Stefan was angry. 'Oh, yes, I know what you mean. You speak exactly like Rubin, that malicious rat of a critic. I'm not supposed to be real or true to life. Well, why should I be? I am contemptuous of reality; if you like, I use it as a potter uses clay, moulding it according to the spasms of my mind; a mind pickled in smoke, alcohol, and disbelief. Life is too finished and dreary, anyway. There is nothing I could add to it; only record, that is, imitate. And I have always hated the idea of plagiarism. As for the nice, rich people, well, why not? I prefer the upper depths, and Heaven help me from descending to the slums. Think of the critics, Daniel; they'd laugh themselves sick: Farkas getting senile, Farkas developing a social conscience, Farkas cashing in on "the people." Oh, no. Let me remain the light recorder of parlour and bedroom gossip, the polished clown, the grinning sage or whatever the critics usually call me. They have forgotten of course *The City Park* and *The Proud Goose,* those early relics. So have I. I have achieved a fine, glittering crust, and the poet that was Stefan Parkas has gently passed away.'

He was conscious of overexcusing himself. Daniel listened with widely open eyes.

Stefan sighed. 'Also, I'm far from being as witty as I used to be in the twenties; but then, the world too has lost its sense of humour. The audience doesn't chuckle any more these days — they just guffaw rather vulgarly. It has gone, that bemused smile in the stalls as if they and my actors shared a slightly erotic secret. Gone like so much else. I see Frederick died last Friday. You see, Daniel: people die nowadays who wouldn't have done so before.'

Daniel gave no answer, but waited like a judge; or rather like a witness who has seen a crime and hasn't decided yet whether to give evidence or not.

So Stefan went on: 'Oh, no, the past is obligatory. My characters, if you care to remember, mostly wear white ties or tiaras. Whenever I moved to the underworld, I felt like an Orpheus who had forgotten to put on his trousers. Oh, I know "my people" all right — without immodesty, Berta in *The City Park* is about the loveliest maidservant ever drawn — and my janitors, policemen, taxi-drivers — you remember Robert in *Big Business*? — are as convincing as my viscounts and generals and their fine ladies. But — who said it, Rubin or some other fool? — I wrote about the humble in a mood of benign charity. "Monsieur Farkas is again kind to the poor," someone in Paris once wrote. It's true I'm afraid, Daniel, but I can't change any more; neither can I wait for the poor to do so. I know I'm old-fashioned. My bedroom scenes are covered with the green dust of an antique shop. That's why I have really been dead for the past ten years.' He wanted to make Daniel feel sorry for him.

There was a slight noise in the next room which startled Farkas; he turned and waited. Somewhere a door opened with a creak, and Anna's voice said, 'Yes, dear, I'll take you to him.' Then a faint rumbling: the wheel-chair. Farkas retreated behind the square table, quickly lit a cigarette and faced the door, which slowly opened. Anna stood

there with a smile of encouragement. She opened the
double door widely and disappeared for a second. Slowly
the wheel-chair appeared, its front wheels with Daniel's
legs wrapped in a blanket. Anna pushed him to the centre
of the door, turned him suddenly and propelled the chair
into the study. The entry was sudden and dramatic.

While Stefan watched with fright and expectation, he
was aware of his own smile. He remembered Anna's warning, and tried to be natural and at ease. But what did
natural mean? How should a brother, distant, alien, a
mere visitor, behave when facing a completely paralyzed
saint. In the old days he had been able to keep his sense
of proportion by repeating to himself the medical name of
Daniel's illness: amyothrapic lateral sclerosis — it sounded
curiously comforting. But now he couldn't remember it,
and there was nothing to do but smile, highly conscious
of his smile, of his cheek muscles contracting, his lips opening, the tiny wrinkles fanning out by his eyes. He thought
of a stage instruction from one of his early plays: 'The
Vicomte flashes a smile.' *The Vicomte,* he thought,
Viscount, Markgraf, Örgróf.

It was a frank, pleasant smile, fit for many occasions:
receiving a dull producer, or soothing the calculated fits
of Gizella, his present mistress, or bewitching a difficult
wine-waiter. But he felt how ill it fitted the room, Daniel
and his wheel-chair. In the centre of the doorway, Anna
stopped for a second; perhaps a latent dramatic instinct
told her to do so, perhaps tact. There she stood behind
the wheel-chair, smiling like a faded masterpiece, stood
there fitting the flat, the chair, the evening, with a touch of
electric light from outside brushing the top of her hair,

smiling. Beneath her sat Daniel, now completely bald; a rigid, prehistoric idol with a colourless face. His stony features seemed ageless, as if time and pain had frozen them. His tongue, a straight fleshy line, showed between his thin lips and gave him the look of a fantastic idiot, a monster from a mad dream-world. Only his eyes were alive, clear and blue, full of articulate and exciting ideas; eyes that cried out for the help of grimaces, gestures, and a warm, many-shaded voice; eyes that stood so incredibly lonely in that stony face as if forgotten there, so alone and alien as if the face were just a mask behind which a cherubic, pretty Daniel made faces and laughed.

Slowly the chair rolled in. Farkas smiled and stepped forward. He heard his heart beating in his hollow chest. 'Oh, God,' he thought. 'How awful!' His smile remained on his face absent-mindedly. He tried to concentrate on Daniel's eyes; he feared Daniel would notice his horror if he kept his gaze on the bald skull or the distorted mouth. 'Does she ever kiss him?' he thought.

Daniel's eyes scrutinized Stefan's face, then quickly wandered to his suit, shirt, tie; then up again to the monocle. Stefan Farkas said: 'Daniel, dear, how grand to see you!' His voice trembled; those eyes, neither frightening nor 'searching,' were so terribly clear and wise, and one felt thoroughly helpless; much more so than ever before. The eyes contracted: it was a smile they gave, not a conventional smile of greeting, but a wise and pleasant smile, and it said: 'Hullo, Stefan, good to see you; you're very elegant and prosperous-looking and you haven't grown older and are obviously still the great international wit, writing literary Sulzberger Punches.' Yes, the eyes said all that; then they pointed to a chair.

Stefan glanced at Anna and she gave him a warning look.

He cleared his throat, pulled out his cuffs and patted his famous bow-tie. 'Well, Daniel,' he said, and sat down with friendly pomposity; 'I suppose it would be no use for me to pretend that I'm pleased about your state; I mean I know all about it — but all the same, I think you are doing marvellously well — after all, everything is relative, and if I were in your shoes I certainly couldn't look as well as you do, and couldn't write. I don't mean a play or a Dante translation, but not even an order to my wine-merchant. I mean, Daniel old boy, your eyes, they seem to be so tremendously alive. Of course, you always had lovely eyes; while take me, Daniel; I have to struggle with this wretched monocle which makes me look exactly like an idiotic aristocrat from one of my own plays.'

He spoke too quickly, as if to excuse himself.

Daniel's eyes said: Stop that. Then they closed for a second: I know I'm half-dead. They opened and shone: You're very amusing all the same, and obviously haven't grown up.

'Well, Daniel,' Stefan Farkas went on. 'It's been a long time; five years. I know all about you, of course — that is, I know that you've left the *Inferno* for the *Purgatory,* which is the exact opposite of what the world has done. I have no real news for you, although I've been to about eight capitals since 1938; they're all the same: masochistic monsters waiting to die. Europe's like the madman of the anecdote, you know, the one who keeps diving into a dry swimming-pool, hoping that it'll be filled with water one fine day. I'm sick and tired of it. Two years ago I

moved from Paris to Switzerland; found it so smug and
clean and nice that I felt like organizing a squad of young
boys and marching them, all yelling, down the main street
of Berne. Now I'd like to have a real rest before they grab
me for being neutral, or reading Rilke, or not reading
Rilke, or just having the impudence to be elderly and un-
interested.'

Anna nodded in approval behind the chair. Daniel's
eyes said: Of course, that would be your attitude.

Stefan swallowed hard and felt his palms becoming hot.

'Actually I'm on my way to San Fernando,' he went on
'You know San Fernando, you must remember it: The
Grandmamma of the Adriatic we used to call it. I'm leaving tonight and hope to spend six or eight weeks there,
circumstances permitting, in search of youth, inspiration,
and mineral waters. I'm getting old, you know, with a
growing preference for past things. Also I couldn't think
of any other place, though I'm a Swiss citizen now and
could travel practically anywhere. But this vulgar war is
spreading everywhere; even to Italy. But my diplomatic
friends tell me San Fernando will be safe for another six
months or so.'

He stopped as Daniel's eyes looked at Anna and then at
the typewriter with the giant keyboard. She understood
and sat down by the machine, watching his eyes. Stefan
rose and stood behind her; thus he did not have to face
those eyes, which had started to move from key to key.

She typed in slow but almost continuous rhythm.

'Y-o-u H-A-V-E-N'T C-H-A-N-G-E-D S-T-E-F-A-N,' she typed,
'D-E-A-R.'

'Oh, well,' Farkas said modestly. 'It only seems so since

everything else has. I've got two more gold crowns in my
jaw, one-and-a-half per cent more glucose in my blood,
and, as you know, I have divorced my third wife. Isn't
that enough?'

The eyes started again.

'I-s I-T?' She stopped and smiled like a mediator to
blunt the edge of the remark. Then she continued. 'S-E-N-D
M-E A P-O-S-T-C-A-R-D F-R-O-M F-L-O-R-E-N-C-E.'

'Yes, certainly, Daniel, certainly,' he replied over-anx-
iously. 'Now then — you mustn't strain yourself — Dante's
much more worthy of your efforts than I. All I want to
know — before — my train is leaving soon — is there anything, I mean, any particular thing you'd like me to do?'

He saw Anna's fingers drumming on the desk, but he
went on: 'I mean, do you want me to see anybody in particular — or is there a book or some magazine you'd spe-
cially like?'

The eyes waited and moved again.

'T-H-A-N-K-S N-O.' She waited. It was a long pause.
Then it went on: 'Y-O-U'R-E V-E-R-Y K-I-N-D S-T-E-F-A-N,' she
typed.

'Nonsense,' Farkas said. 'I mean . . .'; but she lifted her
hand to interrupt him and continued:

'W-R-I-T-I-N-G S-O-M-E-T-H-I-N-G?' the eyes asked.

Farkas cleared his throat.

'Well,' he said, 'you've got me there. I haven't done a
thing since the war began to get less and less funny. But
I might do something in San Fernando; a play, of course.
Herzog leaves me no peace and I promised La Bokor
something spectacular for her falsetto voice and beautiful
tears. I don't think you will approve of it, anyhow.'

She began to type again; this time more slowly.

'W-H-Y N-O-T A-B-O-U-T Y-O-U-R-S-E-L-F?' Daniel asked.

I must go now, Stefan Farkas thought; I must go. He coughed and the glass door of the bookcase faintly mirrored his gesture.

'Now really, Daniel, my dear,' he replied. 'About myself? It would be so dull and tactless. I couldn't possibly be as immodest and overwhelming as Saint Augustine or Rousseau; nor as final as Robitchek, our famous sponger who summed up his life with such Gallic completeness in *Once Upon a Dime*.'

Why am I excusing myself? Stefan thought, and quickly continued, accompanying his words with little elegant stabs of the hand.

'I mean, Daniel,' he said, 'you've always been a genius, while all I've been is the funny man with a certain gift for caricature. Your world is tragic and serene, mine is ridiculous. I . . . ' He felt he must go now. 'I really must leave you. My train . . . '

Anna said quickly: 'Yes, Stefan. You mustn't miss your train.'

'It has been grand seeing you, Daniel,' Farkas said, wondering if he should touch his shoulder. Daniel probably wouldn't feel it. He moved away from the chair and walked to the square table and turned to face his brother once more. The eyes were serious and incredibly expressive: slightly moved and inquisitive; as ever, waiting for an explanation.

Stefan smiled.

'Take care of yourselves, you two,' he said. 'And pity the poor traveller who finds no rest.' He raised his right hand dramatically like a clown imitating a Shakespearean actor. He dropped his hand. The eyes were questioning.

'I'll write to you, of course, and if all goes well I'll be back for Christmas.'

No, you won't, the eyes said. Anna had a look on her face as if she were on the verge of tears. The eyes looked at her and at the typewriter again. She nodded and wrote something.

Stefan did not want to return to the chair any more. 'Yes?' he asked.

'Is that all? Daniel asks,' she said.

Stefan coughed self-consciously. 'Is that all?' he repeated, playing for time, and looked into Daniel's eyes. Daniel sat there, frozen and stony, accusing and yet moved; like some terrible witness to a crime.

And then, in dismissal, he closed his eyes.

Ugo

At eight o'clock there was a hesitant knock on the door. 'Come in,' Farkas said, and slowly the door opened and there stood Ugo the waiter with the dinner-tray. There were tears in his eyes. 'Signor Farkas!' he cried, 'Signor Farkas!' as if something wonderfully sad had happened. He shuffled quickly into the room, holding the tray expertly and elegantly in his left hand, stretching his right hand forward.

'Good evening, Ugo. How are you?' Farkas replied somewhat embarrassed.

'How am I?' Ugo asked, placing the tray on the table and shaking Farkas's hand violently. 'How am *I*?' he repeated with paternal reproach. 'What does it matter? But how are *you*, Signor Farkas? Oh, I'm so glad you're here again.'

Farkas thanked him, and offered Ugo a cigarette to get rid of the waiter's old, moist hand. 'Ugo, too,' he thought. Like the limestone walls of the Regina: there seemed to be cracks in Ugo's face that hadn't been there before. He had always been frail, Ugo with his tail-coat that looked oversize and the large Chaplinesque boots in which he shuffled painfully. He had a small face, Ugo, with light-grey eyes, a flabby nose, and an old mouth, soft and wrinkled, toothless. His hair was sparse and greying; the only touch of dash was provided by the ridiculous side-whiskers. And now, on top of everything else, he had eczema: small, red spots covered his skin, and as he couldn't shave regularly clusters of stubble stood on his chin.

'I have brought you a bottle of Chianti,' Ugo chatted, and fussed with the tray. 'I've hoarded it and kept it hidden ever since I heard you were coming.' He stopped and looked up again at Farkas, his eyes swimming. 'You look very well, Signor Farkas.'

'You look very well yourself,' Farkas lied. 'How are your corns?'

'Oh,' Ugo shrugged his shoulders. 'What does it matter? They hurt. But then, gradually everything hurts.' He was scrutinizing Farkas, waiting discreetly, waiting to see if Farkas had really changed, or grown senile, or unfriendly; but waiting mostly for Farkas to say something brilliant,

witty. Farkas knew it, and he almost felt as though he
were taking an examination or handing his first manuscript to Osvath the editor. For Ugo was not only a waiter;
not in the usual sense. He belonged to that tribe of servants that has been dying out rapidly since 1914; servants
of those cafés which used to be more than just crowded
and smoky catering places, but were homes and clubs and
offices for many; an inspiration, too, and a refuge where
there was exciting warmth, a stimulating communal life
that bred genius and madness and genuine crooks. Under
the gilt-framed, smoke-stained mirrors at small tables with
marble tops scribbled over with signatures, caricatures, or
abrupt financial calculations, there used to sit Farkas's generation, day after day from the early-morning soup, taken
after a bout, until the night grew into a smoky dawn.
There they sat, on the plush sofas, surrounded by local and
foreign papers, large tumblers of coffee, and some better-
class tarts, and with words built up their world. As B. said
once: 'In the Beginning There Was the Café New York:
Then The Word and Isidore, the Head-Waiter.'

When after the hectic first night of *Big Business* in Paris
with old Guitry, someone read out the flattering notices to
Farkas, he wondered what the café at home would think
of it now: it mattered more than the Paris press and old
Guitry's gibberish. András was there with his shiny black
hair and luminous eyes, rotten with disease and spluttering some of the loveliest poetry in the world; and Dezső,
bony, elegant, with his free associations, linking the clouds
to a friar's girth; or Sándor, with his cigar and his women
and the thick blood which gave a little bastard to so many
respectable households. And others, scores of them, group-

ing themselves around some major planet like Farkas or Slezak. Their plays and poems and essays and pictures were made with an eye turned on those circles, because they were the final forum of approval or rejection. They were going downhill, those cafés, and Farkas knew that they would probably be gone before his time was out, having been replaced gradually by clean-looking functional places, narrow Bars-Américains, milk-bars. And he felt satisfaction, because he was jealous of another age which would not understand or enjoy them, anyway. 'Be he cursed who steps into my place,' he used to quote András's bitter poem to himself whenever he thought of his cafés.

And Ugo, whom he had met at the Dôme some thirty years ago, belonged to them; therefore he was not only a waiter, but friend, financial backer if necessary, purveyor of women, confidential messenger, adviser in legal and amorous matters, and, above all, a discreet audience. Later, he moved to Vienna and worked at the Imperial. Farkas met him there regularly, and whenever a new play of his was put on at the Josefstaedter, he would invariably ask Ugo: 'Well, Ugo, how is it?' Ugo respectfully distant, yet assured of his own importance, would reply: 'The first act's rather slow, sir, and die Thimig could be better in the telephone scene.' Ugo was mostly right, although he formed his opinions, before he went to see the play, by carefully listening-in to the café conversation. He knew whom to trust — who was biased for or against Farkas.

Ugo had a Viennese mother who bore him in Pisa, of a 'respectable local businessman,' as Ugo once explained. That mother gave him a certain degree of sensitiveness and an additional language, German. So Ugo knew his way about in Vienna and Prague, and even Budapest. Farkas ran into him at various places during the best part of his life. Once, while sick with flu in Berlin, he even rang up Ugo at the Café Japán in Budapest to ask him how his new play, the opening of which he could not attend, was getting along. 'It's all right,' Ugo shouted into the phone, 'but they giggle at the love scene in the first act. Should they?' And Ugo was not only a critic and a spy on café opinion, but an evangelist too, carrying afar and popularizing all the famous Farkasisms and the best of his anecdotes. God knows how he picked them up, but somehow whenever Farkas said something witty Ugo was either there, just filling his glass, or clearing away the crowded ash-tray; or if in another town he somehow was one of the first to hear about that anecdote or pun; and would then shuffle into the depths of the café to one of the tables that 'mattered' and say, cackling: 'Na, have you heard what Farkas said two days ago in Vienna?'

Ugo was connected with so many of Farkas's memories. Sitting on the terrace of the Mignon by the Danube in thirty-one, with Lóri and Zoltán and a new girl from the National Theatre, drinking a lot of cognac and feeling at his best, telling them the first sketch of *Kingdom for a Hearse* — inventing most of it then and there, mainly for the benefit of the new girl from the National Theatre. Sitting at dusk on the terrace of the Grand, by the Ring in Vienna with Kálmán and Zweig, telling the flying-fish anecdote, requoted and reprinted a thousand times since. Sitting in his room at the Hungária — the first night with Gizella and the last time he was genuinely interested in whether she would sleep with him or not. Ugo was always there, discreetly in the background, filling the glasses, disappearing and reappearing at the right moment.

Ugo now asked, waiting: 'How is the world, sir?'

Farkas could only think of something he had heard three years ago from an unknown young man in the train going to Geneva. It had been published several times since, and he hoped Ugo had not read it. 'Well, Ugo,' he said, putting his hand on Ugo's shoulder, 'I can't make it out. It's like a game of football to me.' He stopped, and was happy because Ugo's face lit up. 'If they want the ball, why kick it? If they don't, why run after it?'

There was a small pause; Ugo nodded because he felt Farkas had not changed, and then started to laugh, gratefully.

The Germans

Thanks to Ugo, Farkas knew quite well what was going on at the Paradiso. Not that much happened — until Leonardo's escape — and anyway, whatever happened was of slight interest to Farkas, who was used to the stereotyped dramas which went on in hotels. San Fernando was always a dull and respectable place, the major part of its clientèle being made up of elderly people who came to drink the curative waters at the well in the main square, to take slow, cautious walks in the gentle hills or just sit on the Corso under the old-fashioned lime trees with a palm tree here and there; sitting and staring numbly at the sea, listening to their hearts or bowels. True, some young and reckless folk came too, in flashy cars, and for a week or two they would noisily fill the Paradiso, criticize the lack of entertainment and modern comfort, and depart. Several cabinet ministers came regularly; many high officials had villas on the slope amidst the vineyards, and the retired officers of the gendarmerie had a rest-house in the woods. Once there was a murder at the Sanatorium, though all eye-witnesses had died long ago and the case had grown into a fabulous legend. But there was nothing of the hectic bustle, with jazz-bands and feste and concerts, of Abbazia or Rimini or — God forbid! — the Lido; and the double beds were occupied by people legally married.

The Benedictine Fathers owned most of San Fernando, and the Abbey on the grey hill stood like a growling watch-dog. Suggestions by Fritti or Foa, the Jew who owned a draper's shop in the main street, for catching up with the times were scornfully turned down by Father Giuseppe. As a final compromise a string quartet played in the pavilion by the sea in the afternoons and on the terrace of the Paradiso at night, and as a further favour permission was granted in 1930 to include a saxophone-player (an elderly lady with spectacles) so that some of the younger guests could dance.

There was no real *plage* at San Fernando, only an old wooden bathhouse with rickety towers stood lonely and out-of-date in the sea, some two hundred yards from the shore, where the deep water began. At night it looked like a medieval castle, with the wind blowing between cracks and crevices and the surf beating loudly against the improvised surf-breakers which surrounded it in a half-circle.

The woodwork was steadily rotting away, and the bridge that led to it from the Corso collapsed several times; but Father Giuseppe preferred to spend large sums on repairs (timber was very expensive) to listening to Fritti or some other modern soul and building a *plage* on the soft, sandy beach behind the willows where the Corso ended. The bathhouse was strictly divided into 'men' and 'women,' and bathers of both sexes could only meet in the sea or on one of the three slippery rafts that lay at anchor just in front of the house. Each part was surrounded on three sides by rows of cabins for undressing in, while the fourth side was open, facing the sea. But in spite of the strict division of sexes, Father Giuseppe's figure, clad in black, would often appear, grim against the sun and sky, watching some of the younger swimmers happily splashing or the women in their half-nakedness as they lay on the rafts, pink or tanned and unashamed. Once he expelled a Miss Olga — a friend of Don Teofilo — who dared to infringe the rules and visit her brother in the men's section.

Rather like a faded print, San Fernando tried to remain true to a tradition. Lombroso once took a cure there, and the Archbishop of Naples was — contemporary documents testify — violently sick on the Corso. In the Regina, the plush couches, now frayed and ramshackle, were once cherry-red, and young ladies sat primly on them, waiting for a waltz. That faded air never left the place, and the Abbey, some four hundred years old, hovered above the walks and plants and clients, reminding them that the sun was fickle and would eventually yield to an even rain when the summer was over. Farkas once remarked that

San Fernando always looked as if the season had just ended, at that hesitant period when the sea grew darker and
the first russet leaves rustled underfoot.

The Paradiso tried to fight all this rather heroically with
its chromium plates and one neon light over the entrance
door: also it had English waterclosets, a wireless set, and
on two occasions an imported gipsy orchestra (Father
Giuseppe being absent, in Rome); and once a couple of
Lesbians came from Innsbruck. But it was all in vain:
Fritti, earthly and businesslike, was ever losing ground
against the Abbey with its timeless scorn. 'People come
here to rest,' Father Giuseppe would explain; 'to meditate
and wash their kidneys and biles.'

So the rhythm of San Fernando remained slow; down
the main street into the little groves framing the square,
then by winding, shaded paths to the serene Corso, the
clients strolled, talking of the food at the Sanatorium, of
someone who had just died, or of their digestion, while the
string quartet discreetly played a song by Schubert or a
march by Souza. True, there were always some children who
yelled and some adolescents who kissed after dark by the
willows, and once one of the imported gipsies chased his
naked wife with a dagger up the Abbey Hill. But the
rhythm soon settled back, and time passed in even beats
from meal to meal, from arrival to departure. A few flashy
visitors, a couple of Lesbians from Innsbruck, and an occasional scandal could not change it. The Abbey stood
strong and grey and timeless, watching, owning most of it,
the hotels, the shops and rich, volcanic soil where the vines
grew and nothing violent happened: there was faded unhappiness in every corner and many of the people who
came stayed to die.

The three Germans created something of a stir at first,
Ugo explained, bringing with them the war and a certain
type of stern romance; but soon they turned out to be dull
and inoffensive. They came in March to recuperate, and
Ugo simply referred to them as 'the strangers,' in contrast
to 'foreigners,' a word which evoked in him respect and
interest. They lived opposite Farkas in three large rooms.
One, the Major, was a pale, sandy-coloured man, flat-
chested, with spectacles. He had a tiresome habit of sniffing, his nose thin and slightly reddish as if he had just
been crying. There was something petulant and apologetic about him, and he spent most of his time writing,
reading, or just receiving letters. Farkas often watched
him when he was sitting in the lounge and did not feel
like dozing or walking. The Major, slightly apart from his
comrades, would busily bend over a small round table, his
thin neck craning forward from a collar that was just one
size too large, and finger a letter that had arrived just
then or perhaps some time ago; or write with a stiff, busy
hand, almost without a pause.

Farkas envied him for such fluency, and could not help
wondering what he could possibly write about day after
day; for the Major wrote one letter a day at least, topping
it occasionally with a picture-card — the Famous View
with the Abbey and the bay, or the Drinking Well under
the palm trees — cards made in 1905 or thereabouts with
vague groups of men and women, ridiculously dressed,
gloomily holding glasses of mineral water — or walking
under the lime trees (the Noted Corso of San Fernando).
He would carefully read his letters and cards, making neat
corrections, Farkas observed, his lips moving as he read,

nodding solemnly or smiling a pale, sandy smile. Then he would meticulously fold the paper, place it in an envelope, address it, and produce a little wallet with stamps, and finally go up to Enrico and hand over his daily work, asking 'Post?' in a raucous accent; and Enrico would smile apologetically and point out that the seven-o'clock delivery hadn't yet arrived. The Major would thank him and walk back to his table and continue reading the letters of the day before, or just sit watching the entrance, waiting for the postman. No one quite seemed to know whom he was writing to, for Enrico was proverbially discreet; also no one was interested. Farkas thought the Major was probably writing to himself.

The second was a captain, named Tropf. The only one whose name Farkas remembered; it amused him. Tropf was tall and well-built, with a tendency to plumpness. He had fair, curly hair and two round eyes, wide apart above a nose that looked like one of the marbles children play with. He had constant surprise on his face, like a rabbit disturbed in a kitchen garden. He was the one, Farkas observed, who did not do anything, but sat surprised and passive as if he had just finished a book or just returned from a brisk walk. The point was that he never read and hardly ever went for walks. Farkas envied him too, for Tropf did not seem to be bored or tired. He sat by his comrades, staring at nothing, his mind obviously a transparent space across which the minimum of interference passed from either outside or in. He looked occasionally at the Major, or the other captain — the young one — in a puzzled way, or watched the slight movement that was going on in the lounge. But there was no reaction in him.

When the time came, the Major said, 'Let's go and eat,' Tropf nodded with surprise and followed the others into the dining-room, or upstairs to sleep, or rarely and with reluctance to the bathhouse; though he never swam, and did not even undress except for taking off his tunic if it got too hot.

The third German, a captain of the Luftwaffe, was the most active of them all. A big fat boy of about twenty, he moved about evaporating sweat, grumbling and behaving as if San Fernando were a pair of tight shoes. 'He is trying to live up to their reputation,' Ugo commented. Farkas found the airman the least interesting: just a big fat boy who ate all the time, drank all the wine, swam, played tennis, and shocked the faded silence of San Fernando by loud belches and songs. He exasperated Fritti with his appetite and thirst. He ate a double breakfast, had elevenses, a snack before lunch, and then could hardly wait for tea. His comrades tried to restrain him, especially the Major, who often admonished him in an undertone between meals; but it was of no avail. Farkas disliked him immensely. The airman represented something he always ridiculed and despised: a fat big stupid boy like an overgrown messy baby. Farkas felt a slight nausea as he watched the young man chewing a sandwich with bits of bread and cheese sticking out of his fat mouth, his eyes seriously intent, concentrating on the elementary pleasure his tongue and palate provided. Yet, he did not look particularly healthy: his cheeks were pallid, and there was something morbid about his skull, closely cropped and shaven at the back, with tiny stubbles peppering it right down to the nape.

Farkas tried to avoid them as much as possible, especially after the second day, when he noticed the fat airman
go up to Enrico and obviously inquire about the new-
comer, then return to his comrades and whisper something
in a fat smacking voice as if words too were something to
eat. The others looked at Farkas, and he quickly walked
out; he knew he would be rude to them if they came up
and tried to ask for an autograph or to make friends. But
he could not quite escape, of course: San Fernando was
too small. Once when he went down to the bathhouse and
was lying in the shade, reading and feeling the salty wind
on his white soft body, he heard their voices, and the fat
one was whispering again. This time he heard him saying
his name, and 'Farkas' sounded like a juicy bit of roast
goose left in its fat to grow cold. He got up, and winding
the towel around his middle, walked quickly to Alfieri, the
beach-master and attendant and an old friend of his: he
asked him for a pedicure in order to stave the Germans off.
The trick worked; they were too shy to approach him
while Alfieri was there, his bronze, elephantine body leaning over Farkas's feet.

Another day he was sitting by the sea, smoking a cigar
and thinking that perhaps after all he should write something, or telegraph for Gizella, who had been waiting for
him the last few years in Geneva, when he heard the
rhythmical steps of the three officers — steps in unison,
echoing loudly down the promenade, like so many small
doors slammed in rapid succession. He felt annoyed, as the
sea was just changing colour, rather beautifully, and his
cigar was drawing well, and perhaps for the first time he
was feeling content with San Fernando. He did not turn,

but sat stiffly, hoping they would not spot him. They did, of course. There was hardly anybody else on the Corso (it was after lunch-time), and Farkas was wearing one of his flamboyant straw hats.

The steps stopped behind his back, started again, and came right up in front of him. Farkas looked up painfully and saw them standing there, three uniformed figures, the Major with his writing pad and fountain pen, Tropf gently surprised, and the airman eating grapes from a paper bag.

'*Entschuldigan Sie, Herr Farkas,*' the Major excused himself solemnly.

Farkas just gazed at them sternly, trying to mesmerize them away.

'My wife has just written me,' the Major continued. 'She says she went to see a play of yours. In Dresden. She enjoyed it tremendously.'

Farkas put on a smile because he knew now what to do. '*Vous dites?*' he asked in a friendly voice. '*Vous dites, mon enfant?*'

There was a pause, and the fat boy gaped and stopped eating. The Major reddened. '*Ma femme,*' he said finally, '*ma femme m'a écrit . . .*' He halted, searching for a word.

Farkas smiled encouragingly. '*Et alors?*'

'*Ma femme,*' the Major continued, while the other two stared at Farkas as if speaking French belonged to a prehistoric past, or were a tactless practice, '*ma femme a vu votre*' — he halted again — '*votre pièce du théâtre. A Dresden. Elle l'aimait beaucoup.*' And he blew out his breath in relief.

Farkas smiled benignly like a teacher. 'Bravo!' he said.

'Bravo!' and watched them click their heels and flee embarrassedly.

Soon they emerged into the general pattern of San Fernando: the steps in unison, the three uniformed figures
against the cream-coloured dusk of the lounge or the sea
with the lime trees: the busy scratching of the Major's pen,
the smacking of the airman's mouth, and the surprised
face of Captain Tropf. It all fitted into the daily pattern of
noise and colour. Farkas, who was cursed with very sensitive nostrils, could smell them afar, especially after it had
been raining.

Ugo, of course, furnished more information in his 'bulletins,' which he delivered after breakfast on the terrace of
the Paradiso when Farkas — always the last guest to come
down — was lighting his first cigar. 'The master race,' Ugo
would begin derisively, and add: 'I prefer a horse-race.' At
his master's side Ugo liked to picture himself as a modest
Panza, and made terrible jokes and puns.

Farkas knew and tried to appreciate them. 'Well, Ugo?'
he asked, 'what's the news in San Fernando?'

Ugo coughed up saliva and swallowed it discreetly.
'Show me your bedroom' — he was often in an epigram-
matic mood — 'and I tell you who you are.'

The bedrooms of the Germans were quite illuminating,
it seemed. They often took breakfast upstairs — except for
the fat airman, who went to church early, or played tennis
— and this gave Ugo a chance to make use of his gifts of
observation.

'Those are the rooms of lonely males,' Ugo said. 'One
can always tell. The Night Before ended abruptly and
without satisfaction — no woman to reach for. The Major

sleeps huddled up in the corner of the bed, arms hanging down, knees drawn up. He does not snore, but speaks violently in his dreams. The other day he rang for breakfast and must have fallen asleep again. When I entered, he had rolled to one side of his bed, leaving more than half of it empty. He crumples his sheet tremendously, Filomena the maid tells me. And Filomena ought to know. When he woke he jumped at seeing me. "*Ja, ja,*" he mumbled, "*ja, ja!*" He always says it. Then he sat up and slowly scrambled out of bed. He wears awful striped pyjamas — fawn and blue — and the jacket is too short and one can see a small bit of his white back as he bends down to put on his slippers. The room smells of that age when men grow flabby inside; when, as Mr. József wrote in his beautiful poem, "the foreign matter is growing fast in my heart as in my teeth." He then combs his hair, blinking myopically into the mirror, brushes his teeth, and settles down with a letter in his hand. "Hm," he remarks every morning while looking at the tray, but I couldn't say if it is in approval or not. He is neat and orderly: the first thing that strikes one are his socks hanging neatly down on a chair — balanced so as not to slip, hanging like hatched chickens. His toilet articles, too, stand in a tidy row on the glass shelf, and the basin is always clean, with a blue sponge and a blue soap-box in each corner.

'The Captain, the one named Tropf, is usually shaving when I arrive with the tray. All men have their own tricks in shaving. This one does it in a khaki shirt, his white rump showing underneath like a 3 laid horizontally. He turns when I enter, says, "*Eine Sekunde,*" and motions me to put the tray down on the table. His face is half-covered

with lather and he is shaving with a complicated movement — his left hand reaching over his head to stretch the
skin on his right cheek, or the other way round, and I
should like to tell him how silly and superfluous it is, not
to speak of the shirt which is slightly raised by the movement, showing more white rump. He uses an old-fashioned razor, not a safety one. The Captain is afraid.

'You can tell who is afraid. To start with, he mostly
locks the door; often I have had to wait after I have
knocked as he forgot to unlock the door when he woke.
Then, he places the chairs in a very peculiar way; one near
the door — one could stumble over it — the second and
third between the bed and the door. The windows are
always left closed at night. That gives the room a heavy,
warm smell, full of smoke and breathing. I don't know,
of course, but I think he sits up in bed at night, staring
into the darkness, listening to noises. Once he rang for
me after midnight. He wanted a glass of cocoa, he said;
but he was only afraid. He was sitting on his bed half-
dressed when I entered, and when I asked what he wanted,
he was obviously playing for time, wanting me to stay as
long as possible. "Ah, yes," he said, "what did I want? Of
course, of course. Now let me see." He reached for his
cigarette case and offered me one. "Now then," he started
again, and I could see that all the time he was listening to
something. "A thunderstorm's coming," he remarked,
half-questioning. "No, sir," I replied. "It's a beautiful
night." "They're so sudden," he insisted, "these storms, so
sudden. One moment it's bright and sunny; the next it's
all rain and thunder."

'I grew impatient, but he went on. "I'm positive there's

a storm rising. The wind is moving the trees, down in the
square. Can't you hear it?" "No, sir," I said. "Excuse me,
sir. The kitchen closes at midnight. If you wanted anything . . . " "Oh, yes," he said. "A glass of cocoa, perhaps."
When I returned later, I was sure he would try to keep
me there, or even ring again under some pretext. He was
still sitting on his bed, half dressed, listening, ready to
escape. "It's a beautiful night, sir," I tried to soothe him.
"And there's no wind." It only made it worse. "Well,
then, what was that sound?" he asked. "What sound?" I
asked. "Like the wind moving the trees in the square."
"I can't hear anything," I said. "Listen," he said: and we
both listened; but there was nothing, unless I am getting
deaf, which is not impossible.

'But what should there be in San Fernando, especially
after midnight? There are no burglars, no ghosts. In the
main square some of the waiters might be sitting on the
benches, in the dark, smoking and resting their feet and
talking. Often I sit there with them myself. We just sit
and rest our feet and discusss the war, the village, or our
feet. But we talk quietly so as not to disturb the guests.
What else could the captain named Tropf hear? Alfieri the
beach-master might be walking home with some fish he
had caught. But everybody would know it was Alfieri, as
his boots make a characteristic thud; also he breaks wind
rather noisily, at regular intervals, a practice he has often
been reprimanded for, but which he cannot help. Who
else? I couldn't say, Signor Farkas; perhaps you could.

'The airman, the fat one, is an entirely different prop-
osition,' Ugo continued. 'Quite the little ape he is, of
course, haughty and religious. There is a picture of the

Virgin over his bed, a gold cross dangles on his fat hairless chest, and Filomena says a Bible lies by his night-lamp. He sleeps messily, spreading across the bed, breathing heavily and snoring with the sound of a seesaw. He cracks bad jokes to the staff, and does gymnastics with a curious expandable contraption before going to Mass. *"Saluto Ugo,"* he roars as a greeting. "Saluto Ugo — a good rhyme, eh?" There you are. He goes to bed early, having made his usual advances — in vain — to Filomena. And if one passes his room at about ten, as I often do, one can hear him praying or masturbating. It is either an even murmur or an uneven gasping. He does the second thing, Filomena, who ought to know, informs me, with clockwork regularity, three times a week, Monday, Wednesday, Friday, excepting great festivals when he wakes very early and goes for a solitary walk before church. Returning from church to have his breakfast, he plays with a rosary, singing coarsely, relieved. *"Saluto Ugo,"* he greets me, slapping my rheumatic shoulders; then he starts devouring large chunks of bread and butter. He is a fool with a certain shrewdness, and he suspects that we can all feel repelled — all of us except Father Giuseppe, who, as a good Catholic, forgives everybody provided they are good Catholics too. Even Don Innocenzo who, being the Chief of the Police, is anxious to be friends with Germans, makes a face behind the airman's back and calls him, with a sneer, Fritz.'

The Brat

Don Innocenzo visited Farkas the very first morning, having sent a query through Fritti 'whether he might pay his compliments.' 'Must he?' Farkas asked Fritti, and in his dressing-gown, received the little man at about eleven. Don Innocenzo strutted into the room like a peacock, dynamic and full of gusto, his handsome face covered with the kind of enthusiasm owners of newly opened restaurants radiate. '*Mes hommages, Signor,*' he cried, after jerking his hand in the customary salute. '*Enchanté, absolument enchanté.*' He spoke bad French. Farkas had met him before, and, as before, viewed him with suspicion, as if the little man were a fox-terrier; and Farkas mistrusted fox-terriers. '*Bon jour,*' he replied curtly. Don Innocenzo flung himself into a chair, sticking out his boots, which were much too shiny; picked up an orange from Farkas's plate and bit into it, without peeling it first. 'Thrilled to have you in San Fernando,' he continued at the same high-pitched level as if he were recounting some exciting news. 'May I have your passport? A formality,' he sighed apologetically; 'you know.'

Farkas felt quite cheerful that morning, after his melancholy arrival; the sun was bright, and through the open window came the scents and sounds of a fine morning. He first felt like being rude to Don Innocenzo, but then changed his mind, remembering his stomach acid which had been liable to become tiresome of late whenever he was rude or excited. He was looking forward to a pleasant breakfast on the sunny terrace. So he gave his passport to the little man and listened with forced interest to his violent ejaculations.

Don Innocenzo was in charge of the police and, as Ugo told Farkas, had acted as Podestà since Signor Bastini was taken to Ravenna, some six months ago, to be treated for his painful boils. A young man of about thirty-five, Don Innocenzo was the 'model citizen' as someone had called him, with a small wiry body and a large handsome head with closely grown, curly hair, a wide, continuously wrinkled forehead, bushy eyebrows, pretty walnut-coloured eyes, curly lips, and a good jaw. He had two deep dimples which reminded Farkas of inverted commas, emphasizing the childish lips. Don Innocenzo was obviously proud of his dimples; he would often smile, or just bare his teeth as if someone had commanded him to do so. He cut a handsome figure in his white summer suit. The chauffeur type, Farkas had labelled him seven years ago, appeals to women by quick uncomplicated deeds rather than by the profundity of his sentiments. He acted all the time, the little man; but according to Farkas everybody did, and the question was simply whether they were correctly cast or not. Don Innocenzo was: he fitted smugly into his profession, régime, locality, and age. He swaggered about in a rhythm that always seemed *crescendo*, and one wondered if he ever rested. Busy, alert, here, there, everywhere: his boots drumming, with a smart noise across the gravel paths of San Fernando, his arm jerking up to the salute, his face ever moving in prearranged grimaces, as if facial gestures, too, were handed out to him

officially. Watching Don Innocenzo, Farkas always imagined the little man giving himself commands. 'Pro-duce
dimpl-es, one-two!' or: 'Wrinkle fore-head, one-two.' He
loved to wrinkle his forehead; this, he thought, gave him
a grave look, as if his job were too responsible for words
and the whole edifice of the régime rested on his shoulders.

They talked about the war that morning; or rather Don
Innocenzo talked, accompanying his statements with restless grimaces which stressed each sentence, ending them
with a vocal exclamation mark, starting each word with a
vocal capital letter. Farkas mostly mumbled neutrally and
wished Don Innocenzo would leave him to finish dressing.
The little man complained about his chiefs 'who wouldn't
let him go and Fight for the Empire, forcing him to stay
and continue his Dull Routine.' 'Sicily is in Danger!' he
cried. 'The Foe At The Gate Of The Fatherland!' Yet he
had to remain behind, inactive and bursting with energy.
'Passports, bah!' he said. 'Petty crimes — a few smugglers,
an occasional brawl at the village, and one or two refu-
gees! The Fatherland Is In Danger And Don Innocenzo
Is Not In The Front Line!'

'Quite,' Farkas murmured, thinking of his breakfast.

'Though there might be some fun one of these days' —
Don Innocenzo suddenly dropped his voice, adopting a
confidential tone, that of a conspirator. 'A convict is at
large . . . and we are waiting FOR HIM!' The last two
words in sudden *crescendo* again, underlined in rapid
succession by a melodramatic movement of his hand, the
wrinkling of his forehead and a wolfish snarl. Suddenly
he started to rub his hands, like a youthful, Fascist edition
of Shylock. 'We are waiting.'

'Hm,' Farkas said. 'And now, if you will excuse me, I'll have my bath.'

The little man jumped to his feet, startling Farkas. '*Con vostro comodo,*' he cried, saluted, shook Farkas's hand and departed.

With clattering steps he left, his forehead wrinkled, his dimples emphasizing his charming though forced smile. 'Brat,' Farkas thought, 'the type of child who pokes out his tongue at strangers, his nose running; beats up the weaker children, breaks windows, and makes Saturday afternoon hell for the rest of the universe.'

Don Innocenzo had never quite grown up. Ugo testified to it, too, and later Giacobbe; and events to come. And when Farkas saw him for the last time, hanging quietly from the old-fashioned lamp-post that stood in front of the hotel, hanging in peace, with a broken neck, his hands dangling helplessly, his eyes open yet blind, his beautifully shined boots catching the greying light and the wind jabbing at his hair — even then he looked a brat, Don Innocenzo: a punished, beaten brat, repentant at last.

'Hey, Signorina Lisabetta,' Don Innocenzo cried one day to the postmistress, a seedy spinster with spectacles; 'how's the baby getting along?'

'What baby?' Signorina Lisabetta asked, and reddened; there was a crowd of four in the post-office.

'The one you're having, I hear, in four months,' Don Innocenzo yelled, and left.

'Once he put a burning cigarette in Don Teofilo's pocket,' Ugo reported, 'and silently watched it burning. When Don Teofilo's pocket — and mind you, he was wearing one of his fancy yachting blazers — started to emit smoke, Don Innocenzo sprang up and ripped off the table-cloth with all the wine and coffee, shouting, "Fire, fire! Call out the Fire Brigade!" '

One Sunday night Don Innocenzo came up to Farkas's table on the terrace: Don Teofilo was there, gnome-like in his wheel-chair, and the sleepy Doctor Schmidt. The refugee girl-violinist with the scar on her face was playing *La Mattinata* behind them as her last number. It was a clear but windy night. There was no one else on the terrace. Farkas had had his overcoat brought down by Ugo. They were drinking a rich red wine, and Don Teofilo was complaining in his growling voice, which so often got derailed into an almost hysterical note, calling for his nurse, or another cigar.

Don Innocenzo suddenly appeared out of the darkness; he was slightly drunk, and as he sat down he pinched Doctor Schmidt's leg as a practical joke. 'Hallouaaaa, music!' he yelled, and *La Mattinata* stopped and there was a frightened silence, as if a crowd were there and suddenly felt overawed. The girl with the violin turned and waited. 'Stop that music!' Don Innocenzo went on, unpleasantly; 'go home, *allez, filez!*' The girl said nothing, put her violin into its case and closed the case with a click; then slowly wandered off with the goggle-eyed pianist.

'I don't want music,' Don Innocenzo explained, and poured himself some wine. 'Do you? Of course not. We're talking now.'

'You're being rude,' Doctor Schmidt remarked in his flat, soothing voice, which sounded as if the rest of mankind were all patients in need of a flat, soothing voice telling them to behave and not to worry.

'Of course I'm rude,' Don Innocenzo replied. 'This is a rude world and one can only get along in it by being rude.' His *r*s were getting vague. Out of habit he smiled, producing his dimples, and lit a cigarette. He smoked as if it were forbidden him, wetting the mouthpiece and gulping the smoke down greedily and trying to puff out perfect circles; but he never succeeded. 'The news is not so good,' he said, and Farkas saw he could not control the drunken twitch of his upper lip. 'My beautiful Sicily, my beautiful Sicily!' he cried, as if Sicily were a favourite toy or his mother. 'Those dirty Angloamericans' — he mixed up his syllables — 'those murderous murderous.' He couldn't find a substantive which expressed his feelings, and so he started again: 'those murderous murderous . . .' He pursed his lips and put his elbows on the table, staring in front of him.

'Now you're properly cast,' Farkas thought.

Don Innocenzo went on: 'Deep vengeance is the daughter of deep silence,' he quoted the proverb mysteriously. 'Deep vengeance!' he shouted, shaking his fist.

'All right, all right,' the Doctor said.

Don Teofilo was bored and felt cold. 'Nurse,' he cried in a wailing voice, 'nurse, where are you?'

She appeared, as always, silently from the immediate background, her ugly flat face showing that type of frozen kindness which is just a thin film for frozen hate.

'Yes, sir?' she asked.

'Nurse,' the Baron said, 'my second rug, I'm cold. Hurry!' She immediately placed a rug on the weak, childish legs which had remained so thin and crippled ever since Don Teofilo had swam an icy lake in Switzerland, while his body grew toad-like.

'How is your fugitive?' Doctor Schmidt asked Don Innocenzo.

'My murderous fugitive,' he replied, and did amazing
things to his forehead, creasing it into writhing furrows.
'A silent stream destroys the bridge,' he produced another
proverb. 'My fugitive' — and then he pulled himself into
alertness. 'Never fear, Professor, we'll get him. We get
everybody; murderous everybody. Some day he'll turn
up here, and I shall be waiting for him.'

'Dirty Communist,' Don Teofilo said, and lit a cigar.

'Murderous murderous murderous,' Don Innocenzo
sank back again into stupor, and tried to throw his cigarette into the Doctor's wine-glass, but missed as the Doctor
drew it away. 'Oh, what's the good of it?' Don Innocenzo
said, with drooping lips. *A che giova?*

Most nights they sat on the terrace of the Paradiso;
Farkas, Don Teofilo, and Doctor Schmidt, with Don
Innocenzo or Father Giuseppe joining them occasionally.
Those nightly talks which lasted till well after midnight
were a major event in San Fernando: a kind of excuse and
compensation to Don Teofilo and the Doctor for the in-
sipid lethargy San Fernando fell into during the autumn
and winter. People would pass the terrace after dinner,
stop, and murmur: 'Look, there they are!' Elderly couples,
arm-in-arm, would stroll by and gape slightly as if the
famous group by the table were exotic animals. 'Don
Teofilo is explaining,' a husband would whisper. 'Signor
Farkas is telling a story. They are all laughing. The
Doctor looks serious.'

Farkas liked neither Don Teofilo nor the Doctor. He
had a very poor opinion of their narrow outlook and petty

world; they were so terribly provincial. 'Two Madame Bovarys,' he described them to Ugo. He adopted a deliberately superior and aloof attitude to them, punctuating his sentences with a slightly insulting 'if you *know* what I mean' or 'if you follow me' and the like. But he went to the terrace almost every night. Don Teofilo, because of his obscene, puffed body, his crippled legs, his nurse, and his wailing, presented a living proof that he, Farkas, was healthy, after all; while as to Doctor Schmidt, Farkas had always liked the company of medical men. Some secret fear made him seek the friendship of men like Professor Adam of Budapest, or Neumann of Vienna — fear that something might happen to him at any time and it was useful to know the best specialists, to have them around. So with Schmidt: the pale, sleepy doctor, who hardly spoke and made no effort to cover up his stupidity, seemed like a lifebelt to Farkas, who knew that he had reached the age when each little failure of the body's mechanism — each missing heartbeat, each slight nausea — were like the ringing of an ominous bell. He liked to discuss ailments with Schmidt, inquiring about the effect of insulin, the behaviour of glucose, or the result a rich meal might have on him; or just any insignificant symptom he might feel. 'By the way, Schmidt,' he would say, 'my tongue was coated this morning, why?'

But most of all he went because the night was long in San Fernando, and Farkas never turned in before one or two in the morning. The hours that came in the wake of midnight were the most precious to him. Then his mind was sufficiently saturated with smoke and alcohol to suppress irrelevancies, and he was able to select and concentrate and formulate the vague raw material brewing in his mind. True, he needed some stimulus: a somewhat isolated table, preferably out-of-doors, with distant music and the wind; company that knew him and was willing to listen and able to appreciate; the dry taste of brandy or good wine. Don Teofilo and the Doctor were very inferior to the usual crowd, but they were impressible, and knew how to listen and agree.

Father Giuseppe came rarely, emerging out of the dusk, a dark, silent figure, almost sinister but for his red, tired peasant face, speaking a *bassa voce* as if the world were a vast confessing-box. He very obviously did not care for Farkas, and probably feared him after the night when Farkas, who had taken more wine than usual, felt naughty and explained to the party how the Freudian analyst, a modern and more efficient variant of the Father Confessor, would eventually undermine the Church. Father Giuseppe was not an able dialectician. His shrewd yet simple peasant mind revolved round the daily task of managing the vast properties of the Abbey, a mind propped up by iron dogmas on which no one had so far challenged him. He listened to Farkas with suspicion. *'Ecco il diavolo,'* he may have thought to himself, but could disprove little of what Farkas suggested, and his biblical quotations sounded increasingly lame. Ever since that night he had been reluctant to come for more than a short while — as if apprehensive that the pink-faced, monocled devil might suddenly and successfully disprove the Holy Trinity, or, what was almost as horrible, the right of the Abbey to own San Fernando.

Anyway, Father Giuseppe was a tired man; he would

have resigned from his earthly task but for the war. He rose at dawn, and then till late in the evening he checked accounts, supervised the delivery of wine or the building of a new fence, admonished the quarrymen, or the land labourers with cold wrath, made several tours of inspection through the woods or to the bathhouse, looking for laziness or promiscuity; his red, tired face becoming ever redder and more tired. The land labourers had secret guards to watch out for him, for they never worked hard enough to please him. The children feared him, too, and the players at the tennis courts, including Schmidt's two gawky daughters — they felt embarrassed when out of the dark woods stepped the familiar black figure, walking slowly by, nodding in acknowledgement of their greeting. After sunset he came down once more from the Abbey. San Fernando knew and waited. If someone looked out of a top-floor window facing west, he could see the solitary black figure walking down the dusty road by the sea, his robe puffed by the wind, his hands clasped behind his back, approaching, as the sun withdrew its rays and receded into a neat, flaming ball, sliding slowly down behind the Abbey Hill, leaving San Fernando alone in the night.

The Girl

It was on the fourth night of his stay that Farkas realized that the refugee girl with the scar on her face lived next door. He had heard her playing, of course, on the second night and after; and he had noted how admirably her routine music fitted San Fernando: the melancholy of a lonely violin as she played all the tunes one expected to hear, touching a chord in those who remembered an ageing summer in Karlsbad or Bad Gastein, or Vichy; the long cumbersome evenings after the early meal when one felt like taking the first train and fleeing back to the warmth and noise of the city. He had not seen her except once when she came by after the restaurant had closed. She had soft blond hair and what Ugo would call 'very intelligent hips.' At any rate, she had a soft round figure and a way of walking very erectly which stressed every line and curve. Farkas, who knew about women as much as was humanly possible (which, he would say, was darned little), looked after her that second longer which determined that he would look again next time and possibly even longer. He did not see her face clearly that first night. But next afternoon on the Corso she came walking along with the goggle-eyed pianist: she looked very pretty in the distance, soft, smoothly tanned, with appetizing limbs, and, as Farkas noted again, a peculiar way of walking which made her breasts and hips vibrate. It wasn't deliberately provocative, and was certainly not vulgar, but there was some queer proudness in her walk; he expected her to stamp her foot in scorn, any moment. Before she reached the bench where Farkas sat smoking, she turned to her companion, and Farkas saw her pretty, soft profile, the childishly puffed lips, the round line of her chin and throat. Farkas was pleased to look at her: she seemed so very young; and Farkas did not mind confessing to himself (and to some of his friends) that he had reached the age at which he was beginning to appreciate sheer youth in women.

But then she turned back and showed her right cheek, which was marred by a deep, raw scar; quite long, starting by the cheekbone and running down diagonally to the jaw. It made that cheek look sunken and lean. It gave Farkas a shock; but then the girl turned away and was young and pretty and sweet again. Yet the memory of the scar lingered, and attracted. It gave the girl an additional dimension: a moment before she had just been a young, sweet girl with an exciting way of walking. Farkas imagined her making innocent silly conversation for which she could be forgiven. He could imagine her hurrying to a rendezvous or crying because of a villainous bank clerk, and eventually getting married and growing plump. But the scar made all the difference; it evoked images of blood and darkness and, definitely, of a dagger. Later, when she told him that it was merely due to an undramatic accident in her childhood, he felt cheated.

Almost every day they met, either on the terrace or on the Corso. She knew that he was watching her and her walk; as she passed by, she became a trifle prouder, and she made a deliberate effort to turn her scarred cheek to him as if intent not to fool him. One night later he sent Ugo to her to ask if she would play the *Fiakerl Lied* for him. She immediately stopped whatever it was she was playing and started the silly Viennese song he had asked for. He turned and smiled and she smiled back, and when it was finished, he clapped discreetly. When the restaurant was closing and she walked by him, he half-rose and said, 'You played very sweetly.' She thanked him and hesitated for a moment, but then hurried on. From then on he tried to shake off Don Teofilo and the Doctor before the music ended, to remain alone and see if she would join him. But somehow it never happened: she always hurried back to the hotel.

One night he was sitting on the balcony, smoking and watching the crowns of the trees swaying in the wind and listening to the distant beating of the surf, when someone drew a curtain next door and opened the windows. He could not help listening, and soon he knew his neighbour was a woman; and then heard her humming *La Mattinata*. She walked up and down for a while, opening cupboards: then a shoe dropped and some jars clinked. And all the while she was humming and it betrayed the kind of unhappiness one feels in hotel rooms which become too familiar yet less and less of a home, sensing the impersonal hostility of the strange room with the bed others have slept in or the wallpaper one has come to hate. 'La-ra-ra-ra-la-rara-ta-tam-tam,' she hummed; then through her nose, more subdued: 'm-hm-ri-ra-la-ra-ratam,' and she stopped and flung herself on the bed.

Nothing is so articulate as the silence of unhappiness, Farkas thought as he sat on the balcony, listening to the girl getting more and more miserable. The night was remarkably quiet; only some dishes were being washed somewhere and the surf was discreetly beating against the Corso. So he heard her sigh once or twice and throw herself to one side, then the other. Then came a lengthy silence in which she might have been staring at the wallpaper or the ceiling. Then on the wall she started to drum with her fingers the rhythm of *La Mattinata*. 'Da-raram-ra-ra-ram-ba-ram-bam.' It went on for slow, clumsy minutes. The bed creaked again and she rose and walked to the washstand. Farkas heard the hissing of a tap. She was brushing her teeth; this sounded more cheerful. Then there was a knock at the door.

The sound was sudden, sombre and full of impending action. Anyway, that was how Farkas felt about it. Possibly the girl's reaction was the same, for she stopped dead and listened. There was another knock, and she sighed and said, '*Entrez.*' Farkas did not know, but he figured that she must be standing in the centre of the room, between the end of the bed and the washstand, looking at the door as it opened.

'*Bon soir*, Tony,' a voice said.

'*Bon soir*, Don Innocenzo,' she said. He advanced into the room, whistling. Then Farkas heard his hand touching her shoulders, which must have been naked. There were a few soft sounds; a hand moving, bodies pressed against one another, the rustling of silk underwear. Then, quite suddenly and with great bitterness, she said: 'It is a beautiful night.'

The Morgans

The middle-aged English couple, Mr. and Mrs. Morgan, were cheerful; practically the only cheerful and sane people at the Paradiso. They wandered about with friendly and interested placidity, always admired the sunsets, the lime trees, or the rock-garden near the well with the little group of dwarfs who smiled idiotically amidst roses and

jasmine. Farkas first noticed them some time after his arrival: the woman, a small, grey-haired lady with spectacles
and a set of ill-fitting false teeth, who wore large unat-
tractive straw hats, smiled at him one day and said, quite
loudly in English, 'Lovely morning!' It sounded odd with
Don Innocenzo and the Germans around, but Farkas
enjoyed it and replied: 'Lovely, indeed!' 'They're always
lovely,' she continued with genuine interest, nodded and
walked away. The man smiled less and wore shaggy
flannels, his trousers drawn up much too high, showing
his thick brown woollen socks. He had a very clear face:
all pink and fresh, and each feature standing apart clearly
as if he wore an invisible magnifying-glass over his face.
He, too, wore a straw hat, somewhat battered, and it never
left him, like the pipe which he kept dangling between his
teeth with an almost tendentious obstinacy, as if the pipe
were a Union Jack or some other symbol.

Their presence was an obvious embarrassment to San
Fernando. They felt it, but behaved with benign understanding. It was not they who were embarrassed. They
would pass the Germans a dozen times daily. The Major
would blush, the airman glare or look away, Tropf blink
in an even more surprised way than usual. But Mr. and
Mrs. Morgan would just smile at them, the same kind yet
thoroughly non-committal smile they bestowed on Ugo
or the sunsets. They had got stuck when Italy declared
war, and should have been interned, but Don Innocenzo
somehow fancied himself in the rôle of a gallant foe and
persuaded the higher authorities to let them off with
'enforced residence.' They were not supposed to leave
San Fernando and had to report regularly at the police

station. They went to church every Sunday, to the delight
of Father Giuseppe, who once, in a sermon admonishing
the villagers for poor attendance, made a veiled reference
to the 'devout fellow-Christians from the North.'

The man spoke to Farkas one morning on the Corso.
They were both watching the crowded streams of small
fish rushing in endless circles in the shallow water. 'Plenty
of fish,' the man said. 'Yes,' Farkas replied. Mr. Morgan
tipped his hat, smiled at him and walked away. Another
day, just before dinner, Farkas was sitting on the Corso
and they came by and sat down on the next bench. She
was knitting something blue and he was just smoking his
pipe, his hat pulled low over his eyes. Then he noticed
Farkas, nodded, waited and said, 'Good evening.' 'Good
evening,' Farkas said. There was another pause, and he
heard her whisper something.

After a while he said, 'Excuse me,' and coughed: 'You're
a playwright, aren't you?' His wife nudged him.

Farkas smiled and replied: 'Yes, I am.'

The man waited, and then continued: 'We've a nephew
who writes plays, too. Dick Morgan. I don't suppose
you've heard of him.'

'No, I'm afraid I haven't,' Farkas said.

'Well, he isn't much of a playwright, Dick isn't,' the
man mused aloud. 'Had one play put on in Manchester.
What was it called, Gladys?'

The woman suddenly leaned forward, beamed, and
dropped her knitting in her lap. '*The Silent Watch* it was
called. And it wasn't in Manchester, it was in Leeds.'

'That's right, Gladys,' the man said. 'Leeds. We've
never seen it. He's in the army now, Dick is.' He paused.

Farkas enjoyed them, so he felt like chatting. 'How do you like this place?'

She said, 'Oh, it's all right,' and the man said, 'Well'; both at the same time, and they laughed sweetly and the man went on: 'Oh, it's all right, I suppose. They've been jolly decent to us. The food's getting a bit dull, though.'

'Very dull,' Farkas said.

'And it's too hot sometimes,' Mr. Morgan continued: he looked across the water and pushed back his hat.

'Very hot,' Farkas agreed.

The same night Farkas was sitting, as usual, on the terrace with Don Teofilo and Doctor Schmidt, and Don Innocenzo came, and he was drunk again. As he sat down, he dropped some ash into Don Teofilo's tea. The English couple arrived a few minutes later, walking slowly by, arm-in-arm and smiling cheerfully. He was wearing a dark jacket and his old straw hat, smoking his pipe. She wore a jersey and had her knitting-bag with her. As they passed, they smiled at Farkas and the man tipped his hat. They sat down a few tables away and ordered tea.

Don Innocenzo was very moody that night; he kept playing silly practical jokes and drove Don Teofilo to despair: he called for nurse oftener than usual, asking for his pills, or another rug, or the evening paper. Don Innocenzo looked at the headlines and grew both violently sad and angry. 'My Beautiful Sicily,' he started again, and clenched his fists, banged the table, and suddenly turned towards the Morgans and yelled: 'You have ravaged my Beautiful Sicily!'

Mr. Morgan looked up and said: 'What was that?' — he was perhaps hard of hearing and had not caught what Don Innocenzo said.

'You're Ravaging, Ravaging, Ravaging!' Don Innocenzo grew more and more furious. 'You're Killing the Flower of Our Manhood, Burning Our Beautiful White Cities!'

Morgan looked at his wife, then lit his pipe, shook his head, and said in a friendly voice, 'I'm sorry.'

'Sorry, sorry, sorry!' Don Innocenzo shouted, and turned to them fully.

'Stop it,' Don Teofilo said, but made it only worse.

'No sorry!' Don Innocenzo cried. 'You're Killing the Flower, the Manhood, the Sicily!'

'I'm not killing anybody,' Mr. Morgan stated patiently, and asked his wife if she wanted milk with her tea.

There was a small pause, then suddenly Don Innocenzo growled something, jumped to his feet, and rushed over to their table. 'Yes, you are!' he shouted.

The music stopped, and Farkas saw Ugo shuffling nearer with an anxious look; and Don Innocenzo leaned forward and hit Morgan across the face with spread fingers. The pipe fell out of the Englishman's mouth, and he slowly bent down to pick it up. There was a dark spot on his cheek where Don Innocenzo had slapped him, and it was getting darker. As he reached down for his pipe, Don Innocenzo tried to step on his hand, but wasn't quick enough. The Englishman lifted his pipe and put it into his pocket and said to his wife, 'Come, my dear'; and as they rose, he said to Don Innocenzo, 'Swine!' and said it with such conviction that Don Innocenzo stood aside and let them pass as if he agreed. They walked away unhurriedly; the man's trousers were again drawn up much too high, showing his socks, and she carried her little knitting-bag firmly.

The Jolly Fellows of Ravenna

The fugitive from the penal islands was a son of San Fernando, a certain Leonardo di Bocca, usually referred to as the brother of Giacobbe. Don Innocenzo's mysterious references to him left Farkas quite cold; the little Fascist seemed to brag about him as if the man were a trophy he had won. 'I am waiting for him,' Don Innocenzo would repeat darkly, as if to assure Farkas that San Fernando, although not so nice as his Beautiful Sicily, nor anywhere near the Battlefield, might still offer some topical excitement.

'Everybody remembers Leonardo,' Ugo explained. 'Some with hate, some with pride. He was born beneath the Abbey Hill, near the Rotten Corner — so-called because the fishermen say all storms come from there. His father was the village chemist, fairly prosperous, I'm told, and an atheist. Leonardo and his elder brother, Giacobbe — who still lives in the old house on the hill — were, at times, the menace of the community. "One might have known," Don Teofilo remarked after the arrest. He had reasons for saying so, for Leonardo one night set fire to Don Teofilo's favourite Siamese cat. Anyway, they were wild boys. Once they pierced holes in all their father's contraceptives, which caused considerable embarrassment to the community and a marked increase in the birth-rate. They were expelled from school in Ravenna for substituting a portrait of Charlie Chaplin for that of the Virgin.

It was all in the papers after the arrest. Both of the boys went to the University at Milano. Giacobbe returned earlier; then Leonardo arrived and tried, they said, to organize a Communist cell in the village. He did not get very far. Father Giuseppe — then a rising young priest — and Don Teofilo, the two largest landowners, had him eliminated. He was sent to the Lipari Islands. That was eight years ago. Now he's escaped.

'The brother, Giacobbe, was tolerated because the authorities did not want to upset the village too much: the boys were popular with the peasants and the fishermen: in any case, Giacobbe seemed to behave harmlessly and he is now just loafing around. He has no friends down here on the main square, and the other landowners (he's still got a few acres of vineyard) shun him like the pest. Luigi the cook meets him now and then, and of course some of the villagers come to him for "legal advice." No one knows what he's doing the whole day: his vineyard is pretty neglected. They say he's got lots of books. He's never taken a wife, and one can see him hanging about the village or Signora Pina's establishment on the Abbey Road. He's a queer one.'

'Um, yes,' Farkas said, and asked Ugo for another portion of butter.

The weather was lovely at last, that week, that slow week in San Fernando before the focus of things and people changed so suddenly and violence came like a flood. The shadows of the trees were black and clear and the sun had a whitish, radiant glare; yet it was never too hot — except for the Morgans, perhaps. There was a brisk breeze every morning and it died down only after lunch, when

Farkas — possibly like everybody else — lay down behind
the green shutters in the semi-dark room, feeling the cold,
clean sheet under his naked body, smoking one last cigar
before falling asleep to the sound of flies and bees and
the sighing of trees in the wind. Farkas went to the bathhouse every morning, where he usually sat on a wooden
bench in the shade, just behind Don Teofilo's vast body,
deep bronze now, like a big brown blot against the sea
and the sky. He wore green sun-glasses and a funny white
cap, Don Teofilo, with his naked body dominant and with
large layers of fat hanging down and half-covering his tiny
legs. Farkas could not help sitting near him, for Don
Teofilo sought his company and had his spies out after
him: the moment Farkas entered the bathhouse, Don
Teofilo's wailing voice would cry out, 'Farkas! Farkas!' and
there was no escape. Once, while Farkas was taking a
shower in one of the side corridors that ran around the
whole edifice, Alfieri came trotting after him and said,
'Signor Farkas, His Excellency is waiting for you.' There
was no escape.

They would talk awhile, or Don Teofilo would read
some of his hopelessly bad poems, which, in contrast to his
wicked, ugly body, emanated *fin-de-siècle* grace and the
scent of lilacs. When Farkas grew too bored, he would
cautiously enter the water by the rickety wooden steps and
swim slowly for about half an hour and land on one of
the rafts — unless the fat German was sprawling there —
and then swim back and rub himself down and return to
the hotel for lunch. As he left the bathhouse, he would
invariably meet Doctor Schmidt, usually on the long
wooden bridge, and Schmidt, who worked hard at the

Sanatorium, would look harassed and sweaty. 'How are you this morning?' he would ask in his flat, sleepy voice. 'I'm very well,' Farkas would reply. 'Good,' Schmidt would say gloomily, as if he had heard bad news, and then Farkas would continue on his way.

Just before going in for lunch, Farkas usually walked slowly down the Corso, then up the dusty road to Signora Pina's place, formerly a doubtful establishment, a semi-*bordello* where some of the younger peasants, fishermen, and waiters had gathered nightly to drink cheap red wine served by Pina's husky waitresses. The war put an end to it: most of the girls were called up, or went to town to cash in on the world-wide prosperity of prostitution, and only Pina remained, for she was much too old. Her place was now a mere café, and Farkas used to go there for a quiet *apéritif* — mainly before lunch and sometimes at night, too, when he felt he could not bear the company at the Paradiso. There he would sit by himself, looking at the tall reeds which rose immediately in front of the terrace, framing a wooden plank which led some fifty yards into the sea. Formerly one could hire a rowing boat plus one of the husky waitresses, who would not only row for one, and sing, but also perform surprisingly urbane erotic feats. But the boats were 'called up,' too, used by the Party fishery just beyond the Abbey Hill.

And after lunch came the siesta in the semi-dark room, disturbed occasionally by Tony, the unhappy neighbour, who cried a lot and pottered about or made love, un-happily, to Don Innocenzo. At four Farkas got up, took a shower, and went down for his iced coffee which, thanks to Ugo, was almost pre-war and *à la Vienna*. The lounge was quite deserted at that time, save for Enrico, dozing, or the fat airman passing through, just back from tennis or church. But the Morgans were there, of course, having tea, ceremoniously, stubbornly, and heroically, helped by Ugo, who, like all international waiters, was Anglophile. They came down from their room a few minutes before four, and she would tell her husband in a sweet, thrilled voice, as if she were making an extraordinary and perhaps naughty suggestion: 'What about tea?' And he would answer with thoughtful enthusiasm: 'That's an excellent idea, Gladys.' Then Ugo served tea, never quite properly, forgetting either the strainer or the slop-basin. Then they started to sip their tea and crunch their toast, talking loudly in English, clinking their cups and spoons cheerfully, hoping, Farkas felt, that the Germans or Don Innocenzo would come in and arrest them for their demonstrative behaviour. Whenever Fritti toddled by, they invariably stopped him. 'Cup of tea?' Mrs. Morgan would ask sweetly, and the manager would look around, blush, and say firmly, 'No, thank you.' After two years of the Morgans, he did not know whether to treat them with polite contempt or careful reverence. 'Divided loyalties,' he explained to Farkas. 'Conflict between patriotism and post-war trade.' And Mr. Morgan would always ask him what the news was: usually in a loud and cheerful voice. 'Have they taken Naples?' 'No, certainly not,' Fritti would answer, and walk off quickly.

Although the Paradiso did not interest him, with the possible exception of Tony whom he greeted regularly now, these were his immediate surroundings, and once or twice, when he vaguely thought of starting work again, he turned each character in his mind, tasting them, inspecting them from each side: would they do? He could not suspect, of course, that soon things would start to move and the spotlights fall on different things and people.

During the third week he became aware of being watched. One Saturday morning he was sitting on the terrace of the Paradiso having breakfast, feeling particularly fit and contented, dividing his attention between his coffee, the *Giornale d'Italia,* and Tony's window, deciding to pay a visit to Signor Foa's shop to buy himself some shaving cream, when he felt somebody's stare on his neck. Farkas was very sensitive in this respect, almost femininely so; and after a while he had to turn and was just in time to catch the quick movement with which a man, sitting some four or five tables away jerked his newspaper in front of his face. Obviously he had been watching Farkas, doing so quite clumsily, in an amateurish way. Farkas smiled to himself and thought that it was probably the *'Ovra della pasta ascuitta,'* the Spaghetti-Gestapo, as the local secret police was nicknamed. When he returned to the hotel, he deliberately passed the man, who pretended to be deeply engrossed in his newspaper and did not look up. Farkas saw for a moment a dark face topped with pitch-black hair sprinkled with handsome grey on the temples. When Farkas got to his room to fetch his swimming-suit, he remembered the man again, and peering out of the window saw him sitting at the table smoking. He looked up, and their stare met for a second; then the man quickly looked away and called for the waiter.

Farkas had quite forgotten about him when next day he saw him again on the Corso. He was having his meditative half-hour by the sea, smoking in silence, pulling his straw hat over his eyes to keep away the sharp sun-rays that bounced from the gentle sea. He had nearly dozed off when he heard quiet steps in the distance. At first he took no notice, but there was no other sound except the faint rustling of the trees, and so the approaching steps forced themselves on his attention. It was the quiet, crunching sound of somebody strolling leisurely, without purpose. When Farkas turned, he saw a white figure some hundred yards away. He recognized him at once, the white linen suit and the very dark hair. He could not see his face well, but noted the way he walked, rather flat-footed and soft, his feet turned outward, his body swaying gently from side to side: a youngish walk it was, a city walk with no primness or pomposity about it. 'Ah, there he is again,' Farkas thought, and turned back to the sea, remembering the two Ovra men who had shadowed him in Rome some years ago, following him practically everywhere, even into a cinema where they breathed down his neck, until he got so tired that he lodged a complaint with the Ministry of Foreign Affairs.

The man dressed in the white linen suit slowly walked past Farkas's bench. He did not stop, or slow down his walk, and went as far as the end of the Corso, where the Yachting Club stood; then slowly returned again. Farkas felt amused and listened to the steps, trying to guess the man's mood and temper. The steps became somewhat hesitant when they neared the bench again; finally they stopped, receded, and stopped again: the man sat down on one of the benches behind Farkas's back. There was now no other sound but the rustling of the trees and the soft splashing of some distant rowing-boats moored in front of the Yachting Club. Farkas remembered how he and Daniel used to play 'Sherlock Holmes' as children; they would stand at a busy street corner, count the passers-by, and follow the twelfth wherever he or she went. Once they had to walk five miles, while Daniel explained that their victim might be Jack the Ripper or the Hound of the Baskervilles in disguise. Finally the hunted man turned and, yelling abuse, slapped their faces, and Daniel kicked him back. Then they decided to use some disguise: Daniel suggested a faint limp, which they adopted, and limped over to Buda following a fat old woman with a market bag, until Daniel got a cramp and they had to stop.

The man in the white suit did not wait for Farkas to move. He sat there for about half an hour while Farkas tried to think of something amusingly sinister he could do to arouse the man's attention. But before he could think of anything, he heard the man getting up. He walked away slowly in the direction of the main square. Farkas had not seen him for two days when he turned up again: this time in the bathhouse. Farkas was reading in the shade, wrapped in a bathing-towel and feeling glad because Don Teofilo was not there, when he saw the man again: he stood in the far corner of the house, near the diving-board, wearing small black swimming-trunks, leaning against the door of a cabin, his arms folded. He was trying to behave naturally and did not watch Farkas conspicuously, but gradually edged nearer and nearer, and finally sat down a few yards away, reading a newspaper and throwing an occasional glance at Farkas. Later, when Farkas went to have his midday shower, he walked firmly and aggressively past the man, who looked up and smiled. This was the first time Farkas had seen his face from so near. It was a handsome though tired face, with a great crumpled forehead and very dark and lovely eyes that stood almost apart from the face in an extra dimension, dark and shining. He had a small nose, and when he smiled Farkas saw his teeth were not too good, with gaps between them. The thick hair on his chest was greying, too.

Farkas did not smile back at him, but made an annoyed grimace. He wanted the man to realize that he knew and disapproved of being followed. Later, when he was walking back to the Paradiso, the man did not come after him, but he was on the Corso in the afternoon, keeping at a discreet distance, and again, later that night, he sat on the terrace while Farkas had his nightly drinks with Don Teofilo and Schmidt. He thought of asking them about the man; but somehow he waited until they went and he could speak to Ugo.

'Who's that police spy, Ugo?' he said, when Ugo brought him another carafe of wine.

The terrace was quite empty. The band was still playing and the girl's violin was sending thin, sentimental waves down the square.

'Which one?' Ugo asked, leaning lower to catch Farkas's whisper, brushing the tablecloth with a dirty napkin.

'The one in the white suit.'

Ugo turned and bent low again.

'That's not a police spy,' he said. 'That's Giacobbe, Giacobbe di Bocca.'

'Well, why does he keep following me?' Farkas said.

'Shall I ask him?' Ugo said.

'No, never mind.' Farkas dismissed him.

Ugo went away and disappeared into the kitchen through the swing door. The terrace was empty now except for Farkas and the man in the white suit: he sat there, his elbow on the arm of his wicker chair, smoking thoughtfully. But Farkas knew he was only waiting for a chance and that in a few minutes perhaps he would rise, embarrassedly walk over to his table, bow and say, 'Excuse me, are you the famous playwright Stefan Farkas?'—or something of the sort. The man did not interest him, nor his unfortunate brother. But he did not feel like going upstairs, and was bored with himself. He would not have minded talking to somebody who would listen decently. Don Teofilo and the Doctor had been very tiresome that evening. The fat gnome kept telling smutty jokes which sounded singularly repulsive coming from him — as if he had lived them all through, personally. The Doctor was sleepier than usual. His eyelids kept closing, and he hardly listened when Farkas, to relieve Don Teofilo's pornographic outbursts, told a subtle anecdote from the seventeenth century.

The man in the white suit got up, and, as Farkas had expected, walked slowly in his direction, still hesitant but apparently set on speaking to him. Farkas did not look up to encourage him, but out of the corner of his eye he could see him approaching and sensed his embarrassment. The man stopped at his elbow and cleared his throat.

'Excuse me,' he said. His voice was very deep and sounded much older than he looked.

'All right,' Farkas said. 'I know. Sit down.'

He looked up. The man stood there, smiling self-consciously, but rather puzzled and delighted. He looked handsome in the dim light, although his suit was very crumpled and soiled. He sat down.

'You've been following me for days,' Farkas said sternly. 'I don't like being followed.'

'I'm sorry,' the man said. 'My name is Giacobbe di Bocca . . . '

'I know,' Farkas said. 'And you've a brother who's escaped. I knew Trotsky in Vienna; I didn't like his accent and the way he played chess, and I regard Communists with the same suspicion as Jesuits.'

The man nodded and did not look puzzled or impressed by Farkas. He said 'Ha' thoughtfully, as though he pondered over a tricky problem. 'So you've heard about my brother.'

'Yes,' Farkas replied. 'And you want me to help you, or him, I suppose.'

'No,' the man said, almost absent-mindedly. He had long, feminine fingers and a sensitive hand. 'No, thank you. I'm sorry if I was a nuisance. I didn't really mean to be. But when I heard that you were here, I suddenly remembered that it's years and years since I had an intelligent conversation. Years,' he added sadly.

There was a small pause. Farkas felt a bit disappointed. Di Bocca did not seem to be the shy, impressed young man he had expected him to be. He sat there quite at ease.

'I so much wanted to meet you,' he continued without enthusiasm, but sincerely. 'As a colleague.'

Farkas cleared his throat ironically.

'Colleague?' he said, took off his monocle, and rubbed it with his silk handkerchief. 'Ah, a writer.'

The man smiled. 'No, not quite,' he said. 'A Reader. With a capital R, so to speak. I read.' He leaned forward earnestly. 'Don't you think there ought to be understanding and co-operation between author and audience, writer and reader? I mean, it's almost as difficult to read intelligently as to write. Yes,' he added thoughtfully, and Farkas did not know if he was serious or just ironical, 'my style has developed a lot lately.'

'Congratulations,' Farkas said, and decided to take it as a joke. 'Are you reading anything good?'

'Oh, yes,' Giacobbe di Bocca said with sudden modesty.

'But you do write as well, don't you?' Farkas asked.

'Oh, well,' the man said, and again seemed to be shy.

'Come on, don't be modest,' Farkas said, and turned to him. 'You remind me of the young poet who went to see an old editor of mine with his novel. The editor asked him what it was all about, whereupon the young man blushed and hummed and hawed. "Come on," my old friend said, "What have *you* to be modest about?" ' Farkas continued: ' "For only the great can afford to be modest." '

Di Bocca laughed; his uneven teeth showed.

'I am not really a writer,' he said. 'It's only part of my reading. Once, long ago, I used to write very bad poems; later, political stuff. Once I wrote about you, too.'

'About me?' Farkas said. 'You must have hated my plays.'

'I am not the hating sort,' the man said, with unnecessary emphasis. 'No, it was a rather long-winded essay, called "The Humour of Capitalism." Long ago it was,' he added. 'And never published, of course.'

'Never mind,' Farkas said. 'So many have written about

me in the same vein. It would have bored everybody. Those who go to see my plays don't read youthful essays, and those who do don't go to see my plays. What did you say? That I'm the typical falsifier of life, the superficial jester of the middle classes, and so forth?'

'Yes,' di Bocca admitted. 'D'you mind?'

'Don't be silly,' Farkas said. 'I don't take my writing seriously.'

'Ha,' the man mused again. It was an irritating habit. But his deep, resonant voice attracted Farkas: it was like a tired bassoon left alone in a deserted concert hall.

'Have you written anything else?' Farkas inquired paternally.

'Oh, yes,' Giacobbe said. 'Several essays. I have been working on one for the last five years. There's nothing much to do in San Fernando, and I am not allowed to travel.'

'What is it about?'

'Punctuation,' the man said, and the word sounded like the title of an heroic ballad. 'You must know something about the subject. How do you feel about semicolons?'

'I mistrust them,' Farkas said. 'They show that the author was too cowardly or too ignorant to finish a sentence.'

'I disagree,' di Bocca said. 'The full stop is often misleadingly final. Think of all the things that could not be said in any one sentence — which keep lurking behind the infinity of a point. The semicolon is more modest; and it gives a rest. The colon, of course, is too obvious; don't you agree? Too obvious, with no subtlety. Like a child rudely pointing with his finger. I hate the three dots,' he added vehemently. 'I hate them. They are so incredibly vulgar, like a man's voice trailing off in an obscene whisper. And pompous, too, suggesting that there are things on earth and in heaven that the author knows, but feels too superior to communicate. I mean, can you imagine Dante or Homer or Goethe dotting their sentences? No, certainly not. It's affected, prim, bourgeois. But the main villain is the exclamation mark. Actually the title of my essay is "The Exclamation Mark: A Symbol of Fascism." You follow me?'

Farkas was annoyed with the last remark, but the deep voice attracted him.

'I think I do,' he answered, with sarcasm.

'I would liquidate them if I were the Minister of Education,' di Bocca continued. 'Liquidate them mercilessly, take them off all proclamations, admonitions, manifestoes, erase them all. They infect man with false pathos and inflated sentiments. Think of d'Annunzio and all the radio speeches and leading articles of the age. You know why the Anglo-Saxons will win this war? Because they tend to dispense with the fellow, with that pompous intruder, that soap-box orator, the Exclamation Mark, who raises his voice and twists his hand in a melodramatic gesture, stampeding the Radio. It has a phallic origin, of course. It radiates id that has run amok.'

'Very interesting,' Farkas said.

The man suddenly changed his tone: he became the polite outsider, the eager admirer. 'Are you working on anything?'

Farkas was vexed by the question: he did not know why.

'Yes, I am,' he lied.

'Oh, really?' di Bocca was almost excited. He leaned nearer, fixing his stare on Farkas's face. 'What sort of thing will it be?'

'A play.' Farkas felt like going.

The man asked: 'A triangle?'

'Yes,' Farkas replied aggressively. 'But I must be going now.'

'Oh, must you really?' di Bocca asked disappointedly.

'Yes, definitely,' Farkas simulated a yawn. 'Well,' he said, 'I'll be seeing you, I suppose.' He forced his voice to be somewhat arrogant. 'You must tell me more about your work.'

'Yes, Signor Farkas,' the man said respectfully, and stood up.

Farkas went upstairs, and after he had undressed he went to the window and looked down. The terrace was dark, the waiters had gone home, but di Bocca still sat there, his cigarette glowing. Farkas was still annoyed.

During the next few days he did not see Giacobbe di Bocca. The first day he did not think of him; but at night, when he went onto the terrace, he caught himself looking around and realized that he was wondering whether the man would be there. He wasn't. Farkas felt a queer disappointment. Later he asked Don Teofilo casually: 'What about the fugitive?'

The fat man shrugged his shoulder. 'He'll turn up. Don Innocenzo says he's got nowhere to go, and they're hunting him all over the country.'

'Do you know his brother?' Farkas asked.

Don Teofilo's face became an imitation Jahveh. 'Scoundrel,' he said. 'Loafer. Bolshie.'

The next day, when Farkas went down to the bathhouse, he turned around once or twice to see if he was being followed. And in the bathhouse he kept interrupting his reading and looking up; he knew all the time that he was waiting for Giacobbe, and this knowledge irritated him. By the third day he felt as angry as a neglected wife and asked Ugo if he had seen di Bocca. Ugo said he hadn't. Farkas went for a long walk on the Abbey Road, fuming and making up little speeches to himself and to an imaginary Giacobbe, and was witty and superior. The same night he had a dream. It was on the Corso. Giacobbe and he were sitting in a perambulator, playing chess. A big fat woman came by with swinging hips, and Giacobbe leaned over him, leering. 'Do you know who that was? That was Signorina Capitalism.' He reddened and said, 'Ah, yes.' Giacobbe's face was big and red. 'I bet you don't know, Stefan, what that means.' 'Oh, yes,' he tried to fend off the other. 'We only call it by a different name; we call it *walda*.' But Giacobbe laughed and stood up and urinated like the little boy of Brussels.

On the fourth day Farkas went, as usual, to Madame Pina's café to have an *apéritif*. As he entered, he immediately spotted di Bocca, who sat with his back turned to the entrance. Farkas hesitated, then sat down at another table and asked loudly for a drink.

Di Bocca turned at once. 'Signor Farkas!' he said rising. 'May I join you or are you waiting for someone?'

'I'm not,' Farkas said. 'You may sit down if you promise not to say much.'

Di Bocca laughed. He had not shaved that morning, and his face was crumpled as if someone had slept on it. His voice was a good deal hoarser than before. Madame Pina brought Farkas's drink, and gave him a curious glance when she saw di Bocca sitting at his table.

'You've got a rotten reputation in this place,' Farkas said. 'I shouldn't be sitting with you.'

Giacobbe blushed.

'I can go away,' he said.

'Don't be silly,' Farkas admonished like an uncle. 'You ought to grow up.'

'I am grown up,' the man replied. 'On some levels, at least. I mean politically and as regards literature. And sexually, too, I suppose. I'm thirty-nine next year.'

'Youngster,' Farkas said. 'Have you ever been married?'

'No,' di Bocca said. 'Why? According to your works, all women are unfaithful to their husbands.'

'Exactly. Marriage makes a man grow up,' Farkas said. 'One cannot know enough about women. They are dangerous, and you have to find the right moment to catch them unawares. They keep dropping clues when you're married to them.'

They had another drink.

'I must go now,' Farkas said lightly. 'But I may be coming down here after dinner.'

'Oh, lovely!' di Bocca said, with enthusiasm. 'We must have another talk.'

The same night di Bocca was sitting in the café near the waterfront, and Farkas walked straight up to him. They drank red wine.

'Well, how is the world?' Di Bocca was in a thoughtful mood and his beard was growing in dark spots on his chin. 'And in particular how are your friends up at the Paradiso?'

'They're all right,' Farkas said and polished his monocle. 'Of course, to you they are all symbols of the Hated System. Pity they don't wear top-hats and smoke fat cigars and kick poor, wonderful workingmen in their pants.'

'They do,' di Bocca said. He was drinking rapidly, in big gulps. His voice was very deep. 'Yachting caps will do for top-hats, and Don Teofilo is fat enough for a symbol, isn't he? But of course you think they are nice.'

'No, I don't,' Farkas said. 'No one really is. Are workers nice?'

'No, I don't suppose they are,' di Bocca said. 'The difference is that they don't pretend to be and don't want to be. Not the genuine ones.' He produced a faded tin box from his pocket, opened it, and fished out a small cigar. 'But tell me, Signor Farkas, do tell me, what is your ambition now?'

Farkas said: 'To finish this carafe of red wine in peace.'

'That is all?'

'Yes. You see, youngster,' he went on paternally, 'the trouble with ambitions is that they are realized.'

'That is a platitude,' di Bocca said, and lit his cigar.

'All platitudes are true,' Farkas said. 'Don't follow to their ruin those intel-l-l-l-lectuals and r-r-r-evolutionaries who get fed up with simple home truths and keep making up new, revised, and falsified versions. Honesty is the best policy and those who rise early may become millionaries.'

'Nonsense,' di Bocca said. 'I know dozens of honest early-risers who have ended in the gutter, or in prison. But to go back to what you were saying about ambitions. Surely you can't be content with finishing some wine, or a cigar, or a walk? You have had all the success in life —

piles of money, fame, and possibly beautiful blonde mistresses.'

'Yes,' Farkas said. 'And you want to suggest that it wasn't, it couldn't be enough.'

'Exactly.'

'Rubbish,' Farkas said. 'It made me reasonably happy. All I want now is to avoid pain, irritation, and vulgarity. I know you have different notions, but as I doubt whether your taste is any better than mine, I prefer to stick to my ideas. After all, all you fellows want for your "people" is piles of money and beautiful blonde mistresses. For me, the idea of lots of manual labourers, mechanics, peasants, and shopkeepers running life for me is repulsive. You have all invented a myth. Rich people, aristocrats, archbishops, are usually full of good taste and kindness and charm.'

'Yes,' di Bocca said. 'Hitler adores flowers and Wagner. Do you really like the clientèle at the Paradiso? Do you think they are full of charm and kindness?'

'Some of them are quite amusing, and none of them wants to place dynamite in my night-pot. The Morgans are sweet, for instance, and there is the little refugee girl. Do you know her?' he asked quickly.

'I've heard her playing, thank you,' di Bocca said. 'That was enough. Oh, but Signor Farkas' — he drank some more wine — 'they're only cork, bobbing on the surface, with no roots of significance, unaware of the deep currents beneath; they will be swept away and you are wasting your gifts of observation. As with an iceberg, below the Paradiso is the big base: beneath the carpet, frayed, anyway, and not the Persian it pretends to be, are the kitchen and the servants' quarters with little Chef Luigi, a thoughtful and sad man, and Filomena with her beautiful breasts and old, wrinkled face; and Tasso the kitchen hand who hasn't slept a wink since August the fifteenth, 1917, when a shell burst beside him. What do you know about them? Ugo could not tell you anything because Ugo, the loyal leech, is a snob like all good servants. And the rest of them; old man Stefano who carries the heavy trunks upstairs year after year and cannot stand straight any more, and Alfonso the pastry-cook who sings and laughs so well. And, beneath and beyond them, the deeper thing, the village you have never thought of visiting.'

'I am not interested in villages.'

Giacobbe drank again. A red drop ran down his chin, onto his white collar. He wiped it off.

'I know, I know. I have seen some of your plays and read others. You're interested in adultery and the kind of jokes which make people laugh as if they were being tickled with a straw. Very well, I'm the last to blame you. If you'll excuse me, like Ugo you're a loyal leech, faithfully serving those people who think they can afford to be generous and let someone poke fun at them for their money. But that was long ago, very long ago. Perhaps you're not quite aware of the changes.'

'Yes, I am, and I don't like them,' Farkas said.

'Of course not. I don't want you to like them; only be interested in them. I lied to you the other night. I do need your help, and I cannot get it unless you know what it is all about. The accent being on "all." I take it for granted that you do not like large pieces of metal filled with explosives to be flung at you from all directions, or to see young and cheerful bodies blown to smithereens, nor the demolition of comfortable residences. I beg you to look at San Fernando in this spirit.'

'I came to San Fernando to rest, not to look,' Farkas replied, with a Shakespearean gesture.

They were getting slightly drunk, sitting on Madame Pina's concrete terrace by the sea. It was a night which later on stood apart and sombre, marking the end of the first slow days; the end of a number of other things as well. There were two carafes of wine on the dirty tablecloth soiled with large reddish spots and the traces of ash. Giacobbe smoked quickly and let the smoke out while he was speaking, the smoke accompanying his words, wrapping them up and sending them high. His face was tired and handsome, each feature slightly more pronounced than it should perhaps have been, standing apart in disharmony as if the small nose resented the dark eyes or the articulate lips. His voice was very hoarse; he nearly whispered at times and had to clear his throat frequently.

'My throat,' he croaked apologetically; 'you must excuse me. Too much talk and smoke. I know you came to rest,' he went on. 'To escape, to be more precise. But can you really? After all, you're a good European. There are no bombs here, none of the pain or danger; but the stink of young corpses is in one's nostrils. You cannot get away; only the moon is neutral, they say, and the battle is nearing us. It is all very well to stand aside for a while, to wash your hands and keep moving to quieter climes. But how long can you move on? How long escape? Geographically you're very confined already, and soon it may catch up with you. And then you will be forced to take sides. You will be forced, I tell you: tonight, next month, next year; it is inevitable. And then the war and the world, a mere nuisance till then, will grow into a tragedy; and you will not be asked questions; and subterfuges, neutral passports, and subtle cynical remarks will not help; you will have to move quickly because you will realize that your life is at stake, alongside other lives, and that there is no chance of dying with your boots off. The barricades are raised. In the meantime I ask your help. It is no slight favour, no usual one. I shall have to make you interested, make you understand.

'My brother Leonardo has escaped, as you know. The police are waiting for him, the police, the State, the army, and the navy, if you like. So am I. All of us who are waiting for him know that he has no friend but me. His former comrades are dead or in exile. He had been on the island for eight years. He was never too strong — always some trouble with his health; and of course his teeth have never recovered from what they did to him. For years he ought to have lived on milk and a careful diet. For eight years he lived on greasy dishwater, spongy bread, and an occasional food parcel I was allowed to send. Anyway, he is at large now, a broken Leonardo, I am sure, who must have crying or vomiting fits, who blinks at the sun of freedom, listens for the sounds of pursuit. I do not know how he's done it. He wasn't very strong, or smart. But he is out somewhere, out in this night, and unless he is incredibly lucky he will be caught before he gets here. Don Innocenzo, too, is waiting for him. The little peacock wants promotion and fame. I am waiting, too, and I need your help. But you must be an ally, first.

'You see, Signor Farkas,' Giacobbe went on, his voice rough as emery paper, 'I couldn't simply trust your "kindness" or "understanding." I am suspicious of mere sentiments. Everyone is capable of them. Even Don Innocenzo can love a cat, or a whore; and Don Teofilo, that wicked toad, worships bees. No, love or sympathy is not enough. You must be convinced that Leonardo and I and, incidentally, San Fernando are right. If you are, I can trust you because you have reached conclusions logically and objectively, and only the stupid betray their conclusions.'

'I'll be glad to do what I can,' Farkas interrupted him, reaching for his glass. 'Though it can be precious little. But don't ask me to be interested. I mean, all my sympathies for your unfortunate brother. But don't expect sympathies for your political views. Politics are like . . .'

'No aphorisms, please.' Giacobbe di Bocca's voice sounded like a creaking door slowly opening. 'I know you're not interested in "politics," which means for you a number of pompous officials, cheating and swanking and getting rich; or tiresome decrees which you can afford to disregard. I know. You're the Distinguished Foreigner everywhere: a very comfortable rôle, placing you high above the natives; and you consider all other men natives, don't you? I remember something I read about you some years ago: you were reported as saying that you had the largest flat in Europe: one room at the Adlon, another at the Crillon in Paris, a third at the Negresco in Nice, and so on. That was years ago. Since then, most of that flat has become pretty uninhabitable, and soon this last "room" of yours will be menaced.

'But my politics are different, you know. They're the

bread of the fishermen, the venereal disease of some of the day-labourers, the lungs of the children, the growing cancer of some of the old. All this and a lot more, all that deep thing upon whose surface you and the Paradiso are bobbing, ignorant of the stream below. I said that I had read some of your works. I understand that life for you is mostly a scatological episode, and history merely an accidental chain of dubious anecdotes. Admittedly, sometimes you see the pathos of love and its bitterness in comic relief. You find it highly amusing to display. Two Elegant Men quarrelling over a Woman, and you believe it significant and timeless, indicating that these things are perhaps the only constant elements in man's record. Well, it may be that Paradise was simply a tense triangle between Adam, Eve, and the Serpent, and everything that has happened since may be explained in terms of Cleopatra's nose, Pompadour's pimples, or the snow-white breasts of Countess Walewska. But you seem to be forgetting that man has suddenly and riotously begun to grow up. I want you to realize that you are hopelessly outdated.'

'I know I am, and I do not propose to catch up,' Farkas said.

'Oh, but that is exactly what I'd like you to do,' Giacobbe said. 'Tonight.' He drank more wine. 'Things might happen in San Fernando, any moment. In a small way, of course; but you are here, a highly competent and notable observer, and that might give us significance. You do write beautifully. It makes me sad to think of those perfectly cut sentences of yours; pearls they are. I do not know what will happen, but we will remember that you are in our midst. Think, what a difference it would have made if Carlyle had actually been present at the storming of the Bastille, or if Petrograd had had other recorders besides Reed. No, you must catch up. Things might happen and your interest might waken, but only to turn to such frivolities as Ugo's remarks or the little Austrian refugee girl's tears. Those things are insignificant. What if Ugo is a pathetic relic of a semi-feudal age; if the Austrian girl is an unhappy leaf at the mercy of every passport official or police agent; what if the three Germans are mildly interesting neurotic cases, or if the English couple maintain an attitude of strong and kind contempt? *You* must grow up, Signor Farkas.'

'My dear youngster,' said Farkas, with a superior smile, pulling out his shirt cuffs, 'I am too old to be able to afford that. Anyway, I believe that despite your "changes" a man trying to kiss a girl is better literature than a mass-meeting in a factory area or the predicaments of your villagers.'

'Ah!' cried Giacobbe, happy and excited, throwing his hand into the smoky air as if to catch some of Farkas's words, 'you're getting to the point, although you're delightfully wrong. Apparently you consider yourself a writer who, because he happens to know the secrets of linking up verbs and nouns prettily, can afford to wander about the face of the earth looking for literary subjects, considering life a confused show where he alone can create order by selecting what is beautiful or interesting. Well, among other changes, this arrogance, too, will have to go. That kind of Caesaromania is just as repugnant as that of the Nazis or of those early priests who bamboozled the world by pretending to find significant clues in the bowels of birds. Signor Farkas,' di Bocca added reproachfully, wagging his forefinger, 'the universe isn't a model you can hire by the hour, undress and leer at.'

'Nonsense,' Farkas said, and took off his monocle. 'The universe is here'—he tapped his forehead—'it is mine, and I can do with it what I please.'

Giacobbe started to giggle like a malicious child: even his voice had a higher pitch. '*Ecco* an idealist,' he said, slapping his knees, like a detective who has just found the murderer. 'You are going to be surprised in your little ivory tower; or shall I say ivory Maginot Line? What ingratitude! Just because, through painful evolution lasting a few thousand years, you happen to differ from a Yahoo by being able to integrate inefficient observations of your world, you have the cheek to declare it to be yours. It was some two hundred years ago that good Bishop Berkeley formulated this territorial demand, proclaiming arrogantly that *esse* is *percipi*. Among other things, he didn't know that man is, as our much wiser colleague on the Avon so marvellously said, "such stuff as dreams are made of"; and that our dreams are those of a savage child. Neither could he know our embarrassing relations to the monkeys, the liquidation of God, the fourth dimension, the quantum theory, or that the history of man depends on the way he works. You exist, Signor Farkas, not because you think, but because you work and you are what you dream.'

'I never dream,' Farkas said, and leaned back, 'and I avoid work as far as possible.'

Giacobbe rubbed his palms together. His voice was getting hoarse again.

'I'm happy you're flippant. I should hate a solemn antagonist. It shows, incidentally, that your ivory seclusion is not even the morbid mire of Proust or the subconscious anarchy of Joyce, but only a *chambre séparée*, at the best, with red plush, some half-naked tarts, and tabetic aristocrats. Not much worth fighting for. Ah, but you'll possibly retort that you wouldn't fight for it, anyway: all you want is a last comfortable window-seat whence you can poke fun at the world. But even satire is going, that art you seem to be so greatly attached to. So long as the stupid gangs on top were all-powerful, holding on high their freak taboos and idiotic totems, one was justified in ridiculing them, as has been done successfully for the last hundred years; as a matter of fact, all good literature has been destructive ever since we succeeded in stepping out of the black magic of the Middle Ages. Swift, Rabelais, Voltaire, helped to clear the rubbish away; but now the *tabula* is almost *rasa*, the cleaning is largely done, and even my eighty-years-old grandmother doesn't believe in the Holy Trinity or the inevitability of private property. The gangs on top are everywhere on the defensive; at their most aggressive they have to turn to subterfuges and pretend to be destructive, or act like Yahoos; which furthers their own destruction. We shall have to be affirmative once more, and shall need new Dantes and Miltons, not scepticism.'

'And transfer Bethlehem to Moscow, dyeing the star red, I suppose?' Farkas said.

'It has been transferred before,' Giacobbe replied dryly; 'to Byzantium, Rome, and even to Avignon. But you must not be concerned with geographical niceties. Anyway, there is no question of transfer; we can leave Bethlehem to the Zionists and the oil companies. But it is par-

ticularly offensive to suggest that man is still the helpless
prisoner of Nature and magic he was two thousand years
ago. Despite the pessimism of churches, business men, and
purists, humanity has, after all, progressed since the times
when sensitive Semites roamed the desert, despaired at the
lack of law, and projected their father-imago to the sky.
The Golden Age is of the future; let us, as soon as possible,
get rid of our savage infancy. Those early panaceas, the
laws of Moses (that first of Victorians), of Christ, that
brilliant Red, and of Mahomet, who describes heaven and
hell with the smart exactitude of a Thomas Cook's catalogue, were, for all their beauty and wisdom, designed to
tame isolated tribesmen in search of a unity which they
had lost somewhere between the penis and the cortex.

'Remember, Signor Farkas, that contrary to popular
misconceptions, it was man who, having cleared a forest,
finding some leisure and discovering the Noun, knelt
down, took some clay, and made God. And so far as those
Laws — carefully edited and censored ever since — some of
them are outright dangerous, most of them impractical,
and all of them calculated to encourage hypocrisy. Pray,
who believes in them except prigs, fanatics, and village
idiots? In God, that mystification of a comparatively simple Oedipus complex? In loving one's neighbours, not
killing, not committing adultery, not coveting the private
property of the man next door, wife, ox, ass, maidservant,
and all? God, for one thing, has been successfuly mobilized
for every possible "sin," and is perhaps the only thing ever
fully nationalized. He has proved to be a staunch ally of
Huns and Barbarians and Nazis. No wonder; if He ex-
ists, He must be an Imperialist, a dictator, relying on a

vast bureaucracy, encouraging nepotism, bribing man into obedience either by sadistic threats of an eternal concentration camp or by promises of a lurid rest-house populated by glorified spinsters, or — as Mahomet was eager to point out — fat harlots, date trees, and plenty of drinks.'

'I see,' Farkas said, and brushed away the heavy, stinking smoke of di Bocca's cigar. 'Praise to Man and his Prophets: Marx, Darwin, Freud, and Giacobbe di Bocca.'

'Well, no,' Giacobbe replied modestly. 'Although the gentlemen you mentioned were far more competent and reliable as observers than a few uneducated fishermen from Galilee or that ambitious falsifier Saul, who turned the manifesto of the vanquished Nazarene into a doctrine of reaction which has been scaring man for much too long now. Those Laws were of service in a scared and sparse world; but did they succeed in lessening misery or fear? New ones are needed, based, not on the lonely savage, but on a community whose ethics are assured by material abundance, properly conditioned reflexes, and a fearless mind that will help us to get rid of lust and lies.'

'B-r-r-r-r!' Farkas shuddered. 'Now you really scare me. Your phalanstery sounds worse than Dachau. All your rosy-cheeked, well-fed, conditioned, and psychoanalyzed party members — I should hate to meet them! And they will be so unhappy without their silly little conflicts.'

'Ah, that one!' Giacobbe grinned. 'Now you trot out that pretty argument, unhappiness. Signor Farkas, you remind me of Professor Battista, of the State Asylum near Milano. A wonderful man, you ought to meet him; I am sure you two would get along nicely. Marvellous man, the Professor, with his proverbial white beard and gold-framed

spectacles. He has some five hundred genuine and guar-
anteed madmen in his establishment at Mombello. Some
of his cases are world-famous. There is one patient who
insists that his skull has changed places with his funda-
ment and vice versa; he keeps shaving the latter, and is
touchy if the former, which he covers with a veil, is referred to. Then there is the one who thinks he is a Business Cycle, and he keeps rushing about in little circles;
and many others, even more fascinating. The Professor
once said to me, after taking me around: "Young man,
wouldn't it be terrible if they all recovered? They'd feel
so unhappy and dull." That's your attitude too.'

Farkas shook his head. 'I have no attitude, youngster.
As you said, I am a flippant, not a solemn opponent. And
it is quite hopeless to try to convert me. There is nothing
to convert me from. I do not wish to become a prophet,
and if I write again it will be the same old-fashioned trash.
All I'm interested in is making a few people smile again.'

'Ah, but wait a moment.' Giacobbe squashed his cigar
in an empty wineglass. 'You mustn't forget that your audience will be vastly changed. The polished crowd is mostly gone, thank God, or is going rapidly. There will be a
different type of listener now, one you probably despise;
but he is going to fill the stalls and dress-circle, eager and
interested, wanting to hear a lot of answers.'

'Sorry,' Farkas said. 'I don't know them myself. And
even if I did, I shouldn't care to write them down.'

'Well, I don't know,' Giacobbe said thoughtfully.
'Things might happen in San Fernando, things that would
perhaps interest you. And there'll be different ways of
writing them up. You might perhaps select the love-affair

of Tony the violinist and Don Innocenzo: the helpless
refugee girl who is blackmailed into bed all the time and
now doesn't mind any more. Or what about Don Teofilo
and the nurse. She hates him, you know, with an old-
fashioned hatred that is rare these days. Or perhaps,' he
said cautiously, 'you might write Leonardo up one day,
Leonardo, broken, toothless, out there somewhere in the
night, possibly on his way to San Fernando, where we are
all waiting for him. Admittedly, he is not the hero-type,
your hero-type, I mean. He is — or rather he used to be
— taller than I am, with a beautiful white forehead and a
great shock of ginger hair. The girls in Milano liked him;
he evoked their better instincts. They used to visit him
when he was sick, take him flowers and pet him. I can't
imagine what he looks like today; not much, I'm afraid.
But even in his case there is a faint love-interest, Signor
Farkas, so don't despair.

'You know Doctor Schmidt's elder girl, don't you, the
tall, gawky, arrogant girl who walks about as if the whole
world had dyspepsia or appendicitis and only her father
could help it? Well, she and Leonardo used to be friendly
that last summer. She must have been seventeen or so,
less bony and less conceited, and they met in the woods,
and one night she came to our cottage. I don't know
what happened; Leonardo was discreet, and soon we had
other things to discuss. But that night I was lying down
upstairs, that night she came, and I heard Leonardo's
laugh and I heard him switch off the lights, and I remember the sweetness of the wind. Not much of love-interest,
I admit, and if he ever comes back here, there will be
nothing more to it, as she is engaged to the Podestà's
nephew.

'Yes, that last summer.' Giacobbe's voice came from a deep, narrow well, an old frog croaking painfully. 'Leonardo had just returned from Milano — in June it was. He had a new white linen suit and he went to the village day after day and talked to the labourers and the quarrymen and helped them if he could. It isn't much of a village, ours. There are about eighty houses, with two hundred rooms; in them live eight hundred people. Forty went to the war, the rest work for the Abbey; sixty per cent of the women do, too. Twenty-five per cent are illiterate, twenty-eight per cent have tuberculosis, twelve per cent venereal disease. Thirty per cent of the children die before they are one year old; abortions average fifteen a year. Two peasants own their vineyard, fifteen are tenants of the Abbey, and the rest are wage-earners. They earn in a day what a box of matches costs in America. They die between forty and fifty; after the last war they almost lynched a tax collector, and once, ten years ago, they chased the Podestà down to the beach, and they throw stones regularly at the church, the militia post, and Don Teofilo. Add to this the fact that Leonardo did not waste his time in Milano and was blessed with a certain amount of revolutionary logic. As a result of all this he was arrested for "plotting against the safety of the State on August 8th, 1935."

'They took us to Ravenna that morning. They had nothing against me, just "wanted to make sure." It was a very hot day. Leonardo wore his new white linen suit, and his beautiful white forehead shone in the strong sun. We went by train, in a reserved third-class compartment, accompanied by four plain-clothes men. They wanted to avoid attention: the holiday season was in full swing, and as we left, another train arrived crammed with fathers and families and prams and luggage; a loud, sweating crowd. I can still remember the posters at the station as we got on the train: COME TO SAN FERNANDO. Antonio was there, the station-master, dressed up as usual as if he had just left a stage where he had been playing Danilo in the *Merry Widow*. It was very hot on the train; all of us sweated. The detectives were quite young fellows, except for the one who squinted and kept biting his fingernails, then looking at them and nibbling away again. I tried to find out what was going to happen, but they wouldn't speak to us. Leonardo sat in the middle of the seat, between two detectives; I had to stand because the old, squinting one had lain down, after taking his shoes off. I remember his socks: they were biscuit-coloured with black, sweaty spots, and his big toe had popped out through a hole and stood up like a lonely fat man.

'We arrived late, although the Glorious Revolution was supposed to have made the trains run punctual. We were taken to police headquarters where we had to wait for a higher official. We sat on a bench in a long bare corridor, with the portraits of the Duce all over the place. He glared at us from all directions, like the mesmerizer in a village circus. The four detectives played some sort of backgammon; their hats pushed back, cigarettes hanging from their lips. It was a beautiful day, and we smelt the scent of roses from a garden and the sun had a friendly warmth now that the midday heat had passed. We did not feel frightened any more. We waited for an hour or so.

'Then the official arrived, a little man with a busy face, and after some time we were shown into his room. He sat behind a simple desk and strained himself to look like the portrait on the wall. He wasn't nasty; he kept consulting a *dossier* and looked at us and frowned; mostly frowned, yes, so consciously and deliberately as though frowning were his main job. Then he asked us questions and never waited for the answer; but he kept asking us as if to assure himself that frowning was not enough. Finally four new men came in, loudly and happily, laughing coarsely and exchanging rude remarks with the official. They wore black uniforms and inspected us two carefully and cheerfully. They even slapped our shoulders and one of them cried joyously: "Well, well, the Bocca Brothers, the Bocca Brothers, ho-ho!" They were jolly, those fellows; the fellows of Ravenna. Two of them had swarthy faces, pockmarks and dirty shirts, and revolvers in their belts. One of them, called Francesco, had a very sharp face, all angles and points, with oily hair and protruding cheekbones. His dark skin was very tight. The second one was the jolliest of the lot, a little plump man he was, with sparkling white teeth. He always laughed, baring his teeth as if we were photographers; and he kept cracking jokes and later on he sang. The third was called Saporito, I think, and was a pansy with wonderful blue eyes and very long eyelashes. The fourth I cannot remember.

'Ah, how jolly they were, those fellows of Ravenna! They took us downstairs, laughing and cracking jokes, and when I asked what was going to happen to us, they burst out into fits of laughter. They all laughed differently, mind you. Francesco roared deeply, in a Falstaffian way, in contrast to his thin, sharp face. Whiteteeth gurgled as if something ticklish had happened some time ago and he had just remembered it. Saporito giggled, closing his large

blue eyes, his shoulders shaking. The fourth I can't remember, but he laughed too. As we walked down the circular staircase, deeper and deeper, descending into a cellar, Whiteteeth started singing an old Venetian song, not
very loudly and not very well either. Rather to himself,
amused and full of expectation, like a lad on his way to
meet a girl. He sang:

> Oh! pescator dell' onda
> > Findelin,
> Vieni a pescar in qua!
> Colla bella sua barca,
> Colla bella se ne va,
> > Findelin! lin, la!

And again:

> Colla bella sua barca,
> Colla bella se ne va,
> > Findelin! li, la!

'The others took it up, and soon they were singing in
chorus "Findelin, li, la!" — not very well, often out of key;
but how jolly they were, those fellows of Ravenna! Their
cheerfulness was quite infectious, and soon Leonardo and
I joined into the singing, exchanging puzzled but glad
glances. I remember Leonardo catching my eye and winking just as we arrived at the bottom of the long stairway,
and how Whiteteeth opened an iron door and stood aside
and bowed to us, saying, "Enter, gentlemen, enter, enter,"
and then continued singing that silly song:

> Enter, enter, enter,
> Colla bella sua barca,
> Colla bella se ne va,
> > Findelin, enter!

'It was a large, whitewashed basement room, and at the end, surprisingly, were large French windows which opened onto a back garden. That was where the scent of roses must have come from — because the first thing I noticed were the roses shining through the window. The sun came in in broad, dusty shafts, throwing strips of shadow across the concrete floor. The room was empty except for a dentist's chair near the windows and a glass cabinet full of instruments.

> *Colla bella sua barca,*
> *Colla bella se ne va,*
> > *Tra-la-la, lin, la!*

'Whiteteeth sang as he led Leonardo to the chair and begged him with comic politeness to sit down. Leonardo did not feel so gay any more and kept looking at the glass cabinet and at me: but something of a moment ago, the gaiety, the wink, the soothing knowledge that nothing bad would happen, remained on his face, mingling with his new fear. For now he was beginning to be afraid. I, too, began to lose my confidence in those jolly fellows of Ravenna, and the sun and the roses and the buzzing flies, all so tremendously alive and reassuring, began to present an obscene contrast. They made me stand by the window, facing Leonardo; and Whiteteeth and the fourth man I can't remember went up to the chair and made jokes while strapping Leonardo's feet and hands. Saporito and Francesco stood beside me, their hands on their guns.

'Whiteteeth went up to the glass cabinet and opened it with a click and fumbled among the instruments: they made cold, metallic sounds. The fourth man asked Leonardo politely if he wanted to take off his jacket. "Such a beautiful jacket," he cried out, stroking the lapel. "Beautiful, beautiful *findelin!*" Whiteteeth sang, absent-mindedly, looking for some instrument, *"tra-la-la,* beautiful, beautiful, beautiful."

'As I stood there in the sun, by the window, facing Leonardo, a great frightened silence crept into me, and all sounds stood apart from it, clear and separate, each movement, each noise, against this big silence in my belly. I began to feel the significance of the moment and to be conscious of myself and of details; I saw the mole on Whiteteeth's chin and sweat-drops on Leonardo's beautiful forehead, and I saw the knot of his shoelaces; I heard the metallic sounds of the instruments and Francesco's breathing; and it was as if the sun and time had broken everything into tiny particles and each stood apart, waiting. But most of all I saw Leonardo's eyes. He stopped looking around as if resigned to his fate. He only looked at me, strongly, strenuously; he did not want to lose my eyes, and whenever I happened to glance at something else — at Whiteteeth, who came back and affixed the driller — or the flies outside in the garden, I had to return with my glance to Leonardo, and there was reproach that I had gone away.

' "Now then," Whiteteeth said, "open your pretty mouth, Leonardo, my son."

'Leonardo looked at me, but I could not help him. "Open up," Whiteteeth said, the drill in his hand. "Be a good boy." Leonardo clamped his jaw, still looking at me. "Open up," Whiteteeth said. His right hand moved up to Leonardo's face, and on the back of his hand a fly was crawling, and Leonardo saw it moving, too, and squinted

at it. Then Whiteteeth's lean fingers expertly pressed Leonardo's jawbone and his mouth opened like a shell, with a small, cracking noise.

'I heard Saporito shifting his weight from one leg to the other; and Leonardo's eyes were in mine again and I heard the drill starting to buzz: I saw the small, revolving end of it touch one of Leonardo's front teeth. First it was an even buzzing, z-z-z-z-z it went, and to its rhythm Whiteteeth hummed and sang, *"findelin, lin-la!"* Then the sound became deeper and rougher; the drill slipped and caught the edge of the tooth. Leonardo was still looking at me. I saw his tonsils, and his tongue was struggling, writhing like a small, fat snake. The buzzing was growing angrier and rougher: the drill was well inside the tooth now and Whiteteeth still sang. I don't know how long we stood there. The others were quiet, too. Francesco lit a cigarette and smoked with wet smacks. Whiteteeth just drilled on, his dark hand static like an immovable shadow across Leonardo's chin. Once Leonardo groaned, and the first thin blood appeared and slowly trickled down his chin and his neck onto his collar. "He should have taken off his jacket," the fourth man said quietly: he was standing on tiptoe to see better. Whiteteeth now stepped aside and pushed Leonardo's head back; and Leonardo was crying now, a lasting, wincing cry which did not stop for quite a time; and he tried to struggle.

'When Whiteteeth got down to the root, he stopped for a second or two. The buzzing stopped, too, and Francesco breathed out, and the silence was very marked and sudden. But then he went on and the buzzing started again, and he drilled right through the gums to the jawbone and the drill made a rattling noise, and when I said, *"Stop it!"* Saporito hit me with his gun and I lost my balance and nearly fell. There was no sound from Leonardo now; he breathed evenly and his head was propped up again, and he kept looking at me; then, for the first time, he was sick, and his mouth was covered with mess. But Whiteteeth went on, and when he could not drill through the jaw-bone, he started to drill sideways, right through the next tooth.

'Then I looked at the back garden again. The sun was losing its brilliance and the wind was rising; evening was not far off. The big fat roses moved in the wind. I kept looking at those big fat roses, and all the time the buzzing went on and Whiteteeth sang, *"colla bella sua barca, colla bella se ne va, findelin, lin, la,"* and when I finally looked back, Leonardo's eyes were waiting, reproachful, and for the first time he was really hurt.'

The Fugitive

That afternoon Farkas went for a walk in the hills be-hind the village, climbing slowly amid the vineyards. It was a rich, sweet-scented day, not excessively hot, but drowsy, with careful sounds: the thuds of footsteps where the men were working, the buzzing of flies and the dis-tant puffing of a train. At five o'clock the wind changed, and the sweetness of the vineyards was touched by the salty breath of the sea. Farkas went to the little valley with the stream and sat under a tree, inspecting the dark green land which rolled down to the sea. He felt the warmth of the grass and of his own body, and sat there over half an hour, airing his mind, letting nothing but the idiotic simplicities of direct observation pass through it. The cloud, he thought, my crumpled sock, he thought, the cigar, he thought, and hardly anything else, feeling at ease and youthful, overcome by that irresponsible and mysterious elation only simple physical pleasure can give. It felt good to tear at the grass, to shift his weight and sink into the soft mossy field, to stretch and lie back and be alone under the uncomplicated sky.

Then he walked back by the footpath to San Fernando. A donkey cart passed with a peasant, who greeted him dully, and beyond the village the church bells were ringing. Slowly the evening came, with the heavy scent of the village, of dust, of cow dung, and of men who had sweated the whole day and were going home in the changing light, waiting for the cool darkness to smoke a cigarette or a pipe and to talk. As he reached the railway, he saw Antonio's wife, Signora Clara, appearing as always in the window, watching the signals change to green, listening to the approaching rattle of a yet unseen train. Farkas quickly crossed the railway line and walked into the station. The railway, those sentimental tracks that led nowhere and everywhere, reminded him of the city, of Gizella; for an unpleasant second of Daniel and Anna, and as usual, of inevitable death; the more so as this station was deserted, with no rush or excitement to distract him from the old meaning of the rails, which his eyes could follow only as far as the forest to the right, while on the left they slanted downhill and seemed to lead straight into the sea below the Abbey Hill.

Then, slowly, the mild sounds of the evening were counterpointed by the approaching train, and Farkas strolled down to the entrance door and walked through and sat on a bench, under the dusty faded posters and torn time-tables fluttering mutely in the breeze. Antonio appeared, too; first his steps echoed inside the building as he came down the stairs; then the door of his office opened and the magnificent moustache took up its usual position, briskly and ceremonially. He did not notice Farkas at first, and the scene was a mixture of the comic and the conspiratory as Farkas sat there, unobserved, watching the station-master act his daily part with enthusiastic sincerity. Apparently the years had hollowed a mark on the platform where he always stood, and he was careful to plant his feet firmly and exactly; he pulled at his tunic, pushed up his starched cuffs, and patted his stomach with military smartness, and he waited, fixing his gaze on the unending tracks. Then he cleared his throat and said, half aloud, *Attention!* to himself, or to the tracks, or perhaps to the world at large, that untidy multitude of men and things. Almost immediately he must have sensed Farkas: he turned, blushed, and their eyes met. Farkas tried to look absent-minded so as not to appear an eavesdropper. Antonio saluted him and quickly jerked his head away. Farkas felt that something ought to be done, or said; but there was no time, for the train was puffing into the station.

The steam rolled in clouds down the platform; through it came a shout from the stoker, whose blackened face ap-

peared through the haze, grinning. Then the door of the
mail van opened and the hands of an unseen man threw
out two big bundles and a few crates. The old, deaf porter, who had arrived meanwhile from nowhere, shuffled
forward and started to fuss with the mail, placing each
bundle and crate on a dilapidated trolley. Antonio did
not move, but relaxed his salute, waiting. Then a guard
stepped down from the last coach. By that time the vapour
had dissolved and the train stood clearly and curiously
immobile against the green hills and the darkening sky.
The guard shouted a greeting to Antonio, who answered
with a nod and a brisk salute, and watched, with Farkas,
as the thin, red-eyed man in his greasy uniform cried, *San
Fernando,* twice, and then walked along the coaches peering in through the windows, opening and shutting doors.
Poor Antonio, Farkas thought with genuine sympathy: no
arrivals; and the warm pity that filled him slowly felt so
good that he wanted to retain some of it. He rose and
lit a cigar, and was throwing the match away when the
guard opened the door of a third-class carriage and with
awful slowness a body rolled out and head forward fell almost noiselessly onto the platform.

The green half-circles of the vineyards and the shining
spot of a lighter shade where a field spread the mildly curv-
ing slope under the darkening sky; across its base the train
with its geometrical austerity of line; the steam clouds
which had again started to roll across the whole vista; the
guard motionless, but full of impending shouts and gestures, of face muscles weaving their accustomed pattern of
horror and dismay; the limp body which at last came to
rest and now seemed as if it had been there all the time,

the head perched in a freak position on the left hand, with grey, closed eyelids, and a grey face, grey and awful and with no control and consciousness; the hand, the left hand, also limp and helpless; and Antonio standing motionless, prelude to a jump, a shout, a run, and the total loss of the part he had been playing, his eyebrows contracting, concertina-like as if to exercise a flabby forehead; and the grunt from above, from the window where, unseen by Farkas, sat Signora Clara, the wife, waiting all these years, waiting, perhaps, for this. That was all that mattered when Leonardo di Bocca arrived at San Fernando.

Giacobbe finished the story later.

Leonardo was taken to the militia post. Farkas had watched him carried away; amidst throaty shouts, violent hands: the quiet body, the limp hand, the sagging mouth. Doctor Merlin of the Sanatorium was called out and Don Innocenzo informed. The Doctor observed utter exhaustion, high fever, and an ugly flesh wound on the left leg, by the shin-bone, a wound caused by a bullet. He gave the man a dressing and some morphine and suggested putting him in the Sanatorium *annexe* until his identity was established. But then Don Innocenzo arrived, did not like the look of the stranger, searched him and found nothing but a dirty wallet with four hundred lire and an identity card bearing the name of Private Giovanni Rosso of an Alpine division, whose leave of absence had expired three days before. Then the stranger recovered consciousness, stared around stupidly with smiling eyes, and fainted again. Don Innocenzo agreed that he should be put in an attic room in the *annexe* until he could be cross-examined. The stranger was carried off, and Don Innocenzo, suspecting a case of desertion, sent a telegram to Ravenna. The next morning the reply came: Private Giovanni Rosso had reported back to his unit two days before, having informed the military police that while in a hotel near Ravenna his clothes and wallet had been stolen.

At noon a militiaman called on Giacobbe and said Don Innocenzo wanted to see him. It was a very hot, clear day, with little shade left under the trees. They walked slowly down the main road, Giacobbe and the militiaman, sweating as they walked, silent at first, Giacobbe was apprehensive: he had heard of the arrival of a stranger, and he knew that Don Innocenzo disliked and suspected him.

'What is it all about?' he asked the militiaman.

'Don't know.'

'Why don't we go to the post? Where are we going?'

'Don't ask me, Signor di Bocca. It is very hot, and talking is difficult. I don't know anything.'

So they went on silently, Giacobbe wondering where they were going. He tried to size up his position: could it be that his frequent meetings with Francesco the quarryman or Ciro the fisherman had been observed? Or had they suspected his concern for the twelve washerwomen whose case was slowly and bitterly brewing in the Abbey and the village? He thought he had been careful. He was not afraid; only annoyed in a way: suppose Don Innocenzo knew all about these last few months, the preparations, the plans, the whispered interviews at night. Suppose he were arrested: could such a subjective turn of events influence the shape of the future? San Fernando was slowly changing its historico-physical state. The boiling point was not far off, but it needed an added effort, and he,

Giacobbe, must make it. Would Francesco be able to carry on, or Alberto the maimed ex-soldier, or any of the others? As they turned into the main square under the glaring sky, he thought of Lenin going into hiding during those last few weeks in Petrograd; of the flicker of a Cossack's eyebrow which had started the first fraternization between the army and the workers; of other 'crossroads' and turns of personal destinies. Then they entered the dark, cool vaulted entrance to the *annexe,* walked up to the fourth floor, and stopped in front of a door. The militiaman knocked. Don Innocenzo's voice said, 'Come in'; and through the slowly opening door Giacobbe saw Don Innocenzo standing, freshly shaved, pink and dynamic, by the table. Behind him, in a chair, he saw his brother Leonardo.

'Come in,' Don Innocenzo said, with a huge smile, his dimples deep and catty. 'Come in, Signor Giacobbe.'

'Good day,' Giacobbe said.

The militiaman closed the door behind him. It was a big room with an angular roof and a small window with white curtains. The sun came in hotly and made the air steamy. There was a Madonna print on the yellow wall. 'How tired he looks!' Giacobbe thought. Their eyes met, and Giacobbe was afraid now, for Leonardo's eyes were smiling.

'Do you know this man?' Don Innocenzo asked.

'No,' Giacobbe said. He has no teeth left, he thought; no more teeth, and a messy beard, and he is so tired.

'Do *you* know *this* man?' Don Innocenzo turned to Leonardo.

There was a pause. His forehead is no longer smooth

and beautiful, Giacobbe thought. For Heaven's sake, don't fumble, he added pleadingly with his eyes; don't give yourself away, please.

'Speak up,' Don Innocenzo said, and hit Leonardo over the ears.

Leonardo's eyes fluttered, and his ears became red.

'No, I don't know him,' he said. He was afraid.

'Dirty liars, both of you,' Don Innocenzo said. 'And stupid, too.'

'I am sure I don't know what you mean, Don Innocenzo,' Giacobbe said humbly. He decided he must become active, to fill out all the awkward pauses. But he felt that there would be no help from Leonardo's tired, scared eyes.

'Shut up,' Don Innocenzo said. 'Talk only when you're asked. I'm not going to waste time.' He walked to the window and said to Leonardo: 'What's your name again?'

Another pause of self-betrayal. It was quite hopeless.

'Giovanni Rosso,' the brother said. 'Please don't hit me again.'

'Giovanni Rosso,' Don Innocenzo repeated. 'So you insist. Very well.' He came up to the table.

'Please,' Leonardo said quietly; he knew he was going to be hurt again and he knew that he could not take it.

'Giovanni Rosso,' Don Innocenzo went on, furrowing his forehead with a pompous grimace. 'Very well, then.' He hit Leonardo again; this time with the back of his hand.

'Please, Don Innocenzo,' Giacobbe said quickly, and stepped forward; he felt his stomach contracting somewhere above his solar plexus and the blood rushing away from his hands and feet, and quite suddenly he was cold. 'Please, sir, there surely must be some mistake.' He was talking quickly, careful not to pause, hoping that words might stop the hands of Don Innocenzo. 'There must be some mistake.'

He could not go on. Don Innocenzo's face was screwed up; he looked like a wicked child, pulling a fly's legs off. His hands moved quickly; *slap-slap* they went, and Leonardo's head lolled to and fro and his eyelids kept fluttering, scared. *Slap-slap* went the hands with increasing fury.

'Please, sir,' Giacobbe said.

Leonardo was crying now, hunching his shoulders, trying to dodge the hands of Don Innocenzo. *Please, sir,* Giacobbe thought, and leaned against the door, feeling sick. *Please, sir, he thought: here is Leonardo. I have waited for Leonardo for all these years and I knew he would come back broken and beaten, but all the same I hoped it would be all right — and slowly he will recover and forget those years. He will come and stay with me, and I shall pamper him and give him lots of milk, and he will sleep in the big bed of our parents — the big bed he always liked and we used to quarrel who was going to sleep in it, and I always hoped he would get it — and will lie there till late in the morning and I shall prepare breakfast: coffee, dark and with no sugar, as he liked it, and fresh bread with dripping or butter, as he always liked it, and some fresh fruit, and I shall bring it up to the room and say gently: 'Leonardo, my dear, breakfast is ready,' and put the tray on his bed, and slowly he will gain strength and hope and confidence again, and leaning on my arm, he will go for little walks in the hills and sit on*

the grass and look at the sea, and the good, strong air will
make him stronger, and then perhaps some months later
he will begin to tell me about all those years on the islands
and I shall tell him about all those years in the village, and
first we shall only tell the silly and irrelevant episodes, re-
peating them, but then later we shall remember the in-
timate pains and hopes and will speak about them, Giacobbe thought, watching Leonardo's head lolling to and
fro.

The Spark

It was the hottest night of all, with a damp wind sweep-
ing the sea and the air like a hot towel. The whole day the
sky had been dusty and lay low over the greying waters. It
was so close that in the morning hardly anybody ventured
to the bathhouse, and Farkas spent the day in his room,
panting, on his bed, drinking iced tea and sucking the
lemons that Ugo brought up at regular intervals. It was
two days after Leonardo's arrival and one day after Giacobbe had told him about the scene at the *annexe,* adding
that Leonardo had been taken to the prison at the militia
post up in the village and that Don Innocenzo was waiting
for further instructions from Ravenna.

The shutters were tightly closed in Farkas's room, thin
blades of light filtered through, and all sounds seemed to
be drowned in the heat. It was remarkably quiet the
whole day. Tony, the little Austrian girl, hardly moved at

all: she sighed a few times, but could not even muster strength, it seemed to Farkas, to articulate her unhappiness. Later, Farkas went downstairs, for his room was growing intolerably stale. The lounge was dark and somewhat cooler. Enrico was asleep behind his desk, his round bald head resting on the desk, like a skull left there absent-mindedly after some anatomical demonstration. The Morgans had tea, bearing the fury of the heat with suppressed cheerfulness, sipping hot tea and fanning themselves with an old copy of the *Illustrated London News*. They smiled at Farkas as he passed.

The afternoon brought no relief, and Farkas felt he could not face the company of Don Teofilo and the Doctor. So he walked carefully and slowly to Madame Pina's establishment on the Abbey Road and had some iced wine and did not enjoy his cigar. There was no one else on the terrace, and his solitude grew marked and sinister. An old waitress kept shuffling by, and the frogs were silent among the reeds. After a while he decided to return to the hotel, although the thought of his bedroom repelled and depressed him; but just after he had paid his bill and was waiting for the old woman to bring his change, a new wind rose among the reeds, a wind suddenly sweet and fresh. The mist gathered into a few bulky clouds, the sky began to clear up, and the first stars appeared with the twilight, polished and pleased. Some militiamen entered and sat down, tired. Farkas walked down the wooden plank and stood there while the new wind blotted the sweat from his chest and forehead. Then he started off to the Paradiso.

When he reached the bottom of the main square, he stopped, for the scene held a strong theatrical quality and he could not help feeling that he was facing a distant stage. On top of the square (the centre of the stage) was the terrace of the Paradiso, with six or seven tables in the foreground illuminated indirectly by the powerful bulbs of the half-covered back part of the restaurant where people sat if it rained. This part had long mirrors along the wall, and they reflected and amplified the lights and gave them radiance, so that the tables and their occupants in the foreground gained an additional depth in space. Their faces were all dark, but the shoulders and the tops of the heads were touched by the brilliant lights. Over the roof of the covered restaurant swayed a huge oak, slanting and tousled. Higher up were the clouds, now angry-black and torn, billowing before the moon. The terrace was framed on the left by the Paradiso, all spotty with shadow and light from the two tall, old-fashioned street-lamps in front of it. To the right the gardens began, with the Kursalon silent and black in the background, untouched by light except that of the restless moon.

There was some movement in the illuminated background of the terrace: Farkas saw vague figures, black and white, appearing and reappearing. They must have been the waiters. The foreground was curiously immobile. As Farkas approached the terrace, he recognized Don Teofilo, his cap and cigar, with Doctor Schmidt sitting opposite him. Standing between them, resting a foot on a chair, was Don Innocenzo. The nurse stood directly behind Don Teofilo's back, holding a book in her hand, trying to catch more of the light. These figures were in the centre. To the right of them sat two figures who turned out to be the Morgans. They did not seem to move either. The man was smoking his pipe, his legs outstretched, his ridiculous straw hat pulled down to his eyes, while Mrs. Morgan just sat and stared. There seemed to be no one else in the main square. Some of the windows had been thrown open in relief now that the heat-wave seemed to be passing.

The sounds of the evening were muffled as Farkas slowly walked up the steep square under the lime trees. There was faint music, softened and diverted by the new wind. The Austrian girl stood on the platform by the piano, as usual leaning over her violin, her soft hair falling over her scarred cheek, playing something Viennese, and then the goggle-eyed pianist started to sing, and as Farkas drew nearer, his hoarse voice became articulate:

'*Tempora mutantur,*' he sang, '*die Zeiten aendern sich, Herr Doktor, fuer Sie und fuer mich.*'

When Farkas was about five yards from the terrace, the music ended, and as if someone had started a new paragraph there was a short silence, immobile as before; but then the spell broke and the scene came to life. There was discreet applause in the background and the Austrian girl brushed her hair from her face and bowed. The pianist half-rose, blinked, and bowed, too. At the same time Don Teofilo scratched his chin and his cigar came to life, emitting a whitish cloud of smoke. Doctor Schmidt cleared his throat and started to stir his coffee busily. Don Innocenzo ended his swashbuckling pose by removing his shiny right boot from the chair and sitting down. The nurse looked up and yawned. Mr. Morgan knocked out his pipe, and Mrs. Morgan called out loudly in English: '*Waiter!*'

Thus Farkas made his entry.

His infallible dramatic instinct told him that there was something in the air; that after all had been introduced, it had arrived, that indefinable moment, with the atmosphere close and electric, waiting for a spark. 'Now,' he said to himself. The night held a thousand clues. He would not have been surprised if he had suddenly discovered Mrs. Rapcsak the prompter crouching somewhere in front of them, peering into her script, whispering, 'To be or not to be,' or 'Dinner is served, Your Highness,' or something of the sort; or if Ede the stage-manager, a pudgy-faced individual, had been standing among the bushes, his coat carelessly thrown over his shoulder, watching with a poker-face the 'Great Scene' which he would always find unsatisfactory.

Don Innocenzo's face was more mobile and self-important than usual. He raised an eyebrow and thrust out his chin, his little eyes darting to and fro as if in deep thought or waiting for an ambush.

Don Teofilo said, 'Aha!' as he saw Farkas, and the others turned. 'There he is,' Don Teofilo said excitedly, and rubbed his fat fingers, which were intersected by numerous rings.

'Good evening,' Farkas said.

'Good evening,' the Doctor replied.

'Take a seat, Signor Farkas,' Don Innocenzo said gravely, waving an upturned palm.

'We've been waiting for you,' Don Teofilo said.

'Waiting,' Don Innocenzo added.

'Waiting?' Farkas asked, conscious how old-fashioned the dialogue sounded.

'The war is over,' Don Innocenzo said.

'Haven't you heard?' Don Teofilo asked. 'The Marshal has asked for an armistice.'

'My Italy,' Don Innocenzo said. Farkas saw that he was drunk again; his lips were wet with saliva. 'My Italy,' and he stared into the darkening square, his face-muscles working busily. He put his elbows on the table and propped up his head with two hands, his face a mask of misery.

'Look at him,' Don Teofilo said, with scorn. 'Here he sits, sorry for himself, doing nothing.'

'There is nothing to do,' Don Innocenzo said in a hollow voice; obviously he was listening to his own voice and liked it. He was working up a good cry. 'Nothing at all. I have phoned to the post and I have phoned to Ravenna. There is nothing to do but wait for Fate.'

'Well, that is very interesting,' Farkas said, and hailed Ugo. 'Carafe, red,' he ordered.

Don Innocenzo said: 'Carafe red,' and he drank from his glass. 'Here we sit drinking red wine, drinking red wine,' he repeated it, 'as if nothing had happened, as if the world had not come to an end.'

He must be pressing his tear glands hard, Farkas thought. The little man's voice is quivering, and soon self-pity will bring the tears. 'Come, take it easy,' he said cheerfully.

'Why don't you do something?' Don Teofilo said.

'Here they come,' Doctor Schmidt said.

They all turned, and Don Innocenzo forgot the uprush of his tears. Across the main square, small under the trees, came three figures, a man in a light suit between two uniformed men.

'Ah, yes,' Don Innocenzo said, his face contorted into an

incredible mask, like the face of a provincial actor trying to express hate, fury, vengeance, all at the same time, working his face up according to some theatrical textbook on 'How to Act,' his forehead wrinkled, his eyes small and stiff, his lips churned up into a sneer. 'There he comes,' he said, and rose and walked away to meet the three men.

'He's mad,' Don Teofilo said.

'Who are they?' Farkas asked.

'The fugitive and his escort,' Doctor Schmidt said, dipping a small soft piece of white bread into his coffee like an impoverished gentlewoman of Vienna. 'Don Innocenzo sent for him.'

There he was, Leonardo di Bocca, in a light suit much too small for him, walking slowly now until they all stopped. Don Innocenzo went up to them and said something to the militiamen, who saluted and turned, leaving Leonardo alone. Farkas now saw that he was supporting himself with a walking-stick. He could not yet see his face, but Don Innocenzo roughly took his arm and brought him forward, towards the terrace. They said something Farkas could not hear and Leonardo shook his head several times.

As they entered the terrace, Don Innocenzo made a comic bow, with an inviting gesture to Leonardo, who smiled embarrassedly. Now Farkas saw his face. He looked much older than he had expected: an old, frail man he was, Leonardo di Bocca. Farkas observed a certain likeness to Giacobbe: there was something about the shape of his skull and the way he walked, softly, although he was limping, dragging his wounded leg. But there was nothing of Giacobbe in the face, a white, frail face with soft contours, a flabby, unhealthy face. He had light eyes, Leonardo, and he wore spectacles, cheap frameless ones, and he had sensitive nostrils and an ugly, toothless, old-woman smile when he opened his mouth. His eyelids kept fluttering as if afraid of being hit, and when he arrived at the table he looked at each of them, at Farkas, Don Teofilo, and the Doctor, and the smile left his face, leaving a speechless, inarticulate horror that said: 'Please, don't hit me.'

Don Innocenzo strutted up behind him: his movements were violent and sharp as if he were being jerked by an invisible marionette player.

'Gentlemen,' he said, 'meet my very good friend the bastard Leonardo di Bocca, the noble fugitive, the champion of little men and peasants, the celebrated dirty swine.' He nudged Leonardo, almost proudly. 'Here he is, gentlemen, after we've caught him trying to sneak off the train, here he is, our fugitive.'

Leonardo smiled again as if he did not know whether this was to be a farcical scene or some sudden and violent tragedy.

Don Teofilo turned his thick head. 'Must you drag him here?' he asked Don Innocenzo.

'Must I?' Don Innocenzo repeated, and gave a gentle push to Leonardo so that he staggered a step forward and mumbled, 'Sorry,' for he had almost fallen on top of Farkas. 'Must I? Of course I must. I want you to have a good look at him, the traitor.' He stepped behind Leonardo's back and made a satanic face. 'Look at him.'

Farkas said: 'I'm going now.'

'No, you're not, Signor Farkas,' Don Innocenzo said.

'This is an historical moment. Leonardo di Bocca returns to his home town. The local boy who made bad,' he laughed. 'Poor little fugitive' — he mimicked pity — 'he told me that he was a certain Private Giovanni Rosso, wounded in Africa, that's what he told me.' He turned to Leonardo: 'What kind of wound is it, my friend?' he asked, pointing at the lame leg.

Leonardo blushed and looked down at his leg and said in a low voice, like a child who knows that it has been caught lying. 'Flesh wound, sir,' he said, 'near the shin-bone, sir.'

'How terrible!' Don Innocenzo cried, with a wide gesture. 'Isn't it terrible, gentlemen?' he repeated to Don Teofilo; then turned and with all his strength kicked Leonardo's crippled leg.

There was a dull sound followed by a quick, surprised groan from Leonardo; he had no time to scream because Don Innocenzo kicked him again before pain could reach his vocal chords. Leonardo dropped his stick; it fell across the table and crashed against the carafe and overturned it. Farkas watched the wine trickling across the folds of the tablecloth towards Don Teofilo. Then he saw Leonardo's knee come up with a jerk as he quickly grabbed the place where he had been kicked. He tried to quell the pain and was gasping now; a short gasp it was, as if he were choking and had to struggle for air. Farkas felt a hand knocking against his shoulder: Leonardo had lost his balance and was groping for support Then Don Innocenzo kicked again, this time at the other leg. This made a different sound: like biscuits crunched it sounded, as Leonardo lurched forward, hopelessly losing his balance. He fell against the table and slid onto an empty chair, lay there struggling. All the while no words were spoken. Leonardo tried to raise himself, his face strained in surprise, his tongue on his lower lip like that of a man trying to lift a heavy weight. His hands kept hitting out for more support, but Don Innocenzo pulled the chair away quickly. Leonardo dropped on the gravel and sat there, silly and helpless, his back towards Don Innocenzo, his legs wide apart.

Don Innocenzo again reminded Farkas of a brat; an intent little boy trying to guzzle ice-cream or a dish of stewed fruit, unable to stop, spooning away with quick mad strokes. He kicked again, then he bent down, and his hands, fingers bent, seized Leonardo's collar with a greedy movement and pulled him up roughly. Strain and surprise grew on the white, frail face, the eyelids fluttered like the frightened wings of a little bird. Don Innocenzo turned him and dumped him on the chair, and he sat there, soft and sack-like, his spectacles slipping down his nose. Don Innocenzo shook him twice. Still no word was spoken, and Farkas wondered when it would come, and why he himself did not speak. But he could not: everything followed so quickly, so logically. He almost felt he knew what would happen next, inevitably. Don Innocenzo propped Leonardo up and hit him several times with the back of his hand. Leonardo's head lolled to and fro as if he were shaking his head reproachfully. Blow followed blow in quick succession, and the sounds merged into one. Now Farkas heard Don Innocenzo panting. He was breathing heavily, like a greedy little boy who knows he should not go on, but cannot stop. *Clap-clap* went his hand, *clap-clap*, like so many little rounds of applause. Then he stopped, and there was silence but for his breathing. He was quite exhausted, and his breath came unevenly.

The wind must have dropped, too, as Farkas listened: there was a great vacuum of silence, a great, deep well of silence, broken only by Don Innocenzo's quick, excited breath. It was a watchful silence as if all San Fernando had stopped and was waiting and watching. But slowly the vacuum filled up as if water deep at the bottom of a well had started to rise with an even sound, and Farkas became aware of a hundred breaths slowly filling the hush. He had never heard anything like it before: Don Innocenzo's breathing was like a solo violin and now the whole orchestra came surging up. At first he thought he was imagining it and he went on watching the white-faced man sprawling limply in the chair, his hands hanging down on either side, like white cloths, his mouth wide open and smeared with the blood that dripped slowly from his nose. Beyond, a few figures stood rigid: the nurse, a waiter. But now Farkas turned, for he knew he was not suffering an hallucination and that there was silence no longer. In a wide line, some hundred yards from the terrace, stood a multitude of men, shadows in the dim light, standing quietly and watching; unreal but for their even breathing. Then someone in one of the back rows sneezed, and it sounded like *Amen*.

Then came silence again: it lasted a few seconds only, as if the men had been holding their breaths. Farkas turned to look at Don Innocenzo again. There he stood, his back to the crowd, facing the white, frail man. His hands were on his hips in the eternal pose of the braggart, unaware of anything but his triumph. 'Dénes would be perfectly cast for him,' Farkas thought. Don Innocenzo smiled as he looked down at his victim, who lay with closed eyes, half-unconscious, utterly defeated. Farkas did not know what was going on in the terrible brat's mind, but his face was covered with the red circles of passion.

'Come on,' Don Innocenzo said. 'Come on, swine.' Leonardo did not move. Then Don Innocenzo turned, and he saw Farkas first and blushed as if he had forgotten himself; and then he saw the crowd. He narrowed his eyes and there was a puzzled furrow over his left eye. Farkas, too, turned back to the multitude. He could not say how many they were, but they stood in thick rows that filled out the space between the Paradiso and the gardens. They were still waiting and silent. 'Good audience tonight,' Farkas thought, and wondered if Don Innocenzo would suddenly break out in the aria from the *Prince of Mantua,* half-sitting on the table, gaily lifting a goblet.

Then he saw that the crowd was slowly pressing nearer, still silent. They halted, and Giacobbe stepped forward and walked unhurriedly towards the terrace, two men at his side. One of them Farkas recognized vaguely: he must have seen him one day on his way to the hills. The other looked like a fisherman: he was gaunt and tanned, with a crow's face. Both of them carried a rifle.

'Leonardo,' said Giacobbe softly, dropping his voice at the end of the name. It wasn't a call, or an exclamation: just a bare name, but Farkas felt it was rich with meaning. It might have meant, 'Good evening, my dear brother Leonardo.'

'What's all this?' Don Innocenzo asked.

Giacobbe ignored him. He stepped over to the white-faced man and inspected him closely. 'Yes, of course,' he said absent-mindedly.

'What's this?' Don Innocenzo shouted, and pulled Giacobbe away roughly. 'What's this?'

Giacobbe said to Farkas: 'You see?'

He leaned over the white face and lifted one eyelid with his finger. 'Leonardo,' he said again; this time very tenderly. 'It's going to be all right,' he said, and turned back to the crowd. He raised his voice:

'We shall now proceed,' he announced sadly, 'to hang Don Innocenzo.'

The crowd grunted and pressed nearer. Farkas could almost feel their warm breath. They were about ten yards from the terrace, and those in the first rows came under the lights. Only the faces were lit: the bodies remained half-dark, partly covered by the shrubs that lined the terrace. Farkas saw Alfieri, gigantic, bald, looking ill at ease in his clothes, holding a spade on his shoulder: and Foa the shopkeeper, dishevelled and biblical, and one of the younger waiters at the Paradiso, a short, bow-legged youth whose name he did not remember.

Don Innocenzo's face was still a pompous, frowning face, as if irritated by an intrusion; except for his mouth, which seemed to have separated itself from the rest and dropped into a soft, childish line of dread. He looked at Giacobbe and started to say something, but changed his mind. His hand quickly dived into his pocket and produced a whistle. Then he turned and jumping over a chair blew the whistle and waited. The sound was sharp and echoed long and slowly. But there was no answer, whatever he may have expected: his Blackshirts, an army, or divine help. He blew it again, and the crowd replied by pressing nearer, fanning out in a widening circle. Don Innocenzo started to run now; towards the Kursalon, his steps making the only sound in the night: *clap-clap* went the busy little boots, almost like his knuckles when he was beating Leonardo. *Clap-clap*, and then he halted.

Giacobbe made no move. He watched the little figure darting away across the gardens. Farkas turned to look, too. The gardens were spotty with light and shadow as the hesitant moonlight dripped through the foliage. Through this treacherous light Don Innocenzo started to run again. He was a good runner, with quick, long strides, and he sprinted towards the Kursalon, beyond which the woods started. He was blowing his whistle all the time. That and his steps were the only sounds.

But just before he reached the covered promenade which encircled the Kursalon, he stopped again. Farkas now saw that there, too, were men in a close line, almost touching one another's shoulders. Don Innocenzo hesitated and turned southward, where the main square sloped steeply along the Sanatorium to the rock-gardens with the idiotic dwarfs. The line of men (silent and untouched by light) moved forward with slow, inevitable steps that crunched on the gravel. Don Innocenzo blew his whistle shrilly and dashed towards the Sanatorium, darting and ducking, shooting out among the trees which hid him for a second now and then. But there, too, he came up against the silent multitude. Farkas saw hands reaching out, but Don Innocenzo swerved and ducked again, and, changing his direction, made straight for the rock-gardens with the idiotic dwarfs. But the night was full of men, and the spotty background of light and shadow was like a swamp full of unexpected perils. The circle of men was drawing nearer. Don Innocenzo turned and turned again and ran — this time towards the main street; but there the crowd was thickest; and he quickly turned to make his way back to the terrace. By then the men were upon him. Farkas heard the whistle stabbing the night with sharp sounds and saw the crowd, like surf, roll onward and recede towards the old-fashioned street-lamps, so decorative and out-of-date, under the Paradiso.

There were no details any longer: only a mass of arms and hands moving in unison with a single purpose, their harmony disturbed only by a struggling spot in their midst. The whistle repeated its shrill, gurgling sound; then a slap was heard, one final slap squashing the shrill noise. The crowd surged on, nearer to Farkas. Now he could see an occasional face wrought with wrinkles of light, inexpressive but intent. It was curious how silent they were; silent, yet emotional; not businesslike, nor a lynching, hysterical rabble; and yet both, bearing with their silence a touch of inevitable doom. As before, Farkas felt that this was the logic of things and that nothing else could happen, and the numb audience — Don Teofilo, the Doctor, the nurse, the waiters, and himself — could do nothing but cling to their seats and wait for the curtain. He was conscious of the quick violence of the action and its blurred details. But he made an effort to notice the dying glow of Don Teofilo's cigar, left forlorn on the ashtray; the sound of a window opened above, in the Para-

diso; a sudden whiff of kitchen smell; and like a drowning man he searched for some significant scene of the past,
but could remember nothing.

The crowd thinned out, then surged back to its focal
point as if sucked by a retreating blast. The pale circle of
light under the street-lamps was filled with hands and
heads and shoulders; in their midst a struggling Don Innocenzo, half-raised, his hands hitting out frantically. Then
someone quickly climbed the lamp-post and a rope came
writhing down. Another pair of hands caught it and two
dark heads came up with Don Innocenzo, turning him towards the terrace. The crowd engulfed him again with its
surf-like and harmonious movement. Now he started to
shout. '*Viva Il Duce!*' he shouted, his arms struggling free
and shooting out in a dramatic gesture. 'Ham,' Farkas
thought. 'Dénes would play that part much more con-
vincingly.' Don Innocenzo was thrown upward and his
head caught the noose, like a fish snapping a bait. '*Viva Il
Duce!*' he shouted; 'Long Live the Empire!' he said, and
was covered by two men who rose out of the multitude
into the light.

The crowd backed now, except for the man who had
climbed the lamp-post; they cleared a circular space
around it. It was all over, and they stepped back as if to
inspect their work. There he hung, his chin resting on his
chest, in the timeless humility of death, his limp hands
turned out, the tips of his boots meeting: an embarrassed
child waiting for punishment.

First Interval

Like the tide that receded, leaving a refuse of shells and seaweed, the crowd had gone, leaving darkness and silence stiff with inanimate things that betrayed the recent violence. Farkas stood on his balcony overlooking the main square. An overturned chair, some foliage trampled underfoot, the red wine spilled over the cloth, and the lonely body hanging on the lamp-post; all had its meaning.

They went as quickly as they had come, dispersing, it seemed, according to some careful plan. Giacobbe went, too, helping to carry his brother to the Sanatorium, where Doctor Schmidt was going to do his best. The nurse pushed Don Teofilo to his villa behind the Kursalon. He was stiff with fright, and clung to the arms of his wheelchair, staring about him with round eyes at Giacobbe, the crowd, and their victim.

Giacobbe asked Farkas to go to his room, and said he would come and see him next morning. He was pale, trying in vain to suppress the excitement that had overcome him now that action was over. His upper lip twitched, and his voice was not only extremely hoarse, but trembling as well. He wore an open-necked shirt and a dark suit greasy and crumpled.

When Farkas returned to the Paradiso, the lights were on in the lounge. Three men stood by the porter's desk with old-fashioned rifles slung over their shoulders. They nodded to Farkas with grim friendliness as he passed. One of them was a youth of seventeen, Benito the grocer's errand boy, whom Farkas had often seen dashing away on his bicycle. Enrico was at his post, sleepy and polite as ever, his red, inflamed eyes blinking, as if there had been a sudden influx of distinguished and fussy Americans and he did not know how to put them up. The manager's door by the lift was wide open, and Farkas saw a small sad man wearing a cook's cap and jacket sitting at Fritti's desk, telephoning.

The three Germans sat at their usual table, in pyjamas and dressing-gowns, unkempt, their faces baggy with the wrinkles of lost sleep. The Major had forgotten his spectacles and was constantly narrowing his eyes, which gave him a look of acute suspicion. The Captain was just surprised, his mouth half-open, and he kept scratching his tousled hair. The airman's face was puffed, with red spots, and he glowered, chewing some undistinguishable piece of food. Two more men and Filomena stood behind them with revolvers. One of them was Stefano the luggage-man, whose face Farkas had never seen before, as it was usually hidden behind trunks, piles of umbrellas, overcoats and hatboxes. Filomena, her beautiful breasts stiff with pride and excitement, her old apple-face screwed into a permanent grin, kept talking to the Germans: Farkas could not hear what she was saying, but her voice held the joy of irony.

'Herr Farkas,' the Major cried as he recognized him. 'Herr Farkas, *das ist ja unerhoert.*' Farkas thoroughly enjoyed having pretended not to understand German the other day. *'Bonne nuit, cheribibi,'* he replied solemnly, and walked on without stopping. The Morgans, too, were there, having some tea. Mrs. Morgan looked clean and alert, and fussed with the teapot. Her husband sat silent and pleased, watching her with childish sleepiness on his face. 'Cup of tea?' she cried out to Farkas, and the Germans jumped slightly. 'No, thank you,' Farkas said. 'I say, what's all this?' the man asked. 'A slight case of revolution,' said Farkas, and went.

Now he stood on the balcony, watching the sky settle at last. The clouds stopped their race and grouped themselves around the moon. He felt tired. As he was about to step inside, the girl next door spoke from the window.

'May I see you for a moment?' she said.

Farkas said, 'Certainly,' walked back into the room, switched on the light on his night-table, and hid his dark-green pyjamas under the pillow. There was a knock, and he walked to the door and let her in. She wore a white dressing-gown and had combed out her hair, which fell in long waves. She did not look at Farkas, but crossed the room to the window and stood there for a second, looking out. Then she turned and leaned against the wall. Her face was in semi-darkness.

Farkas looked at her and tried to imagine what she would be like lying on his bed. She said: 'I'm terribly sorry to barge in like this. You will forgive me, won't you? It was terrible to be alone tonight.' She rested her body on her right foot, in a primitive pose like a girl carrying water in an earthenware jug, walking to a desert well, her breasts bare; a biblical pose it was, and Farkas thought: What would it be like to touch her warm body, especially that deep arch in her back? And he thought of her lying beside him; her hands under her head, staring at the ceiling, in silence, enveloped in a conflict of satisfaction and remorse, then starting to talk at last; possibly telling him the story of her life. How her father, a distinguished bank manager of Vienna or perhaps a retired army officer (we used to have a car, you know), died, leaving her mother (she was still beautiful, you know) struggling hard to make ends meet, and how she went to the Carmelite School, and how one day she met a young man (he was really terribly nice) named Franz, and how she used to go to his rooms near the Graben.

Farkas wondered what variations there could be: would she ask if he had really known Reinhardt, or mention that she had seen him once in the Kaerntner Strasse with Slezak the singer and wanted his autograph, but had not had the courage to ask for it, or what? Years ago in Prague, a Sudeten waitress was sent to his room by the night-porter, a short fleshy girl with the most beautiful thighs Farkas had ever seen. She started to talk the moment she entered, beginning with her early childhood in Karlsbad and how she used to be pinched by fat old men; and she never stopped talking as she undressed and sat on Farkas's lap; and even while they were making love she kept talking, and in the end Farkas wagged a finger at her and said: 'If you don't shut up at once, I'll write a short story about you.'

Perhaps she has a variation, he thought as they stood there. The silence between them was like the touch of a girl-manicurist's hand on one's own, when one suddenly realizes that the impersonal, businesslike touch is that of a woman. The room suddenly became that First Paragraph, in brackets, preceding Scene One. Objects such as *bed* and *easy-chair* and *bottle of brandy on the table* became italicized in his mind and THE YOUNG GIRL (fair, about twenty-five, labouring under heavy emotion) stood by the window facing THE AUTHOR (elderly, elegant).

'Herr Farkas,' she said quietly, 'can you think of any reason why I shouldn't commit suicide?'

She has some dramatic instinct, at least, he thought; plunging *in medias res* without bothering about dull expositions. He began to enjoy himself. *Outside*, he continued his mental stage instructions, *warm night with young girl's lover hanging from a lamp-post.* There were many ways to go on now that the dominant note was struck; he could direct the theme into an alley of pathetic stuff, with him reminding her, in the Great Scene, of the warmth of the sun, the laughter of new-born babies, the taste of strong coffee, and all the other generous gifts of life; or maintaining the style of the later Farkas, be flippant, full of chuckles and cynicism.

'No, I can't,' he said realizing that he spoke those words because he was afraid that she was too absorbed in her own story and would only listen to him if he shocked her, and that she had perhaps made up her mind to dominate the scene and leave the stage eventually, with the pathos of forthcoming death. No, my dear, he said to himself, I shall keep the lead, and he felt like Bors, the great Shakespearean actor, who always resented the fact that Hamlet had a mother and that he could therefore not quite walk away with the play.

She looked at him pleadingly. 'Please,' she said. 'Won't you take me seriously?'

'My dear girl,' he said, and pulled at his cuffs, 'there

are many dastardly things one can do to women. One can leave them with illegitimate children, one can beat them and betray them. Only one mustn't take them seriously. It makes them grow old prematurely.'

She was wagging her head.

'He didn't take me seriously,' she said, and sat down on a chair and talked fluently as if Farkas were an old acquaintance. 'Certainly not. "Don Innocenzo," I asked him that first morning, "will you please prolong my visa?" He looked at the passport and said, "I see that you were born in Vienna; it's a marvellous city." I was so worried, and he talked about Vienna. They were all like that: Poschl, the official who gave me my exit-permit. I went to see him, and my heart was beating terribly fast. "Ah, little girl," Poschl cried, "my pretty little Miss Levy wants to depart from our town; isn't it a shame?" And he laughed and stroked me and came to my room next night with the permit. Or in Prague, the first year, Jurchek, the lawyer who had fixed my contract. "Doctor Jurchek," I used to ask — and I was terribly serious, it was terribly important to be able to stay: "Doctor Jurchek, will it be all right?" He pinched my chin and took off his glasses and later his shoes as well, and said: "A sweet girl like you should not worry about things like the police."

'But *he* was the worst,' she went on; 'this one here. "*Et alors,* my little Jewess," he would mock me at the end of each month, "well, well, my little pluto-bolshevik world-conspirator, arch-enemy of the Axis," he would say, and finger my passport gaily. "Don Innocenzo, please," I always begged him (and by then he was coming to see me almost every night), "please, please, this is very important." "Ah, little Jewess," he once replied with a smile, "suppose I had you deported, my little negroid-semitic hybrid, suppose I sent you to the gas chambers of Poland?" He was always mocking me.'

She continued: 'No, certainly not; he did not take me seriously. He would say, "Little pig, tonight you were very, very vehement with your kisses; of course, tomorrow your permit expires." You don't mind my telling you all this?' She looked up at Farkas, but did not wait for a reply. 'Only a few days ago he said, "Tell me, little Jewess, suppose we lose the war, will you then grant me a visa if I come and make love to you?" I wanted to go down tonight,' the girl said, with a sudden quietness in her voice, 'and talk to him. "Good-bye, Don Innocenzo," I wanted to say, "you wicked boy, good-bye," and stroke his hand for the last time; but I was scared lest he might speak to me, dead though he was, speak to me from the lamp-post and say, "Ah, *voilà* petite Jewess, why are you so tender? Ah, of course, tomorrow the visa expires." '

'Aren't women wonderful!' Farkas interrupted her before she could cry, and offered her a cigarette. 'Nothing makes them so tender as a brute. Come bully me and be my love. But seriously: Don Innocenzo was a despicable cad. It is much better for the world, including yourself, that he's dead. You should be rejoicing now. No more visa troubles. They might even make you an honorary citizen of San Fernando. Or did you really enjoy being blackmailed every month?'

She made an intelligent grimace, full of resignation and without sentimentality. 'I never enjoy myself, Herr Farkas,' she said. 'I'm notoriously unhappy. When I cross the path of a black cat, which is a disaster according to our superstitions, the cat hangs its head, rushes home, and says to its family, "What do you think, Antonia Levy crossed my path tonight, what an omen!" You say I should be rejoicing, no more war and no more permits. But what then? There is nowhere for me to go. I shall be thirty next month; I feel ugly and isolated. I hate playing the violin to elderly invalids. There is nowhere I could return. Mamma died last year. Every morning when I wake it is like Monday morning — like going to school unprepared and frightened.'

'Have a brandy,' Farkas said. 'And stop being sorry for yourself.' He poured her a drink. 'Life isn't particularly pleasant, but I can offer no proof that death is. It all depends on what you want. If it's a Big Purple Holiday, with no worries and a tall, rich, kind English duke, lots of decorative dogs and no headaches, you'd better give up now. Your type always has something to worry about. If it isn't Mamma, then it is Franz, or the permit, the visa, the hairdresser, the getting old, the wrinkles under the eyes, and so on. But the idea of lying in a dark ditch with worms nibbling at you isn't exactly uplifting either. If you have come to me for a visa to the After-life, you're definitely at the wrong address.'

'Oh, but you are so clever and wise, Herr Farkas,' she sighed. 'And people do say, don't they, that they're fed-up with themselves?'

Farkas went up to her and lifted her chin severely. Her skin was warm.

'My dear girl,' he said, looking into her eyes, 'your *Weltschmerz* is an utter bore. Some of my best friends have died in the last four years, and some of them were great men. In addition, every day a large number of hopeful and vigorous young men die a violent and unwanted death. Yours would be no loss to the world. Even in normal times it would only be reported in the local news column between the birth of some triplets and the price of cabbage. You will eventually grow quite old and lose your teeth and the lustre of your hair. The world will continue to be unkind and uncomfortable. All I could offer you is half my bed and an autograph.'

She looked up at him and went quite pale, hating him for what he had said. For a moment he thought she would start crying. She swallowed hard and her lips were a thin line. 'Thank you,' she said, 'for restoring my confidence. I shall take it as a compliment.' She drank, shook her hair, and said 'ah,' as the brandy started to warm her inside. She made a malicious face. 'And I shall need some money, too,' she added, staring at him.

Bravo, he thought. 'That's better,' he said. 'Of course, money. That's all right.'

'And no autograph, please,' she said. 'And you will forget, of course, what I have been telling you.' She is a very poor actress, he thought. 'I had been racking my brains for days,' she went on dryly, 'how to meet you. Tonight I was so frightened that any excuse sounded all right. You soon found me out.'

'Yes,' he said, pouring another drink. 'You see, most women behave like some of my characters; or rather the way they would behave if I didn't brush them up. What about Don Innocenzo?'

'I loathed him,' she said. 'He wasn't even a brute, you know.'

Like Marianne you are, Farkas thought, Marianne the honest harlot in *The Proud Goose*. Gizella could play her nicely. He must have hurt her a lot, but he knew that he wanted to. Gizella once told him, at a moment when she had asked him for some sign of kindness: 'If only once you'd say, "Darling, I'd always love you, never leave you, always protect you"; if you'd only say it once.' But Gizella had miserable literary taste.

He looked at her as she drank with the artificial hardness she had put on to support her miserable act of the little tart, trying to hide the whining, hapless fugitive that she was, who would eventually rush back to her room and bury her head in the pillows and call for Mamma. He was satisfied now; the scene had gone off the way he wanted it to, as if he had written it in advance. He even felt sorry for her, although he knew that she was the type who could easily be consoled and put at ease.

'Look here,' he said, 'stop that act.'

She looked up with a mixture of fright and suspicion, and wanted to say something bitter, but he walked up to her and sat on the arm of her chair and added in a deep voice, the way he wanted to say it, 'Poor little Tony,' and she bowed her head and laid it in her open palms and wept the way she had wanted to weep ever since she had entered the room, while he stroked her soft hair, catching a glimpse of the two of them in the mirror; and he made a move with his hand, like the magician in *Rabbits from a Hat*, meanng presto! *voilà!* I've done it again. But, unfortunately, he felt really ashamed now.

The Theme

Sitting at the lunch-table in the dazzling sunshine, Giacobbe, hoarse, unshaved, with a nervous twitch in his left eye, leaned over a map drawn in pencil. By three o'clock this morning San Fernando village and summer resort was effectively controlled by what we now call the Committee's National Liberation forces, of which I am Commander-in-Chief. Of course, we had a plan all the time, carefully worked out by myself, Chef Luigi, Francesco, the leader of the quarrymen, and Alberto, the war cripple from the desert campaign. By a happy coincidence the quarrymen were all in the village yesterday, waiting for a decision concerning a game of football to be played next Sunday. As for us, we had a meeting, anyway, with the husbands of the washerwomen — you will hear about them later. To put it briefly, yesterday by four o'clock we had a considerable crowd of men concentrated. Thus, when the great news was announced over the wireless at about five o'clock and Foa rushed to us on his bicycle to let us know, we were able to deploy our forces without delay, while the Forces of Reaction were either stunned, drunk, or in bed. Counting our immediate strength, we found we had eighty men for tactical purposes. They were unarmed, of course, save for two rifles and a large number of pickaxes and spades. Our strategic reserves were known to be over a hundred, including the fishermen who had been fairly well organized by Ciro, our local poet, whom you should have met, by the way. The establishment of quick communications was the first job; so, having been elected Commander, I took ten good men and occupied the post-office and telephone exchange. It was an easy task, of course, as it was already closed to the public, and Signorina Lisabetta, a stupid spinster with spectacles interested in nothing but her forthcoming retirement and some vicious parrots, was having dinner on the first floor over the offices. Francesco, Alberto, and I went upstairs and asked her in the name of Freedom for the keys to her office. I am sorry to say that she resisted, first by screaming for help, then by throwing at us a large coffee-pot, and, no doubt by mistake, a parrot. Francesco had to disarm her, while I tried to explain that our intrusion had purely political reasons. She wouldn't believe me, called us bandits, but when Francesco got her on the sofa, she began to suspect rape and stopped struggling. She lay there, bony and repulsive as such a State employee would be, her spectacles riding on the tip of her nose, panting heavily, her legs twitching with excitement. 'All three of you?' she asked hoarsely, fearing the best, I suspect; but Francesco asked for the keys again, which threw her into a fit, and the struggle started afresh. Finally we got the keys, and having gagged and bound Signorina Lisabetta we locked her in her bedroom, went downstairs, and installed ourselves in the post-office. It was the eve of September the ninth, nineteen hundred and forty-three.

The post-office was thus transformed into our headquarters, a sort of Smolny Institute. I was to remain there to co-ordinate all movements with Alberto and Francesco as field commanders, so to speak. I took charge of the telephone exchange myself, with some measure of difficulty, as I had had no previous experience in operating such intricate machinery. But on the whole, everything went reasonably well. I made contact with the fishermen, told them the news, and asked them to stand by for further instructions. Then I rang the garage and called out the lorry-drivers, who were all-important for our mobility.

Briefly, this was our task: (1) to disarm the forces of reaction and arrest their leaders; (2) to establish effective control of all strategic points; (3) to set up a working committee for the solution of San Fernando's problems, such as the release of the washerwomen and Leonardo, and, finally, to establish law and order before the arrival of Allied troops. The Chef Luigi, who has been in charge of our intelligence, arrived a few minutes after he had been notified. The code word for our operation was *Speranza*. He was still wearing his cook's cap and jacket when he arrived, but believe me, no one in this place has so much quiet dignity as the Chef Luigi. We had a quick conference; in the light of what he told us about Don Innocenzo's inactive reaction to the news, a new, simple scheme of attack was decided upon.

The first job, we decided again, was to disarm the militia, consisting of fifteen men, all armed but dispersed. Five of them were known to be having drinks at Pina's; three were patrolling the Abbey Road, two were somewhere else, presumably near the main square; one, a squinting scatter-brain named Ignazio, was in bed with the wife of one of those patrolling the Abbey Road, and four were at the militia post at the top of the village. I rang Pina first, and having told her the news about the armistice asked for information about the five militiamen. Dear old Pina, although a bad type of exploiter herself, was always sympathetic to the grievances of the village. I knew I could trust her. She told me that you were just leaving and that the five men were sitting there quietly, having ordered the first round of drinks. I asked her to keep them occupied and then dispatched Private Alberto with fifteen men in a lorry.

Alberto had sufficient military experience to cope with such a task; but his main problem was to do his job quickly, thoroughly, and, if possible, without arousing attention. He went and surrounded Pina's place in a narrow circle, posting five men in front of the house with the lorry while the rest went around and waded through the reeds, closing the trap from the sea. 'No Dunkirk there,' Alberto later reported with pride. They caught their first Fascist soon after their arrival, before launching the general attack: he was just stepping onto the plank which leads into the sea, to relieve himself, when Alberto's men got there. 'Hey, Augusto,' one of them called out to him while he stood there, legs spread apart, swaying slightly. 'Who is it?' he asked, and before he knew what had happened, he was overcome and disarmed. They put him in the one rowing-boat that was left poor Pina, and two men stayed with him as guards, covering him up with their jackets to muffle his groans. His rifle and pistol came in handy: they were the first pieces of booty and gave Alberto confidence. He entered the café from the sea accompanied by four men, while the others went around the house and entered it from the front, one by one, trying to look as innocent as possible, sitting down at separate tables in pairs. They were all quarrymen, by the way; short, stocky men; but there is no one tougher than a San Fernando quarryman.

The terrace was empty (you had already left), and the four Fascists sat near the sea with Pina leaning over them and — Alberto swears — telling them dirty jokes to keep them occupied. Alas, such are the dialectics of history. An old bordello-keeper with dirty anecdotes helps the cause of freedom and justice. Alberto's entry was hardly noticed. The Fascists were gurgling with laughter, slapping the table and Pina's fat bottom, clamouring for more jokes. Now, this Pina woman always had a sense of humour. I don't know how often you have talked to her, or if your Italian is good enough for you to appreciate her quick, dry wit, her superb cynicism which makes of the world a large, not too attractive bordello where men and women are but slaves of their lust, combining it with material greed. She's an old-fashioned one, this Pina, a relic of the Boccaccio age, perhaps, when shrewd women used to control the community by carefully regulating the supply of their sex; she has often reminded me of one of those ancient woodcuts showing a Renaissance bedroom with a friar hiding behind a curtain, a maid, her breasts uncovered, sitting in her bed, sweet and naïve, and some old nurse — an early Pina — beckoning the friar.

Anyway, there she was, telling smutty stories to the Forces of Reaction. She had noticed Alberto and his men. She sat on top of the table, and when the Fascists continued to clamour for more, she crossed her old, fat legs and asked them loudly if they had heard the one about the king's mental disease. 'The what?' one of the men asked, and slowly their laughter trickled away into their throats, leaving an awkward silence. They looked around, and one of them, a fat, sweaty individual named Andrea, said: 'Pina, you'd better be careful.' 'I am careful, you fool,' she replied in the grand manner; 'but what has that to do with the king's mental disease?' Her voice was very loud, triumphant, fit for an opera. The fat man sobered up. 'You mustn't talk like that,' he said. 'You might get into trouble.' The others snorted in assent. 'I don't think she will,' Alberto interrupted, and stepped up to them.

People — especially the Fascists — had always been embarrassed about Alberto ever since he came back from Africa with two pink, round obscene clumps of flesh instead of the hands which had been blown off by a hand-grenade. He was the immediate reminder that war was a bloody thing and not a glorious adventure. They looked at him as he stood there, his mutilated hands resting on his hips. 'Hey, Alberto,' the fat one cried; 'looked at the bottom of a jug?' 'Haven't touched a drop,' Alberto replied, then reached out with his pink clumps of flesh, picked up the fat man's glass clumsily, and lifting it high said: 'To hell with the Germans!' and drank. He was enjoying himself, the good Alberto, and would have continued his somewhat theatrical triumph, but fortunately remembered that time was short and precious. So he gave a sign and the quarrymen closed in on the four Fascists. The fat one jumped up and reached for his rifle, but it was much too late. One of the quarrymen hit him over the head with a pickaxe, and he fell on the floor. The others just stared mutely, and were duly disarmed and led to the lorry.

Meanwhile Francesco and Ciro had been busy, too. The

lorry-drivers had all turned out, bless their hearts, and we were able to move simultaneously. Francesco, coughing with excitement, his grey, taut face red with tuberculosis and happiness, took twenty men and went to the village, to the militia post. Ciro, the poet-fisherman, took another lorry with fifteen men. His task was to pick up the stray militia patrols if he could and go back to the fishery which he was to take over in the name of the people; to re-organize his men and establish a nucleus of resistance on the Abbey Hill. Another ten good men, a motley crowd, was led by Benito, the grocer's errand boy, and the Jew, Foa, who had been hauled out of bed by my telephone call and who came panting to the post-office, his biblical lion's head all aflame, carrying the rifle he had been hiding under a sack of dried peas. They went off to neutralize the retired gendarme officers' rest-house in the woods, just by the tennis court — a nest of apoplectic reactionaries — and then to occupy the railway station and the signal-box. At the same time Alfieri, the beach-master, volunteered to immobilize the sea escape routes by stealing all the row-ing-boats and sailing-boats from the Royal Yachting Club and anchoring them behind the bathhouse, an excellent defensive position accessible by the wooden bridge only. Chef Luigi for his part returned to the Paradiso to take over there, to watch Don Innocenzo or any developments and to move the moment we had all arrived. Happily he didn't need any extra men, as he was well supported by a number of kitchen hands and waiters.

I remained at the post-office with fifteen or twenty men and a lorry, to be used as reinforcement if necessary. There I was, Farkas, alone in the post-office, with the men waiting outside and making coffee in a tin can over a primus stove they had found in Signorina Lisabetta's kitchen. There was nothing to do but wait for the others to come back. I had not been frightened up till then, I was too busy going over the plan, seeing the men, giving them orders, making and receiving calls. But now it was different: I was alone, and through the window I could look down at San Fernando and its lights and trees, down to the sea and over to the Abbey which stood big and impassive. I was whistling to myself, the *Marseillaise*, the *International*, and *La Bandiera Rossa*, terribly out of key I was whistling, and I knew that I was afraid; there was a lump in my stomach and I was feeling cold. I went over the situation once more for the hundredth time, cataloguing the objective and subjective elements, thinking first in abstract terms, such as war, misery, bitterness; then of the immediate background, of the washerwomen locked up in the Abbey, their husbands and their violent impatient words, and of the villagers in general who made such beautiful corn and fat grapes and yet ate grey, spongy bread and drank cheap wine that tasted like vinegar; and of Alberto's pink clumps of flesh and his grim talk and of the fishermen who never spoke except through Ciro; Ciro the poet, who would come and visit me at nights and by the petroleum lamp read his verses, so cumbersome and heavy, yet with a primordial simplicity in them which made him sound like a child talking to himself.

And most of all I thought of Leonardo, locked up in prison waiting for his doom, who would be liberated and come and find us happy and free and there would be a *festa* in his honour; yes, the feast occupied my thoughts that night, a great, real festival with long tables in the garden, scores of people, coloured paper lamps, and gar- lands over our heads and good wine standing in neat carafes hazy with ice; and rich, fat food and singing and speeches; a real big feast without the sense of remorse and fear, and Leonardo there, sitting at the head of the table in a new white suit, his beautiful white forehead shining once again; Leonardo unbroken and erect and full of vigour and interest. Lenin, forgive my stupid sentimen- tality, but that was how I thought about that night, in such terms, in terms of feasts and laughter and good wine and no guilt; not as an historical trend, not as fetters rent asunder, not as vengeance and killing, but as a big, beau- tiful feast with long tables and paper lamps and Leonardo.

But then I thought of *them*, of Don Innocenzo, his self- assured arrogance, his conscious power, his boots and jokes and cruelty: of Father Giuseppe, the shadow over San Fernando, never tiring and omnipresent, checking up on people's work and dreams and sins. Were they really to be gone from their august posts before the night was out? I asked and knew no assurance. Up and down San Fernando our men were moving with the grim efficiency I had always hoped for, yet always doubted. Will they be able to conquer, or have I unleashed something that may end in tragi-comic failure? They were willing to act, those men; surprisingly so, and it looked as if these last twenty years had passed over them without affecting their bitterness and readiness, just as the last hundred years had not really seen many changes here save for their growing knowledge that the fields and their masters and their God were one day to be stripped of their frightening omnipotence.

Francesco came back first, glowing with sick excitement, proud and almost swaggering. They had found four Fascists who surrendered meekly when they heard the news. The post was first surrounded and Francesco entered with five men and told them briefly what had happened, adding on his own that the Duce had shot himself on hearing that the Fuehrer had taken poison; that the Allies were in Rome and approaching Berlin and General Montgomery might arrive in San Fernando any moment now, accompanied by the Chief Rabbi of London and the Navy; and the militiamen had the choice either of fleeing to Japan in a submarine or surrendering honourably to the people of San Fernando. They listened numbly, and one of them, Pietro, a tall individual from Ravenna, asked for proofs, whereupon one of the quarrymen shot him. 'You see,' Francesco explained to the others, 'do you think we should have dared if the things I've just told you weren't true?' This sounded logical, and they all said they would lay down their arms if allowed to go unmolested. Francesco said, 'Very well,' and took their arms (five rifles and three revolvers) and the key to the stores, adding that, as there was danger that some misled villagers might take justice into their own hands, it was in their interest to remain in protective custody; and locked them up in the neighbouring prison.

There was only one hitch in Francesco's triumph: he found the prison empty and discovered that Leonardo had suddenly been taken down to the Paradiso upon an urgent summons from Don Innocenzo. I became terribly excited: I knew that there was no time to be wasted on personal matters, and that there was the plan and we should not precipitate events. I rang through at once to Chef Luigi and asked him about Leonardo; he replied that Leonardo had indeed just arrived escorted by two militiamen and that Don Innocenzo was drunk, but there was no reason to worry, as the terrace was still fairly crowded, and that you, Farkas, were there with Don Innocenzo and the others. So I made him promise to keep a watch on Leonardo and let me know at once if anything suspicious happened. It was getting late, and no news from either Ciro or Foa's party which had gone to the rest-house and the station. I rang the fishery: 'Ciro hasn't arrived yet,' they said. I sent two men on bicycles out to the Abbey Road to see what had happened and report at once; then rang the railway station, but there was no reply. Then I talked things over with Francesco and asked his opinion. While we were discussing matters, Alberto arrived from Pina's café with his five militiamen; our men locked them up in the shed behind the post-office and Alberto joined in our conference. We had now dealt with most of the militiamen, and there was no indication that we had been rumbled.

Then Foa rang. He was greatly agitated. 'Here Foa — *speranza*,' he announced himself, combining his name with the password. 'Everything under control,' he reported. 'We have occupied the railway station and the rest-house. No casualties; Antonio and Colonel Peruggio, manager of the rest-house, are our prisoners.' I asked him to leave a strong guard at both places and return at once with the rest of his men. In the meanwhile, we decided the time had come to call out the villagers and end our operations with a mass demonstration on the main square. Alberto was charged with this task: he was to rush back to the village, arouse the men he trusted, and start marching them down at once, meeting us by the church.

It was getting late, and I was worried that Don Innocenzo and the rest might go home and we should not find them at the Paradiso; also I was worried about Leonardo. Still there was no news from Ciro, but we could not wait any longer. Slowly we started to line up in marching formations, while the lorries went off to fetch the villagers. I left two good men at the telephone exchange, and we walked out to the main street and the men lined up, eight abreast, and under the dusty trees one could hear their quiet but triumphant whispers and the shuffling of a good many feet. Foa arrived and joined us with his men, and now there was nothing else to do but wait for Alberto, hoping that Ciro was all right and would catch up with us later.

While we waited, Foa, his biblical shock of hair trembling in the darkness, quickly told his story. They had first gone to the rest-house with Benito, the grocer's boy, a bright lad, leading the way through the woods. They stopped some few yards in front of the white villa and decided to reconnoitre. One of the quarrymen, a former electrician, climbed a tree and cut the telephone wires, for the rest-house was known to have a direct line to Ravenna. Meanwhile, four men, armed with pickaxes and Foa's rifle and an old revolver and led by Benito and Foa, went up to the front door, while the rest hung around in the gardens, keeping an eye on the windows and the tradesmen's entrance. Before they rang the bell, Benito crept to the large French window which threw some light into the night. He saw some ten or twelve people sitting at tables playing cards. There was the Colonel, a tall, red-faced man, and all the others, mostly elderly men and women, stiff in fine clothes and dresses and all washed and brushed, playing cards as if the world were standing still.

Then Foa rang the bell and the Colonel himself answered it. 'He was wearing one of those striped artificial silk shirts I had sold him in thirty-eight,' Foa said. 'He looked tall and bald and forbidding and was surprised to see me. "Foa?" he asked, "what the devil are you doing here?" I became rather confused and said, "Well, you see, Your Excellency, it is like this." But Benito was impatient, as he hated the old man and pushed through beside me and said: "You're in protective custody." I wondered how the boy had picked up those fancy words. "That's right," I added, wondering whether to call him "Your Excellency" again, "there's been a revolution." Meanwhile Benito simply walked in towards the drawing-room accompanied by two quarrymen, one of them carrying my rifle. "What the devil is this, get out at once," the Colonel shouted, trying to catch up with Benito, but one of the quarrymen pushed him against a glass cabinet that stood in the hall, full of little knick-knacks — mostly china dogs and lace and cups and what-not, and he crashed against this fine glass cabinet and broke the glass and some of the dogs too. "You see, Your Excellency," I tried to tell him, and I'll be damned if I know why I kept addressing him like that, "there is nothing to do, Your Excellency." But I shall always remember him, the Colonel, as he would come to my shop in his white summer uniform, his spurs tinkling along the main street, his horsewhip and monocle and stern bald skull, and the way he would say, "Well, Foa, what about those braces?" as if he had lent me the braces and everything else and was demanding them back. The people in the drawing-room were apparently deaf; they must have been very deaf, for they had taken no notice of our entry, the crash and the shouting. They just went on playing cards.

'I shall never forget the scene,' Foa went on, 'those fine people, all washed and brushed, sitting by the green baize tables in silence, glaring at the cards. They were playing bridge or some such outlandish game, and as Benito, the two quarrymen, and I entered, leaving the Colonel in charge of the others, I saw one old lady in a print frock, the very best type of satin, leaning forward and saying very loudly: *"Four clubs."* Then she saw us; the others looked up, too, and each of them gaped and had a funny line between the eyes; which was not surprising, as there we stood, Benito with his thin legs hanging down from his baggy plus-fours, his freckles, his large ears; and the two quarrymen, dark with cropped hair and no collars, one of them chewing a toothpick, my rifle in his hand; and last, but not least, myself — the only one they knew well. There was silence in the room, but from the garden came the angry voice of the Colonel, silenced by a loud slap. Then Benito stepped forward, kicked over one of the tables and said, in French, *"Rien ne va plus"* — God knows where the kid picks up those high-class words, but it sounded very impressive. Unfortunately, those people did not hear it; they must have been very deaf. An old man — I remember him, he came to buy a toothbrush one day —

rose with an annoyed face. Benito was flushed, and
shouted: "You're under arrest." The lady in the print
satin frock said anxiously: "What is all this about?"
"You're under arrest," Benito cried furiously, "arrest,
arrest!" The old man stepped up to him and asked:
"What is it you wanted?" So Benito pushed him into an
armchair and shouted for the last time. "You're under
arrest." '

Foa continued: 'We decided it was no use wasting time
shouting at all those people, so we left some quarrymen
guarding the house, while the Colonel was locked up in
the lavatory, the only room without a window. We proceeded to the railway station; the time was well chosen,
for the Ravenna night train was not due for another fifteen
minutes and Antonio was drinking wine upstairs. The
station was empty but for the old porter, who was asleep
in the waiting-room. We strolled down the platform, all
of us, and had a good look in all directions for stray
Fascists or strangers; there was no one. As we marched
along the platform, Signora Clara spotted us. You know
how she sits in her window all day, waiting for the trains,
staring at arrivals or departures. "Good evening, *bella
signora*," I greeted her. "Is your husband in?" "Yes," she
replied flatly. "May we disturb him for a moment," I
asked, "on important official business?" "Certainly," she
said.

'So up we went and knocked at the door and Antonio
came to let us in, in his shirt-sleeves with a large paper
napkin round his neck, saying: "I'm having a snack now,
Foa; then I shall be busy, the Ravenna train, you know" —
but Benito, that wicked youth, just would not let him

finish. "Never mind the Ravenna train," he said, "never mind, you're not the station-master any more." Antonio looked at him and at us and stopped rubbing one of his back teeth with his tongue and said: "What sort of silly joke is this?" Benito said: "Tell me, Signor Antonio" — I wonder how the boy thinks these things up!— "tell me, do you think Hitler is a great man?" "Of course he is a great man," Antonio reddened; "now look here . . .! Do you think . . ." Benito interrupted him, "that he is a very great man?" "A very great man indeed," Antonio replied, and pulled himself into a stiff pose. "Good," Benito said, "that's all we wanted to know"; and spat into Antonio's face. I can't tell you where he got the cheek, the boy Benito, but he spat at him again, and there it was, and Antonio realized that something had happened, and the saliva ran down his cheeks like tears. Then the quarrymen took over and stripped Antonio and took his beautiful uniform and his keys and borrowed some cigars they found on the dresser and took Antonio himself and locked him up in the luggage room with a few old suitcases and two cases of wine. Signora Clara did not say a word all the time; she just stood by the window, her enormous hair piled up, and Benito apologized for the intrusion and explained the new situation, adding that women like her would gain real freedom from household drudgery in the new era; but she just did not care and said nothing.'

Giacobbe continued: It was time to march, and those last moments were long and curious; you know how time feels at times. Those moments were the longest in my life, as I waited for Alberto and the villagers; the longest but not the slowest; for the Chef Luigi had just sent a message that Don Innocenzo was beating Leonardo up. I remember the moon coming up behind the trees, coming up from under a cloud. I quickly ran back to the post-office and rang the fishery, and someone said Ciro had been shot and was dying and fifty fishermen were on their way to join us. I asked what had happened to Ciro and someone said, 'Hold on,' and gave the phone to Ciro, and he said, 'How is everything, Giacobbe?' 'Fine,' I said. 'What's the matter with you?' 'Come and see me,' he said, 'when all is finished; there is a beautiful moon tonight and I can watch the stars,' he said typically. There was nothing I could do about Ciro, for time was running short. I went out again and told them we would start now and they should be very quiet and refrain from violence and be worthy of the Cause. Then the fishermen arrived, walking through the woods in gaunt, silent pairs, and told us that Ciro was in a very bad state, but would not see a doctor and it would not make a difference anyway, as he was dying. And then the villagers arrived. So we started to march down the main street, eight abreast, a hundred and fifty all told, carrying pickaxes and spades and even scythes, marching mutely down the road in the long night.

Theme with Variations

Giacobbe went on: So we marched under the sympathetic stars, making hardly any sound. Some of the villagers came barefoot, and all were told to keep quiet. The procession was headed by Alberto, Francesco, two of the fishermen, and myself. It was a long night; indeed, the longest in my life, as we marched towards the main square, Don Innocenzo, Leonardo, and a number of other things as well, revenge and freedom. First I thought about myself; rather mechanically in the tempo of the silent steps and our marching bodies, and under my thoughts I felt my distant stomach, squeezed and twisted by the comparative calmness that now followed the busy night — a calmness which for the first time since I had been afraid in the post-office was not filled up by our business, our activities and doings, but grew up to the stars. What did I think of? *Now it has come*, I said to myself, *now we shall do it, now it has come, we are marching*. But then I felt that it was no use escaping to such abstractions and that the past and the future, their concrete associations and practical queries, would have to be discussed now. So I thought of my father as he sat one night in his favourite chair, leaning on his hand, his small cigar hanging between his lips, his tired eyes half-open behind his pince-nez. I thought what a pity that he could not be here; and why a father dies so young and misunderstood, watching the child grow but not quite grow up, watching him from behind his pince-nez across the awkward gulf that divided them and unable to live long enough and see him succeed, or settle his mind and grope his way to his first original conclusions. What a pity he could not be here, I thought, how we could talk and I should understand his tiredness and his head wagging at the child's savage anarchy; and he would now understand what I had meant one night in 1916 by crying in the dark attic room. Now he could advise and direct me, I thought, because he was always that sort of man; and now at last he could confirm or deny whether now, as I neared forty, I often moved my hand or brushed my hair or spoke the way he used to; whether I had carried on something of him.

And I thought of Leonardo whom I had seen so broken the other day at the *Annexe* when Don Innocenzo was beating him. I had not been allowed to see him since, and those few days passed slowly and anxiously while he was up in the prison, so near, yet I wasn't able to talk to him, and I was scared they would take him to Ravenna and shoot him or send him back to the islands and he would have come in vain. But now he will be free, I thought, and soon lie in a crisp white bed, behind green, cool shutters, and tomorrow I will go and see him and we will talk. And then soon, in a few days' time, perhaps, we will have a big *festa* and Leonardo will be there at the head of the table, rested, and his veins and nerves slowly regaining life and vigour. I thought of them, of my father and Leonardo, in two brief flashes; I felt them as one might catch a sudden whiff of scent from a flower, or the smell of bread with all its long and interwoven associations of politics or love.

Then I heard the steps again and felt the lump in my stomach, and was again aware of us, marching down the main street towards the square; in my mind I saw the multitude behind me approaching the square in mute triumph, and I saw such words as *how* and *why* flashing through my mind. Yes, I was asking myself, marching down the main street, *why* have these people what is popularly called risen; *how* is it that the villagers, the fishermen, the quarrymen, their lives entangled in the narrow routine of their immediate problems, have suddenly acted historically? They were simple people, the people of San Fernando; and by 'people' I don't mean the beautiful blab of the Narodniks or of sentimental upper-class renegades; I meant those of us who worked, owning nothing, providing thereby the near and distant few with that mysterious surplus which made misery and wars and held us all in chains, preventing the growth of men and minds. They were simple, even stupid and superstitious, and frightened of lord and priest. If you looked at them jerking their hands to their hats to salute Don Teofilo or Father Giuseppe, if you saw how they bent their tired backs in humility, how their eyes reflected the cowed hatred of the dog-man, you wondered how it was that these people, at this one particular moment, had acted with such iron logic according to the scientific rules which the two indignant and prophetic Germans had formulated in England nearly a hundred years before.

But San Fernando knew nothing of surplus value or the accumulation of primitive capital, of the knell that was to sound, rending the greedy system asunder. But then, apples had been falling from trees before Newton was born. And after the last war some townsfolk came and leaflets came, and San Fernando listened with suspicious reverence, and looked for the 'buts' and the 'ifs,' for traps and hitches, and a fisherman once called one of the Milano agitators 'Right Honourable Signor Comrade.' No, they did not understand the theories then. But theories are good only if they are deduced from the tangible world, and the world around San Fernando was the best agitator of all. Yet it was so very difficult; some of us tried to explain patiently, tried to dispel suspicion and fear, and chart them maps of behaviour. But by the time the first wind of revolt had reached here and the first glimpse of understanding had dawned in the villagers' minds, the Fascists had come, and with them a new silence and humility. So I wondered.

The people of San Fernando did not perhaps understand the theories and could not explain their world, but they had come to the point when even without the guidance of theory they felt like changing their world. That was what I was thinking about, marching down the main street. Of course, there were the general *motifs* of history, the breakdown of authority and of older values in 1918, the new hopes held out and the failure of such well-meaning friends as the Ravenna deputy who used to come and talk sonorously about the brotherhood of men and the Kingdom of God on earth, putting each sentence in inverted commas as if he spoke only in direct quotations derived from some impeccable divine authority. But he failed, the good man, because he was weak and inconsistent, and the babies of San Fernando kept arriving and the place was small and the men could not go overseas any more and each night a thinner slice of bread was cut, fewer olives dished out, less wine drunk on Saturday night to forget the busy week. Then came the Blackshirts, and their mouths were full of thunderous promise, full of fat words about Rebirth and Honour and Rome. To all this San Fernando listened dully, and the people, being simple, kept looking for a link between the word and the world.

The Black Men changed nothing. They were friendly to the Abbey and to Don Teofilo, and the villagers saw that their bread grew no bigger and the children kept squeezing into the dark, damp rooms that always smell of cheap wine and bodies. They saw no change; there was no change for them. The Black Men just shouted, and petrified the old misery with efficient haste. The land and the sea remained with the old owners, though a new prison was built, and they increased the number of street-lamps and the Abbey Road was rebuilt with asphalt. But the villagers did not like the prison, and were not allowed with their carts on the new road, staying on the old footpath, frightened by the new motor-cars and cyclists. San Fernando needed no people from Ravenna or Milano to understand that there could be no change unless the land changed its masters.

Then, later, there had been Leonardo. They did not really understand him or like him, the villagers. But they saw him being dragged away. First the village dismissed him as a 'queer gentleman'; but in direct proportion to the growing gulf between the promises and the deeds of the masters, Leonardo's memory grew and became somehow identified with grievance and anxiety and hopes. Then they saw the bribery and the corruption that went on in the Abbey and at the Podestà's office; in thirty-one there was that drought and *filossera* — very badly — in thirty-five and this year again; and the Zacconi family were evicted in thirty-eight, and all the smaller, daily symptoms; and when they appeared, the villagers stopped and argued and shut up, but they were inclined to remember Leonardo.

The slogans of the Blackshirts were even less real than those of Father Giuseppe, who had managed to preserve some slight popularity. After all, rain was needed, or a long spell of sun, or a child was sick with fever, and in the darkness there remained nothing but to crouch in a corner and kiss the crucifix, or light a candle for Saint Benedict; thus the magic of the Abbey still functioned, and Father Giuseppe knew it and reminded the village that sin could only be exorcised by sweat and suffering; so they went on sweating for him and suffering for themselves. Slowly, beneath it all, the quantitative changes grew, imperceptibly, though, but growing slowly towards the point when a qualitative change must occur. The years passed much as before: people were a bit more afraid of the Podestà, there were more taxes and the Black Men came and talked in big, resonant words which no one understood. But then the war started, on a small scale at first, in Africa and with triumph, and the Black Slogans blared through loudspeakers put up in the village. Abyssinia fell, with a distant uncle of one of the village girls castrated by those savages, and the rents were raised by the Abbey and again new taxes came and the fishermen's wages were cut: that was 'triumph' for San Fernando; the excitement of war never quite arrived, filtering through in dull trickles only.

Then the big war came and it wasn't popular. Not as if the people of San Fernando were 'good' or 'pacifist,' but being concerned with tangible realities only, with the dry facts of life, they did not like the idea of killing or being killed *en masse,* and no amount of 'glory' and 'empire' could change that. Then, the first men were called up; they went silently, without flowers or jokes, their women accompanying them to the station in black, unsmiling. The trains left, and the women stood and looked after them and did not wave or cry. Then the first news of someone killed arrived, and the neighbours stood in groups in the wife's kitchen and did not even try to cheer her up. She did not weep, just looked at the official letter and then spoke without complaint because she suspected that this was inevitable, an act of God, like the *filossera* or the drought. Then other villagers were killed, too, and the first news of defeat reached San Fernando, and someone on a visit from Ravenna made a rude remark about the King-Emperor. Oh, yes, and then young Filippo, the husband of Rosalia, the village beauty, had to go to Germany to work, and he did not write for weeks, and when he did, he was full of complaints and asked for the warm socks he knew his father had kept from the last war. Then, last year the *filossera* was exceptionally wicked, and the village went to the vineyards and watched the grapes rotting, and there came the first signs of collective anger when they were told that they could have no copper sulphate to fight the pest. And there were no potatoes either, and the bread became thinner, half the pre-war size, and had to be made of potatoes and rye and very little flour. Francesco's wife came back from Ravenna crying because they had asked two hundred lire for a pair of standard shoes, and the old men grumbled, too, for coffee was not coffee any more but toasted beans, acorns, and chicory. The quantitative changes grew; the pot started to boil.

Another visitor from Ravenna, a fat old woman, spoke of epidemics of tuberculosis, and next year some stranger said in Milano they had a strike — the first one for twenty years; and one winter morning, as I was passing through the village, someone spat and cursed the *tedeschi*. And I remember the day when Alfieri organized an auction of cats — he had two of them — and some twenty people came down to the bathhouse, and they said they had had no meat for months and inspected the cats carefully, fingering their chests and behinds, and discussing whether they should be fried or roasted, and what methods could be used to get rid of the smell. Alfieri sold them for seventy and ninety lire respectively, and I watched the crowd go, headed by two husky women carrying their cats in baskets tied up awkwardly with string. The animals squealed and screamed as if sensing their impending doom, and one of the militiamen sternly ordered the women off the main street so as not to annoy the guests at the Sanatorium or the Paradiso.

But beyond these general and partly objective motives other forces were operating in San Fernando. Revolts do not happen through an impersonal mechanism; nor are they spontaneous explosions, random caprices of vigorous or gifted individuals. It is a mixture, and in San Fernando the mixture was both the 'same as before,' following the pattern of Paris or Petrograd, yet something new and of its own as well. Historical forces were working quietly, growing like a tree, heading for the moment when bud blossoms into flower, when evolution makes a jump. At the same time there were men and women to accelerate the process. There was Francesco, of whom you have heard already. He had returned to the village one day, after twenty years in Torino; he came, old and grey and tubercular, but he knew how to organize, how to translate impersonal truth into the language of the quarrymen. They used to stay together when work was over and listen to Francesco, and you would be surprised how quickly they grasped the meaning of his words, how easily they drove his arguments to the logical conclusions.

Have you ever seen quarrymen working? Under the ruthless sun, twelve or fourteen hours a day, heaving their heavy axes and shovels, hitting at the hard rock they hate, repeating the awful movement a myriad times a day, up and down and up and down, and their spine unwillingly following their arms and shoulders; and hunching in one another's pale shade, finding no coolness, munching a dry sandwich and gargling with the cheap wine to keep fresh; and starting again and pushing their heavy loads on the carts, with the lifeless stones breaking the sun into many dazzling knives so that their eyeballs hurt until late at night, with circles of light swimming on their eyelids long after they have closed them, seeking the oblivion of sleep.

On Saturdays they lined up below the Abbey and took their wages and went. They got just enough for the rent, the dry sandwiches, ten or fifteen cigarettes a day; and Saturday nights they filled themselves with wine and made an awful din and went home — often sick on the way — cursing the moon, and beat up their wives or children and woke late Sunday morning with a sour taste in their mouths. Sundays they hung about dully in neat suits, bent under the sense of guilt and boredom, watching the wind change and thinking of Monday and how the week would soon start again, sapping their Sunday mood. For them it was quite easy to understand Francesco; they listened and nodded and said, *Naturally,* and did not need much proof.

Or take Ciro and his fishermen. They went out in all

weathers. Their work was less dull and tiring, and the sea made them silent, but gave them an ear for song and a heart full of mystic signs and fears. They thought all real power was outside them, up in heavens: the favourable wind, the stilling of the storm, the mastering of the waves, and the sex-life of fishes were outside their control; all they could do was be alert and efficient not to miss the rare chances; and to be humble and fulfil the hereditary rules of behaviour towards the elements: to light candles and go to church and say special prayers, storm-stilling, wave-calming, fish-catching prayers. But they had long ceased to trust Father Giuseppe. They paid tribute to the Abbey and its ways, as if to appease. But they felt God often revealed himself directly and suddenly, and Father Giuseppe could not intervene or help while they were out at sea facing the caprices, the mean moods of God, alone.

They had their own sect, secret and well-organized; no outsider was permitted to join, not even their women. Ciro told me about it. It was a harmless sect; they would meet regularly, either in Ciro's hut or on the deserted beach north of the Abbey Hill. Someone would read the Bible and then start to sing, and the others joined in the singing, the same two or three bars of a hymn, sitting close together, swaying and closing their eyes, until the music covered their consciousness and they forgot where they were and what they were, swaying and singing and sweat pouring down their faces; finally they stopped and felt easier and cleaner and less humble. They all loved Ciro, his dark wisp of hair and dark verses, his jokes and his almost sexual affection for the sea and his fellows.

Or Alfieri; take Alfieri, that bald giant who spends the

summer bending over urban feet, pedicuring them. Such a job itself is enough to make a revolutionary of anyone; especially him who is tall and strong and used to be proud of his strength, which he had wasted walking about the bathhouse with that enormous towel around his torso, handing out keys to the cabins and sun-oil, and watching out for some wretched guest who might suddenly try to drown himself a few yards from the raft; watching their weak, flabby bodies, sunken chests, and pimply backs as they came from the town with loud, penetrating voices and unruly children, messing up Alfieri's clean bathhouse with cigarette butts and greasy sandwich papers.

And take the Chef Luigi, that thoughtful little man at your hotel, and the others there whose life is a caricature of the feudal age; how they lived on forced smiles to please the tourists and Fritti; how they saw money thrown away on ridiculous unending meals and concocted drinks; how they were forced to crawl for tips and how they hated it, for there is nothing so hard as accepting small gifts from strangers — especially if you are proud and thoughtful yourself. They did not need much to make them bitter, the Chef Luigi and his friends; and you people up in the lounge and the restaurant and the bedrooms never knew or cared what it took to prepare and serve two boiled eggs; what happened to the messy disorder of your bedroom after you'd left, whistling a tune, for the bathhouse or the Corso; and how many hours of wretched toil preceded your waking and ensued the moment you switched off the light; that down below dishes were washed and the grey muck of crushed cigarettes scratched off the ash-trays and linen sorted out and boots blacked and the rest. They did not need much.

But what really started it were the washerwomen. Women are always inclined towards anarchy and they are the last to be frightened by that executive committee of property-owners, the State. They suspect and secretly despise the authority of men because they know that the centre of the universe is their lap and their kitchen; that men might make politics, but women make men. But seriously: women, with their preponderance of the thalamus, their animal instincts and supernatural sensory powers, are often the first to sense the moment when the old order of things starts cracking; and they know the strength inherent in their weakness and thus stand gloriously in the first ranks of great rebellions. The first riots near the end of a lost war are always started by them; they know that not only an army but the world as a whole marches on its stomach. It was the women of Vyborg who were first to strike in Petrograd and it was the women of Naples who last year lay down across the tramway lines to stop their men for embarking for Africa. I wish I could take two years off and write a monograph on women in revolutions; about their basic realism, about their militant temper, far more aggressive than that of man and repressed into a potential explosive by centuries of habit which have made the female, that greatest of predatory animals, into the tamed slave of man.

The washerwomen were only carrying on the fine tradition of Rosa Luxemburg or Krupskaya or Pankhurst. There are twelve of them, most of them married to villagers, and they work for the Abbey. The factual background is simple enough: they work long hours and are paid miserably. The laundry is in a dark cellar; the wet steam turns it into an inferno, and there they work, year in year out, rubbing and scrubbing lace surplices and damask tablecloths and sheets and underwear; the steam gets into their eyes and throats and hair and pores. Three years' work there and a woman looks as though she, too, had been laundered and wrung out and left to dry. They all have pale lips and matted hair. Colour has left them, and when they emerge at the end of the day their lungs hurt at the first breath. Their hands are terrible — purple and bitten by bad soap — as if they had eczema. Their backs ache constantly, and at forty they look sixty. Yet they are the toughest lot in the village. You should watch them one night coming home in a silent line, their black scarfs sinister about their pale faces. They come and their men wait for them and hardly a word is spoken. They are the only women who hardly ever gossip — except on Sundays, perhaps, when after the midday meal they mellow a bit and sit outside and slowly become human again. You cannot blame them if they are agnostics. They have to wash the Abbot's old-fashioned pants, and it doesn't make them sympathetic to the idea of ecclesiastical infallibility.

They had been in a morose mood ever since the return of Alberto, the maimed soldier. His wife is Beatrice, and she is very beautiful. There aren't many beauties in our village. The women are all squat, short-necked, and big-breasted, but Rosalia and Beatrice, the two sisters, are exceptions. The villagers think Rosalia is more beautiful than her sister, but I don't agree: she's got big, stupid cow's eyes, while there is an unhappy wisdom in Beatrice's face as if she knew all the secrets, as if she had come to San Fernando by mistake, a fairy princess, perhaps, who had renounced her knight and her castle and come to us to suffer. Which is nonsense, of course, as she is a most legitimate daughter of old Orlando, a mean old farmer with a squint. Anyway, there she is, Beatrice with her black hair, black as night or sin, as they say, framing in wild, uncombed locks her perfect face. She has large shining eyes and a sad, full mouth, and when she walks in front of you, you can't help thinking of her standing by a forest stream naked.

Beatrice and Alberto married shortly before the war, and there was a gay wedding, and we all teased the blushing Alberto and gave him useful advice. Only Beatrice was quiet and full of secrets, though I am sure she loved her man. But that's the way she is, quiet and full of secrets, but one can tell by her wild hair and her walk that she has strength and lust. Last year her man was called up. She went to see him off, silent and angry as if she was thinking of the coming emptiness of the nights. She felt offended and spoke harshly even to Alberto and would hardly kiss him for the last time. Then, a few months ago, he returned, his strong hands turned into shapeless lumps of mutilated flesh, and the villagers say Beatrice just looked at those hands and slowly returned to the house; and they all said she was cruel — all except Alberto, who seemed to understand and did not mind.

She had started working for the Abbey some months before his return, and she never liked the laundry, and, what was unusual, she said so. The others told her to keep quiet, or leave, but she soon got into trouble with Father Leo, a thin, birdlike individual, a sort of housekeeper and overseer in the kitchen and laundry. I can't remember what exactly happened. She talked back at him, or would not finish her work on a Saturday. But next Sunday Father Giuseppe in his sermon spoke sharply of 'the lack of humility in our youth,' and 'the promiscuity of our women,' and everybody knew that he meant Beatrice, who was sitting in one of the front pews, beautiful and self-assured and her gaze never wavering when the priest looked at her.

Then the real trouble started, last Friday. It was a frightfully hot day, as you will remember. I stayed indoors until the evening, behind closed shutters, sipping cool wine and thinking of the quarrymen out in the heat, the quarrymen and all the others out in the fields and the vineyards, and how little I could do to alleviate their plight, and what would be needed to make such work worth while.

Later, I went up to the village. There was a crowd at Alberto's house, and as I approached them I sensed trouble: they were very excited and they were all men, with only a few women standing on the other side of the street. What had happened was this: the washerwomen had gone on strike and the Abbey had called out the militia and had the women locked up in the cellar and wouldn't let them go unless they asked for forgiveness, paid a fine, and finished their work.

That first night rumours were wild, as no one knew what exactly had happened. Alberto and two other husbands went to see Father Giuseppe, but were curtly told that they could not see their women (apparently possessed by evil spirits) and should return to the village. Six militiamen were hanging about with rifles, and the men had no choice but to return. Later, more news filtered out through some of the militiamen — highly exaggerated and coloured by malice. Beatrice, it was said, had attacked Father Leo and nearly killed him, and there was a real fight when the militiamen arrived and fired their rifles, and some of the women were wounded. All this turned out to be untrue.

The facts leaked out later: the trouble had started in the morning when Father Leo, in a bilious mood, had gone down to the laundry, nagged the women, asked them to hurry up, and ended by informing them that as from Monday they wouldn't get any afternoon coffee, a meagre privilege they had been enjoying, as it meant a break, a stroll in the garden, a rest for their backs and eyes. When they heard that, there was an angry murmur, and Beatrice stopped working, went up to Father Leo, and placing her hands on her hips said she would quit. 'Don't be naughty,' Father Leo scolded her. 'I'm not naughty,' Beatrice answered dryly. 'Unless we get our coffee, I'll stop working in this filthy place and make the others stop too.' She sounded ominously ferocious and deliberately rude. The other women tried to make her shut up, but it was too late. Father Leo turned and slapped Beatrice's face, whereupon Beatrice quietly bent down, picked up a bucket full of soapy water, and poured it over the priest's head. Then she made a speech. No one knows what she said — Father Leo had fled and the women were too excited to remember. Anyway, Father Giuseppe, who appeared a few minutes later, found her standing on an upturned bucket, 'gesticulating wildly, spitting forth sinful words with a foaming mouth, using sacrilegious language,' all of which is grossly exaggerated. Apparently all she told them was to stop being fools and letting themselves be exploited (Sinful Word Number One), and that they should stop working unless they got their coffee. Father Giuseppe's appearance froze the atmosphere, and even Beatrice seemed overawed and stepped down from the bucket, waiting. 'I have just heard what has happened on this holy ground,' he said coolly. 'You will finish your work. You, Beatrice, will go and ask Father Leo's forgiveness and be grateful that he is a generous soul who asks nothing else. Then you will leave and never return.'

Beatrice had apparently regained her courage and said cheekily that Father Giuseppe's suggestion about leaving suited her well enough, but that she wouldn't dream of asking anybody's forgiveness, least of all Father Leo's. There was a pause. Oh, I wish I had been there! It was one of those pauses when history is made. Father Giuseppe seemed speechless at first, glaring at the rebel, his arms folded. 'Beatrice,' he raised his voice, 'you will do as I told you.' 'And if I don't?' she asked. 'Come on, women,' she encouraged the others, 'let's go home. I'd like to see if they dare to be nasty to a war-cripple's wife.' Father Giuseppe looked at the others, and he must have felt that he was losing ground, because he quickly stepped outside and locked the door behind him.

Poor old Father Giuseppe, I can't blame him. He, too, is acting historically these days, and if he does so exaggeratedly it is the fault of the times which darken the shadows, deepen the gulfs, raise people high and cast them low. These are rebellious days; the pulse of the world is beating faster and dull normality has gone. These are

times when men everywhere must face questions no one
has asked them before; when history, like a rampaging
elephant, enters all the pious china shops, smashing everything to bits; when even the isolated Eskimos hear the
drone of the planes and the blare of loud-speakers; when,
at last, no one is allowed to creep back into ignorance and
smug irresponsibility. It is only starting, but soon even
you and all the other hedonists and *Schoengeister* and 'men
of letters' will be forced to take sides, to evacuate your
esoteric oases, to give up your big beautiful souls and get
down to brass tacks, which is freeing all the San Fernandos
from hunger and mass murder and stupidity, and doing it
without keeping an eye on posterity, or some fussy critic;
doing it without clinging to your big, interesting, complicated, subtle souls. There was never anything quite like
this; it is Change *par excellence*. The bud is ready to
blossom, the ape to grow up, and that lukewarm hypocrisy
of manners which has been wrongly identified with civili-
zation will have to be shelved for the duration. Meanwhile, those who are thrown into the arena have to act
according to patterns of environment and heredity. Thus,
Father Giuseppe, charming scholar, fine connoisseur, and
devout Catholic though he may be, must play his part of
villain — unless, by divine interference, he decides to visit
a psychoanalyst, confess his complexes, accept that the only
dogma is that of heresy, give up his job as a slave-driver,
and join us; which is very unlikely. Therefore I shall forgive him, miserable prisoner that he is, forgive him but
fight him to the last round.

Father Giuseppe called in the militia: they entered the
laundry and found the women in a much wilder mood.

They gave notice, demanded immediate release, and two weeks' wages. It was refused. One of the militiamen asked them to be 'sensible,' which was met with ironic laughter. That made the man furious, and he grabbed Beatrice by the breast and pushed her against a table. She fell, but jumped to her feet and started to throw wet napkins and bits of underwear at the men; the other women followed suit. The men were helpless; one of them tried to advance, but was hit by a large piece of soap, whereupon he fired his revolver at the ceiling; but it did not help and another man was hit by a large brush. Finally they fled, locking the door. At night Alberto and his two friends were thrown out by Father Giuseppe. Next morning the men had a meeting and decided to send old Orlando, Beatrice's father, to the Abbey, telling him to be humble and ask for the women's release. Mind you, this decision was reached only after violent arguments, but most of the men were still in a conciliatory mood. Old Orlando returned with burning ears: Father Giuseppe would not even see him and had sent out Father Leo, who made Orlando a lengthy harangue full of long quotations from the Bible. It all amounted to the same; and what's more, the priest made a not-too-veiled threat that the Abbey might take criminal action and have the women tried and imprisoned 'for Communist agitation.'

This ended the peaceful mood of the men. They weren't frightened any more and they were thinking of their women in the cellar, without proper food or sleep, and they were getting angry. They had another meeting and asked Francesco, Ciro, and myself to be present. An 'action committee' was formed, and I found myself the chairman.

I made a speech welcoming the fact that for the first time in twenty years San Fernando was organizing itself, and I used very careful words; I did not want to scare them. But the pot was boiling, the bud ready to blossom. There was a pause, and then Alberto said he knew what I had meant and he was sure the others knew, too. Francesco spoke, too, in a sly, slow voice, and he said the black-robed devils up on the hill will regret one day what they have done, the priest and their friends the militia, 'the whole dirty gang.' I looked around and still there was no fright in those men and I could have wept for happiness; I could have wept because they were not frightened and felt strong, as they squatted there on the sandy beach north of the Abbey Hill.

Later they went; only Alberto, Ciro, Alfieri, and myself remained, and we spoke openly of what might happen. I gave them a brief report on the national situation and showed them a 'Letter from Spartacus'; the first revolutionary leaflet that had reached me for twenty years. The same night we had another meeting in the quarry. Ciro came again, and Alberto and two more from the village, and old Foa turned up with Benito, and Francesco brought along one of the lorry-drivers, and I brought the Chef Luigi. Alberto told us that the women had sent a message through Benito, who had managed to sneak in to them the night before while the guards were having their dinner at Pina's café. They were in fine spirits, the women, although they had had practically nothing to eat the whole day, and Father Giuseppe had seen Don Innocenzo and presented the women with an ultimatum that unless they started work by Monday morning, they would be handed over to the authorities. The women said they were not frightened, but expected us to help them. So we decided to call a mass demonstration for next Monday. The rôles were allotted, each man given his task, and we felt confident that the Abbey would have to yield. Francesco suggested a general strike, but I felt that was premature. Let there first be a demonstration, I said; let the men see how strong they are.

Oh, but they knew it already, they had known it during those few hasty meetings; they sat and listened and looked around and saw themselves. They had not realized before how many they were; they had been used to working isolated or in smallish groups, and had never met all together and never seen their strength. They started counting heads and counting pickaxes and shovels, and Alberto had a rifle and I had a revolver and old Foa had another rifle and someone had a rusty cavalry sword, a relic of the last war. They were counting heads; and that was my last all-pervading impression, those few days until last night, when from the windy football ground we started to move — that growing knowledge of strength. It was the most magnificent thing in my life to see those men, until then quiet, scared, ignorant, mean, quarrelsome, dirty, and suspicious; until then isolated and insignificant. The long process was at last coming to an end, and they felt it. They had no inkling two days ago that within twenty-four hours they would hear about the armistice with the Allies; but they knew something irrevocable had come about, a synthesis they hadn't known before, a unity that was new.

On the surface there was nothing but their anxiety for Beatrice and eleven other washerwomen. But these men held themselves back, crushed their spontaneous anger which could have driven them to haste and folly; they checked themselves and met and made plans and thus acted historically. And beneath the immediate purpose lay hidden the heritage of centuries; old misery, repression, and revenge. The bones and nerves of those men carried within them the premature deaths of their ancestors, the kicks and slaps administered to earlier generations, their exclusion from all beauty and knowledge; their blood carried the memory of scores of futile corpses fallen in futile wars, and their raw fingers remembered the past. They did not know all this, but they could feel it and acted accordingly. They had grown up during those few days, and now nothing could ever drive them back to infancy. Whether they failed or not, it could never again be as it was before. So they met and talked and planned and waited, and when last night the Jew, Foa, came racing to us to tell us about the armistice, no one was surprised. They nodded, and made their revolt.

From Farkas's Diary for Ninth September, 1943

Giacobbe has just left after telling me about the 'revolution.' It's all very confusing and historical. I always start writing diaries at such moments; true for a day or two only until history settles and becomes a bore. Did it, didn't I, in Sarajevo in nineteen-fourteen, Munich in eighteen, Vienna in thirty-four? It's a lovely day, clear and warm.

Last night's putrid heat and depression gone. Woke at eight after violent dreams about chasing the Austrian girl. Got up to see if Don Innocenzo's body was still down there. They had cleared it away: the main square and the Paradiso terrace looked very neat and orderly, almost exag· geratedly so. First thing that struck me were the flags over the Kursalon, and the Sanatorium, British, American, Russian, and Italian flags, somewhat primitive, obviously hand-made. They have muddled up the Union Jack, and the Soviet sickle looks rather like an unripe banana.

Rang for breakfast, slightly interested whether any ser· vice. Thought that probably new 'hotel commissar' would inform me that I'd jolly well got to go and get food myself; exploitation over. Remembered Budapest, Hotel Astoria, 1919, with gramophone playing the *Internationale* the whole day and the square faces of new men thronging in the hall. Surprise: Ugo appeared almost at once, with usual tray, but *very* excited. He doesn't like it, and fears repercussions. 'There's going to be trouble,' he kept say· ing, 'revolutions are like a . . .' he started an aphorism, but gave it up. Told me Fritti was arrested last night by Luigi and two others of the staff, but was reinstated later after 'hotel council' was formed under Luigi to regulate wages, hours, food for staff, annual holidays, old-age pensions, and the building of new bathroom in servants' quarters. Council will control Fritti in all matters affecting welfare of staff, and he must co-operate until 'nationalization of hotels.' Luigi dropped hints that Paradiso might be requi· sitioned altogether for Allied troops. Ugo said: 'They're all mad, expecting the Allies so far north.' Anyway, the three Germans have been put in prison. The Morgans were woken this morning at seven by delegation consisting of Luigi, one of the quarrymen, and Foa (who speaks English), in order to express anti-Fascist Committee's sympathies for past privations, and give Morgans freedom of SF. The Morgans were at first terrified seeing the Committee, believing the worst had come; it took a good ten minutes to clear up misunderstanding. Morgans are to be transferred to State apartments, given double rations, and free entrance to mineral baths. Morgan himself was asked to become Liaison Officer between Committee and Allies; he accepted. Mrs. Morgan promised to knit cardigans for fishermen.

Went for a walk after breakfast. Met no one in lounge except Enrico, sleepy as ever. Fritti was nowhere to be seen, and in front of the hotel two young men stood on guard in their shirtsleeves; one of them had a rifle. San Fernando looked very peaceful; apparently Giacobbe and friends want to create good impression. As I walked down past the Paradiso, saw Austrian girl leaning out of window, quickly withdrawing as she saw me. Probably ashamed of exhibition of tears and soul last night. On the square small groups of people, mostly elderly ones from Sanatorium, excitedly discussing the end of the war. One tried to stop me with 'What do you say to the news?' 'What news?' I asked innocently. 'Haven't you heard? The war is over.' 'What war?' I said, and walked away. All shops closed, even barber's, which annoyed me as I wanted haircut. Walked up main street, everything very quiet. Later met an open lorry which drove along slowly with three men standing on top, one of them with rifle. They saluted in passing. Embarrassing.

Met Doctor Merlin of Sanatorium — little bald man, nose always running. He was very pleased. Had heard from someone Allies had landed in Trieste and Livorno and captured Rome. Fine rest I'm going to have. We walked together to post-office (guarded by two men, who let us enter after I had explained I only wanted stamps). Postmistress back at her desk, slightly shaken. Said she had a very disturbed night in answer to my 'And how are you this morning, Signorina?'

Back to hotel. Fritti came trotting out from his office, beaming. *'Mon cher Maestro,'* he warbled, 'isn't it glorious? The Cloud has passed at last. We're free, FREE again. *Vive la démocratie!'* he shouted. *'Vive l'Angleterre, Vive l'Amérique,'* and after a pause: *'Vive l'U.S.S.R.!'* Hotel-managers, harlots, crooners, always Anglophile. Fritti seems to be one of the 'I've always been pro-British.' Never heard him talk about 'Cloud' before; it was always the 'Glorious Rebirth,' and the 'Magnificent Revolution.' Met Mrs. Morgan going upstairs. Dear soul, she had a tremendous hortensia on her bosom and a small Union Jack in her hand. 'Isn't it lovely?' she cried. 'The war is over in Italy and we've got such a lovely room now, a private bath with such funny gadgets and even a queer footbath.' The only wireless in the hotel has been confiscated by Committee. Thank God for that, Germans won't pollute air with rasping news bulletins and 'Lili Marlene.' Went upstairs to rest before lunch — actually to listen if any sound from Austrian girl. Lay on bed, drinking cognac and soda with ice, listening; but not a sound. Hope she hasn't taken it too badly.

Lunch with Giacobbe. He left at four, leaving me limp,

my ears buzzing. He talked for two solid hours, never stopping. Obviously he wants me to get interested, perhaps write religious drama about him and San Fernando. Poor Giacobbe. But Daniel would like him.

Don Teofilo arrived for tea, in white linen suit, very merry, with British decoration (phoney, I think) from last war, carrying old *Times*, fanning himself with it conspicuously. Forced smile on his face, his eyes darting in all directions as if afraid of something falling on his head. He sweated heavily, mopping his round, bronzed skull with large white handkerchief embroidered in colours of House of Savoya. Service quite good; waiters slightly less respectful, all except Ugo. Don Teofilo talked in whispers, his fat lips smacking each word as if they had highly erotic content. He's worried; the Committee sent for him this morning; he had to be wheeled to village, thought he might never come back alive; was received by two villagers and Alberto. 'I expressed my hope,' he said, 'that they would have due respect for my age, crippled legs, long patriotic service, intimate connections with Sir Austen Chamberlain. Also I reminded them of my distant relationship to Garibaldi and my friendship with Nitti, last Liberal Premier. I added that the new Government was always my cup of tea, including Marshal Badoglio, and said the people of San Fernando could count on my intervention in Rome. I suggested leaving for the capital at once. They thanked me for coming, asked who Austen Chamberlain was; sounded quite polite at first but the soldier Alberto had the impudence to remind me of my intimate friendship with Don Innocenzo and the Podestà, and enumerated a catalogue of what he called the "amaz-

ing total of benefits" I was supposed to have derived from my connection with the Fascist régime. I
tried to explain to them that I was never interested in
politics, except in a higher sense, that is, the supreme
interests of the Nation. I had never made a secret of my
dislike of the methods of the Fascists, and I had said so in
July when the Duce was dismissed, but there was precious
little I, a crippled veteran of the last war, could do, etc.'

Don Teofilo bored me more than ever. I'm sure he'll
be forgiven by the new crowd, though they may take some
of his land away and force him to contribute to the party
(whichever party it is). But he'll get away with his past
record. There are always chaps like him who somehow
manage to float with every current. Don Teofilo ended
our tea-party by asking me would I mind if he deposited
with me the 'family jewels, carriers and symbols of a proud
tradition, and practically the only convertible capital' he
possessed. I refused. He blushed and looked quite
pathetic for a moment; but then put on a sulking, snob-
bish smile, coughed, and said I must forget his hasty re-
quest, but he was rather upset; yelled at the nurse, and
rolled off. I watched her: her face was stony and repressed
as ever. I wondered how long she'd stick it.

Rested after tea. More rumours later: the Allied land-
ings at Spezia and Genova. But Ugo, who turned up at six,
said: 'There's going to be trouble. The men are planning
to organize a mass demonstration on the Abbey Hill tonight and get their women.'

Went for another walk at six. Much cooler. Austrian
girl nowhere to be seen. Hell. Corso deserted, sea calm.
All sailing-boats, rowing-boats, yachts moored off bath-

house. Two or three youths patrolling the bridge. Felt quite hopelessly out of place; decided to leave this week. One catch: Austrian girl! Must talk to her again before going away. Always been fond of unhappy women. Shall I go to Geneva and meet Gizella? Her calculated lust and almost mathematical affection! She would wait in a hotel, in a négligée, with champagne and lobster. Everything prepared as if she'd applied a Five-Years' Plan to her sex-life: best available drink, food, scent, négligée, proper amount of flesh exposed, right tightness of dressing-gown at hips, all effects carefully planned with a wooden, self-conscious intensity which always made me wish to find Gizella drunk, in dirty rags, clutching a beer bottle in a Marseilles *bordello* — quite out of question, of course. Perhaps I should, at last, write my piece about Vulgarity, a subject which has always interested me. Goethe with *das ewig Weibliche* missed the essential point, although very near to it.

Meanwhile there's a revolution. Returned to hotel. Found urgent message from Father Giuseppe asking me to come and see him at the Abbey. Note very polite, insistent, careful not to sound desperate. What he hopes from me, beyond me. Asked Enrico to get hold of Giacobbe. The Great Rebel was at the Sanatorium and came over to the hotel when he got my message. Showed him Father Giuseppe's note; he knew about it and said he thought I ought to go and talk to Giuseppe, see what he wants, do my best to effect the release of the women. Asked Giacobbe if he was mad, taking me for an ambassador; he laughed at me. 'You will help us; you can't help helping us,' he said, adding that he would take me as far as the fishery whence a lorry could drive me up to the Abbey. 'You must see Ciro,' he pleaded. 'For a second only. He's going to die tonight.'

Rang Father Giuseppe; told him I would come at night. He sounded uncommonly glad and much too polite; asked me to stay to dinner. I agreed. At seven we started off with Giacobbe in a lorry driven by a silent, square-faced man in dark blue shirt. Giacobbe talked about Ciro and how he had been shot. On the night of the revolt they had driven along the Abbey Road, trying to pick up stray militiamen. Just past Pina's place they saw three of them cycling along. The men suggested rounding them up right away, but Ciro said they were probably armed and he'd better go and try to talk them over. He got out of the lorry, walked up to them when they stopped, and said: 'Brethren, the dawn has come; the night is over; the spark that slept so long has burst out to the stars.' They didn't know what he meant. 'Ciro could never understand,' Giacobbe remarked sadly, 'that poetry should be written before or after a revolution, never instead of it. The militiamen saw the lorry slowly driving nearer and one of the fishermen shouted at them, telling them the news and asking them to surrender. They shot Ciro through the lung and now he is slowly bleeding to death; the doctors have given him up.'

Arrived at fishery at seven-fifteen; little groups stood by entrance, gaunt, dark men, fussing with their nets, silently. They greeted us, unsmiling. We walked behind the building to the waterfront, and there lay Ciro on a straw mattress, very white and peaceful, staring at the sky. We walked up to him.

Giacobbe knelt down and said: 'Ciro, how are you?'

'Very well,' the fisherman said.

'This is Signor Farkas, you've heard about him, haven't you?'

'Yes, certainly,' Ciro said and looked at me. 'Good evening, Signor; I am sorry I cannot get up and receive you properly, and I am deeply honoured.'

I did not know what to say. Weeping women, funerals, dying men, and unlocked lavatory doors always leave me confused.

'Well, old man,' Giacobbe went on, 'now you're comfortable, I hope, and soon you'll be better.'

'Shame on you,' Ciro replied. 'You always told me it was stupid to pretend. You know I'm dying.'

Giacobbe patted his hand. The sea was very beautiful and calm and there were little groups of men all around the dying man, standing silently with their nets, or hands in pockets, slightly suspicious of us. An old woman came and gave a drink to Ciro.

'I have written a poem,' Ciro said.

'Yes?' Giacobbe said.

Ciro fumbled under the blanket and produced a crumpled piece of paper.

'You mustn't strain yourself,' Giacobbe said.

Ciro shook his head and started to read out his poem. I can't remember exactly, but it went something like this:

'*Grey is the face of the fishermen,*
Red is the blood they spit
As they sit by night and their nets they mend.
They mend and knit, by the sea they sit.

> *They knit by the sea, at night, and mend.*
> *Grey is their face and friend they've none,*
> *No friend, no friend, no friend.*
> *No friend but the fish they kill, no friend*
> *But the germ in their lungs that's killing them.*
> *No friend as they sit and their nets they mend.*
> *Red is the blood they cough.*
> *Red is the face of the fishermen*
> *As they say, enough.'*

When he had finished, he smiled and fingered the paper and folded it up with slow, shaking hands and gave it to Giacobbe, who said in a low voice: 'Thank you.'

'I must go now,' I said. I stepped nearer to the dying man and tried to smile encouragingly and said: 'That was a very beautiful poem, Signor Ciro, a very beautiful poem.' He smiled gratefully.

As I walked away, the sea was calm, beautiful. At the corner of the building I stopped and turned back: Ciro waved his hand.

Drove up to the Abbey: the road deserted, but met patrols. The secondary road leading to the railway station was blocked by a lorry; by it camped four men, cooking food over an open fire. They shouted a greeting to my driver. Driver said: 'Tonight we'll get the women.' Was getting cool as we drove up the hill. Haven't been to the Abbey since last time when shown around by Father Giuseppe. There is a room where present Pope slept one night.

Father Giuseppe was waiting in front of a side door by the chapel. (Lorry did not take me quite up to door, stopped, driver asked me to walk rest of the way, no apology!) Father Giuseppe looked more of an apple than ever, his round, red face over the black robe like a toy made of apple and of some odd bits of funereal cloth. He had a cold. Shook my hands warmly and led the way through a vaulted corridor, across an open courtyard, then up the wide, chilly staircase. Abbot himself wanted to see me, he explained. Met Abbot when last time in San Fernando, at some silly banquet, but couldn't remember him clearly.

We climbed up dark, broad stairs to third floor. No wonder they get colds, place so draughty. Walked some endless corridors, with Father Giuseppe talking of perfectly neutral subjects (his bees, the coming wine harvest, etc.). Finally he stopped and knocked and waited, and then let me enter. Room tremendously large, with oak beams, huge lumps of massive furniture, good carpets, two large pictures (one, by somebody *quattrocento*, of the Holy Family, another of the Abbot); a large, crowded room, yet evidently uncomfortable and disorderly, stuffed with books, newspapers, dishes, ash-trays, cats. Took me a good minute to discover among the rubbish the Abbot himself, sitting amid piles of cushions, cats, and books, near the far corner. I knew his presence by the fine rustling of silk as he moved his heavy robe. He cleared his throat and said: *'Entrez, cher Signor Farkas, entrez.'*

He had grown terribly old, the Abbot, I observed with a certain degree of elation. His aquiline face was as of fine, old parchment, cracked by scores of minute wrinkles; it was a white face, a face withered by wisdom, with sharp cheekbones; his neck like that of an old woman. Only his eyes were very clear and clever and quite youthful. No senility there.

'So glad you've come, Signor Farkas,' he said; his voice was surprisingly firm, coming from that withered face. 'You will help San Fernando to regain peace and order? Of course you will, Signor; although an agnostic, you have the mind of an aristocrat and a sense of humour which must opt for ancient values and not for the grim and dull anarchy of new ideas. I read your short stories last year, in Italian.'

I sat down in a large limp plush easy-chair. Father Giuseppe behind Abbot's chair, put on a firm, appreciative smile.

'Thank you,' I murmured. 'But . . .'

'I liked those stories very much,' the Abbot said. Father Giuseppe nodded behind him. 'You're only an agnostic on the surface and it's because you are afraid of being ridiculed by the sinners who fill the theatres. But both Father Giuseppe' (another nod) 'and I remember the privilege of seeing in Rome your magnificent play, *The Valley's Faith*. Pity all your writing isn't like that play.'

Lighting a cigarette, I replied: 'Sorry. It was an awful fiasco, that play.'

'Was it?' the Abbot said, and moved: the heavy silks rustled. 'All the more reason for writing more of the kind. Surely you're not interested in following the popular fashion? Fashion used to follow you.'

Oh, God, I thought, what does he want from me? I was very suspicious of all these compliments. 'Nothing's so shattering,' Rubin once wrote, 'as compliments from the wrong people.'

'Faith isn't fashionable any longer,' I said. 'So my agents tell me.'

Angry rustling.

'Ah, but that's where you're wrong, my son,' the Abbot said, impatiently pushing away a cat (or a book). 'Look into people's hearts and you'll find the trust in reason, the belief in disbelief gone. No wonder; disbelief has lasted only a short while, a mere second in the story of the Church. All those wretches thought it would give them surer values and a stronger creed. It didn't, and on the ruins they are now everywhere building up the foundations of more altars and more crosses.' (More nods from Father Giuseppe.) 'As always, when material progress made people soft, they thought, the fools, they could take an optimistic view of their kingdom on earth and dispense with the Church.' (Cat purrs.) 'Ah, but it is gone, that short, pitiful period of materialism. Fright and danger bring back faith to the simple; and great scientists find, behind the pattern of stars and electrons, the unmistakable hand of Him.' (Nods.) 'Former rebels, sceptics, and other misled youths turn their heads in shame from past heresies and look for a new God; youths who grinned at us and made blasphemy a passport to their barren land, a sort of trade-mark for cleverness, they, too, feel fear and hesitation and go now to a different type of desert, and through our ancient technique find Him.' (Nods, purrs, rustling.) 'For a while they will still hesitate; their silly cleverness, their rationalism, will linger; they will call old things by new names, search for excuses and subterfuges, walk the painful maze, but they will eventually return to the generous bosom of the Holy See; and we shall forgive them, as we always do, and they will help to lead men back to the crossroads where, four hundred years ago, they took the wrong turning.'

'Quite,' I said, wondering why everybody in San Fernando picked on me, trying to sell their creeds like so many commercial travellers. All I am interested in is having a rest. (And the way an Austrian girl walks.)

'I should like you to go down,' the Abbot continued remorselessly, while I continued the commercial travellers' association and thought of him reaching out, shop-assistant-like, and showing me drapery called Roman Catholicism, saying, 'Please, my dear sir, feel the fabric, it is the best in town and you may have it cheap, as we are having a Sale' — 'I should like you to go and tell those demented people to be sensible and not to commit folly. I have been informed of the horrible crimes they perpetrated last night, the murder of Don Innocenzo, a charming youth, efficient administrator, and faithful son of the Church; and of others. They will have to pay for that; but let them not make things worse for themselves by challenging the Church. I know that they harbour some grievances against the war and the late-lamented Mussolini, although he gave them security and organized work and leisure' (Violent nods from Father Giuseppe), 'and if they had the sense to compare their present comfort with that of their fathers or grandfathers, they would have realized long ago, with gratitude, how much better off they were.

'Really, I don't know what's happened to them,' the Abbot added amid more rustles and nods. 'Fifty years ago they had no rights, no cinemas, no electric light, no sewers; they couldn't read or write, and politics were strictly forbidden to them. Now they have the brazen impudence to believe that they can abuse the fact of their poverty and turn themselves into a fiction called The People, and step into the place of experience, piety, and culture. You see, here you have another argument for going back to the pre-Renaissance era. The overhasty extension of privileges and material welfare only whetted the appetite of the greedy and vulgar masses; further, the highly dangerous popularization of the written word has not only dragged literature from the heights of a Dante to the gutter of pornography, but has filled the minds of the rabble with the slogans of the Anti-Christ.' (Thoughtful nods, a cat moves away. Where do I come in?) 'But then,' the Abbot said in a tired voice, 'I do not wish to discuss history in general. We're only concerned with some half-witted and misled citizens of our small community, citizens who have been inflamed by dangerous agitators and murderers. I understand they wish to stage a demonstration in front of the Abbey tonight. They must have lost their senses.'

'Excuse me for interrupting,' I said, 'but I think it is simply a matter of *cherchez la femme*. There seem to be some women detained here and the village wants their release.'

Impatient rustling.

The room was growing dark by now, and Father Giuseppe stepped away to switch on the table-lamp. The former gloom was suddenly filled with details I hadn't noticed before: more books, newspapers, cats.

'My dear Signor Farkas,' the Abbot said, 'those women are just as ignorant and misled as the villagers. We shall hand them over to the authorities as soon as law and order are re-established. If the men wish to demonstrate they can do so. If they dare to attack the Abbey, nothing will prevent them but our Faith and the Cross. However, I do

not think it will come to that.' He sighed. 'Those poor
people are children of the Church — all except the criminal, heathen few who incited them. But I do not want
them to incur an even heavier punishment. I should like
you to go and talk to their so-called leaders. I understand
you know some of them, especially that brigand Giacobbe
di Bocca. Pray explain to him that he will bring nothing
but disaster on the village; that he should restrain his
gang and await, in good order, the arrival of the authorities.'

'What makes you think I'd have any influence on them,
Bocca or any of the others?' I asked.

The Abbot smiled. 'I remember the Priest Marius in
your play, *The Valley's Faith*. His power of persuasion
was remarkable.'

Sly old fox.

'I can never be as good as my characters are, Your
Grace.' I was glad I remembered the proper title. I had
almost called him 'Your Excellency' or something idiotic.
'They are as good as I should like to be; much better than
I am.'

Impatient rustling.

'The Church will be grateful, my son,' he said. 'San
Fernando will be grateful, too.'

I looked at Father Giuseppe, and he nodded busily to
emphasize the old man's arguments.

'Will you forgive them,' I asked, 'though they knew
what they were doing?'

More sly smiling.

'I will,' he said cautiously. 'But I could not interfere
with secular justice, of course. There have been several
cases of homicide.'

'There have been several cases of homicide farther south,' I replied, 'and farther east and farther north and west.'

'We are not interfering there either,' the Abbot said, and quickly moved an old, white hand. 'The Church stands above war; it is neutral. We pray for both sides.'

And he bowed his head piously. The silk robe rustled, and I was about to light another cigarette when he heard the shots. One first, then a pause, then in quick succession two, three, four rifle shots. Father Giuseppe quickly walked to the window, and I rose. I watched the Abbot's face: he looked surprised, made no move; but he knew it was a rifle. 'What is it?' he asked slowly while I was walking to the window. 'May the Lord have mercy on their souls,' Father Giuseppe remarked, looking down. I repeat, *remarked:* his voice carried those words of pity in such a dry, wooden way, as if he were saying, 'The milkman is late.' I looked out. In the gathering dusk there stood a crowd, a hundred or so, facing the chapel in wide, sickle-like rows, half-surrounding the dusty space in the centre of which lay a solitary figure. From where I was, he looked like a Red Indian, with his ear to the ground: his open palms touched the dust, his head, turned in profile, lay on his right ear, and his eyes were intently closed.

Then the rifle barked again: it came from one of the third-floor windows of the Abbey. The crowd did not move; it was petrified at the sight of the man dying in the dust. I looked at Father Giuseppe; he frowned. Then someone shouted, from the place whence the shots had cracked, '*Go home.*' That broke the immobility of the scene. The crowd surged forward, then stopped again.

Three men stepped forward, leaned over the quiet man. One of them lifted his arm and let it go; it fell back in comic resignation, as if to say: 'Ah, hell, leave me alone.' They turned him on his back. His arms were limp, his body soft, and now he lay facing the sky. I could not see his face clearly, but I knew that he had a moustache. The night was growing darker. Then they lifted him and carried him to a lorry that stood by the road, waiting. Father Giuseppe said: 'One of the militiamen must have fired the shots; they sought sanctuary here last night. They were very frightened.'

The crowd turned to the quiet man as he was lifted onto the lorry, and then, as one man, they turned again to face the Abbey. Someone shouted from the first row: 'Who are you? You killed him.' There was silence, then the answer came: 'Go home, you dogs.' Father Giuseppe leaned out to see better, then drew his head back again. He said to the Abbot: 'One of the militiamen has shot a villager. I must go down at once.' He did not wait for an answer, and walked with quick, small steps to the door. I heard his steps echoing down the endless stone corridor. 'You see, my son,' said the Abbot. I went back to the window.

From there one could see exactly what was happening, although the details were blurred. The first row of the crowd still stood quietly, craning their necks upward, wanting to see who had killed their comrade. But those at the back pushed forward; and a shout rose, deep and inarticulate, a shout with no sense or meaning, but very expressive all the same; like the groan of a wounded beast it sounded, raw and pitiful. Somebody in the first row turned, and I saw his suppliant hands, raised high to stem the surge, but soon he was engulfed himself. It was like watching a game of football, and I could not help remembering Pluhar of the Broadcasting Company, who was so brilliant at reporting matches, completely carried away himself and disregarding the microphone, yelling encouragement and admonitions and even curses. 'Come on, Joe,' he would shout; 'what the hell d'you think you're doing? Come on, don't dribble; shoot, for Heaven's sake shoot!' I, too, felt like yelling: 'Come on, don't dribble; shoot for Heaven's sake!' — not because of any particular sympathy for this or the other team, but the excitement of violent moves and countermoves carried me away too.

I leaned low to see better. The crowd swept on and the door did not halt them: they only grew into a funny pear-shaped mass, narrowing at the entrance and slowing down a bit. But the movement was continuous, and soon there was an awful crash and I could hear steps in the inner courtyard. 'They would not dare,' the Abbot said as I turned. 'They would not dare,' he added incredulously, without the slightest fear, but completely baffled. 'I'd better go down and see,' I said, and went to the door and opened it and listened. I heard footsteps echoing somewhere down below, and suddenly a confusion of voices, the high-pitched murmur of a council of war. I walked down to the end of the corridor, and when I arrived at the top of the stairs, I saw ten or fifteen men running upstairs towards me. I was scared now and stepped back, and saw Alfieri, dishevelled, red-faced, leading the gang. They stopped when they saw me and Alfieri recognized me, bless his heart.

'Signor Farkas,' he panted, 'where is he, the bastard?'

'I don't know,' I said; 'probably down that corridor,' and pointed.

They raced on. Heavy boots made a terrible din. Behind me I heard a door open and a small, sweet-faced friar peered out above his rimless spectacles. 'Go back!' I shouted at him, and he disappeared. I walked on and leaning over the bannisters tried to see what was going on in the courtyard. I saw some villagers at the far end leading to the side door of the chapel and the gardens. Four or five men stood in the centre, by the fountain, talking. I thought Father Giuseppe might be one of them, but I wasn't sure. It was getting quite dark. They talked in low voices as though they had forgotten the violence of the immediate past. Then down the corridor came footsteps again: Alfieri was returning with his men. They were walking comparatively slowly, so I knew they had not found the killer. But as they passed a side corridor one of them yelled, '*There he goes!*'; the others stopped, turned and raced away with clattering steps. Come on, Joe, don't dribble, I thought again, and felt slightly sick.

I started to walk downstairs, slowly, and just before I got to the courtyard, I called out loudly: '*Giacobbe di Bocca!*'

'Yes,' he yelled back at once, 'Signor Farkas?' and came quickly towards me.

Needless to say, I was very glad to see him. I did not want to be mistaken for a militiaman or a friar or the Abbot or, in fact, for anybody but Signor Farkas.

'Yes, Farkas?' Giacobbe said, and I could see, despite the growing gloom of the night, his excited face and tousled hair. His voice was deep like a bassoon.

'What's all this?' I asked.

'I wish I knew,' he said. 'We came up here — I couldn't hold them back any longer — and we had just arrived, full of peace and goodwill, wanting nothing but our women, when somebody started shooting at us and killed Francesco. I couldn't stop them; I couldn't. They have gone to get their women; and the killer.'

The women they got first. I sat down in a wicker chair by the fountain, with Giacobbe alternating between yelling despair and hoarse moderation, both of which seemed to impress no one. For a while there were few men left in the courtyard, and I wondered what had happened to Father Giuseppe. I asked Giacobbe: he did not know either. Then we heard the noise of an approaching multitude, cheers and shouts and then the short, happy laugh of a woman. They came back through a small wooden gate at the right-hand corner of the courtyard, some thirty-five men and the women, Beatrice and all.

'Now let's all go home,' Giacobbe stepped onto the rim of the fountain, balancing himself with some difficulty; 'men, we've got our women free; violence must stop now. Let's all go home.'

Someone answered with a rude, jocular remark, and someone else kissed a woman and others teased him and laughed. The violence was partly gone from them, but their laughter was still nervous and they were looking around, realizing perhaps for the first time that they were in the Abbey, looking around and sniffing and wondering, perhaps, whether to be impressed or not.

Then the killer came; rather he was dragged down the steps by Alfieri and his men. His boots brushed the stone steps, stammered downstairs. It was getting very dark. 'Here he is!' Alfieri cried. 'Found him hiding in a bathroom, up there.' Again the night was filled with swift violence, loud steps and shouts. 'Where is he? Come on! Hang him! Hang the devil!' I watched the sounds grow into a wild cacophony — I could see nothing but occasional vague shadows, upraised hands, lurching bodies. The tumult increased and the night began to smell sickeningly of death. Giacobbe cried once more *'Let's go home, men,'* but no one paid any heed to him. All I could see was the general direction of the black, shapeless movement. They pushed on towards the entrance door. I listened for the victim's voice, but there was no telling who cried for help or for vengeance. Then someone flashed a torch: into the thin ray came heads and eyes, hands and ears, all isolated and horribly significant against the inky darkness, as if a vast giant had been dismembered and his limbs flung into the light. But the thin ray moved on and fell into a corner, and I saw the backs of busy men, all doing something I could not see.

'Let's go, men,' Giacobbe's muffled voice creaked somewhere, and I thought again, Come on, Joe, what d'you think you're doing with that ball? There came the sound of hammering. The torch wavered, and I heard a long, shrill shriek; like the scratch of a knife on glass. The light focused on the door; the men moved away and I saw that they had nailed the killer by his hands to the half-open door. He kicked out with his legs a few times, but he was helpless, like a fly pinned down by a little boy. I could not see any more, as the torchlight went out. The crowd started to shuffle out, and I went with them. When I got

outside, I heard the door caught by a gust of wind and under its weight start to close with a creak. One could hear it gathering speed until it shut with a bang.

From Farkas's Diary for Tenth September, 1943

Last night I decided to leave this wretched place at once. I was sick with the whole scene at the Abbey — haven't seen so much unadulterated violence since the first war. Coming home (on a lorry with heaps of screaming women) I was thinking of poor Frici's brilliant skit, *The Defender of Little Men,* about an indignant, naïve busy-body who goes to the front in the last war and sends an angry report, saying that conditions are appalling, with grown-up people living in queer, trench-like holes, wearing odd uniform garments and shooting from rifles at — think of it! — other people. 'Couldn't see a single policeman around,' he ends indignantly.

Of course, it is no good behaving like a caricature. But I hate violence and haven't the slightest interest in the endeavour of the natives. I know that they're right and cannot be blamed; that their violence is a heritage and the reaction to past wickedness and stupidity. But who am I to be involved? First, I shouldn't have listened to Giacobbe's pep-talks; second, I shouldn't have gone to see the Abbot and listened to *his* pep-talk; and third, I should have left last night. Instead of which I am still here and can't make up my mind to go.

I don't know what's keeping me back. There is a train

to Ravenna and thence to Milano tonight. True, it probably isn't safe to travel, but neither is it safe to stay. Giacobbe and friends live in a Marxist coma. They have buried the dead, hold meetings, form Lilliputian cabinets (they made Alfieri the Naval Commissioner), draft declarations and greetings, prepare a Five-Year Plan for the development of land and sea, and most of all, wait for the British and American armies to arrive and confirm them in their power. Meanwhile, reports from various radio stations continue to be thoroughly confusing, and there is no indication that the Allies care a hoot about San Fernando. And why should they? But Giacobbe and friends only listen to rumours. Today there were 'only' five major ones — Allies landing in Dalmatia and at Rimini, all the German armies in Italy surrendering, Rome *definitely* captured, etc. These people go about their business cheerfully. 'The war is over,' they say, 'the People rose' — and identify all sources and forms of oppression and misery with the former régime, firmly believing that the logical and only way was the one they took: hang Don Innocenzo, shoot anybody resisting, break into the Abbey, and walk about with loud enthusiasm, clutching one another in some Proletarian Happy Ending.

Which is all very well, but not my business. I ought to go to Switzerland (Gizella or no Gizella) and have a proper rest. I am not young enough to get excited over these things, or to be able to afford to get excited at all. Why, then, can't I leave? I know I shan't catch that bloody train tonight. Haven't even given notice, made no move to pack or pay my bills or order a car. Didn't go out in the morning, staying behind closed shutters, lying in bed smoking and feeling restless.

It was a very long morning: as if waiting for something that was indefinitely late. I knew I wasn't waiting for anything in particular — except for a decision, some abrupt move that would make me jump out of this emotional mud bath. I thought of that man nailed to the door; of the Abbot's rustling silk robe; of the Austrian girl; but slowly all organized thinking ceased. It was the perfect intellectual void; Joyce could write a tetralogy about it. I rose and walked up and down and lit an occasional cigarette; then started to make disorder, with systematic thoroughness, placing a vase here, a book there, a collar on the table, my socks in the bathtub: all the while it felt as if I were talking to someone or dictating a speech, my body acting mechanically, trying to reduce all outside interference. I touched pieces of furniture as I walked, caressed the curtains, decided to open the shutters, decided not to, thinking *Abbot* and *her walk* and scores of other disconnected idiocies, to keep down, I think, my real consciousness, let it simmer down below, not allowing it to come up with some frightening decision or demand. Rather like someone trying to fall asleep, fighting against intelligent thoughts.

All the while I knew I was deliberately disorganizing my mind; like a young man I was, unhappy on a Sunday afternoon, humming stupidly, talking to himself or to the walls, inspecting the whites of his eyes, picking up a book to read a paragraph and no more, standing by the window listening to the indifferent sounds of a courtyard. And all the while a nagging pressure in my stomach. I took some salts; but I knew belches could not help. Then I went and took a cold shower and shaved.

As I was shaving, I realized this was going to end either by my leaving tonight in a frightful rush or starting to work again. And I knew it was really going to be the latter, and I said so half aloud to reassure myself. Already I felt better. I have always hated packing and paying bills and spending hours on a train, *partir c'est* really *mourir un peu*. I felt better because the decision stopped some of the restlessness, the hesitation, the urge to get rid of something, San Fernando, perhaps, or the whole failure of my visit. I will start work today, I said as I was shaving; and my mind became filled with images and titles and characters, all upside down and in total confusion, but I knew it was that highly electrical state of mind in which it would be a pleasure to fish out some useful bits; to try and fit them together, to find others, and generally to start on the long and happy process of preparation — the only happy period of creation, the period preceding the getting-down to details, the pen-and-paper-taking period when one has to be disciplined and exact. There were two titles, good enough to do something about them, with their appendix of an idea in embryonic form, pregnant with clues and curtains. There was 'Triangle' — the Hoeppler Case, that is, the Perfect and Only Triangle, the Real and Genuine Triangle, with Hoeppler as lover of both the wife and the husband, thus closing the usually missing side.

I took an empty cigarette box and wrote

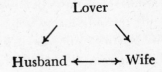

and then started to dress. There was nothing more to it
yet; but already I sensed some of the dialogue, saw a din-
ner-scene, felt the general tone of it. One could play with
the idea. Each side of the 'triangle' accusing the other two
of adultery; the jealousy of the husband when the wife
confesses her lover is the same as his; three principal characters only, with an incidental butler or maid or mother to
help out. I thought about it for a few minutes while I
dressed, thinking of the real Hoeppler (too dull and ob-
scenely selfish to be worth while copying fully) and of the
Bachs — he a millionaire, a connoisseur, a pervert only because of his total suspicion of and boredom in women; she
full of remorse, honesties, doubts, convincing herself at
last that she is doing the right thing by yielding to Hoeppler, etc.

Then, while knotting my tie, I started to inspect the
second title, 'Corpus Delicti' — about the man who travels
about Europe to collect all his former love-letters from the
addressees. It was too epic, of course — but Longleys and
Bauer have been clamouring for a novel since last Janu-
ary, and it might do. A bit too clever it was, and I thought
of a chapter in Brussels with dear old Solange refusing to
part with her bundle of letters; and it was then that I suddenly remembered that old theme of which I had told no
one but Pallenberg shortly before he had died in that awful crash. He was slightly dyspeptic that night and said
maliciously that my idea reminded him of Molnár's *Devil,*
which made me so angry that I deliberately forgot about
it for years. It wasn't at all like *The Devil!* It was about an
old man who revisits years after a place he had once been
happy in (I had the Tatra Mountains in mind as a back-

ground), ready to face every disillusionment, places and faces grown old and shabby, because he, too, had grown old and bitter — but finding the exact opposite, a lovely, lively place full of new buildings, flowers, and colour, full of happy and vigorous people, which makes him terribly cross. He is an old masochist who goes to seek a nostalgic confirmation that the place he had cherished in his memory had grown worn out and aged as he had; ready to resign himself to his impending doom, but only in a doomed world which could hardly survive.

As he finds the Tatras bursting with laughter and energy, he grows almost mental, and in his bitterness precipitates everyone into disaster and destruction. There was the Young Girl, eighteen or so, a lovely neurotic case, but recovering. In one of those beautiful midnight scenes with a doctor, she is about to find mental peace, but the Old Man steps in and convinces her that she is of no use, that this is the end for her, and finally makes her commit suicide. Then there is the Elderly Couple who decide to have a child, after all, filled with that autumn optimism that comes to people over forty; but the Old Man dissuades them in a Goya-like description of future wars. Then there was the Poet whom Daddy wants to make manager of a vacuum-cleaner factory, and the Old Man forces him to give up poetry and beauty, etcetera. I couldn't remember all the characters — there was Somebody Political and Somebody Tubercular and Somebody Military, and but for Pallenberg I should have written it ten years ago.

I had lunch in my room and tried to remember what title I had given to that idea. I knew I had had one and even Pallenberg had liked it. But I just couldn't remember, although one by one many other details came back to me: the name of the Young Girl (Elisa) and the second-act curtain. But I couldn't remember the title, or anything about the Old Man. It annoyed me. Whenever I tried to think of the Old Man in my mind, Pallenberg intruded; but I knew I hadn't imagined him originally as Pallenberg: yes, he could have played the character well, but even at that time I should have preferred Krauss or Bassermann.

After lunch I went for a walk. San Fernando was very quiet in the early afternoon light, with friendly though battered shutters, green in the sun. I like green shutters; they are associated with sun and youth. Had a haircut, after all. The barber I call Il Trovatore is a handsome man of forty with a very fat wife at the cash desk. He was most enthusiastic about the 'glorious revolution.' He is like a small-town Figaro, full of dramatic gestures and rhetoric — due, possibly, to the presence of so many mirrors. 'Sir, my dear sir,' he cried, nibbling with the scissors at the back of my neck, 'at last the chains have been broken! Leave it long?' he added, meaning my hair. 'The Germans must lose,' he said later; 'look at the way they cut their hair' — and giggled, enjoying his little joke.

From what I hear, San Fernando seems to be waiting for the Allies, British Home Fleet, Red Army, United States Air Force, and all, ignoring all the confusing news Radio Roma put out. Il Trovatore said the war had ended and this could only mean freedom, equality, justice, happiness, and the nationalization of the brilliantine industry.

There were more burials today — the whole village

turned out to say 'farewell' to little Francesco, who was killed in front of the Abbey. Still vague as to what actually happened. Doctor Merlin of the Sanatorium (who was having a shampoo in the next chair) said three militiamen who had fled to the Abbey on Sunday night lost their heads when they saw the demonstrators, believing they had come to pick them up, so one of them opened fire. The Abbey was silent, Merlin said, completely isolated, and practically everybody was on strike today.

Met Alfieri on my way to the Corso. He said tomorrow he was going on a sea patrol with some of the fishermen 'to direct the British Navy into the bay.'

No sign of the Austrian girl.

Lay down for a sleep before dinner. It was very hot again. Woke at nine bathed in sweat, after a most peculiar dream; lay staring at ceiling, trying to recapitulate. It started near an unknown theatre, a large *fin-de-siècle* building, gilded and illuminated. I was going towards that theatre. It was dark, almost night, but the sky was lit up with neon lights, and suddenly I saw my own name, flashed in large electric letters: STEFAN FARKAS, it flashed and blacked out, while underneath, another group of letters said: HIS NEW PLAY WITH . . . Neither the title nor the names of the actors could be seen. I was wondering which of my plays was on. There was a great crowd surging to the entrance: all poorly dressed beggars, in rags, with bruised faces. Some of them were bleeding, some carried scythes and flags and pickaxes. Some wore top-hats in queer contrast to the filthy rags they had on. Behind the theatre a tall, pointed mountain peak rose, quite suddenly and unexpectedly, a white peak, phosphorescent with the blue of snow; yet at the same time I heard the beating of the surf as if the sea were near.

I was very interested to know which play was on, so I tried to get nearer. But the crowd was thick and restless, and I saw that most of them just entered at one door and came out by another, increasing the confusion and my difficulties, perpetuating the circle-like movement. 'Let me through!' I shouted, but no one took any notice of me. 'I'm the author!' I cried; 'the author!' and one of the men turned, and he was Don Innocenzo, yellow-faced and dead, yet talking, moving. 'Your passport,' he said. 'Don't be silly,' I said. 'I'm the author.' Then I saw some posters, faded and yellow, with the names of the cast. It said in very large letters: 'DEFINITELY FOR THE LAST TIME — MAX PALLENBERG,' and as I read through the names of the other characters, I saw that all of them were played by Pallenberg: there were no other names than his, in gradually diminishing print. Then there was another poster and it said: 'Definitely for the Last Time —MAX PALLENBERG as Max Pallenberg in MAX PALLENBERG's *Max Pallenberg*.'

Somehow I was pushed aside and carried away by the crowd, and found myself in a narrow side street, deserted but for a dog barking at the moon, which stood rigidly over the mountain. I was running fast, sweating as I ran, looking for the stage door, diving into doorways, only to find them all locked. The moonlight was very strong and the street flooded with light, and as I paused to recover my breath, I saw a shadow across the road, standing rigidly, waiting. I wasn't afraid, because I knew him. I raised my hand; the shadow did the same. I turned; he turned, too. I lifted my knee; he lifted his, too. 'Hey, you,' I shouted to him, 'where is the stage door?' 'Hey, you,' he echoed, 'where is the stage door?' I started to walk again; from the corner of my eye I could see him following me. I was murmuring to myself: there was murmuring across the road. When I got to a corner, I knew I should find the stage door; and I quickened my steps, and as I turned into an alley I almost bumped into the shadow. 'Excuse me,' I said. He echoed my words. I saw that the dog which a minute ago was barking at the moon had sneaked up behind him, whining. 'Do you know what play is on tonight?' I asked. He smiled and bowed with a face like Molnár's Devil and said: '*Voilà!*' I cried: 'That's not true!' and started to run, and there was light in one of the doorways, but as I got there it went out again.

I entered; it was pitch-black and I was feeling my way and the walls were warm and rough, but then the dog sneaked up to me and I felt its cold wet nose. I struck a match, and there was another poster on the wall, ragged and yellow as if it had been there for long years. Its torn corners were flapping in the draught. All I could see by the light of the match was, 'STEFAN FARKAS'S NEW PLAY,' but before I could read the title the shadow appeared again and blocked the way. I cried something and the match flickered and went out. Suddenly I was holding the shadow in my arms and felt a naked back and I was naked, too, and filled with great yearning and warmth, warm and comfortable as she put her soft, childish arms around me, pressing closer and closer. I started kissing her cheeks: they felt soft and smelt of fresh peaches, and her hair was like silk. But suddenly my lips came to a horrid rough edge on her face, a bitter, sharp crack as if she had a bottomless hole on her face. It tasted salty, like raw, salted meat, only much more terrible, and I tried to withdraw, but my body could not get away, and her arms were strong and I was forced to keep my lips on that raw crack across her face. The moon had gone and the dog had stopped whining. I tore myself free and raced along the dark doorway, running as fast as I could, feeling the dog between my legs, its soft, hairy coat, and it kept running with me. I knew the doorway was full of cases and broken glass and chairs — mainly chairs in long rows as in the theatre (and I tried to run in a straight line, as I knew people must be sitting in those chairs and I wanted to avoid bumping into their knees). Then I looked and to the left there was the stage. I saw an empty seat and quickly sat down, panting.

The stage was empty but for a large chair with its back turned to the audience. I turned to my neighbour: 'You're late,' he said. I could not see his face, but I knew that he was a clever old man and would help me and give all the information I needed. 'What's on?' I asked. 'Hush,' he said. 'Look,' he added, and pointed, and I looked at the stage, and suddenly out of the armchair emerged Daniel in an elegant morning-coat, a red carnation in his button-hole, and he grinned and bent down and picked up a piece of paper and asked, 'You've lost something, Madame?' and everybody looked at me, and I felt very embarrassed and said aloud, 'No,' whereupon Daniel shrugged his shoulders and disappeared behind the chair. Then the curtain came down and there was tremendous applause, but the lights did not go up. It became even darker, and I felt terribly lost; the darkness was full of small, darker crystals, bursting from each other, swimming in circles. I wanted to talk to my neighbour, but I could not see if he was still there. The applause died down; there was a hush, and the curtain rose again on a dark stage. The curtain looked like the skirt of an old-fashioned Viennese woman. I whispered to my neighbour: 'What was the title of my play?' He gave no answer, but he knew it. 'Who is the old man in my play?' I asked. 'Sh,' he said. 'Be quiet. Don't keep asking me.' He was talking fast, in whispers. 'Hush. Be quiet. Don't ask me. The barricades are raised. The interpolation of the opposites are set. The Like is like an As If, and it reminds us of That, and the Here is a similar to the There, eh? Don't ask me. The Somethings of the Something. All fresh, happy — a new world, but it is of no use. You must take a pen and stab yourself to death. There is no other way. The Something of the Something.' He stopped talking, and yet I listened carefully and knew what he meant. He was suddenly on the stage, talking to a large crowd of peasants, wild-eyed, excited, wearing Jacobin caps. 'Go and drown yourselves!' he thundered at them. He was terribly familiar as he stood on the stage with his back to me. I cried out to him, 'Is that all?' and just as he was about to turn his face, the curtain fell, there was thunderous applause and I woke.

The Prodigal Brother

The same night Giacobbe came to see Farkas. He looked tired and he had not shaved for two days. His voice was almost gone; he could only whisper, and he coughed a great deal. The skin of his face was criss-crossed with deep lines, especially by his nose. Only his eyes, dark and luminous and alive, were full of excitement; they seemed to live apart from the rest of the face, ignoring the deep lines, the sagging skin, the stubble on the chin, the tired voice.

Farkas asked him how everything was. Giacobbe seemed absent-minded and unhappy. Yes, the village was in splendid spirits; they were forgetting the dead and felt strong with a lust for building and work. 'They're frighteningly logical,' he added. 'It'll be all right.' He wouldn't talk of the village any more. He had something else on his mind, answering Farkas's polite questions almost mechanically. Yes, the Committee had started its work. No, the Abbey wouldn't co-operate. Yes, they were waiting for the Allies; and so on.

Finally Farkas asked him about the *festa*.

'Oh, yes, the feast,' Giacobbe said, touching his forehead delicately with his index finger and thumb. 'Yes, there'll be a feast. But first we must set Leonardo right.'

'How is he?'

Giacobbe sighed.

'His leg is better,' he said. 'Much better. At first we were afraid it would have to be amputated; but it isn't necessary. He's got a nice room for himself. He sleeps most of the time; if awake, he asks for flowers, to look at them. I'm very worried about him.'

'He must be terribly tired and shaken. He needs rest.'

'Yes, rest,' Giacobbe said. 'I know, rest. But there is something in him that worries me. We had a long talk last night. He's changed.'

'Who hasn't?' Farkas said. 'Now stop worrying.'

Giacobbe smiled gratefully.

'I'd very much like you to come with me and see Leonardo,' he said pleadingly. 'Perhaps you can tell me what it is. Please.'

Farkas protested. He said he had definitely made up his mind to keep aloof. He remembered the night at the Abbey and it made him feel sick. He said so.

'Oh, but it will be very interesting for you,' Giacobbe said.

'You talk like a pimp,' Farkas said angrily. 'Trying to sell me a revolution, lock, stock, and barrel, as if it were a whore. Aren't you ashamed, youngster?'

'You said you weren't interested in revolts,' Giacobbe replied. 'Perhaps revolutionaries are more to your taste.'

'Sorry,' Farkas said. 'Anyway, I've got to work today. I am writing a new play.'

'What about?' Giacobbe asked greedily. He had regained some of his sardonic superiority. 'Pretty women, slick men, etcetera?'

'Mainly etcetera.'

Giacobbe got up.

'Please, Farkas,' he repeated. 'Don't let me down. He's in a very strange state. He might need persuasion; and you could help.'

As he uttered the word 'persuasion,' Farkas felt a queer response, somewhere deep in himself. The word was echoed and died down in the pit of his stomach.

'Persuasion?' he asked, conscious of his sudden interest, and disturbed by it.

'Yes. Please do come.'

They argued on, but Farkas knew he would have to give in finally. He gave evasive answers, but half-promised to think it over. Giacobbe said he'd fetch him at nine, and left, sad and hoarse and absent-minded, to attend a meeting.

Left alone, Farkas sat in the armchair by the window, trying to forget about San Fernando and Giacobbe. He had a writing-pad on his knee, a pencil in his hand. He wanted to make a brief, structural sketch of the play. The room was getting dark, but he did not put on the lights: he knew he wasn't quite ready. Again he wanted to remember the title, but could not. So he wrote down:

?

A PLAY IN 3 ACTS
by
Stefan Farkas
1943

Scene: the Tatra Mountains, a hotel. Time: any time. Characters:

Here he stopped. He was trying to think of the Old Man, but his thoughts were circling around, like vultures over a corpse, he said to himself, and was unable to go on. The Old Man, he said half aloud, hoping for help from oral associations. Young Girl, Elisa, Elderly Couple, Poet, Military Man, *Revolutionary*. He wrote down these seven characters in a neat row. He had beautiful handwriting, and as he looked at the small round chiselled letters he felt pleased. The first page of the pad looked neat and promising; and the rest of the white expanse was inviting. 'The Universe,' he thought, smiling indulgently; 'here and mine. The perfect means to power. I can make them weep or laugh; I can create murder, or faith, or just jokes.' Behind that page, somewhere, there was Telch the agent, Oscar the producer, actors, stagehands, rehearsals in a cold, dark, deserted hall, the first notices in the press, the critics; and one night the crowd, their faces reddened by the footlights as the curtain slowly rose. Act one, he thought. Scene one. In brackets, the scenery — the Lounge of the Hotel. Incidental characters, or leave the lengthy exposition and start *in medias res*? 'All I need is a good line,' he thought proudly, 'and I can start.'

Instead of a good line, Giacobbe came, somewhat happier. The meeting had been most satisfactory, he said, and after a pause: 'You will come, won't you?'

'You slave-driver!' Farkas sighed.

Leonardo occupied a second-floor room. Farkas hated hospitals and sanatoria, their clean, acid smell, the softly walking, ugly nurses who carried horrible things on trays and in pots, the pomposity and matter-of-factness of the doctors, the colour of the linoleum. The whole dry factual atmosphere. The intimacy of death. The arrogant division between the staff, who knew what it was all about, and the Candidates, as Farkas called the sick. Whenever he entered a hospital or sanatorium, he had a sneaking fear that out of a trapdoor a doctor would jump and rush him to an operating theatre and convince him that he had some vicious and complicated disease and must be operated on. He was attracted by doctors, but they frightened him. They knew too much, or at least they pretended to. 'Aha, the shape of your nose!' they seemed to think when they looked at him. 'Aha, the colour of your ears!' He walked quickly along with Giacobbe, cursing himself for coming and hoping it wouldn't last long.

He hardly recognized Leonardo. True, he had only seen him for a brief moment on the terrace: he had been very ill then, and now, shaven and washed, in neat blue-and-white pyjamas, Leonardo looked cheerful and very ordinary. The table-lamp was the only source of light, and it showed Leonardo's white face: a cheerful, rested face, slightly puffed and covered with the pink haze of fever. His nose seemed to be rather big, and whenever he opened his mouth he became ugly, for he had no teeth left. His forehead was attractive, and his hands, which rested quietly on the bed-cover, were delicate and feminine.

At first they talked of neutral subjects; of the weather, the food, Doctor Schmidt's gawky daughter who was getting married next month, vague and polite generalities. Leonardo had a pleasant voice, and he spoke animatedly; what struck Farkas was his cheerful detachment, as if he didn't care, wasn't impressed, and took everything for granted. He was not embarrassed at all. Giacobbe, on the other hand, was obviously and unusually ill at ease. He couldn't sit still, smoked nervously, and kept fumbling with books. Farkas watched him as he looked at his sick brother. He would not face him squarely; he looked at Leonardo almost secretly when his brother was turning to Farkas. There was something feminine in Giacobbe's behaviour; his tired, tough face became soft and anxious and full of love when he looked at Leonardo.

Then, suddenly, he took advantage of a small pause and said: 'We had another meeting tonight.'

He sounded apologetic.

'Well, well,' Leonardo said. 'Another meeting? San Fernando Meets Democracy. Hurrah!' He was obviously amused.

Giacobbe lowered his eyes.

'There was a discussion about the need for collectivization and the merging of small holdings,' he said. 'Most of them agreed. Pity you couldn't come.'

'Yes,' Leonardo said. 'And who took part in the discussion? Or was it one of your monologues?' He wasn't directly ironic; only amused and detached.

Giacobbe's fingers twisted the fringe of the bed-cover.

'A soldier named Alberto spoke,' he said meekly. 'And Alfieri, too, and four or five peasants.'

'Bravo!' Leonardo cried. 'There's nothing like self-education. In my time, the peasants didn't know whether collectivization was a swear word or a female ailment. Congratulations. Agitation and enlightenment under Fascism is no mean achievement. How did you do it? With the usual catechisms? "How to Become a Communist in Ten Lessons," and "Teach Yourself Dialectical Materialism"?' He sat up, his eyes gleaming. 'I can just imagine you, dear brother, explaining the Hegelian system to the day-labourers with the help of some popular simile. Food — thesis, digestive juice — antithesis, excreta — synthesis.'

'Are you making fun of me?' Giacobbe asked.

'No, of course I'm not,' the brother said. 'Only don't be so damn serious about it.'

'It is damn serious.'

'Oh, come, Giacobbe!' He sank back on his pillows and looked out into the night. 'The main square is so lovely.

You haven't told me anything about San Fernando. I hear they've built a tennis-court by the Corso. What's the wine like this year? I shall want some wine, later. And I'd like to go on excursions, Giacobbe. We could go together — to the hills and the other side of the bay, as we used to. I would like to tell you many things. We haven't seen one another for eight years. A terribly long time. You haven't said much about yourself. You've grown fatter, I see, and you haven't married. You should have.'

'You see,' Giacobbe suddenly turned to Farkas, 'he's changed.' He dropped his voice.

'We have all changed,' Farkas said.

'Eight years is a long time.' Leonardo stared out of the window. 'I shall never be able to tell. I wish I had written a diary, but of course one couldn't. Just an ordinary diary. I could give it to you now and you would read it and understand. As it is, you never will. You have grown fatter and you haven't married, but on the whole you have stayed the way I always imagined you would be when I came back. But I have changed; I travelled a lot, you know — in my mind, of course — while the world stood still on the islands. Nothing happened on the islands. It wasn't bad or good; it just *wasn't*. Everything stood still: night came, winter came, meals came, new men came. But at the bottom of it everything stood still, so you had to go on mental trips; you couldn't stay still. So I've changed. Don't be disappointed.'

'We were waiting for you,' Giacobbe replied. 'Ask Signor Farkas, he knows.'

'Well, I've come,' Leonardo said.

'You've changed,' Giacobbe said stubbornly.

'Yes,' Leonardo said. 'Mind you, it wasn't bad out there — not after Keller arrived. At first I was scared. I didn't know how much more pain and terror might come and how much I could endure. One can take a lot; and it wasn't too bad. When they beat me on the islands again, I was surprised how little afraid I was. They beat me much less than I thought they would, and it hurt me much less than what they did to my teeth in Ravenna. I used to come back to my cell quite elated. I said to myself: That wasn't too bad. And they didn't beat me often; four or five times in the first month; then gradually they gave it up. I was a good boy.'

He looked at Farkas.

'It is funny, Signor, how quickly one gets used to it; to the heat and the stench of the cellar, to the rotting food, the back-breaking work, the lack of every comfort and beauty — it's funny. One forgets about clean sheets, bathtubs, civilized meals. You are grateful if they don't hurt you; and every night, that first year, I thanked God that I hadn't been beaten or tortured. The horizon narrows, and in that static world one stretches out every second of rest, of sleep, of eating, of passing water, of smoking a cigarette. One learns the trick of doing one's duty with as little exertion as possible; of shielding oneself against the sun or the flies. Take flies, now. They come and stay and you can't exterminate them. But every night I took my shoe and squashed a couple of dozen on the wall. It's fun killing them, and one goes to bed thinking that one has reduced the race of flies considerably. One hasn't, of course. I was killing flies for eight years and they got no fewer; but they didn't get more numerous either. Oh, well, the

first year or two it was bad. One was revolted by the
stench and the heat; one planned escapes, but never made
them. One remembered the outside world; one was interested in the news, in girls, people. It was a mixed period,
the first few years, a mixture of bitterness, fear, and hope.
Mainly one hoped. Your letters were wonderful, Giacobbe. Funny that you were the only one to write. The
others teased me a lot: they had wives or mothers or sweet-
hearts to write to them. I had a brother who sent me cigarettes and socks and newspapers and chocolates. They
teased me a lot. I loved your letters. I went to a corner
to read them and I often wept — just as the others did over
letters from their mothers or wives. Sometimes I wished
I had a photograph of you.'

Farkas looked at Giacobbe; he sat, his head hanging
down, listening.

'It was bad and good,' Leonardo went on. He settled
comfortably, his face relaxed; he was obviously bent on
talking as much as he could. He now stared at the ceiling
as if to read a text from it. 'I was conscious of time and
myself and the world. Later it was neither good nor bad;
there was no time and no self. But at the beginning I was
conscious of it all. Of the cell, which I came to know and
ceased to hate: the concrete bunk and the brown, stiff
blanket, the hole in the ground and the grills on the window; the size and the shape and the colour of the walls and
the smells in the corners. I often thought of people like
the Count of Monte Cristo and the Man in the Iron Mask,
and other romantic prisoners; and it gave me comfort to
think how many millions had been in prison for millions
of years since the beginning of time. From then on I learnt

to regard myself, not as an isolated, unique martyr, but as one of a multitude, and then self-consciousness began to diminish. Keller, in one of his jocular moods, talked of his plan of forming a new party, the Party of Ex-Convicts and Ex-Martyrs, who would wear striped shirts and yell "Sing-Sing" instead of "Heil." Its aim would have been to turn the world into a large penal island, while Party members would retire to Monte Carlo and enjoy perfect anarchy.'

Leonardo covered his eyes for a moment.

'Perhaps the worst thing was hope; hope of getting out soon, hope of starting all over again. I often thought of San Fernando and tried to read between your cautious lines. Later, I wasn't so hopeful, or interested. About the end of the third year, it all got blunted; everything was broken into routine and my mind settled during the day, trotting after the automatic movements of the body like a dog. The sea, the sparse grass, the cliffs — the mind registered them faithfully, felt like a worn-out gramophone record, ceased to make comments, to use adjectives, to speculate. The world and its language was reduced to basic essentials. The sound of a bell, the whistling of the guards, the shuffling of feet, the bending-down, the lifting-up, the hurting back, the shade at noon while we had a brief rest, the occasional breeze, the changing of the blueness of the sky, the growing shadows in the evening, the voice of somebody you knew better than the others, mail, the running into a quiet corner, the tearing-open of an envelope, the established technique of getting the full joy out of reading a letter or a newspaper — first quickly, deliberately leaving out details, then again and again and again. For a long time — until Keller's arrival — I used in speech or thinking only four or five hundred words. It was like being harassed before falling asleep: one thinks of the harsh or frightening morrow and finds solace in a shrug and the pulling of the cover over one's head, the expulsion of complicated thoughts. That's how it was: gradually I reduced myself to an almost automatic condition. I wasn't scared or interested any more. News came of you, of the world. The *filossera* was bad, the League of Nations had met, aeroplanes had crossed the ocean, the régime seemed like staying forever; but all of it was out of focus, as if one had receded to a second childhood with the world mysterious and alien. People in the outside world were the adults; we on the island the children.' He sighed.

'There were periods of revolt, of course. The heat and the guards and the fellows got on one's nerves. One had moods and fits. One day I remembered my body, and at night lay naked in my bunk, inspecting my limbs and muscles. It was a young body, but it had started to get flabby and tired. I knew youth was going from it, prematurely. The supple strength had become a cramped reflex; the soft skin, bitten by so much sun, had become shrivelled in parts, and cracked because of the wind. My belly was bloated because of too much water and maize bread. I began to smell, and one night I cried, for I knew that the sweet-scented body which could do everything, jump and race, lift weights and love, was going to pieces. I remembered how young I really was; I remembered the girls I had made love to and those I had not yet met but wanted to love. Those were my best days, and I thought of long excursions and bicycle races, of rich meals and of dancing through a feast; of making love till the early lights of the morning. That night I beat my body in helpless fury and tore at my loins.'

'Poor brother,' Giacobbe said.

'And one dreamed,' Leonardo went on. 'All of us had similar dreams, dreams of anguish and pursuit and gushing lust; but most frequently of all, the Dream of Return — of being back at home; whether it was Milano, or San Fernando, or Ljubljana, or Paris (we were an international crowd), it was somehow the same in its essentials. One dreamt that one was at home again; one was happy, yet anxious; one met dear friends and relatives; sometimes one walked down a familiar street holding father's hand, listening to explanations about the changes. Where is that shop, that old grocery store? Where is that statue? Where is that girl named Teresa? — one asked, and somebody explained. Many had that dream. And as one walked, or listened, or just floated, suddenly one realized that it was *too early*, that one should not have come back — not yet, because *they* were still around, they with their boots and dark shirts, black or brown or green, they were still around, still hunting for someone, perhaps for oneself, and one had to flee, and as one fled one cursed oneself; oh, hell, why did I come back? I could have stayed in safety, in dull, yearning homesick safety; but how safe it was, and there were no pursuing boots and shirts, and if only one had waited a *little longer*, a few months only or a few weeks, until *they* were all defeated, or had perished in some natural catastrophe! We all dreamt that dream. And of course we all prayed.'

'That's bad,' Giacobbe said.

'There were some really religious ones, but the majority were tough and faithless; but we all prayed. It was pure superstition, of course; white magic.. At night, just after the lights went out, one could feel, and sometimes even hear, the words murmured inwardly, the magic, healing words, asking some big, soft god to speed the mail, to cure the cough, to bring a northern breeze, or take away the boil; words to placate the guards, the climate, fear. It was mechanical, a routine: the island sank back in savage totemism. I prayed, too, according to strict rules: three "Our Fathers," and three to the Virgin, and one short tail-piece, dealing with the particular problem of the day. "Please," one would say, "let them not send me to the road today; it will be too hot and I feel very weak." Or: "Please give me diarrhoea so that I can stay in the cell, in the cool cell alone with myself." And: "Please don't make my tooth hurt any more." '

Leonardo sat up.

'At one time I wondered if I'd be pardoned; I wondered on what terms. For months I was a good boy, an exemplary one. But time lost its sense — a year, or two, or five, is there a difference, one asked? But you wrote letters, Giacobbe, and said all the village was proud of me. It felt good to be a martyr. Once I had a long period of awakened political interest — was it before or after Spain, or Munich? I cannot say. I don't know what started it. Perhaps Joujou, the Frenchman, the only intelligent fellow in the camp, who came and talked to me. I had a great yearning for books. They gave me a Bible and Mussolini's autobiography. I read the Bible and picked out its revo-

lutionary message and learnt some of it by heart; but it
wasn't enough. I wanted many books; I wanted to know.
Things I had known slowly faded away: one day I realized
with fright that I had forgotten the first paragraph of the
Communist Manifesto and couldn't do geometry any
more. I remembered my reading schedule for the year I
was arrested. There was Carlyle and Macaulay and Feuer-
bach and Lenin, and Heidegger, I think; and wasn't there
an article by Marx about Palmerston? And that little
booklet, just translated, by Einstein? And shouldn't I re-
read *Salammbo*? This fit was worse than the grief at my
body. There wasn't much time, I felt, and one ought to
know so much. I used to ask Joujou; he was shrewd and
intelligent, but had little real knowledge. He was an old-
fashioned syndicalist and he had a few quotations up his
sleeve and he used to produce them like a magician producing the ace of spades. *"La propriété c'est le vol,"* he
would say. Or, *"La religion est l'opium du peuple."* But
then Keller arrived.'

'Keller?' Giacobbe asked with suspicion. 'Who is
Keller?'

Leonardo smiled. 'You'll know in a moment.' He
sighed. 'You wouldn't have liked him.'

'Why not?'

Leonardo shrugged his shoulders. 'He was too weak.'

'What year it was he came I can't remember; was it two,
three years ago, or less? Manfred Keller. He was an Austrian and he was up for five years. "I'll be out in three,"
he said; and he was. He died that cold winter not so long
ago — when was it? He was dark, with very black hair
smoothly pasted over his skull, strong black eyebrows, and,

later, a beard. He was stocky and strong, with flat, white hands. He had very white teeth, except for those that had been smashed. He was in very bad shape when he arrived, all bruises and black eyes and an arm broken. They'd beaten him terribly at Milano, where he was arrested. One night they just threw him into the cell which I had occupied all by myself for almost a week, as poor Romano had coughed out his miserable lungs and died. I washed Keller and put him to bed and slowly he regained consciousness. "Thank you, *mein Sohn*," he said, and passed out again. He always called me "*mein Sohn*." Keller was very silent about himself, at first. He was a good worker and picked up the ropes very fast. He seemed to know his way about: knew how to bribe the guards for cigarettes, how to shirk work, and so on. Slowly he told me about his life. He'd been more inside prison than out, starting at the age of seventeen, just before the end of the last war. In 1920 he was caught in Hungary and served his first long sentence in the Csillag Prison at Szeged. "My heart goes soft if I think of Szeged," he confessed. "Like an old tart remembering the night she lost her virginity. Szeged, the old *Csillag* — those damp, mouldy walls, that beautiful view of the Tisza. I lost my first tooth there."

'At seventeen he was arrested by the Habsburg Police for being a pacifist; in Hungary he was gaoled, first by the Liberals, released by the Communists; almost shot by mistake; then sent to Szeged by the Horthy gang. He went to Germany, was beaten half dead by the Black Reichswehr for being a Socialist; by the Social Democrats, who took him for a Communist; by the Communists, who took him for a Social Democrat. In Munich one of the Fehme gang

whipped him for being a Jew; in Hamburg a converted
Moslem denounced him as an agent of the Comintern.
Fleeing to Paris, he was arrested; they mistook him for a
Hungarian agent involved in the great franc forgery. Ten
years later, the Nazis picked on him in Berlin again. Later,
he went to Spain and was in prison three times there, having been taken for everything he was and wasn't. Back in
France, someone wrote a fulminating article about him,
calling him an anarchist; genuine Trotskyites shunned
him because, in 1937, he had applied for a Soviet visa to
attend the summer season in Moscow; for he loved the
theatre. Later, he refused the visa because he had been
seen with a White Russian girl who was known, by everyone but himself, to be a Franco spy. In Cluny he was
trampled down by a mounted policeman; just before the
war he was expelled from France because he knew the
young Pole who assassinated Von Rath. He left the Party
after the Molotov-Ribbentrop Pact, and since then had
been "the loneliest man in Europe" (to quote him), "the
only one who did not belong anywhere — to no country,
no party, no organization, to no Union, no Club, Association, Circle, Clique." He volunteered to serve in the
French army when war broke out, but was refused as an
"enemy alien," interned, and handed over by Vichy to the
Germans. When could that have been? Oh, yes, three
years ago. How funny; I should have thought he was on
the island much longer; much longer.'

There was a pause, and Giacobbe drew his chair nearer
to the bed.

'Tell me about this Keller,' he said.

'Well, it's not so easy,' Leonardo replied cheerfully,

pleased that Giacobbe was interested. 'He tried to be flippant about everything, as he was much too damned serious about everything. He said it was hopeless, this battling. "I have tried it all," he said. "It was a failure; it couldn't be anything else. This is an era of transition; only those can stay firm and strong who are either very stupid and aloof or able to view life historically." He was the outcast *par excellence,* swaying like a rope-walker between two worlds, many worlds. "I was born into a six-roomed flat," he told me once, "with maids and nurses, silver plate and annual holidays to the mountains, and fine clothes, and Papa smoked Havana cigars and rode in a limousine. Thus, I had to do everything with pure intellect, reach my conclusions in contradiction to my temper and wishes. For a while it worked. But deep underneath, the childish ego longed for Papa's cigars and the limousine. The fight must be left to them, to the real ones who, because of the immediate problems, could never long for things fake and soft; for battling is as natural to them as breathing. For me it was a duel, a bitter fight with shame, and compensation with forced heroics to prove myself — heroics and doubts, but not the real stuff."

'He must have suffered a lot. He would distribute leaflets in Wedding, under the nose of the Nazis, and then later pass a party of top-hatted revellers and feel a longing for soft lights and dumb blondes. He spoke at thousands of meetings, and always felt like a cheat, like some dubious *agent provocateur.* He refused all help from home, lived in hovels, ruined his gastric system, read ferociously; but it all did not help. "The delusion," he said, "comes from starting to build on not-quite-the-truth, on minute imprecisions which multiply themselves until the whole thing is a damned lie, full of half-truths or just plain lies. *Mein Sohn,* there is nothing I cannot deny; and there was nothing I needed more than a dogma." He felt a stranger everywhere, a fish on land, gasping to destruction. He could deny everything by something else, everybody by somebody else. "They all spoke some of the truth," he said, "but only some of it. That is because we want to know, not only the How, but the Why as well; and there is no answer to that except by irrational experience, which is rare, fickle, and savage." He denied Christ by Judas, whom he admired as a great purist, and so on; Descartes by Kant and Kant by Hegel and Hegel by Marx and Marx by Kautsky and Kautsky by Luxemburg and Luxemburg by Lenin and Lenin by Trotsky and Trotsky by Stalin and Stalin by himself and Himself by Himself, and so on in a vicious circle. He would have believed in Christianity but for the Christians, in Communism but for the Communists, himself but for himself. He quoted Adler to debunk Freud and *vice versa,* and Jung to debunk both. He went the whole way with the neo-mystics, studied Yoghi and Taoism until he realized that he was drifting into a spiritual Fascism; then he turned back to realism and science, only to get into a dead end by arriving at Rhine and telepathy.

'Finally he went slightly mad. It was a sardonic, nihilistic madness, an extreme individualism; yet he kept mistrusting the individual, "that helpless victim of his endocrine system. A grain of desiccated thyroid more or less, and the thin line between cretin and genius is gone. What can you expect of such an unreliable moron?" At one par-

ticular stage (in Holland) he arrived at a complete theo-
retical vacuum when nothing mattered any more but some
sort of abstract movement, without members. It was all a
joke, but he played it on himself in all seriousness. He
planned to form a Society for the Prevention of Cruelty to
Humans; later he had a new idea and called it "The
Movement for the Fossilization of Men," and he sold it to
a dangerously mad Flemish millionaire. Their main
slogan was: "THE ONLY WAY TO RETURN TO NATURE:
FOSSILIZE EVERYONE."

'In Paris he played about with the idea of forming a
Union for proving Teleological Causation; it had three
members apart from himself, and they went about ful-
filling the programme by taking off their pants during
High Mass at Notre Dame, by making elaborate plans for
travelling to Tibet, purchasing valuable equipment and
maps, hiring guides, mules, and two retired Indian majors;
only to prove their case by changing their minds at the
last minute and going to Biarritz instead. Or so he told
me. Perhaps he was making it all up; but I think he was
perfectly capable of anything in order to get out of his
mental deadlock. He gave up the "movement-period" because he discovered that all movements swung eventually
to the right; that Popes, Caliphs, Consuls, and Generals
stepped into the place of the Prophets, and started to ad-
minister and organize the truth until you could not see
the wood for the trees. When the war came, he was happy, hoping he could drown himself in army routine. The
French would not have him, as he was a reliable anti-
Fascist, so he hung about and was arrested and interned at
Montpellier. When the Germans came, he was handed over

to them: *"un petit cadeau de Vichy!"* but he escaped on the way to Innsbruck and somehow got into Italy. The Fascists picked him up in Milano; they had him on their files. He was on everybody's files.

'He was quite happy on the island, especially when he realized that he wouldn't last very long. There was a cancerous growth on his tongue, and it was steadily growing worse. The camp doctor said he could not operate, but would try to arrange for Keller to be taken to a shore hospital. Keller did not care, till the pain started. He would lie on his bunk at night, his tongue slightly bloated, hissing painfully: "I'll wait another fortnight" he would say without fear or self-pity; "then, if I don't get better, I'll take strychnine." He did so three weeks later, and it wasn't strychnine, but some slower and pleasanter kind of poison. He could hardly speak and had frightful pains; the doctor gave him an extra dose of morphine. "I'm rotting away," Keller said that last night. "Tonight I'll pack up and go. You won't stop me, *mein Sohn.*" I promised not to try. I sat on his bunk and watched him fumbling with his phial. I was holding his hand. "Before I disappear" (he spoke with great difficulty) "into the Void, or the Collective Consciousness, or just old-fashioned hell, here are some famous last words. Get out of here before you go quite mental, *mein Sohn,* and don't fight for anybody anywhere. Don't let them get you into anything. Go to the desert, live with a Bedouin girl, or go back to your village and grow grapes. Discover the sun and the fruits and laughter. Subscribe to the collected works of Mickey Mouse. Burn all your books and don't buy any new ones. See your dentist regularly, and do please remember that men of your type are usually impotent by forty-two. Buy a large dog, and watch the sunsets. Let me be a warning to you. I left myself behind at the age of seventeen, like an umbrella, and never found myself again." He was getting tired and he spoke quickly, hissing as if he had a lisp. "At school there was Moeldinger whose ambition was to sleep with la Duse, and Brettl who collected stamps, and Vikorsky who played ping-pong. All I leave behind are empty words and a vast number of files and dossiers in the police headquarters of Europe. Now put out the oil lamp and hold my hand more firmly."

'Six months later I escaped,' Leonardo went on. 'It wasn't really an escape. The camp doctor arranged it all. He was a clever man with a large family and an eye on the future. The Tunisian campaign was over, then the Duce fell, and he wanted to insure himself in case the democracies won. So he selected two or three better-known politicals, including for some reason myself, and helped us one by one to get ashore. I was the third to leave: the doctor sent in a report about my health, saying that my appendix must be taken out. So I was shipped ashore; the rest was easy. With the doctor's help I sneaked out of hospital one day. The doctor gave me a gun, some money, and his visiting card, and asked me to remember him to Democracy. Somehow I got to Ravenna, where I stayed at a small hotel for one night. But my trail had already been picked up, and a fat unpleasant policeman came around to my room and asked for my papers. I had to shoot, and hit him in the belly. He was so fat that it did not help much, and he shot back and hit my leg; but I got away. I hid in and near Ravenna for nearly a week. My leg was getting nasty and I was feverish. I wanted to come here and hide at your place until the war was over. I wanted to come to discover the sun again and laughter and buy a large dog and grow grapes. I got on a peasant's cart and was taken to the next village, and I had to have food and a decent rest; so I went to a roadside *albergo* the peasant recommended, and there was a soldier on leave next door, and the second night I stole his clothes and papers, got back to Ravenna, took a train and came here.

'I'm sorry I broke down at the end. My leg had got worse and I had a bad fever. For over an hour I was alone in the train. It felt like a hot bath, and I became very tired and all the fight went from me. I just sat, listening to my throbbing leg, getting sleepier and sleepier. I thought of you, Giacobbe, and of our house and of the reeds by the Abbey Hill. It is difficult to explain how exactly it was, but I suddenly felt silly playing the rôle of a fugitive: just as silly as I had been playing the revolutionary. Sitting in that train I did not want to hurt anybody; just sit in the sun and drink some of our wine, not caring a hoot if the Government wore black shirts or white, or if the peasants had less land than the Abbey. It was a big sweet tiredness, coming home on the train, wanting nothing any more, struggling no more, listening to my throbbing leg and the rails, feeling happy and uncomplicated. I knew that soon I was going to faint, and that I must collect myself and keep awake, otherwise they would pick me up and send me back; but there was just no more strength in me. If a Fascist had suddenly pounced upon me, I should have smiled and asked his pardon.'

The Persuasive Guest

For five minutes Farkas had watched his left foot getting numb; he only heard vaguely what Leonardo was saying and his thoughts were hopping from subject to subject; yet he felt an indefinable interest in what was going on in the neat white room, in its objects and people, and for a while he took a mental inventory of everything as if he wanted them for later reference. A vague interest was growing inside him, and as he felt increasingly aware of it, he tried to fight it down. Oh, what a bore; ah, why did I come; ah, to hell with these people, he said to himself, and made little resigned movements mentally. He felt Leonardo's gaze upon him all the time; he was talking not to his brother but to Farkas, as if he felt an ally in him and wanted to make an appeal for help.

When he finished, there was a pause. Farkas sighed and looked at the elder brother. Giacobbe sat on the edge of his chair, his fists resting on his knees, listening intently. He shook his head in dismay. He went 'tst-tst' with his tongue, leaned over the bed and patted his brother's white hand.

'Poor old Leonardo,' he said hoarsely, 'you have suffered such a lot. But you'll be better. You are tired and disillusioned, and I, cruel idiot, expect you to be full of verve and enthusiasm.' He spoke like an irritating family doctor who was not taking the patient seriously.

'I am not tired,' Leonardo replied. 'And I'm full of

enthusiasm.' He turned to Farkas as if seeking for a witness. 'I hadn't had a woman for eight years, to begin with.'

'Ye-es,' Giacobbe said knowingly, and patted his brother's hand again. 'Of course.'

Leonardo became irritated. 'You don't take me seriously.'

'Of course I do,' Giacobbe said. 'You must rest. Then, one day, we'll talk it over again.'

'There is nothing to talk over,' Leonardo was annoyed. 'I've made it clear, haven't I? I want to live a normal, healthy, uncomplicated life.'

'Yes. So does everybody else. Including ostriches.'

'I am not an ostrich,' Leonardo said. 'And I don't give a damn what everybody else does or doesn't do. Oh, Giacobbe, you must understand. We must get along well together. You're up to your neck in *Zeitgeist,* war, revolts, the People, and all. I don't mind what you do, but please don't count on me.'

'Poor boy,' Giacobbe murmured, unperturbed. 'So tired, so disillusioned. It'll change.'

Leonardo sat up. His face was getting red.

'Signor Farkas,' he said, 'you do understand me, don't you? Explain to him, please. I want to live like a normal human being; I don't want to fight windmills or Fascists. I had enough. I want to be left alone. Can't he understand?'

'Please, Leonardo.' His brother rose and sat on the edge of the bed. He was very serious now. 'Please, brother, let us not quarrel. It will be done in the way you want it. I am sorry if I sounded insistent. I did not mean to hurt or upset you. I will leave you in peace. No one will interfere with your plans. You may do whatever you feel like. Of course you may. Please, Leonardo.'

He turned away and faced Farkas, and his face was grave; but still that of a family doctor. He closed his eyes significantly for a second to tell Farkas: Oh, well, he's tired and sick, poor boy.

Farkas cleared his throat. He thought: *your cue now.*

'Whatever happens,' he said to Leonardo (his foot was pricking), 'don't change your mind.'

'Yes?' Leonardo turned to him hopefully.

'Whatever happens, don't change,' Farkas went on. He knew he was going to hurt Giacobbe. 'You're perfectly right. Let others make fools of themselves. Do what you feel is right and fitting.'

He lifted his foot and gave a light stamp to wake it up. He felt Giacobbe's hostile stare.

'Yes, Signor Farkas,' Leonardo said meekly.

'Now look here . . . ' Giacobbe started, but Farkas interrupted him with a brisk gesture.

'One moment, please'; and he turned to Leonardo again. 'Don't be a fool again. The People always act in a feminine way, emotionally and without gratitude. You gave your best years to them; now it's time to stop being an adolescent.'

If Daniel could hear me, he thought.

'Let's go,' Giacobbe interrupted nervously. 'He is tired and . . . '

'Please go on, sir,' Leonardo said, happily. 'I'm not really tired.'

'No, I think we'd better be off,' Farkas said. 'I'll send you a bottle of cognac tomorrow.'

Déjà vu, he thought. He felt contented and quite at ease. I must look into this contentment, he said to himself. Later, as he walked down the steps with Giacobbe, in silence, he realized that he must have hurt him badly; but he did not feel at all like apologizing.

'That was very interesting,' Giacobbe said bitterly. They walked under the lime trees in the main square. 'I did not know you had such strong opinions.'

'My dear fellow,' Farkas replied, 'the only thing I feel strongly about is not to have strong opinions.'

'Why weren't you flippant up there?' Giacobbe asked. 'And, anyway,' he added darkly, 'whom were you trying to persuade? That poor misled boy?'

Farkas gave no answer. Giacobbe's last remark had disturbed him.

'Or me?' Giacobbe asked in a loud voice.

Farkas thought of the writing-pad, lying on his table upstairs, the first page half-covered with his writing.

'I don't know what you're talking about,' he said rudely.

Giacobbe stopped and scratched his chest through his open shirt.

'Oh, well, I'm sorry,' he said, in a low voice. 'I must be nervous. I rather hoped . . .'

'Yes?' Farkas said.

Giacobbe looked at the Sanatorium.

'Oh, never mind,' he said. 'I'm sorry I dragged you along. It must have been an awful bore for you.'

'Not at all,' Farkas said.

'Good night, then,' Giacobbe said. He looked pathetic in the dim light, scratching his chest.

'Do you think he'll be all right?' he asked anxiously.

'Of course he'll be all right.'

Giacobbe sighed. 'Well, thank God for that.'

Farkas said: 'Now you remind me of the story about the little girl at school who asked the teacher if girls of thirteen could have babies. When the teacher said, "No, my child," the little girl gave a big, big sigh of relief and said: "Well, thank God for that"; and sat down.'

He was really hurting Giacobbe now, and he enjoyed it.

Giacobbe looked at him in the darkness. 'Aren't you afraid?' he said, in a small voice.

'Of what?' Farkas said.

Slowly Giacobbe turned and said 'Good night, then,' and went.

His walk was tired and Farkas watched him for a moment. He looked a small figure now, in the dim light, walking with feet turned outward, pathetically, like an old man. Once he turned; but Farkas did not wave. He, too, turned, towards the terrace, and started to climb the steep path.

It was ten-thirty and the terrace was quite empty. Don Teofilo and the Doctor hadn't come since the revolution, and many others, too, had stayed indoors and had their meals served upstairs. The band had not played since Sunday night, but when Farkas entered he saw Tony sitting in the far corner with her back to him, reading a newspaper. Farkas walked quietly over and sat at the table next to hers. She did not look up, pretending not to have noticed him. Farkas turned towards the kitchen and Ugo started to toddle towards him, but Farkas stopped him by signalling their code sign (a lifted thumb) for a carafe of red wine; Ugo turned and shuffled off to the kitchen. Farkas lit a cigar and stared into the main square, trying to remember the title of that play. He couldn't; nevertheless he felt easier now after his visit to Leonardo, with an ease he could not quite explain. All the time he was aware of the girl, though he was careful not to look at her. He heard her glass clink once; the slight smacking of her lips as she smoked, and the quiet, incidental rustle of her frock. They hadn't spoken since Sunday night; she must feel ashamed and accuse herself of having acted like a fool, he thought. Once or twice he felt her gaze upon himself; but he made no move. Slowly the minutes passed; the space of silence between them came to be stuffed with significance. They were almost alone on the terrace, a waiter or two in the background, and soon this silence felt awkward, like a foreign word that sounded obscene in one's own language.

The girl spoke first. 'Excuse me,' she said.

Farkas turned to her. 'Yes?'

There was no embarrassment in her. 'Nothing. Only I felt so silly sitting like this, silently.'

'You weren't silent at all,' Farkas said. 'Your thoughts were shouting like a town crier.'

She gave a small laugh. 'Can you read minds?'

'Of course I can. When I sat down next to you, you were self-conscious and even angry. How impudent, you thought: the whole terrace is empty and he must insist on sitting so close. I thought he was a gentleman and had forgotten the other night. Correct?'

'Go on.' She crushed out her cigarette.

Farkas said: 'Then you secretly inspected my hair and thought that it was only half as nice as on the photographs.'

She laughed. 'How did you guess?'

'It *is* only half as nice. Then, you slowly looked me over. Nice old man, you said to yourself. A writer. Then you tried to remember what I had written, but couldn't.'

The girl quickly protested. 'Wrong. I could. You wrote . . . what was it called? Oh, yes. *"Die Liebe Ist Nicht So Einfach."* '

'That's by Fodor,' he said.

'Oh. Oh, yes, of course. How stupid of me. You wrote . . .'

'Never mind,' he interrupted her. 'You couldn't remember them all, and less than that wouldn't do. However, later, you tried to think of a way of speaking. First you thought of asking for a match.'

'That's right.'

'Then you remembered your lighter, which was lying on the table when I came in; so you tried to think of some other excuse. You couldn't. So you just spoke. Which was very sweet of you, considering how badly I behaved the other night.'

The girl shook her hair. 'I'm very impressed and slightly frightened. Please don't go on mind-reading.'

'Why not?'

'I have ugly thoughts,' she said.

'Yes.' He wagged his head. 'It is awful to have wished somebody to die and then he does die.'

She was silent.

'Please, don't,' she said finally.

'Don't be childish,' he said paternally. 'I'm an old friend. We have practically shared the same room for some weeks now. You know, it used to be one big room in the old days. They put up a thin wall, perhaps eight years ago, and turned it into two. I know you quite well.'

She turned her face away. Her scar was a pale, purple line in a white expanse.

'You are not ashamed, are you?' he asked.

'I wish you hadn't told me,' she replied. 'I wanted to talk to you about many things. I knew you must be wise. I hoped you could help. But now I can't tell you anything.'

'You don't have to.' He crossed his arms. 'I know it all.' He lowered his voice. 'You poor child.'

Her hand came up to her eyes. She started to cry softly.

'You didn't love him really. You didn't even hate him.' He bent forward and almost whispered. 'He attracted you because he scared you; because he seemed so utterly strong and fearless, our Don Innocenzo. You've been used to fellow-travellers, to cowed fugitives who would jump at the sound of a ringing bell and lie awake at nights listening to approaching steps, and who were beaten before the fight because they knew they would be beaten. And he seemed so strong, the little brat.'

'How did you know?' she said.

'My hobby is *Menschenkunde*, humanology; the highest of all natural sciences.'

She sniffed and looked for a handkerchief in a small bag and dabbed her nose. She reminded Farkas of Anna now; she was so very desirable.

'I ought to be offended,' she said. 'So you only talk to me because you are collecting material for another play or something.'

Farkas was annoyed. 'What made you say that?'

'It's pretty obvious, isn't it?' she said.

Farkas rose and sat at her table. 'Don't be so conceited. I am writing a play now, but all my characters are fixed and . . .'

'What is your play about?' she asked.

He was even more annoyed. He did not want to talk about that.

'Oh, well,' he said. 'About an old man who is jealous of youth and happiness.'

'A sad play?' she asked. She had forgotten her tears.

'For my characters, yes. Let's talk about something else.'

'Have you done a lot of it?' she insisted.

'It's going quite well.' Blast that girl, he thought. 'The first act is nearly finished,' he lied.

'When you sit so quietly in your room — are you working then?' she asked.

He paused. *This wasn't the idea,* he said to himself; *not at all.*

'Yes,' he said.

'I, too, listen sometimes. I was wondering what you were doing so quietly. Yesterday and the day before yesterday and the day before that.'

'Yes, I was working.'

'Very quietly,' she said.

'Well,' he said sharply, 'did you expect me to play the bassoon?'

She looked up surprised and apprehensively. But he did not want to hurt her.

'As a matter of fact,' he went on in a quieter tone, 'I haven't been doing much the last two days.'

'I know,' she said and sighed. 'You were listening.'

'Yes, I was.'

'I must be a nuisance, disturbing you. I am sorry.'

'You were a nuisance. I was afraid for you.'

She looked at him behind a wave of soft hair that fell and covered her scarred cheek. 'Were you?' she asked.

'Yes.'

'Why?'

'I was afraid,' he said, 'that you'd kill yourself.'

'You must be psychic.'

He shrugged his shoulders. 'Nonsense. I heard you putting a bottle on your glass-topped night-table. I heard you getting a glass of water. I heard you draw the curtains and walk up and down and then sit and start a letter, but stop halfway, tear it up, and continue pacing. Then you lay on your bed and waited. I heard you open the bottle, with a hollow, sucking noise. I heard you change your mind and start pacing up and down again.'

'Yes, I did change my mind.' She made an impatient face. 'I think I shall move to another room tomorrow.'

'It's quite unnecessary.' He patted her hand. 'You won't do it, anyway. You're not the type. The last few days you were set on taking an overdose, but you knew I was probably listening and would come rushing in at the decisive moment. You realized how silly you would look. Death is terribly dull unless it actually happens; suicide is outright silly if it doesn't succeed. And you knew it wouldn't. Not that you're a coward. It isn't a question of cowardice; it's a question of logic. If we were more logical, all of us would take an overdose or turn on the gas. The greatest thing in self-preservation is stupidity, the omission to finish one's conclusions. The man struggling against drowning or ducking to avoid a shell is, at that moment, the perfect idiot; all the blood goes from his brain, rushing to the particular limb he needs most for keeping alive. That is what happens to us, in a less violent manner, all the time. If the man struggling to come to the surface stopped to think it over, to think to the bitter end, think of the misery of survival, of the pain of living, of the growing chance of violent death or simply of slow disintegration into senility and disease, think of the thousands of days, of toothaches and headaches, of cancer or diabetes, of the pain of cities and the idiocy of rural life, he'd give up and quietly drown. But you wouldn't do it because you are a woman, and women hate logic.'

'I feel a fool now,' she said after a pause.

'What made you change your mind?' he asked.

'I don't know,' she said simply. 'I suppose I was afraid.'

He nodded as if to say: Aren't young people reckless?

'Yes, I suppose you were afraid,' he mused aloud. 'Afraid of death. It's curious, you know, how misinformed one is. We've got all the proofs of life's misery, even at its most normal; on the other hand, there is no proof whatsoever that death would involve the slightest inconvenience. You know there's no hell; or, if you do believe in it, you can safely prepare yourself for this other possibility by keeping to the comparatively easy rules laid down by the churches. Yet the churches could not produce a single saint to draw the conclusions, and take the overdose or drown himself. The best they could do was to go and convert savages and perhaps be roasted over a bonfire, with a smile. What hypocrisy! They talk to us about the frightfulness of life and the glory of death; and yet they cling to their own frightful little existences. And you are not even a saint. You're just an unhappy little girl, roughly handled by history, pushed about without shelter or love, left to herself to fight all the witches, trolls, and dragons, inviting by her helplessness the worst instincts of men. My poor child, I've known many like you: they float down the highways of Europe like autumn leaves. They were born into security and comfort; they grew up and went to skating-rinks where their young breasts were touched by young rakes; they walked home in the snow, red-faced and glowing that mysterious little happiness busy hormones produce at seventeen; they stopped at corners to buy hot chestnuts; they went to concerts and to the Opera Ball, and were taken by anxious mothers to the Semmering or Abbazia. It was all so beautiful and easy; at night they would look at their firm bodies in the long mirrors and be proud and stroke themselves and hope for some young rake to come and take it all — not suspecting, of course, that in a span of time which would seem to a tortoise or an elephant a mere week, their proud bodies would shrivel up and the young rakes turn into messy invalids.

'But, above all, The Something Awful had happened and the world, which used to be the business of Papa and his friends only, came in bursting the whole friendly framework of home. And Papa was interned or fled; and some of his friends were made to wash the pavements, and the young rakes were shot, or did not greet one any more. The world collapsed and you had to move — to Prague and Bucharest and Zagreb and other places — and you had to learn the meaning of the Monster named Frontier and the Good Fairy called Visa. And Mamma died on the way

to Belgrade and Uncle Samuel went broke in Paris and
Cousins Helga and Franz wrote snooty letters from America. And you knew that there was no return; that nothing
would ever rebuild that home, or resurrect Mamma, or
revive the unsuspecting friendly glow; and that the young
proud bodies became a means of bargain to appease Monsters and Good Fairies. Don't I know them all?'

She cried the way heroines in novelettes cry; cleanly
and silently, with a trembling light in her eyes. She
dabbed her eyes and blew her nose discreetly.

'What will happen to us?' she asked.

Farkas said: 'Nothing is certain but death, they say in
my country. I've got ten years at the best, which I propose
to spend as a contemplative corpse, trying to keep warm
and drugged by smoke and drinks and words. I shall chew
over my memories which are flippant and without consequence. Some of my plays will be produced for another
generation; later, perhaps revived as curios of a diluvian
age. Most of my books have found a place in libraries,
public and private; but no one will read them except, for
a while, matrons and old fools. Not that it really matters:
who reads Balzac or Flaubert except a few exhibitionists?
As far as San Fernando goes, it too will die, in a way. It
has been dying for years now, and glorious revolt will take
over and turn it into a health resort for the proletariat;
and workers with failing hearts and pancreases will come,
be sad, and die, just as the bourgeois with failing hearts
and pancreases have done up till now. And you? Well, my
dear child, you're still young, although I fail to see what
good that can do to anyone. You can wait, and the war
will be over one day, and you may return to Vienna and

find it tolerably changed and dreary and alien. If all goes exceptionally well, you will meet a nice man, so that you can spend the rest of your life cooking meals and bearing children for him until the children grow up to go to another war. In about five years' time you will start living on memories: the skating-rink and the rest, and all of them will seem as historical as the Congress of Vienna; The Something Awful, Don Innocenzo, whom you will miss, and others like me, the old-fashioned cynic who lived next door.'

'Aren't you cheerful?' she said. 'What you need is . . . '

'I don't,' he said quickly. 'There were at least a dozen women who tried to convince me that if I took them into my house, shared my bed and breakfast and other meals with them, paid their expenses, took them for walks and summer holidays, listened to their gibberish and so forth, I should be happy and free from worries. A curious argument.'

'Aren't you bitter?' she said.

'That's an implicit fact one mustn't question,' he said. 'It's just as if you were to ask Freud how he had slept last night, or Dunne what time it was.'

All I need now, he thought, is a good curtain — one which would leave me completely free to choose the next scene; to say something light and warm and take her to my room. But to his great annoyance she rose. 'It's getting cool now,' she said sadly. 'Thank you very much. I hope we'll be friends.' Before he could answer, she quick ly walked off the terrace.

The Dance

The murmur of voices, an occasional shout and drumming steps woke Farkas next morning. Through the shutters the rays of a fresh, young sun came in, and he lay on the bed, with closed eyes, listening. The noise grew and reverberated with excitement. 'Oh, dear,' Farkas thought, contemplating asking Fritti (or the Committee) to put up a large notice on the Paradiso's entrance door, saying, 'Don't Disturb.' He got out of bed, combed his hair, brushed his teeth, and put on his dressing-gown, listening not so much to the crowd outside as to the girl next door. She was moving about the room. Some wooden object — a brush or a coat-hanger — made a flat noise.

Then he went over to his writing-pad. 'Good morning,' he greeted it, and picked up a pencil. The first page was only half-covered with writing. It said as the night before:

?

by

Stefan Farkas

1943

He lifted the writing-pad and crossed out the query and wrote: *The Something of the Something. Or: The Something. Or just: Some Thing.* Then he rang for breakfast and walked to the window and opened the shutters. The sun was strong and fresh: San Fernando looked very green and blue, divided by sharp light and shadow. There was a large crowd dispersed all over the main square. A lorry, beflagged, stood in front of the Paradiso, with some peasants in it. Others, quarrymen, villagers, fishermen, with women and children and grandmothers, dressed in their Sunday best, stood in groups of five or six, waiting and shouting and joking. Farkas saw Alberto the maimed soldier, flushed, wearing an improvised armband, running to and fro, giving orders, trying to create some sort of order, laughing, occasionally frowning importantly. In the olive grove a table had been put up and five men sat around it, leaning over some papers. Two village lads were climbing the lamp-posts trying to fasten long, coloured bits of cotton or some other material, which later turned out to be rather garbled versions of Allied flags. In the distance two trumpets were experimenting, slashing the fresh sunny air with sharp notes. Farkas did not see Giacobbe or Alfieri.

As he turned to the left, he heard the shutters of the girl's window opening, and her soft hair showed as she peered out. She was pale, like a child who's been sick for a time and now discovers the sun again. She did not look particularly miserable: there was no tragic line over the childish face and her soft lips were half open, rather pathetically, ready to smile, he felt, at words of encouragement, or at a joke.

'Good morning,' he said cheerfully, and she turned to him quietly. She obviously knew that he had been at the window.

'Lovely morning. What are they doing?' she asked, looking down at the busy crowd.

'No idea,' Farkas replied. 'They look peaceful.'

As he spoke, some of the peasant women saw them, giggled, nudged one another, and stared. 'We mustn't shock the working class,' Farkas said to the girl. 'They think it's immoral to get up so late.' And to ease the embarrassment of the moment, he leaned forward and shouted to the women: 'Good morning, San Fernando!' and waved his hand. The women shouted back: 'Good morning,' and giggled again. All the other groups turned and looked up, and Farkas saw, wherever he looked, squat, dark faces screwed up in smiles. Like a choir, their shout came up happily: *'Good morning!'* Some of them pointed with their fingers. An old toothless man spat ceremoniously and lifted his hat; 'Good morning, Signor Farkas, it is a very fine morning! The Allies are coming.' 'Yes, sir,' said one of the young lads hanging on a lamp-post almost on a level with Farkas's window. 'Yes, sir, they're coming.' Full-throated and out of key, he started to sing — something which might have been anything. Farkas grunted at them and withdrew. The girl had gone, some time ago.

It was so much like a Sunday: the fresh sun, the gaiety of the light, the festive, cheerful crowd, the suggestion of a brass band in the distance. All this reminded Farkas of an old summer in Vienna, when Daniel and he had stood on the Ring watching a military band marching by. He hummed as he shaved, and thought of his play. 'This afternoon,' he sang, 'I shall go-o-o for a walk in the hills and get it clear.' Then there was a knock and Farkas said, 'Come in,' and Ugo, surprisingly well-shaven entered, balancing a tray.

'Morning, sir,' he greeted, panting.

'Morning, Ugo. What's all the excitement?'

The waiter placed the tray on the table and started to arrange the dishes. 'They are all like drunkards,' he grumbled. 'The milk was an hour late and there will be only a cold lunch. They are waiting for the British.'

Farkas watched him in the mirror. 'Aren't you pleased?'

Ugo's face became anxious. 'Sir,' he replied with dignity, 'you know my sentiments. Of course I'm pleased. But will the British be?'

'Why shouldn't they be?'

Ugo made a wry face. 'Look at that rabble. Not one in ten wears a tie. I know the British. I've had a talk with Chef Luigi. I've told him about lamb chops and mint sauce; I've told him about mosquito nets and I've told him about early morning tea. D'you think he's done something about it? Of course not. He said he was too busy. Busy about what? Now the British will come; right, that's all very well. There'll be speeches which they will not understand; there will be at least seven speakers, and Don Teofilo has been up since seven, ever since the news got around, buttonholing Giacobbe di Bocca and the others and insisting on being on the reception committee. Seven speakers but no roast lamb and no early morning tea. They're going to requisition the hotel.'

'So I'll be put out?' Farkas asked, powdering his face.

'Not you, sir,' Ugo replied. 'They are proud of you. They talk of you as one of the sights. Immediately after the General View, the Drinking Well, and the Abbey, you count as the main attraction, they say. No, not you, but some of the others. Fritti's been busy telling them to move over to the Regina, which is half empty, anyway.

It's all nonsense. They don't even know how many British will be coming — twenty? — three hundred? — three thousand? All they think about is speeches and flags and who's going to be on the reception committee.'

After breakfast Farkas went downstairs. In the entrance door stood Mr. and Mrs. Morgan and greeted him with large toothy smiles. The man wore a dark suit and was painfully brushed and washed. There was a line of ribbons on his chest and a flower in his buttonhole. The woman wore a gay printed frock which stood slightly apart from her as if unwilling to touch her too closely. She was clutching a small Union Jack which she waved at Farkas.

'Isn't it wonderful?' she cried. 'Our boys are coming.'

'Yes, isn't it?' Farkas said politely.

'Now we'll be going home,' Morgan said absent-mindedly, and the smile got stuck on his face.

'They've been *so* nice,' she went on. 'So very nice. They came and told us the news early in the morning. A big fleet is coming, they said.'

'The good old Fleet,' added Morgan.

'Duncan's going to make a speech,' she said. 'They've asked him to.'

Morgan blushed. 'I've never been good at speeches.' He scratched his chin embarrassedly. 'We'll be going now, Gladys.' He jerked himself into fresh excitement, and patted her shoulder.

'Yes,' she said, and looked at him; and the way she said it made Farkas feel the full value of monosyllabic words.

The square grew more and more confusing and noisy. Another lorry arrived with more laughing and shouting. Farkas stood in front of the hotel, hesitating whether to go on. Messengers came running by, sweating boys with armbands; the crowd got thicker and more continuous, and as Farkas scanned the square he saw them coming from all directions: from the main street, the Kursalon, from behind the Sanatorium. It was all movement and colour, but not too obvious and rich, with blue, black, and white dominant, but touched by the yellow sun and the moist living green that poured from the foliage into the shadows. They came in pairs, or in groups of three and four. Some of them were running, others strolled embarrassedly; perhaps they had never dared to come down to the square before. Children came and screamed, and a young plump woman slapped a little girl's face and she started to cry, until her small fretting voice was lapped up by the high-pitched murmur of the mass. The flags were everywhere: on the Sanatorium and the Regina, and hanging down from the lamp-posts, long, rough, coloured tongues, green-white-red and red-blue and just red, and they added another dimension to the scene, deepened the dominant blue of the sky and the blackness and whiteness of women and men, deepened the laughter and the murmur of the voices, flapping briskly, writhing in the slight wind.

'You're not laughing because you're happy,' Farkas thought, watching two small old men giggling; 'you're happy because you're laughing.' He was constantly checking himself, controlling some volition to walk down and shake hands and share the laughter. He was full of irony and suspicion, in order to defend himself against that deep, coloured mirth which descended with increasing tempo on the whole scene, carrying with itself some mediaeval gusto, some old-fashioned, guiltless desire to feast, with oxen roasting over open fires, rich red wine gushing from great kegs, while a squire watched, from the topmost window of his tower, the serfs making merry. Farkas hadn't seen a merry crowd for a very long time, and he kept defending himself with memories; he thought again of the Sunday on the Ring with Daniel, of the snug little burghers taking their children for a walk, the gentiles in their cabs and the coy bustles of the women, all merging into a circle-like movement, a grand *rondo,* accompanied by the Guards' band playing the Radetzky March. 'Look what happened to Daniel,' he added to himself, watching San Fernando.

There were no clouds in the sky: dully the blue expanse covered the square with no promise of rain. 'How they're going to sweat,' he thought. 'By four o'clock the men's collars will get soft.' But then he remembered that most of them did not wear any. The crowd grew again, and the isolated groups merged into one another. The trumpets started to play, although for a while it still sounded like tuning-up. Another lorry came, and two carts; someone known and popular must have been on one of them, for there was renewed cheering. Then the crowd on the main street parted, and Farkas saw men marching down, three abreast, small, stocky men wearing no hats or collars, carrying pickaxes and shovels; some of them had rifles. Then a large white sign, painted on a piece of linen and stuck on two poles, was lifted high, and it read: 'VELCOM IN SAN FERNANDO,' and there was applause at the sight of it, although obviously hardly anybody knew what the first word meant. The men marched on towards the Corso and the crowd followed them shouting encouragements. Children were raised high and one of them shrieked, *'Papa!'* 'By four o'clock,' Farkas consoled himself.

Somewhere singing began, vague and multicoloured, with the melody lost among the trees; but it was approaching like a wave as the crowd on the square took it up. Slowly they receded towards the sea, and the square began to empty, though they were still coming in pairs and small groups. Their steps crunched on the gravel paths and they kicked up a low, white dust. The shutters were all open in the Sanatorium and elderly heads appeared carefully and some of them waved and some of them didn't. A fourth lorry came down the main street honking its horn. 'Hey, Augusto!' someone yelled at the driver; there was commotion and a cluster of young men got hold of the back of the lorry and climbed on top, their legs and buttocks hanging like grapes as it started off again. It was getting hotter.

Later, much later, when the rain came, as if the weather had made up its mind to follow the mood of the square, and when Farkas remembered the dead and the rattle of the machine guns, he thought of this Sunday scene, the colours, the dust and the noise; of how he was thinking, 'By four o'clock they will be sweating.' Later, much later, when the wind came and he felt chilly and even frightened that so short a time could change so much, with all the vigour and movement gone, all the dull blueness of the sky, with the dust inexorably turned into mud: for the rain came down the eaves and pipes and ran down the slope towards the shore, and the silence was still alive with the shuffling, hurrying steps, the trumpets and shouts of the morning; and the torn flags lay like violated girls. But it was later; much later.

Meanwhile they waited in festive mood.

The main square was soon deserted but for a few young lads busy with more flags, and Farkas, who was slowly strolling towards the sea. After all, he decided to follow the crowd, with caution and reserve, intent on keeping apart. At the corner of the main street he was halted by Il Trovatore the barber, who was dressed in a black suit, wore a red tie and a flower, and was dragging a fat child along. He had given himself a real Sunday shave, it seemed, and his chin was covered with powder.

'Signor Farkas!' he cried in great excitement. 'What excellent news, what tremendous news!' And as if to balance the pathos, to the child he added: 'Come on, don't lag behind.'

'Are you going to the Corso?' Farkas asked.

'Indeed I am,' Il Trovatore cried, pointing to the sea as if to command a cavalry charge. 'Forward to the Corso! The Allies are coming!' And again as a balance: 'Don't pick your nose, child!'

They were walking together now.

'I know the British!' the barber said confidentially. 'I know them well. Didn't we fight together last time? I was there,' he boomed, raising his voice as if speaking to a vast audience, 'on the Isonzo and the Piave, fighting the Real Enemy of the Nation. I know them, Signor Farkas.' Then, as a proof, he continued in English: 'Haircut, shave, moustache, hurrah! Haircut, shave, shampoo, tea, water-closet, hallo boy, good day, hurrah! Don't I know them?' And to the child, with a jerk: 'Come *on*.'

He leaned nearer to Farkas and spoke intimately.

'The Fleet, the big English Fleet, is arriving personally. T-r-r-emendous guns and t-r-r-emendous dreadnoughts. Woe to the Germans and the Fascists! Tremendous!' he added to himself, running out of breath.

'Who said they were coming?' Farkas asked.

The barber stopped.

'Everybody,' he said. 'Signor Foa, that eminent victim of racial persecution, Alberto, and, of course, Don Teofilo. Everybody *knows*. There can be no doubt. Signor Tiavoli, a friend of my wife, heard it over the wireless. The big English Fleet itself. T-r-r-emendous!'

The Corso was packed with people. In thick rows they crowded the waterfront, in confusion and in constant movement. The centre of gravitation was the bridge of the bathhouse, but they spread out everywhere and filled the once quiet promenade under the trees. They stood on the benches, and children were raised high, and there were shouts and laughter and the scream of children who had got away from their parents, feeling bored, and were chasing one another among the flower-beds. Farkas shrank back when he saw the multitude, and was thinking of turning back when he heard his name called out and saw Don Teofilo in his wheel-chair. The nurse stood behind him, full of hate and contempt.

'Farkas!' the invalid cried. 'Come here. Please.'

Farkas walked up to him. Don Teofilo, too, wore festive clothes: a dark-blue blazer with the insignia of the Yachting Club, an elegant cap and cream-coloured flannel trousers. Big fat sweatdrops stood on his dark-brown forehead.

'Farkas, this is impossible!' he panted. He sounded very excited. 'One cannot get through. These people have no manners.'

'Where do you want to go, anyway?' Farkas inquired.

'To the bridge, of course,' Don Teofilo said. 'They can't leave me out of this. Di Bocca promised a proper place for me on the Reception Committee. They may be here any moment, and I can't get through.'

'How do you know they're coming, the Allies?'

'Why, everybody knows it.' Don Teofilo dismissed the question with a gesture. 'Everybody. It was even on the wireless. I didn't hear it myself, but everybody else did. They are going to Rimini — but a small flotilla will stop here. After all, this is the best bay on the Adriatic; or practically the best. Where is that man Giacobbe, where is Giacobbe?' His voice became nagging and plaintive. 'Hey, you!' he cried to a group of women standing on a bench. They turned. 'Have you seen Giacobbe di Bocca?'

'No, sir,' one of them replied. 'We haven't.'

'Where is he?' Don Teofilo was losing control of his nerves. 'I must get through. Farkas, come, help me. Nurse, come on.'

Suddenly a long shout went up at the far end, and it spread quickly over the crowd. 'Bravo!' They took it up in a thousand voices, deep basses and shrill sopranos. Most of them did not know what it was all about, yet they shouted happily, letting themselves go. The women standing on the benches turned to one another, their faces glowing, shouting, '*Bravo! Hurrah!*' and finally just roaring some inarticulate yell. They were enjoying themselves no end, like children left to themselves by punitive

parents who have gone away indefinitely to a cinema or a
party. 'Bravo! Hurrah! A-a-o-o-o-o-e-e-e-a-o-i-e-e-e-a-a!'
The children stopped playing among the flower-beds,
rushed to the crowd, furrowing a path between legs, thighs,
skirts, screaming with delight, looking at one another as
the women did and almost winking with joy, all sharing
some delicious freedom and happiness, all trespassing
something, they did not quite know what.

'What is it? What is it?' Don Teofilo cried, trying to
raise himself. 'Have they come, have they arrived? You
up there, what is it? Can you see anything?'

A woman looked at him and continued shouting: only
she turned the inarticulate yell into a happy, puzzled,
shoulder-shrugging: 'I-o-o-o!' meaning: 'I don't know.'

Somewhere applause started; it sounded like flat, fleshy
little objects dropping, until the whole crowd took it up,
and soon the Corso roared, with a thousand strong hands
clapping.

'What is it?' Don Teofilo cried.

'Signor Farkas, Mister Farkas,' a voice called. It was
Benito, the grocer's errand boy, wearing white linen slacks,
a striped silk shirt, and a red tie. His sleeves were rolled
up and his large ears seemed to tremble with happiness
and excitement. 'Signor Farkas,' he said breathlessly as he
ducked under a bench and climbing across some children
arrived at last. 'Please, Signor Farkas, come forward, you
must be in the front row.'

'Who are you?' Farkas said, to cool him down.

'Benito Guardia, at your service,' he said, saluting.
'Please, Signor Farkas, I've been looking for you everywhere; you mustn't stay here. I've got orders to take you

there. Hey! Make way for Signor Farkas!' he yelled at the
nearest group.

'Don't bother,' Farkas said, but Benito grabbed his arm
affectionately and tugged him towards the sea. 'Make
way!' he yelled again. The groups turned: they were still
clapping, and seeing Farkas their faces reflected a sudden
awe, and for a moment they were unhappy. 'Yes, sir,' a
peasant said, and elbowed a path into the mass of bodies.
'Yes, sir.'

'I don't really . . .' Farkas protested. 'Don Teofilo,
perhaps . . .'

'What is it, where are you going?' Don Teofilo cried,
quite confused now. 'Nurse! Bocca! Farkas!' he cried
hectically.

Benito took no notice of him. 'Please, sir,' he said, with
a friendly but overexcited grin. 'This way; it'll be all
right; away you!' he shouted at an old woman. 'Make
way for the illustrious Signor Farkas!'

Farkas couldn't extricate himself. 'Don Teofilo' he
tried half-heartedly.

'He'll be all right,' Benito answered. He felt important
now: an important official guiding an important guest to
an important function. 'Attention!' he kept yelling, dragging Farkas along. 'Attention, make way! This way, sir,
please, sir, all right, sir?'

Finally they got to the waterfront. Here the crowd was
thickest. The children simply sat on the edge of the promenade, hanging their legs over the smooth, friendly water,
clapping and yelling, making jokes. All the benches were
occupied; most people stood on them, some of them on the
tips of their toes, craning their necks, eager to see. A small

motor-boat was coming in slowly, towards the wooden landing-stage by the bridge.

Farkas still could not stop and he gave up trying. Benito fought for him like a lion, pushing peasants away, stepping over children and kicking some of them. They pressed their way along towards the bridge, which seemed to groan under the weight of the crowd. By the landing-stage there was a small circular space left free, with a table and some chairs. There were flags again, at both ends of the bridge and on top of the bathhouse, flapping lazily, and another large sign across the whole width of the bathhouse, saying: 'VELCOM IN SAN FERNANDO.' Farkas noticed Chef Luigi and Alberto and the Morgans standing by the table, leaning over the railing of the bridge, shouting towards the motor-boat, which chugged along heavily. Then the band struck up and the brassy notes crashed through the limp air.

'This way, sir,' Benito cried for the hundredth time.

The cheers and applause rose again as Giacobbe in a white linen suit and Alfieri wearing some pseudo-naval outfit stepped out onto the landing-stage. Alfieri had a large grin on his face, answering some joke from the bridge as he tied up the boat. Giacobbe smiled vaguely.

The two had gone out on a scouting trip, Benito explained to Farkas, in the motor-boat (requisitioned by the Committee and renamed *Matteotti*) to look out for the British Navy. They dared not go far and only cruised along the edge of the bay, or some miles beyond it, finding nothing, as later turned out, except two fishing-boats. 'They're always late!' Alberto cried to the crowd on the bridge; 'the British, they're always late!' The crowd laughed happily and passed on the message, which ran across the ranks of the multitude in almost visible waves. Giacobbe gave orders to Benito and two other lads, who apparently formed the communications squad, to go and tell the people that the British Navy hadn't been spotted yet; that they should have patience. Benito, his forehead getting redder and covered with large lentil-shaped freckles, saluted, yelled to his 'adjutants,' and dived into the multitude.

Giacobbe immediately saw Farkas, quite awkward in the crowd and being pressed against the rickety wooden railing of the bridge. The sun was rising high by then, and Farkas felt the sun rays pricking his sensitive skin. He thought he would stay for a few minutes, then sneak out — although he had no idea how he would be able to.

Giacobbe wriggled his way to him. He seemed pleased.

'Good morning,' he said. 'I'm glad you've come.'

'I haven't,' Farkas replied. 'I was forcibly dragged here by one of your storm-troopers.'

Giacobbe laughed. 'Come this way,' he said.

Meanwhile two quarrymen were working up an argument somewhere in the vicinity, and their raucous voices were slightly apart from the general din. 'General *Monte* Gomery,' one of them said. 'Of course he's Italian.'

'He isn't,' the second said.

'Oh, yes, he is,' the first said.

'Well, what do you think of it?' Giacobbe asked Farkas.

'No, he isn't,' the second quarryman insisted.

'Of what?' Farkas asked; 'the crowd and the Allies and history?'

'Yes.'

'Are you happy?' Farkas asked.

'Very happy,' the other replied. 'I've got a terrible headache, I'm nearly suffocating of heat and thirst, I'm worried about my brother, who couldn't come, and I'm apprehensive whether the British will arrive or not. I'm very happy.'

'Hopeless,' Farkas murmured. 'I'm going home. I feel a sunstroke approaching.'

Giacobbe looked at him. 'As you like,' he said. 'You're hopeless, too.' And he laughed, to blunt the edge of his last remark. Then Chef Luigi's sad, sharp face was thrust between them and he asked something. Farkas slowly made his way out.

'No, he isn't,' the second quarryman was still arguing.

So this is Giacobbe's historical happy ending, Farkas thought to himself; the Great Clinch with Democracy with music swelling *crescendo* and the grateful audience brushing away a discreet tear, grateful that virtue has triumphed, the villains have been punished, and the honest poor rewarded. As Farkas pushed himself forward, the sun and the noise and the crowd made him no longer quite aloof. He had to absorb the scene through all his senses, as if to collect material for some later work. He was soon doing it purposely, though unaware of the exact reasons for acting so. In the foreground of his mind he was aware of a vague spot, which felt like Giacobbe: a white-clad figure, arguing with him silently, while his eyes, ear, skin, and nose sucked up the scene like blotting-paper. 'So this is . . .' was a theme running under his conscious thoughts, running softly, soundlessly, in circles, recurring and edging into what he was seeing and hearing and smelling.

He is happy, Giacobbe, he thought, although he has a headache and other troubles; so is the crowd, although they, out there on the shore, have headaches, too, and bellyaches and other troubles. Some three hundred they were, if not more, standing in thick rows, waiting. They were happy; Farkas could feel their happiness. That was the chief emotion emanating from the scene, subduing all others, making people forget, making them concentrate on waiting on the Corso where they had not dared coming before. They stood on the benches fine people used to sit on: that made them happy too. They did not have to work today, and there was relief in the air, a slight sense of irresponsibility: they, out there, knew, of course, that even if the mysterious and much-discussed *Inglesi* did arrive, tomorrow the women would have to get up at six, as always, to clean and cook and deal with their men and children; that the men would have to return to work and tend the fields, or the grapes, or their nets. But they were absorbed in this cheerful, sunny waiting. They were all together now, and felt strong. They had heard strange words like 'freedom' and 'ownership' and 'democracy' before — a strange language spoken by the educated Giacobbe and some others; and although it was more comprehensible than the elegant but alien dialect of the townsfolk, they were still mysterious and awesome, those words of Giacobbe. But slowly they gained an immediate meaning. They discovered a link, in this cheerful waiting in common, a link between the mysterious words and the tangible world around them. They had only suspected what it really was, this link, and made no effort to ask questions of others, or of themselves; but some primitive and power-

ful evaluation was going on in them, and if one had
stripped the extremely simple truth of all the bubbling
nonsense they were feeling or saying, it would have
amounted to something like this: 'This is good, this waiting and laughter,' and 'That was bad, that war and hunger.'

Their happiness was loud, Farkas thought. No sense of
guilt on the faces, no awkwardness. A mother or two
would slap a child's face for treading on the flower-beds:
some of the benches were dusted and covered with a newspaper before they were stood on; but, on the whole, they
were beginning to feel at home, in a wonderful new home,
and gradually their self-confidence grew. The eyes Farkas
met were no longer so servile and shifty as before. They
looked straight at him, although they knew who he was;
they made way for him, but more in friendship than in
respect. 'Well, how is it? Have you seen anything, sir?' a
man in a back row asked him anxiously as he passed. Then
someone, a strong, big-breasted woman, patted his shoulder. 'The Allies are coming,' she half-sang, and patted
him again. The crowd immediately around her broke out
in hoarse cheering. Farkas just smiled, his smile becoming slightly rigid.

Then a young man, who must have heard of the Morgans but had never seen them, mistook him for Mr. Morgan, suddenly put his strong, warm arm around his shoulders, and shouted wildly: *'Viva l'Inglese!* Long live His
Excellency the Englishman!' Farkas gently protested.
'Look at his noble features!' the young man yelled, as if
he were a barker at a fun fair and Farkas the Bearded
Lady or an elephant. 'Look! Evidently he is extremely

cultured and courageous! Look, friends, look at his elegant
suit and beautiful necktie. Hurrah for His Excellency.'
Farkas could not help accepting the little demonstration
in good grace, smiling rigidly and throwing kisses at two
small infants perching on their mothers' arms. It took
him more than fifteen minutes to get off the bridge.

In the cool under the trees, he turned back to look once
more. As the light was less dazzling here, he saw more
details. 'By four o'clock they are going to sweat,' he consoled himself. 'Some of them might even faint. Their
digestions will be upset even if the British do arrive.
There will be sickness and hatred and greed as before,' he
added, to comfort himself. 'There will be murder and
idiocy; there will be lonely and lost souls at twilight; there
will be longing of ageing men and panic of climacteric
women; there will be pain and doubt and fear all the
same.' He was defending himself. He knew that he was
not quite aloof, that some crust of defence had been
broken.

Suddenly, leaning against a tree, he remembered
François, who, some thirty years ago, had complained to
him that he was hopelessly stuck in his novel as he felt
unable truthfully to render dialogue between two chim-
ney-sweepers. Farkas wondered if he could render this
crowd: the colours and the smells he knew, the light blue
of the sky, light with no substance, as if it were reflecting
the sea and not the other way round, a light and happy
blue with fluffy streaks of clouds, all of it mingling with
the faint vapour that rose from the water; the brown-red
of the woodwork of the bridge and the tightly packed
spots of black and yellow and pink of people; and the

deep, cool green of the foliage on shore. But it was thoroughly inadequate; Farkas knew that the word 'blue' was not blue; anyway, he had a profound suspicion of sensory epithets. François, for instance, believed that the words 'olive oil' should be substituted for 'love' and 'rhododendron' for 'God.' But there was little he could do to petrify the physical moment, the light, happy colours, the tension of waiting and joy of released excitement; the notes of gaiety, the touch of hot hands and warm woodwork. He tried to close his eyes and thus reduce the too many sources of sensation; to listen and smell, and feel the touch of the dry body of the trees.

The voices and the laughter merged now into a coherent chord, as if all the people of San Fernando were musical instruments, carefully tuned and directed by a maestro of genius. The music of their voices ran in ripples as he listened; here and there the shrill pitch of a woman's laughter or the yapping of a child upset the quieter harmony of the whole — but soon it would settle again. Occasional words, like 'mamma,' or '*sì, sì,*' separated themselves and came floating along like bullets in slow-motion. 'Pardon me, good friend,' somebody said distinctly quite near. 'Not at all,' the other replied.

He opened his eyes, for he could not reduce the cacophony to a choir or an orchestra any more. Quite near, the brass band had started to play again. He could see the yellow glitter of instruments from behind the darker columns of tree-trunks and bodies and foliage. They were playing some quick folk-song he had once heard. Loud cheering greeted this music; faces everywhere turned towards the band, a new, quickening move-

ment ran across the tight rows. 'Hurrah!' a young girl
shouted, and they all sounded like their own children.
Somewhere dancing began: he knew it by the sudden
definite rhythm that followed the crude air and was taken
up by one of the distant groups, and a rhythmical hopping
expanded. They formed circles, several of them, and danced
round and round; more and more circles joined up; and
soon a general wriggling, hopping, undulating mass followed the sharp stammering notes of the brass. He saw
the faces of the younger women, their flushed cheeks and
wild hair, and how their big, red mouths opened in the
ecstasy of united movement. Some of them closed their
eyes and looked like women making love; others had a
dark devil in their sockets, a glinting, coaxing devil, proud
and provoking; and scores of young breasts followed the
hopping of the feet. To and fro they danced, whirling
round the trees, knocking against the children who gaped
and giggled and old people who grinned toothlessly and
made disapproving, remembering remarks. Here and
there a hand was flung into the air, a dark shock of hair
flapped in the wind, and soon the swishing of skirts became a steady undertone to the dance, swishing and whirling, showing the strong, naked, dirty feet, brown and
crusted as they stepped and were lifted and stepped down
again.

Then, quite without warning, one particular spot in the
whole moving, dancing mass gained meaning, as if Farkas
had come, in a foreign newspaper, across his own name.
He looked again and saw Tony. She was dancing with
others, in a white dress, her yellow locks alien in the dark
crowd. She did not know the dance well and laughed em-

barrassedly, but soon, by watching those strong, dirty feet, she caught the rhythm and merged into the writing circles. A young, wavy-haired boy danced next her, gripping her hand and pulling her after him, and she followed gratefully. Now and then they looked at each other and laughed, although the sound of it did not reach Farkas. The young peasant twirled her around and caught her hips and pressed her against him, only to let her go again.

Farkas was angry, and he knew he was angry; it was a growling feeling in his stomach. Tony's group was pressed nearer, and he wanted to turn and walk away, lest she should think he was spying; but anger made him stay. His eyes followed her. She looked so very young and appetizing in that white dress. Suddenly she was tugged across a small space, almost fell over a squatting child, and as she spun round she saw Farkas. She stopped smiling for a second. He knew he must have seemed out of place and tried to screw his face into an ironic grin, and said to himself, *I could not do that dance.* Next moment she smiled again, not so carefree any longer but rather self-conscious, yet intent to go on and show Farkas how well she danced. She was jerked away and her face turned back again, and she looked at Farkas and waved her free hand and shrugged her shoulder as though to say: 'I don't know how I got into this.'

Farkas's anger slowly receded; now he had control of it, and could even produce one of his celebrated sardonic smiles; then the whole group lurched forward and she got free somehow and in one lovely spiral she almost fell against Farkas. She said nothing, just looked up at him, panting; then she laughed, stopped to catch her breath and laughed happily and laughed again and stopped and blew out her breath and shook her young, yellow hair and caught his hand. 'Come on,' she said, and she smelled beautifully young to him; 'come on.' He started to say, 'My dear child,' and meant to say something clever, lest she should drag him away to join the dance. Then they heard the plane and he never finished the sentence.

At first it was only a distant noise, a faint buzzing which few heard. Then suddenly, above the music and the general hullabaloo, the roar of an engine approached from above. The dancing stopped dead, though the band went on playing. Heads turned skyward, and there was a general movement in the direction of the shore. 'Don't push,' somebody said. Tony stepped closer to Farkas. They both looked at the sky between the trees. They could not see the whole expanse of the sky, nor the plane; but they knew it was diving on top of them, by the way the roar thinned out into a scream, and the scream was rushing down at an incredible speed.

Hands framed eyes, and almost simultaneously with the silence of the band there rose a great shout, Bravo! Bravo! and someone cried: 'Look, an aeroplane.' A child pushed his way between Tony and Farkas. 'Mamma,' he cried in a nagging voice, 'what is it?' There was no answer. 'Hurrah!' a little group, quite near, cried. 'Hurrah for the valiant English Air Force,' someone added. And again the same unknown voice from behind a neighbouring tree: 'Don't push.'

Now the plane was screaming right above their heads, and inside their heads, too; its noise was frighteningly near. The shouting stopped, and people, for a moment, were afraid the plane was going to crash. But the engine gave a pained groan, like an insulted beast, and levelled out, and its engine regained the smooth buzzing. Tony leaned against Farkas, craning her neck to see the plane. He felt her warm body, marvellously young and appetizing, and looked at her small pink ears; and slowly put his hand on her naked arm. She did not mind.

For a moment — a moment only — all his senses concentrated on that warm arm; so warm and young, with warm, rich blood inside, he felt. He tried to imagine her in bed; her soft long hair falling in waves, her face clean, childish, without make-up, her warm limbs and childish lips. He thought of a rainy afternoon, the best time for making love, with the memory of an old sun and of light in one's body; of a room, grey and quiet behind the autumn twilight, with the rest of humanity going about its business, leaving them isolated in the friendly universe of the bed. He would take her to Geneva, or somewhere, he decided, and immediately he added: Should I? He saw them in the train: she flushed, happy, embarrassed, hoping that now he would stay with her forever and protect her; he full of vague misgivings as to the wisdom of the new affair. They would go to Geneva and stay until the end of the war. He might finish the play (he would have to), and she could potter about, discover serenity and the Lake and his semi-sadistic loving fits, to which she would submit with the martyr smile of a mother. He tried to make some calculations; how long could she last? Six months? And then? Present her with a flower shop in Berne, or Vienna? She would make no difficulties, he felt; be too proud to cry in front of him. Or would it last longer, a year? And should he take her at all?

Gizella would arrive one day, perfectly composed and elegant and cool. Only a slight twitch in her left eye as she sized Tony up. She would be unhappy about Tony's figure and hair and youth, but thoroughly pleased about the scar. She would suggest a walk (she was always at her most attractive in a beige sports suit and flat-heeled shoes) and she would start: 'My dear Stefan, how nice the child is! How long will she last? I'd like to know so as to make arrangements. This beastly war forces me to stay in Switzerland; but I *could* go to Berne, of course, much as I hate it. Incidentally, where did she get that scar? It wasn't you, was it?' Yes, Gizella.

He pressed the soft arm, while the plane approached again. Tony, he said to himself. Yes, I will take her. Quite clear that she attracted him. For a long time past he hadn't felt so much uncomplicated desire for a woman. Gizella was so entirely different; it was she who imposed her calculated lust upon him; he had, more or less, drifted into the affair, and let Gizella take care of agents, bills, contracts, shoppings, and sex. He needed someone, and Gizella, with her suspicious mind and body, her sly panic at getting old and dropping out of the shrill bustle that went on between stage and society, was there like the irritating female voice when one dialled TIM. He needed her because, despite all her faults, Gizella was accommodating: she knew when to shut up, leave the room or the country, or stroke his brow. True, it was all carefully planned, and driven by panic and snobbery, but she made no difficulties and could be exciting — especially when her elegant body became slowly hot and made her forget, for a brief time, her age and cocktail parties.

He could not say what Tony would be like. She sounded bright and had some superficial culture; there was
pride in her, he felt; pride that had grown a hard crust
under so much humiliation. But her 'soul' did not interest him; it was her soft, warm body and her walk and
her hair; and something else he did not yet know, something he had been missing all the time, some soft and ever-
present sympathy and forgiveness in her. He knew she
would forgive him anything he might do, and cry silently
and discreetly in another room, not to disturb him. He
could see her sitting by his bed when he was laid up with
a cold and reading the thermometer and preparing a com-
press or a laxative.

Yet, somewhere in this brief moment, a small clock
seemed to be ticking, and the moment grew, and he said
to himself, Now it is a crossroads, now my free will can
decide, now the future is in my hand, and it is one of those
rare moments when one thinks one is consciously influ-
encing life, one's own and others'. Often, when he was
writing, he had the same sense of standing at a crossroads,
a sense of power. Should Angela sleep with Victor, or
shouldn't she? and thus change the whole course of the
second act. If so, there would be murder at the end and
a new character named Inspector Kropatchek might be
born. If I made Angela refuse Victor's invitation to his
rooms, the second act would peter out in domestic mirth.
The decision rests with me, he had thought then, writing
that play; on me alone, and its consequences will be momentous. Thousands of people will chuckle and go smugly home, warmed by a pleasant comedy of bad manners —
or else they will listen grimly and depressed, feel pity for

Angela and themselves. It is all in my power. That was how he had felt then, writing *Amen*; that was how he felt now, touching her arm. She smiled at him. The choice was reduced to this: he might slowly draw her closer and quite simply say: 'I would like you to come with me to Switzerland tomorrow. I love you.' Or say something else and let her arm go. Life could be reduced to such situations. Yes, I will take her, he thought. His visit to San Fernando had been an utter failure. He had had a few pleasant walks and meals; but he had seen terror and death and listened to a good deal of dull and dangerous talk. Was that all? He could not leave with such failure; he must have some justification for having come. 'I will take Tony,' he said.

The cheering rose again, and now Farkas saw the plane flying at roof-level over the bathhouse, coming towards the shore. 'For Saint Antonio's sake, don't push,' the mysterious voice said again; then Farkas heard the new noise, the rut-tut-tut of guns. He did not recognize it at first; it sounded like the belching of a fabulous beast. He saw the smooth surface of the water getting goose-flesh and it was sprinkled with jumping drops; like jumping beans the bullets danced on the surface as the guns rattled. The cheering somehow still did not die; it had all happened too quickly.

Farkas watched carefully, and concentrated his attention on the route the little bullets were splashing as they approached. He felt no fear: he had no time for it. He knew vaguely what was happening, but as he had never been machine-gunned before, his reaction lagged. The bullets came nearer and pattered over the noisy row of children, women, and men who were sitting on the water-front dangling their feet over the sea. The rut-tut-tut-tut was now accompanied, not by a quick, splashing noise as before, but by hard stony knocks, for not all the bullets hit the sea or the soft flesh of children, women, and men; some missed their target and knocked at the stony rind of the promenade.

Marvellous, Farkas thought as he was watching, mar-vellous how a few hundred small steel tubes filled with a certain combination of chemicals can effect such a variety of changes. Some twenty seconds ago the crowd was surg-ing forward, hailing with cheers, waving and shouting, the conquering friend who had come at last. Those in the first row had been particularly content; they had a ringside seat and were comfortable but for an occasional sharp pebble pressing against their buttocks. True, they had had no lunch yet and were sweating considerably. One of them, a vineyard labourer named Zacconi, had a sore throat; the wife of the peasant Faenza had acute gall-stone, but would not go and lie down and miss the fun for anything in the world. Paolo, the younger son of Alber-to's brother-in-law, a fat, cropped-haired boy who had just discovered the first sweet notion of love, had a bad tooth which he was fingering constantly despite the repeated ad-monitions of his mother. He had that dirty index finger in his mouth when the bullets hit him: one, near his eye, which went through and killed him, some ten or eleven in his chest, riddling his lungs, and the rest in his shoul-ders. A dozen bullets completely wasted. First he fell back under the impact of the little steel tubes, then some-how regained his balance (or so it seemed) and lurched forward, falling headlong into the water. He disappeared for a moment or two, rose again, his sweet, round bottom bobbing cheerfully until he slowly sank.

Marvellous, the little steel tubes. Rut-tut-tut-tut — the splash, the silence of soft flesh, and the contact with the stones of the promenade. A few seconds only, and how profound a change! There was the Caruzzo girl: only twelve, but much too developed for her age, to the grief of her parents. She had large, soft breasts already, and her hips were forming with alarming plasticity. Only two of the bullets hit her, both in the abdomen. She, too, fell forward, and as her parents were at the other end of the Corso, she was sadly overlooked in the screaming, push-ing, surprised panic that ensued, and drowned before fully recovering consciousness, which she had lost a moment before falling, with a deep, silent gasp which said inward-ly: 'Holy Mother, what is it?' At twelve-thirty-one and twenty-eight seconds she was an overdeveloped, soft-breasted child, who would surely be led (in a year or two) to a lonely haystack beneath the hills, a soft, sweet-smell-ing haystack where some young lad would have taken her without protest and she would have lain with open, happy eyes, staring at the sky beyond his head, staring and pray-ing for a long, happy life for the child she would one day bear. At twelve-thirty-one and thirty-five seconds she was going under in the cool water, leaving behind the sudden gasps, the unfettered terror of voices and bodies; the dis-tant but approaching cry of her Medusa-faced mother, pushing her way across the struggling, fleeing mass, her eyes darting wildly, the control of her nerves gone, scratch-ing and hitting her way through the mass, calling Rosina, calling Rosina. All that was gone as from twelve-thirty-one and thirty-five seconds, as she slowly sank into the cold, velvety water, feeling nothing, knowing nothing, wishing nothing, her hopeful and excitable breasts sinking slowly, carefully, with the haystack beneath the hill dry and sweet-scented and empty.

Such marvellous changes the little bullets brought about during their short, spluttering journey! There was the vine-grower, Stefani, an elderly man of fifty with a black moustache and black eyes slightly popping out of his head, whence his nickname, the Carp. He had been discussing taxes with his friend, Pietro, another farmer, when the bullets found his throat and back. (He was sitting half-turned from the water, pressing a point home to his friend.) The Carp wasn't particularly interested in this festive waiting; he was a sour realist, suspicious of feasts, and he had only come under pressure from his mother-in-law, a tiresome, lazy old woman eager for gossip and light entertainment. Now that he was there, he had dragged his friend to the waterfront, ordered some children to move off, and squeezed a place for them.

'Now, then,' he argued, 'I do not purport to know what our Giacobbe is doing about taxes, or if he'll be able to do anything at all. There have always been taxes, there always will be taxes, the only difference being that they steadily increase with each change in Government. Because, my friend' — he tapped the other's chest with his finger — 'why do Governments change? Why? I ask you, why?' he repeated, to prepare a climax. 'Because' — he drew out the word in triumph — 'because they need a pretext for raising taxes. And as long as they keep raising them, my friend, what difference does it make whether they do it with the help of the Germans, the English, or the Patagonians? As it is . . .' the Carp continued, irritated, getting hold of Pietro's lapel and pulled at it. 'As it is . . .' Then he looked and saw the plane and the noise grew tremendous, and suddenly he felt a sharp pain hitting first his throat, by his Adam's apple, and then his back. His hand flew to his throat and he felt it hot and wet and alien, and then he seemed to be choking with some warm liquid and had to cough, and he felt a slashing pain zig-zagging down his throat, and slowly, in a gathering cloud, nausea overcame him and Pietro's lapel, the water, the voices receded as fast they could down a long, dark tunnel.

Another typical example of the change the little bullets effected was the case of the young girl Paola, who was sitting with her sister Carlotta and Filomena the chamber-maid at the Paradiso with her beautiful young bosom and old, wrinkled face. They were sitting by the water, near the bridge. The two girls giggled a lot, and their faces grew redder and redder under the sun. Filomena was squeezed in behind them, crouching most uncomfortably in her gay Sunday frock which was much too tight and short, and she had to keep a scarf over her breasts lest Il Trovatore the barber should see them, for he kept watch-ing her while absent-mindedly answering the endless in-quiries of his plump son.

Paola and Carlotta were arguing about the *Inglesi*.

'They're all blond,' Paola said dreamily. 'Very tall with large teeth.'

'How do you know?' the other mocked her.

'I've seen them in the picture-paper. Very tall and thin.

They've got long, extremely bony legs, and, the paper said, a Bible with their whisky.'

'I don't fancy bony men with Bibles and whisky,' Carlotta said.

'They're not all bony,' Filomena interposed. 'Far from it. Many of them are small and fat. I know,' she added significantly, giving up shielding her breasts from Il Trovatore's stare.

'You see,' Carlotta teased her sister. 'You see, you know-all.'

'The picture-paper showed them bony.' Paola asserted herself, and reddened even more. *'Enormously* tall and bony,' she added to support her case, and looked for other details. 'They're rich,' she went on, conscious of Filomena's scepticism. 'Enor-mously rich, the paper said. They live in Londra.'

'London,' Filomena said dryly. 'All I said was that they're not *all* tall and bony, but often small and fat. What about Churchill?'

There was a pause and Paola thought hard. 'Oh, well,' she said with a shrug, 'obviously he's a Jew. Of course,' she brightened up.

'Foa is a Jew,' Carlotta said, to show that she, too, knew something of the subject.

'Churchill isn't,' Filomena said, and tried to shift away from the barber's gaze. 'He is just one of those small, fat Englishmen.'

While they went on arguing, Paola tucked her big toe into the water, splashing it. She was angry with her sister for her insistent mockery, and she thought of a long line of enormously tall bony men stepping ashore, blond and foreign; and one of them would perhaps come and ask her for a dance; and marry her, and take her to London, so that she could one day write a letter to Filomena and Carlotta, a cool, matter-of-fact letter explaining how tall and bony the English all were. Then she heard the plane. Like the others she listened and looked in puzzled excitement, and joined in the general cheering. She was slightly worried now they had really come and Filomena and Carlotta might be right. She imagined a whole regiment of small, fat Englishmen coming ashore. 'Please, Saint Anthony,' she said, watching the plane dive, 'please, sir, don't make them small and fat, don't let Carlotta be right.' She waved her hand and heard her heart going drip-drop in her throat. Then suddenly something happened to the world: something knocked at her heart, which stopped, and she waited for it to start again; but it didn't, and then she was dead.

Marvellous changes. Farkas saw the first red and bronze spots of blood emerging from nowhere, and when the noise approached until it seemed and sounded right in front of his face, he quickly ducked behind a tree, drawing Tony with him. He felt her very near now, and through her white frock came the busy ticking of a heart. She said nothing, but her breath came in quick, small gasps, and she, too, must have understood what was happening. 'Don't worry,' he said quickly, and closed his eyes. Above their heads there was a clattering noise, like hail clattering on roofs and pavements, except that it was softer, and it soon stopped. 'Oh, God,' she said. He felt her hair against his cheek and his hand went up to stroke it. 'I will take her,' he thought; then suddenly she felt limp in his arms.

He opened his eyes; the noise, the shouts, the violence of hands and legs, were tremendous. They all fled blindly, in many whirlpools, losing all coherence and identity. It was no longer a crowd; only countless panicky individuals driven by the inexorable urge to hide, to find safe cover, to be as far as possible from the waterfront. 'Let's go!' he shouted at Tony. She leaned heavily on him. 'Are you all right?' he asked. He could not see her face; she was leaning on him with her back turned to him. She nodded her head. He could not concentrate on her: they stood in the centre of a rushing man-vortex: they could not move. Now she turned to him. She was very white; her scarred cheek dominating, with the sweet innocence of the dance irrevocably gone. 'What was it?' she cried. The noise, the crowd, the panic around them, grew. Farkas put his arm round her shoulders and stood on tiptoe, trying to find a gap somewhere. He did not quite know what had happened, although he had seen the bullets splashing their way across the water and saw some blood, and knew that there must be dead somewhere, dead and seriously hurt. A thin voice was wailing at an even pitch; 'Rosina,' a woman cried in despair, *'Rosina mia, Rosina!'*

The Corso echoed quick, heavy, thudding steps. The voices of fear whirled around and Farkas caught some — 'Come on!' and, 'My God!' and, 'Help!' — but he could not concentrate. Now that the first frozen spell was broken, he became sharply aware of his own body. He heard his heart beating madly, he felt his knees trembling, and there were sweat-drops sliding down his forehead. 'Come on,' he said, and tried to push forward. But the crowd immediately in front of him pressed on thickly.

They trampled over the flower-beds, and then, thinning out by the grove, ran as soon as space was free. To the left four or five men were trying to get to the sea, and behind them came the call again, *'Rosina mia, Rosina!'* Farkas saw a pale, thin woman darting between the men, her sharp nose nearly white, her dark eyes jumping to and fro, jumping much as those bullets had. A tall man waved his hand above the others. 'Let me go!' he shouted.

The confusion increased. Here the crowd was thick, driven by cross-currents, and it was only at the edge of it, some fifteen yards away, that some could get free and sprint on. The crowd carried Farkas and Tony onward in the direction of the olive grove. Some still hunched their backs as if afraid of being hit; some kept stumbling and craning their necks skyward, looking for the plane. Farkas tried the authoritative method. 'Excuse me,' he called out sternly, 'will you please let us through?' No one heard him. *'Rosina!'* the woman cried. A man dug into Farkas's back with his elbow. 'Stop that!' Farkas shouted, and turned and saw an old man, his face devoid of coherence, ferreting his way blindly. 'They have come,' he muttered, 'they have come.' *'Rosina mia,'* the woman cried, farther away now. Somebody fell over a bench and overturned it. Others turned quickly and saw the gap and jumped over the bench one by one, clumsily. 'Sheep,' Farkas thought. Finally he and Tony were carried with a great sudden wave to the grove; the mass loosened up, and Farkas could walk.

'Well,' he said, and blew out his breath. He was still supporting her, and he did not withdraw his hand. She felt so warm and so marvellously young. 'Look, Tony,' he began, and then saw the back of her white dress, so crisp and clean and white before, covered now with an ugly brown spot spreading slowly. It had the shape of a brown, dirty sponge. For a moment he did not understand and felt disgust. He withdrew his hand and looked at it and it was sticky with blood. 'I've been hit,' she said, and smiled apologetically. She looked straight up to him and then almost shyly away, as if she knew some delicious secret; and then she fell forward.

He caught her in time; she was heavy in his arms, all the marvellous youth and vigour gone. Limp and messy she looked, her hair falling forward in a big wave. 'Tony,' he said, and was frightened. The brown, sponge-like spot was spreading all over her back, and her linen frock was lapping it up. He looked around for help. A man was running past them and turned to Farkas.

'It was the Germans,' he panted, 'I saw the cross on the belly of the plane.' He stumbled over his own feet and nearly fell.

'Come and help me,' Farkas shouted at him.

The man stopped. 'It was the Germans,' he said, as if to excuse himself.

'Come here!' Farkas yelled.

The man nodded. 'Yes, sir,' and came over to him.

'She's been hit,' Farkas said. 'We must carry her to the Sanatorium.'

The man said, 'Yes, sir,' and got hold of Tony's feet and lifted her, and Farkas held her under her arms and felt the wetness of her frock. They walked with difficulty; people kept running by, brushing and knocking against them. The man helping him was a small, foxy man with a red nose. His face was grey and his lips were wet with saliva. 'Yes, sir,' he kept mumbling. 'This way, sir,' he added.

Farkas thought of the Sanatorium: of Doctor Schmidt and a white room and Tony lying there, pale and rested — rather like Leonardo. 'It'll be all right,' he said to her. 'We'll be there soon, Tony. All right? You're not too heavy, no.' He knew he was talking incoherently. She was heavy, and he felt his heart beating in his throat. I'm not so young, you know, he thought, not so young. Look at her dress. She's been hit. Doctor Schmidt. White room. I will take her to Geneva. Goodness, she's heavy. I must stop for a second. 'Look here, I think we . . .' he said to the man; and then he stopped because he saw the man's face as he looked at Tony.

'What's the matter?' Farkas cried. 'What's the matter?'

The man shook his head and leaned forward to inspect her face once more. 'Oh,' he said disapprovingly, pursing his lips. 'Oh. But she's gone, sir.' And he looked up at Farkas and was scared that Farkas might punish him.

'What are you talking about?' Farkas said; but he knew.

They carried her to the lawn near the rock-garden with the idiotic dwarfs. People still kept running by, in pairs and small groups, spreading out in the main square and hurrying up the main street and by the Sanatorium and the Kursalon, all hurrying to the village. Part of the panic was gone: here the sky was wide and they did not feel so trapped as under the close trees of the Corso.

They laid her down on the grass and Farkas knelt down to examine her face. She was ugly, because she was dead; her mouth was open and her eyes dull and dumb and dead.

'Shall I bring the doctor, sir?' the red-nosed man asked.

'No,' Farkas said. 'Go away.'

The man said 'Yes, sir' and went; his steps were small and soft on the grass. Farkas sat down, and closed her eyes.

Curtain

An hour later the Germans arrived. First came a dozen motor-cyclists in field-grey uniform, their faces nearly covered by goggles, rifles across their shoulders; then two light tanks with an open staff-car between them. In it sat an officer whose face Farkas could not see clearly from his window, and Father Giuseppe. Behind them rolled two trucks full of soldiers, with a mortar and two machine guns. The staff-car stopped on the main square; the rest roared on to the Corso. Most of the people had gone by then; only a few couples loitered, rather aimlessly, along the walls of the Regina, hesitant to return to the village and attracted by terror.

'As the cyclists reached the sea,' Ugo later told Farkas, 'they found it pretty deserted but for eight bodies laid out in a neat row by the music pavilion, with Doctor Merlin of the Sanatorium and a nurse attending to some thirty wounded lying or sitting on benches. The motor-cyclists rode up to the bridge. Some shots rang out from the bathhouse, hitting nobody. A fusillade followed, and when two of the cyclists advanced, ducking behind their cycles, the bridge blew up, leaving a gap of forty yards or so between the shore and the bathhouse. At the same time the

Allied flags were hoisted on top of one of the towers of the bathhouse. They did not stay long. As soon as the tanks moved up, they fired a salvo which ripped off the wooden tower, flags and all. The shooting from the bathhouse continued sporadically, but as the Germans did not answer, it stopped. The officer in charge of the Germans walked down to the Corso with Fritti and Father Giuseppe. They were deep in conversation and inspected the casualties. The officer ordered the trucks to pick up the wounded and take them to the Sanatorium. Then he gave some instructions to his men, who took up positions along the Corso, with one tank and the mortar standing where the bridge used to join the shore, mounting their guns at point-blank range on the bathhouse. They did not shoot, though; they just waited. The second tank and some of the troops went off to the village. On the Corso the Germans sat down and started to make coffee and eat their rations. They were mostly elderly men; they looked tired and silent. The bathhouse kept silent, too. They saw Giacobbe and forty men out there waiting; waiting for what?'

Then Ugo went, confused, for Farkas said nothing and did not seem to listen or care. It started to rain. It was a quiet, unhappy rain that made no sound. The square under Farkas's window soon turned into an even grey, with countless shiny spots where the rain saturated the dust of the morning and it gathered in a wet, heavy mess. Slowly the lights changed and the brightness was all gone. Farkas sipped his tea, sitting on his bed, like a clumsy old man visiting rich relatives. He felt empty, and as soon as Ugo left he put out the light.

As he sat, his eyes went on a circular excursion around

the room. They stopped at his elegant pigskin suitcases on top of the cupboard. He nodded. Obviously, there was little left to do now. It was justifiable to think of suitcases, of packing, of paying bills and leaving. The room was getting chilly. Outside a heavy truck rumbled by.

As he crushed his cigarette against the side of the imitation copper ash-tray, there was a knock on the door. 'Come in,' he said.

Ugo entered, hesitant, a grey, sloppy figure in the lighter framework of the door, illuminated indirectly by the lamp in the corridor.

'Signor Farkas?' he whispered, blinking in the darkness.

'Yes, Ugo, I'm here. What is it again?'

The waiter entered and closed the door.

'Don't put on the light,' Farkas said, clearing his throat. 'I'm resting my eyes.'

'Yes, sir. I came for the tea things.'

He shuffled nearer and leaning over the table pottered with a cup. 'The Colonel wants to see you.'

'What Colonel?' Farkas asked.

'The German. He's downstairs in Signor Fritti's office.'

Farkas turned. 'What does he want?'

'I don't know, sir,' Ugo said. 'He is nice, I think.'

'All right.'

'Will you be having dinner upstairs, sir?' the waiter asked. He was carrying the tray with both hands.

'Yes,' Farkas said. 'And tell Fritti I'm leaving tomorrow.'

Ugo stopped. 'You're leaving, sir?' he asked.

'Yes, I'm leaving.' Farkas's voice was irritated.

The waiter said: 'Oh.'

'What's the matter with you?' Farkas asked.

'Nothing,' Ugo said.

Farkas switched on the table-lamp.

'Tell the Colonel I'll see him in a few minutes' time.'

'Yes, sir.'

Ugo closed the door behind him with his right heel, slowly. Farkas looked and then waited a few seconds. Then he went to the bathroom and looked into the mirror. He washed his hands and combed his hair and returned to his room to put on his jacket.

The corridor was empty, and he quickly walked to Tony's door and listened; the hotel was quiet. Softly he turned the knob and entered. The room was dark except for the light grey square of the window. He walked across the room and closed the shutters and the window. Now it was completely dark. He turned and leaned against the window-sill. Slowly the whiteness of the bed emerged from the darkness. He stood for a few minutes, his arms folded, resting his weight on his right foot: he listened, but the hotel was exceptionally quiet and the square sounded quiet and the rain sounded quiet. There was a faint, sweet scent in the room. He went to the door and put on the light. The room was much smaller than his: a narrow bed with a night-table, a dressing-table, a small cupboard, an old-fashioned washstand, two chairs, and a table: that was all. Here she had lived, and the room was full of clues. On the night-table stood a decanter with water and a glass, and there was a small bottle with pills, and a book. He walked over and picked up the book: it was a time-table, an old time-table, frayed and soiled. On the cover she had written a few numbers: 38, 57, 109. He turned to page 38: *Trains to Paris and London*. She wanted to go to London and Paris, and she knew she would never, never go to London and Paris, and she had played with this old time-table. Trains to Paris and trains to Cherbourg and Marseilles and boats to America and Australia and God knows where. Like Lili, he thought, Lili in *Amen,* Lili, the little waitress who wanted to go places and see things. He put the book back and looked at her bed. It was unmade: she had slept in it that morning. The pillows were crumpled and the sheet furrowed and a light-blue nightgown lay across it, curiously alive. He lifted it and held it against the grey light and it hung in his hands, warm and soft. From the washstand hung two stockings she must have washed the night before, and in the corner stood shoes in a neat line. He walked to the table, and there was a picture, framed in silver, of an old fat woman, presumably her mother. He opened her cupboard; it was crammed with light dresses, and he fingered them for a few seconds and drew them apart as if he were looking for a hidden corpse, or the murderer. Ah, well, he thought. He put out the light again and sat on her bed for a while, holding her pillow in his lap. Then he went downstairs.

The Colonel was a handsome man with almond-shaped eyes, very light and blue, a graceful nose and a moustache. He reminded Farkas of an unhappy tiger, with his curiously cut eyes and his lazy, attractive movements.

'Herr Farkas?' he said. He had a beautiful deep voice. He rose from behind Fritti's desk as Farkas entered. 'Good evening.' He reached out his long, bony fingers. His fingernails were filed into triangles. 'Glad to make your acquaintance.'

'Good evening,' Farkas said, and shook the German's hand.

'I'm Colonel Rabe,' the officer went on. 'I've heard a great deal of you,' he added.

Farkas sat down without waiting for an invitation.

'Yes?' he said.

The Colonel blushed. He was handsome, the Colonel, in an awkward, unmilitary way. His hair was greying at the parting and above the temples. His uniform was not particularly tidy: there were two or three conspicuous stains on the tunic, and his collar was unbuttoned and his boots badly needed a shine. He did not look straight into Farkas's eyes; he kept looking elsewhere and his long fingers would plough into his tousled hair. He drew his chair to the side of the desk to create more intimacy. At first he seemed to be absorbed in his thoughts, resting his hands on his square, bony knees; then he looked up for a second at Farkas's face. He fumbled in the breast pocket of his tunic and produced a crumpled paper packet of cigarettes.

'Smoke?' he asked.

'No, thanks,' Farkas said. 'I'd rather smoke a cigar.' He took out his pigskin case, made a careful choice and lit a cigar. 'Would you like one?' he asked.

The Colonel had just lit a cigarette. 'No, thank you very much.' He held out a match to Farkas's cigar. His hand shook a little.

'Would you like a drink?' the Colonel asked.

'No, thanks,' Farkas said, and watched him through the smoke.

The German looked up with a shy, forced smile. 'I saw

a play of yours while on leave in Vienna. Brilliant play.'
He looked away and started to pluck at his moustache.
'Brilliant, though the production isn't what it used to be.'

'No,' Farkas said. 'Things generally aren't what they
used to be.'

The Colonel gave a soundless, nasal laugh; but he became serious again. 'No, we all miss Thimig and Jaray
and *die* Darvas. All the same, it was a delightful evening.'
He looked up for a second. He smoked carefully, as if this
were his last cigarette. 'I'm sorry I had to ask you to come
and see me.' He paused, and was about to continue when
Farkas cut in.

'It's quite all right,' he said. 'I should have come, anyway.'

The other looked up again. His large mouth smiled
politely; his eyes remained unhappy and tigerish.

'Really?' he asked gratefully.

'Yes,' Farkas said. 'I want to leave tomorrow. I supposed I'd have to ask your permission, or something.'

The Colonel started to scratch his knee.

'That's quite all right, Herr Farkas,' he said. 'Quite all
right. You're very popular in Vienna and Berlin.'

'Am I?' Farkas said. 'Very gratifying.'

There was a pause.

'Where do you propose to go?' the Colonel asked.

'To Switzerland.'

'Lovely country,' the German said. 'Which part?'

'Geneva.'

'Of course,' the other said. 'Haven't you got a villa
there? Reinhardt used to visit you there, didn't he?'

'Yes, I suppose he did.'

There was another pause.

'But what is it you wanted to see me for?' Farkas asked.

'Oh, yes.' The Colonel was staring at his boots. 'I must tell you that it was Father Giuseppe who suggested it. Nice man, the Father. He thinks very highly of you.'

'Yes?' Farkas said curtly.

The German got hold of the left side of his long moustache and brushed it rapidly between two fingers. 'You know this man di Bocca?'

'Giacobbe?' Farkas asked. 'Yes. Why?'

The German sighed and brushed his hair from his forehead.

'Oh, it's one of those things again,' he said. 'Everywhere, these vicious circles. When the Abbot was clever enough to send that message through to Ravenna, asking for help against the rebels, I said to myself at once, it's one of those things again, one of those circles. Somebody shoots at somebody and he has to be shot lest he shoots somebody else; but if he is shot, somebody else starts shooting again out of revenge, and the whole thing goes on. There's no way out. We had to come, of course, and we have to shoot several somebodies. But it's good mathematics to shoot as few as possible, so as to have fewer new somebodies shooting at us, or at our friends next time. It'll never stop, unless somebody shoots everybody else.'

And if I had the guts and the verve and the passion, Farkas thought, I would shoot you right now; for you have killed Tony. But I will not shoot you because I possess no weapon and your hands are stronger than mine and, what is worse, I like you because I pity you; and somebody, one day, soon perhaps, will shoot you, anyway.

'No one is free from fear any longer,' the German went on, staring at his boots again. 'It started with a few shots; but owing to the size of the average European family, the somebodies grew to thousands. It is all like a momentous vendetta; and no one can stop it, now or ever. There is the fear of losing one's life and the fear of disgrace, or disobedience, or punishment. It is terrible,' he added, shaking his head, 'terrible, this fear. It has erased the borderline between coward and hero, hero and fanatic, fanatic and madman.'

'Well,' Farkas said. 'I'm just an old-fashioned coward, scared of loud noises, darkness, of being shot at or suffering pain. If I weren't, I should, somehow or other, kill you; for you have killed a dear friend of mine.'

The German blushed. 'Have I?' he said. 'How?'

'Your plane,' Farkas said. 'That dirty plane you sent over. But never mind, I am a coward, physical and moral. So we can go on chatting.'

'I am sorry,' the Colonel said. 'It had to be done. I am really sorry.'

'Don't be silly,' Farkas said. 'I am quite incapable of hate, or anger. I want to get out of here quickly: nothing else matters.'

'I'm not to be blamed,' the German went on. 'Really I'm not. I had to give that order. It's one of those things; everybody is afraid. I am afraid. One could say, I am afraid, therefore I am. Slowly, this dread envelops us all, like a shadow, this sense of standing on the edge of nothing. Everything shifts save dread and its core, anxiety. We should all be lost without it, without this horizon of fear; there is nothing but fear till death us do part.'

Farkas cleared his throat.

'I'd rather not stay much longer, if you don't mind,' he said. 'What is it you wanted?'

'Oh, yes.' The German rubbed his eyes with his knuckles, lifted the crumpled packet and fished out a cigarette. 'Bocca.' He sighed. 'Well, again, what do you expect me to do? Now here is this San Fernando. We didn't start the trouble. These wretched peasants went crazy; there has been outright rebellion, a great deal of violence, and several of our friends have been murdered or molested. I am here to restore order and punish the guilty.'

'You were certainly unexpected and most unwelcome,' Farkas said. 'They don't like Germans here. They were waiting for the British.'

The officer shrugged his shoulder and fingered his moustache.

'The British are hundreds of miles away,' he said. 'Fritti started a rumour and those half-wits believed it. Anyway, the British, too, would have had to restore order and punish the guilty. Wouldn't they?'

'It depends what you call punishment.'

The German blushed again.

'Come, come,' he said. 'The punishment for murder is the same everywhere.'

'It depends what you call murder,' Farkas said.

'Homicide outside the law,' the Colonel said.

'It depends what you call law,' Farkas said. 'Anyway, what do you want me for?'

The German rose and walked to the door and back again. 'I'd like you to go and talk to those people.'

'What people?'

'Giacobbe di Bocca and his friends.'

'What for?'

The Colonel said: 'I'd like you to persuade them to surrender.' He swallowed hard. 'I know it's a painful duty, but you're the only one who knew them well and whom they trust. I don't want any more bloodshed. All I want is Giacobbe, and his brother whom we've got already. They can't get away, the others. They would be shot to bits by my tanks if they tried. All I want is surrender and Giacobbe, who will be shot.'

'Listen,' Farkas said angrily. 'I've told you I'm quite incapable of hate and anger, but I can be seriously annoyed, and I am annoyed right now. What do you take me for? I am not a diplomat and I came here to rest and work and I have nothing to do with those people, or with you. I want to leave tomorrow and I propose to spend my time, until then, in my room and alone. Why don't you send them Giuseppe or Don Teofilo? Why don't you go yourself? It's your job.'

The German shook his head. 'They wouldn't listen to Father Giuseppe or Don Teofilo or to me. I know they wouldn't. They're in a bitter, heroic mood, ready for suicide. There are forty of them, locked up in that ridiculous bathhouse. They're desperate. They need somebody to bring them to reason.'

'And to the gallows,' Farkas said. 'Well, I'm not going to play the pimp for your hangman.'

The German drew a chair near to Farkas and sat down.

'Let's please not argue,' he said in his beautiful deep voice. 'You know perfectly well that you're the only one who could persuade them.'

'I wish you wouldn't use that word,' Farkas said irritatedly. 'I hate it.'

'Words make no difference. I don't want any more bloodshed; I don't want atrocities; I want a simple trial and an execution, strictly legal — and then to return to Ravenna.'

Farkas rose. 'Ask somebody else,' he said.

The Colonel looked at him, then blushed again and scratched his knee again. He said shyly: 'You want to leave, Herr Farkas, don't you?'

'Yes, of course.'

'You know it depends on me.'

Farkas said coldly: 'I think I've still got some friends who might help me if I wired them.'

The German nearly whispered in his embarrassment. 'Of course. But it would take time. In the meanwhile, I'm in charge here. And of course, I might send a report saying that your part in this affair wasn't quite unambiguous. Then it would take even longer.'

He looked away, like a child who has just admitted some major offence. It's hopeless, Farkas thought, looking at the officer's handsome, tired face; it's quite hopeless. He gave orders and the result was the death of Tony; he is blackmailing me now, and yet I cannot make myself feel hate or anger. I cannot raise my soft hands to strike him, or even shout at him, or be rude. I don't like him any more; although I still pity him. He is so terribly scared; he probably doesn't sleep at night, listening to voices inside him. I don't like him, but I feel nothing violent about him; he leaves me utterly disinterested and cold. All I want now is to leave, to leave this bloody place behind me and never to think of it again.

'Aren't you afraid,' he said softly, 'of me?'

The Colonel did not look up.

'What do you mean?' he mumbled.

'I have every reason to kick you,' Farkas said pleasantly. 'And more.'

'But look . . . ' the German said.

'You killed a girl I was very fond of,' Farkas went on. 'And now you are blackmailing me into doing a dirty job.'

'I shall take you to Ravenna myself,' the Colonel said. 'Tomorrow.'

He is not afraid of me, Farkas thought. If only . . . he thought; if at least I had the eyes of Daniel.

'Let's go,' he said.

'One of my men will take you out in a boat,' the Colonel said.

Outside, it was still raining, discreetly, with hardly any sound. A soldier in field-grey uniform was waiting for them, and the Colonel talked to him in German and the soldier saluted and looked at Farkas and saluted again. He was an ugly man, this soldier, his uniform much too big for him.

'Well, good luck,' the Colonel said to Farkas. 'I'll see you tomorrow.'

'Yes,' said Farkas.

He started off in the rain with the soldier trotting after him. When they got to the corner of the main street, Farkas turned for a moment. The Colonel still stood in the entrance, capless, and he waved. He looked a tall, lonely figure in the rain, but Farkas did not wave back. The soldier said something in a guttural northern dialect, but he did not answer him either. Their steps were

soft on the wet road. San Fernando looked very quiet,
with an occasional figure walking across the main square;
Farkas could not see whether they were soldiers or civil-
ians. All the windows seemed to be closed; nothing remained of the warmth and glory of the morning: the flags
lay in the mud like violated girls.

They walked to the grove and Farkas looked at the
small square lawn where, three hours before, he had laid
Tony down. Then, there had been sun, and the lawn
was green and silky, and despite the ugliness of death, she
was beautiful in her white dress, lying on that little lawn.
They had carried her away later, but he had not followed
them and remained sitting on the lawn; and now it was
covered with the even greyness of the rain and a small
dirty pool was forming in the middle of it.

Then they got to the Corso, so alien with the soldiers
and the tanks, and there was a rowing-boat waiting near
the bridge. The water had a dirty colour. Then they were
off: the oars made a soft, obscene sound as the soldier,
slightly nervous now, rowed Farkas out to the bathhouse.
He put up a long pole with a piece of white cloth on it,
and as he faced Farkas and the shore, he kept glancing
over his shoulder to the bathhouse, which stood out vaguely against the dark sky. The rain suddenly got milder and
sparser, but the sky remained dark with long, angry rows
of clouds merging from a light, watery grey into angry
brown near the horizon. Between the darkest row and
the thin, vaguely etched shoreline by the Abbey Hill,
there was an almost chalk-white space, finely interwoven
with rays of light. This lighter strip was like a window
opening into another, ghostly world, standing apart from

the puffed clouds which hung immobile over Farkas's head, and by their different tone of colour seemed to divide the panorama into separate shafts of light. It was a curiously motionless scene. The only moving thing was Farkas's boat, which slid slowly over the choppy waves while the oars made their soft, obscene sound, like old lips smacking at a young body.

'It's going to rain some more,' the soldier said. He wore spectacles.

'Yes,' Farkas said. He felt chilly over the water and turned up the collar of his overcoat.

The bridge was in a sorry mess. The explosion had blown away most of it, leaving the rest mutilated. Bits of wood were floating near the boat, and by the bathhouse the broken ends of crossbars rose raggedly, like the fangs of a sea monster. Long, sharp splinters were hanging from them: and all this against the inflated angry brown clouds. The little motor-boat which had brought Giacobbe and Alfieri back from their patrol earlier in the day was squashed against the landing-stage, bent and curved under the impact of the explosion, and the sea washed through it, entering by the miniature portholes and leaving by a gaping crack; the choppy waves kept entering and leaving, every time washing away another bit of woodwork.

They approached the end of the bridge and the soldier stopped rowing, and turned nervously as if afraid of being shot in the back. Along this side of the house ran a covered balcony on which some of the 'family cabins' opened. The door of one of them stood ajar, and somebody's head appeared slowly. Farkas waved his hand rather foolishly, as if he were paying a visit to some old friends. They were quite near now, drifting on the waves, and a man stepped out of the cabin with a rifle in his hand.

'I have come to see Signor di Bocca,' Farkas cried, and rose to let the man see him fully, but he had to sit down again as the boat was rocking uncertainly.

'Yes, Signor Farkas,' the man answered.

The German moved his oars unwillingly, but the boat somehow slid alongside the bathhouse.

'Good evening, Farkas,' Giacobbe's voice said suddenly.

Farkas looked up and saw him leaning forward over the side wall.

'Good evening,' Farkas said, and stood up. 'I have come to see you.'

Giacobbe and the man with the rifle bent down. Farkas grabbed their extended hands and stepped onto a piece of woodwork that jutted out from the side of the balcony. The others drew him up with a sudden jerk. Farkas turned back and called out to the German: 'You'd better wait here.' And to Giacobbe: 'Don't shoot him, will you?'

Giacobbe made no answer. 'Come this way,' he said.

He led the way towards the inner corridor that ran round the bathhouse with more cabins and showers and lavatories. At the end four men squatted in the gloom, turning towards Farkas with no smiles or greeting. Giacobbe opened a door and they entered one of the larger family cabins, perhaps five yards by five, with wooden bench along each wall, and a broken mirror at the far end. The wooden boards were old and grey and damp, bent and broken in places and fitting together not too well; one could peep into the cabin next door between each loose board, and beneath their feet the grey-green waves shone through with a chill.

Farkas knew this cabin. He had had his regular one, Number 9, whenever he came to bathe, but one Sunday morning the place was overcrowded and Alfieri had put him in this large, unfriendly, dark place, where no sun came in except in careful watery shafts of light through the roof. He remembered this cabin because of the many obscene words and crude drawings on the walls, especially by the mirror, where somebody with thick, childish pencil lines had drawn three fat couples engaged in various forms of love-making. The artist had wanted to be quite explicit, so he had written above each figure the name of the person he had meant to portray. The first and fattest couple was Father Giuseppe and an unknown woman labelled Sister Maria, the second was Alfieri and Lisabetta the postmistress; the third was partly erased.

A few rifles lay in the corner and in a big pile some towels.

'Wait outside,' Giacobbe told the man with the rifle.

'I've brought a message for you,' Farkas said as soon as they were alone.

'I thought so,' Giacobbe said. 'Sit down.'

Farkas sat on one of the benches, near the mirror. Giacobbe remained standing in the centre of the cabin. A faint glow of light penetrated from the roof, and they could hear the slight patter of the rain.

He looked very tired, Giacobbe. His strangely contrasted features, so disjointed now, were covered with a network of light and shadow. His eyes looked two dark circles, and Farkas could not see his pupils; only the small oval of the whites shone. His lips sagged downward in a despairing curve, like those of a defiant child nearly in tears. His hair was wet and tousled: he must have been standing in the rain. His white suit was soiled and torn and water kept dripping from the edge of his sleeve; he wore no collar. He started to pace up and down and his shoes made a smacking sound, as they were full of water.

'Have you got a cigarette?' he asked.

'Of course,' Farkas said. 'Here you are.'

He came over to Farkas and took a cigarette. His hand was shaking badly.

'Here,' Farkas said, 'you'd better take the whole lot,' and handed him the box.

'Thanks,' Giacobbe said, and pocketed the cigarettes. He produced a lighter, but it did not work.

'Here you are,' Farkas said, and his lighter gave a sharp, efficient click. The flame lit up Giacobbe's face for a moment.

'Well,' he said, and breathed in the smoke deeply and gratefully. 'Let's hear your message.'

He walked away again and stopped in the middle of the cabins.

'The officer commanding the Germans asked me to go and see him,' Farkas said. 'This evening. He seems to be quite a nice fellow. We had a long conversation about fear.'

'Marvellous, isn't it?' Giacobbe said — 'to have nice, long conversations with nice Germans between a little slaughter here and there.'

'Don't be bitter,' Farkas said. 'I can't help it if I found him nice and we had a talk. Anyway, he could have shot you to bits long ago. He's got two tanks and several guns lined up along the Corso, pointing at you.'

'Well,' Giacobbe said. 'What's the verdict?'

'He said he wanted me to come here and persuade you to surrender,' Farkas went on. 'At first I refused; I told him I'm fed up with playing the ambassador for everybody. Then he argued that I'm probably the only man you would listen to. I can't think what made him say that; probably Father Giuseppe — anyway, there it is. He wants all of you to surrender and come ashore by nine o'clock tonight. He will send out some rowing-boats. He said no harm would come to anybody.' He stopped and looked up.

Giacobbe stepped nearer.

'Except you,' Farkas went on — 'you and Leonardo.'

'I see,' Giacobbe said.

'I am not going to persuade you or anybody,' Farkas continued quickly after a pause. 'I want to get back as soon as I can. I am leaving tomorrow for Ravenna and thence for Switzerland. All I want is to give you the message. I can't tell you if you should trust this German or not. He said he wanted to avoid unnecessary bloodshed and to punish nobody but the leaders of the rebellion.'

'Nine o'clock?' Giacobbe asked. 'By nine o'clock, you said?'

'Yes, nine o'clock,' Farkas replied. 'It's seven now.'

Giacobbe started to walk up and down; finally he stopped and sat down in the far corner and brushed the back of his head against the wall.

'I take it you must enjoy this,' he said finally, without looking at Farkas, who did not know if he had his eyes closed or not. They were two black, blind circles. 'The perfect dramatic situation.'

'Don't be silly,' Farkas said. 'First of all, I dislike dramatic situations in my private life; secondly, this is anything but perfect. It is a conflict of guns, not of hearts, therefore no conflict at all. It is an ugly and pathetic thing, and I deeply sympathize with you, but I am not a war correspondent. Anyway, I wish you wouldn't be bitter.'

'There are forty-five of us here,' Giacobbe went on, ignoring Farkas's last remark. 'The choice is quite simple. Do you think the German could be persuaded to let Leonardo go? He's a sick man and innocent.'

'I don't think so,' Farkas replied.

'Shall we be hanged?' Giacobbe asked.

'No,' Farkas said. 'You'll be shot.'

Giacobbe's head fell forward.

'Do you remember this morning?' he asked, in a very low voice.

'Can't hear you,' Farkas said.

Giacobbe looked up. 'Do you remember this morning?'

'Yes, I do,' Farkas answered. 'I am very sorry.'

'Do you remember the sun and the flags?' Giacobbe asked. 'The flags and the laughter. Have you ever seen such a happy crowd? It was so very beautiful.'

'Very beautiful.'

'They were so very happy,' Giacobbe went on. 'So very, very happy. They have never been so happy, never in their lives. That was this morning at ten and at eleven and twelve, and then the plane came. Benito came on his bicycle, crying, and said the Germans were returning. Then we blew up the bridge and came here because there was nowhere else to go. It was hopeless, of course, and we knew it, but we had to come and hide behind these thin walls and wait. We saw when they took the dead and the wounded and we saw the tanks moving up.'

Quietly he broke down. His left hand squeezed the edge of the bench and his right hand went up to cover his face, and he sobbed in a deep, sick voice, his head shaking in little convulsions, sobbing quietly, unashamed, as if he were alone. He went on talking, babbling in between, but Farkas could not understand him: little bits of words came out, torn, garbled words. Farkas kept his eyes on the hand squeezing the edge of the bench. The sound of sobbing was muffled as Giacobbe tried to suppress it, and it sounded hollow and deep and sick as if he tried to push it back inside his chest, but some of it tore itself free and broke through Giacobbe's closed lips and from under his right hand, small bits of sobbing that sounded like painful coughs. The waves shone through between the loose boards of the floor, and outside the rain fell with a steady hiss and where it hit the roof, it sounded like peas drumming on parchment. I haven't wept for years, Farkas thought. When did I weep last? he asked himself; oh, it must be twenty, thirty, forty years ago. Then Giacobbe stopped crying and the sudden quietness made Farkas look up.

He rose and walked over to Giacobbe.

As he walked, he heard his own footsteps, and he knew once before he had walked towards someone, someone who was sobbing and whom he had not consoled. When was it, he asked himself, was it thirty or forty years ago? One couldn't possibly remember; it must have been thirty years ago or more, and the picture of Daniel came into his

mind, the picture of Daniel as he sat on the edge of the
sofa in the dining-room after he had come back from the
doctor. He was sitting on the edge of the sofa, hunched
up, with his beautiful fair hair hanging over his eyes,
staring in front of him as if he did not hear Farkas coming. Then he looked up and said, in a dull voice: 'I'm going to be completely paralyzed, Stefan.' Farkas stopped
by the dining-table and said: 'What did the doctor say?'
Daniel gave no answer, just lifted his left hand, lifted it
high, slowly looking at it, and he tried to move his fingers
and could not. 'The fingers are gone already,' he said.
'The fingers are gone, and slowly it will creep all over me.'
Farkas said nothing, and Daniel slowly let his hand fall
and started to cry, so softly and beautifully, with as much
taste as if he were singing a song. He did not cover his
face and did not try to suppress the tears; he did not sob,
or jerk convulsively; he just sat there, clutching the edge
of the sofa, crying softly in a constant flow of harmonic
sounds, his face not distorted, his face smooth and serene
as if he were singing a song; he even looked at Farkas, with
a look that asked, not for compassion, or help; just looked
at him to see if he was still there. Farkas just stood and
stared and could not understand Daniel, or his tears, and
could not move to go and sit by him and pat his hand, or
kiss him, or say something as simple and harmonic as the
crying of Daniel.

He halted in front of Giacobbe.

'People will remember you,' he said; for what else could
he say?

Giacobbe looked up; his face was terribly messy; he
looked like an overgrown child. He wiped his nose with
the back of his hand.

'I wasn't crying,' he said and paused — 'for myself.'

'I know you weren't,' Farkas said, and sat beside him. He put his hand on Giacobbe's shoulder.

'I wasn't,' Giacobbe repeated. 'I was crying for the village. They were so completely happy. Now it is gone, and it will never come again; never. They can lose only once, these people, only once in such an utterly complete way, and they are defeated for ever and ever. What if peace really comes one day? They will always remember today.

'I'm sorry,' he added, as if he had realized for the first time that he had been crying in front of someone else. 'My nerves are in a pretty bad way. It's been too much.'

'I wish I had a drink on me,' Farkas said.

'You are very kind, Farkas,' Giacobbe said, and looked at him. 'Very kind.'

He rose.

'I shall go and tell them now,' he said vaguely. 'Tell them to go back to the village.' He turned around to Farkas. 'I'd better go now. Are you coming?'

'Must I?' Farkas asked.

'No,' Giacobbe said, 'you needn't. But I'd like you to stay with me until they've all gone.'

'All right,' Farkas said.

'I won't be long,' Giacobbe said, and walked out.

In half an hour he returned, much quieter, with a grim calmness. They went out to the open corridor and watched the others go ashore. The Germans sent six small rowing-boats, six fat little boats, and five or six men sat in each, one of them rowing. The boats slid slowly over the choppy waves with the rain beating finely upon them, upon the roof of the bathhouse where it made a thousandfold and persistent noise, like so many water-taps someone has left turned on at night. The sea wasn't as quiet as when Farkas had come, the waves rose higher near the shore: the tide was coming in, and as the waves rose they turned from grey into a white streak and they washed against the floor of the bathhouse too, swishing like heavy skirts. The light was fading and an even, grey night was descending. The trees of the Corso merged into a single, lacy line, with an occasional flutter among the higher leaves. Farkas could see one of the tanks which stood near the entrance to the bridge, and some soldiers beside it watching the boats coming in.

'It won't be long now,' Giacobbe said. 'Let's go inside for a while.'

In one of the boats Farkas saw Alfieri and the Jew Foa. Like the rest, they sat numbly, staring in front of them. All boats had left by now.

Farkas wanted to say, 'It's getting too cold for me,' but changed his mind.

'They'll be back for us in half an hour,' Giacobbe said.

Farkas felt the wetness of his soles and of his overcoat. His hand, deep in his pocket, touched the silk lining, torn at one corner, touching upon the usual pocket dirt, little fluffy balls of dust and tobacco and bits of paper. The edge of his collar was getting wet, too, and it rubbed against his neck. He ran his index finger round inside the collar.

'Let's go,' Giacobbe said, and slowly started to walk. Farkas followed him. They turned into the inner corridor that led round the bathhouse. It was dark there, and Gia-

cobbe lit a match and took Farkas's arm. His eyes slowly
grew accustomed and soon saw a faint light filtering in between the boards of the wall. Then they turned left and
walked along a short passage out to the side facing the
open sea. It was much colder here. The sea was endless
and deserted, with small, white-headed waves lifting themselves and falling again, grey-green and endless, losing
themselves in the undulating line of low clouds along the
horizon, puffed and rolling clouds which were fast losing
their last colour. That chalky, empty gap in the clouds
by the Abbey Hill was gone, filled with loose and growing
blackness; the whole sky seemed to have moved nearer,
spreading low over the twisting waves. Farkas's collar was
beginning to irritate.

They walked along the central row of cabins, Giacobbe
now slightly ahead. The whole place had the sad quietude
of someone betrayed and forgotten. Farkas remembered
the blazing sun of the morning, the tanned bodies of other
mornings, the blue friendliness of another sea. There in
the corner, in front of the open door of his office, Alfieri
used to sit, wrapped up in a huge bathing-towel, looking
like an inflated Gandhi, bending over the feet of white-
skinned townsfolk, hating them quietly and politely. Near
the springboard, in another corner, Don Teofilo used to
sprawl his obscene toad body, his wailing voice echoing
down the corridors as he shouted for the nurse.

Now, for the first time this evening, Farkas heard the
wind. It came from the north, from the 'Rotten Corner'
by the Abbey. It skimmed the surface of the sea, hit
against the walls of the bathhouse, and whistled through
countless cracks and crevices. It was a cold wind, smelling

of an early autumn, of dead leaves and wet hills. It caught an old newspaper and whipped it along, rolling it near Farkas until it stopped by the leg of a bench. His collar was getting very irksome; he loosened the knot of his tie and ran his finger round inside the collar once more.

The footsteps of Giacobbe echoed with a hollow sound. He walked to the edge and touched the railing and looked at the unfriendly sea. The wind caught his hair and lifted it and he looked like a mad musician with his big, dark hair fluttering. Then he turned and walked back towards Farkas.

He seemed to be much quieter now; his face was almost rigid, showing no suppressed emotions, only a kind of businesslike determination, as if he had arranged everything and there was nothing to worry about any more.

'They behaved marvellously,' he said. Giacobbe spoke with surprising ease. His voice was matter-of-fact. 'Most sensibly. I told them the position. First they unanimously refused to surrender, but then I explained to them again and ordered them to return. They were very disappointed that they could not go on fighting. Mr. Morgan cursed in English and Foa wept and kept yelling, "Let me get at them, please, dear, honourable sir, let me get at them." I calmed him down. I told them they would be safe and I told them something about the necessity of changing tactics according to the objective facts. Little Foa argued; he always does. And yes, I told them about your part – how ready you were to help. They cheered.'

'Thank you,' Farkas said, and sat on a bench. 'Could I have a cigarette?'

'Oh, I am sorry,' the other said. 'They're yours, of course. Here you are.'

'I only want one,' Farkas said. 'Before we go.'

'Yes,' Giacobbe said, and started to pace up and down again. 'Before we go.'

His steps echoed sharply. He stopped by the railing, looked out at the sea, then turned and folded his arms. His voice came strongly, as if helped along by the wind.

'I only wish Leonardo could have been here,' he said. 'I'm sure he would have changed his mind; he would have understood that there are no doubts; that this is the real thing.'

He came back again. There was the wind, the sea, the manifold rain and the human steps, hitting hard on the wet, shiny boards.

'But he will know,' Giacobbe went on. 'He'll understand, never fear. I could not convince him with a few words. Words are never enough. But he'll know.'

My feet are getting very cold, Farkas thought; my collar is a damned nuisance, but I can't let him down and just go. He won't have a priest; he must have somebody.

He imagined Giacobbe sitting in a chair, tied up tightly, shot in the back of the head. Giacobbe started to walk again.

'Oh, yes, he'll know,' he continued. 'He'll understand how easy it is to lose oneself in a maze of useless abstractions, of First Principles and Ultimate Realities and Essences; how easy to be lured away by the pretty pattern of formal logic, how pleasant to play with big words that go round and round and mean nothing. He will know that it is hopeless to seek the permanence of abstract Truth, or Beauty, or the immoral void of wine and whores. Every-

thing changes, moving towards unity, in which man is but
the highest form of change in the changing world; there is
unity beneath crystals and stones and daffodils and apes
and Dante, one great unity of change, and all is matter,
including man, but no matter is quite inanimate; and
man is the slave of chromosomes and economics and reflexes, yet inside the once rigid atom electrons dance a
beautiful, incalculable ballet.'

All right, go on, youngster, Farkas thought; you won't
have a priest, but you can have me as an audience. Go on
and relieve yourself.

If only my feet weren't so cold, he added to himself.

'Oh, yes, he will know,' he repeated it stubbornly as
if to convince himself, 'and you will know, too. You tried
to help him, poor wretched, half-educated Leonardo, and
tried to persuade him to give up the vulgar job of revolution and to adopt an attitude of cynical detachment. What
plagiarism, Farkas! Poor Pyrrho tried it before by preach-
ing ataraxy, that deep, aloof happiness to be achieved, he
said, by throwing passion and curiosity overboard.'

All right, go on. I shall finish my cigarette in five minutes' time, Farkas thought. Then you will have to shut
up: for ever.

'You know, Farkas' — Giacobbe came nearer again —
'this reminds me of the anecdote about Pietro the peasant,
this detachment of yours. He complained to the doctor
that he was unable to eat. The doctor said, "Let's see,"
and gave him a chunk of bread. Pietro gobbled it up in
no time. "Well, what are you complaining about?" the
doctor said. "You can eat beautifully!" Pietro answered,
"Oh, well, if I've got food!" If only we had seclusion and

peace for fornication and philosophy. But we haven't; we shan't have for some time.'

He walked away again. His voice came from afar off.

'Oh, no, that won't do, lofty cleverness and subtleties and flippancy. Man is neither a sexy beast nor a mixture of Plato and the Archangel Gabriel. His place is humbler, but surer; clearly fixed in the great hierarchy, somewhere between a piece of coal and a Bach fugue; and his job is to live and help to live.'

Back he was again. If only my feet . . . Farkas started to think.

'Of course, you're even more difficult than Leonardo,' Giacobbe said accusingly. 'You're not even interested in understanding the world, and, least of all, changing it. You're not interested in values; therefore, what good would it do to tell you that no values are absolute and immutable, that they change by century and continent? Rockefeller was a major villain of his age; yet there are thousands of lives his Institutes saved. Nobel was a model benefactor, yet his dynamite maimed millions. Goethe was the only integrated man of his century, yet he refused a loan to Beethoven. And Hitler loves flowers; Socrates was a homosexual, and, as far as I know, Saint Francis of Assissi may have been an addict to satyriasis. But the answer to dialectics is not escape; it is to realize the main trend, which happens to be the struggle of the humble to own the world collectively, and help it along. The Germans out there with their tanks are therefore bad; Father Giuseppe, Don Teofilo, are bad, too. So are neutrals like you; and I am good. And this goodness does not mean an abstract halo over my head, but drawing the logical conclusions. Therefore I am not going ashore and you are staying with me.'

If only my feet . . . Farkas thought again. 'What was that?' he asked. He shuddered; his overcoat felt wet inside and his feet were quite numbed.

Giacobbe came slowly back to him and stopped in front of the bench.

'I said, I'm not going ashore' — he sounded very friendly and firm — 'and you are staying with me.'

Farkas scratched his shoulder. 'What do you mean?'

'We're staying here, I said.' Giacobbe sat down next to him. 'That's simple, isn't it? Don't you understand?'

'No, I don't. I'm certainly going ashore, very soon. You'd better come, too.'

'We're not going,' Giacobbe said emphatically. 'It's so simple. I thought of it after I'd left you in the cabin. I knew we had been defeated — I knew it long ago. Now the end has come, with surrender, the humiliating march back to the village, and execution for Leonardo and myself. It is utter defeat. The Germans came with their tanks and guns and the loveliness of the morning went. The incident is finished; a minor episode that happened in a ridiculous Italian village has ended. Some people rose, triumphed, and were defeated. It has all happened before and is probably happening somewhere else right now, with no consequences, no moral. Only with us it won't be like that.'

He slid nearer on the bench. Farkas saw his dark, tired face, wet and dirty. He fixed his eyes on Giacobbe's chin and said to himself, I must go. He was frightened now; but not of Giacobbe. He had a vague, horrible feeling that if he tried to move; he wouldn't be able to. He lifted his hand and tried to move his fingers; they were cold and numb, but moved perfectly.

'Farkas, you mustn't go,' Giacobbe said. His voice was low from so near. 'You mustn't. *We* are unknown and nameless; just another incident in the backwater of the war. No paper would write about us; no communiqué would be given, no broadcast made. A little revolt, quickly quelled with a few corpses, and two men shot at dawn. You mustn't let us die like this. Thousands die on the hills and in the valleys; their uniform makes them unknown; they are not even dead, only Casualties; thousands die in camps and gas-chambers. They all die for the same thing, but they don't know as I do.'

'We'd better go,' Farkas said meekly. He felt embarrassed, as if Giacobbe had tried to borrow some money. But the fright was still in him.

'Farkas, please,' the man's voice was low and deep, 'please stay. Who would remember us? But you're famous, world-famous, very famous.'

'You're mad,' Farkas said.

'Farkas, please, *please,*' Giacobbe begged him. 'I know I could not convince you with words; my thoughts are Chinese to you. I know San Fernando and I and Leonardo are only an incident for you; at the best, characters for a play. I know you are bound by no links to us, to anybody. But then think of the gesture, of the pose. All *I* could become is a target for a firing-squad, but *you* could become a martyr, a Byron, if you stayed here to die.'

'You're mad,' Farkas said, and looked fully in the eyes of Giacobbe. He felt weak and raised his hand slightly to move his fingers. 'They've got tanks and guns and would shoot us to bits.'

'Exactly,' Giacobbe said. 'The boat will come for us soon. I'll open fire on them — they will first hesitate because of you, but I'll go on shooting until they have to shoot back.'

'Let's go,' Farkas said.

'Farkas, please,' Giacobbe said. 'Please agree to stay. I won't let you go, anyway. My mind is set. I know what I want and I'll make you stay even if I have to shoot you. Please.'

'I must go,' Farkas said.

'Farkas, look.' Giacobbe took his arm and pulled Farkas towards him. 'You don't realize what I mean. I'm perfectly serious. I'm as good as dead, with no chance of escape. Tomorrow I'll be shot in the back, sitting in a chair. I want to stay and die here.'

'I must go,' Farkas said.

'Why?'

Farkas looked away. His mind was working mechanically on established lines. He heard his own voice. 'My dear fellow,' he said, 'I'm cold and miserable. I don't want to die here, or anywhere else. I've got to go to Switzerland' — he slowed down, remembering Tony — 'I've got to finish a play, I . . .'

He felt Giacobbe's rigid gaze upon himself. He slightly turned his head towards the other.

'Go on,' Giacobbe said.

'A play to be finished,' Farkas repeated. 'I want to go to Switzerland; I don't want to die here, or anywhere else; I've got a good many years to live, I . . .' He lifted his hand again; his fingers were wet and cold, but moved.

'Yes?' Giacobbe said.

'A play to be finished,' Farkas said. 'Your idea is ridiculous. I want to go now.'

'Why?' Giacobbe asked softly.

The rain was stronger now.

'What business is it of yours?' Farkas said. His voice was getting numb and mechanical. 'I told you, didn't I? I want to be in Ravenna tomorrow.'

'Why?' Giacobbe said again.

Farkas made a great effort to speak. 'Because' — he swallowed hard — 'I like young girls, big meals, hot baths, and Swiss mornings.'

'Is that all?' Giacobbe asked.

Farkas felt the blood slowly draining away from his face. Inside his pockets he moved his cold fingers; inside his shoes he tried to move his numb toes. His heart was beating fast. I am for ever running away from that question, he thought angrily, unpunished.

'I am going,' he said sharply. He rose and turned and slowly walked towards the exit.

'Don't go,' Giacobbe called after him unhurriedly and with kindness. 'Don't go, please. I should have to shoot you.'

Farkas heard his steps behind him, unhurried, kind steps. He was walking along the central rows of cabins, by the shower and some benches; there was a stool Alfieri used to sit on and behind it his 'office,' a dark cubby-hole with towels and keys and little bottles of sun-oil and scissors and a broken tin can in which Alfieri cooked his food, and some cheese on one of the top shelves. One had to cross this dark cabin before leaving or entering.

He quickened his steps. He didn't turn back.

'Farkas,' Giacobbe called. He was catching up with him.

I must go, Farkas thought. He's mad. He was half-running now. He was surprised that he could run with ease. He felt pleased about it, breathing evenly as if preparing for a long run. He was almost at the cubby-hole.

'Farkas!' Giacobbe cried after him.

Get to the bridge and there shout for help; they could hear him, out there on shore, Farkas thought. His breath was even: he was pleased; he could even try to run faster. He hadn't run for years.

'Farkas, stop!' Giacobbe cried. He was close behind him. 'You can't get away.'

He quickly stepped inside Alfieri's office and turned for a second and saw Giacobbe walking along the cabins, his black hair flapping in the wind, and he saw that Giacobbe had a gun in his hand. It's a question of time, Farkas thought. A question of time. Piles of towels lay in a heap in the corner. The shelves were empty: Alfieri must have taken his belongings and knick-knacks. Hide in one of the cabins until the German comes. He stopped for a moment, listening to his own breathing: still it was even. Giacobbe's steps were just outside the door. He hesitated for a moment, then hurried on, opened the entrance door, and stepped out into the vestibule. Through the windows he could see the maimed bridge, thrusting on end, less its broken bars jutting towards the shore like fangs. The water was deserted. 'Farkas,' came the call again. He turned to the left and started to run, lightly, keeping his hands, balled into fists, on his chest as he used to — oh, when was it? — forty or thirty years ago, sprinting around the dusty school grounds with Daniel. He ran lightly and with ease and he was pleased. My legs are light, he thought. If he could see me! But he wasn't thinking of anybody. Behind him the door opened: Giacobbe was following him, though lagging behind a bit. Question of time, Farkas thought. The corridor was some forty yards long; he would have to reach the inner corridor, dark and complicated with side passages, and then hide in a dark cabin and wait; wait.

Slowly his body became heavier. Of course, I can't go on very long, he thought, and quickened his pace. There! He reached the dark, murky corner and turned. It was pitch-dark in here; much darker than when some time ago he had arrived and walked along with Giacobbe. For a few seconds he saw nothing, but slowly fine rays of light emerged from the darkness: rays of the evening that was slowly passing into night. Behind him, as he turned his head for a moment, was the pale, light square of an opening, staring into the sea and to the shore. He sprinted on; then stopped, listened. The unhurried steps approached evenly. He hesitated for a moment, then opened the next door and peered in: it was one of the small cabins, dark and shapeless, with a faint glint of grey-green across the boards of the floor, the grey-green of the waves, quieter now. He quickly entered and closed the door behind him; and waited.

Slowly the steps knocked nearer on the dark wooden floor. Giacobbe must have been some twenty yards away: he could not see which door he had gone through. He listened: only the slow, even steps, without hurry or anger, almost strolling, almost sure of themselves. Then the voice again:

'Farkas!' Giacobbe called.

He suppressed his breathing for a few seconds and, leaning against the wall, listened. The steps were a few yards away. Question of time, he said. That is all. Even if he found me, I could argue for time.

'Farkas!' the steps halted.

'Farkas, I am going to find you,' Giacobbe shouted. So he did not know he was so near.

'Farkas, please.'

Giacobbe opened a door, waited, and closed it again. His steps moved on. Farkas pressed his eyes between two boards where there was a narrow crevice, but he could not see anything. The steps moved again; another door opened and closed, and then another.

'Farkas!' the call came.

The steps turned and returned in his direction. Now Giacobbe was opening a door some four or five cabins away. Question of time, Farkas thought, and suddenly felt very weak: a cold, sour nausea overcame him, and he groped his way to the bench and sat down. The cold, sour weakness crept up from his stomach, up his spine to his nape and down his throat, and his fingers felt sticky and cold. Small stars swam in front of his eyes: he brushed the back of his head and could not suppress a belch. I shouldn't have run, he thought. Now he is going to find me. He blinked and ran his tongue over his lips. Another door was opened and closed; quite near, but he could not say how near. 'Farkas,' the gentle voice said, invitingly. The weakness spread to his limbs; he blew out his breath, he said 'Phew!' and fumbled in his pocket for a handkerchief; his hair felt sticky too, and his collar — his collar was the worst; he undid his tie and unbuttoned his shirt at the neck and ran his hand around his throat. His feet started prickling; but the swimming stars left, one by one. He blinked again and his door opened gently.

'Farkas,' said the gentle voice. 'Are you there?'

'Yes,' he said. 'Leave me alone. I'm sick.'

'Come out, please,' Giacobbe said. 'Into the fresh air.'

'Look, Giacobbe' — he tried to get up, and had to try again. He felt very faint now; he touched the wet walls to support himself. 'Look, Giacobbe,' he repeated.

He felt Giacobbe's hand touching his arm and getting hold of it kindly and leading him out into the corridor.

'You shouldn't have run away,' Giacobbe said. 'I'm not going to hurt you.'

He led Farkas along the dark corridor; at the end of it Farkas saw the large, grey square of the opening. Their steps were slow on the floor. The nausea was inside his throat now; he was afraid of vomiting; slowly sounds receded and the world felt muffled and sour; like being under an anaesthetic, counting twelve, thirteen, fourteen, and then getting the numbers garbled, saying sixteen, eighteen, seventeen, twelve, twenty-three.

'Look, Giacobbe,' he mumbled. 'Let me go, I'm sick. It's no use keeping me here.' He was frightened that Giacobbe would not hear him properly; that he was mixing up his sentences. He made an effort and raised his voice. 'I'll do what I can for you. I'll talk to the Germans. I'll write . . . yes, I'll write a play about you, if you like.' He knew that the last bit of his sentence was shapeless and senseless mumbling. 'It'd be much more use . . . useful' — he tried it again — 'useful.'

'Never mind,' Giacobbe said. 'There are times when the only useful thing is to die.'

He felt Giacobbe stopping.

'Are you afraid, Farkas?' he said.

'Yes,' he said. 'Are you?'

The cold nausea left his head and crept back to his stomach. He felt his brain clearing up a bit.

'Yes, I am,' Giacobbe said.

Farkas felt him unbuttoning his overcoat; he felt silly and ashamed. 'What are you doing?' he murmured — 'what are you doing, you pig?'

He felt Giacobbe's cold, dry hand on his forehead; it was marvellous to feel those cold, dry hands. 'Thank you,' he said. The hand gently stroked his forehead and his hair and his cheek, gently and delicately and with so much kindness; the nausea was fading away and Farkas nearly felt like kissing that hand. He leaned against the wall; the hand was so cold and dry and kind. Question of time, Farkas thought.

'Don't be afraid,' Giacobbe said. Farkas felt him moving, and then there was a sharp, quick push: he saw a flash of light and heard the cracking report of a gun. Almost at once he felt wet warmth around his stomach, a sweet, wet warmth that spread slowly. The nausea was gone, though his head did not get clearer. He felt no pain; he was very, very tired. I'm going to faint, he thought.

'I'd better sit down,' he said, surprised how far away his voice sounded.

He felt Giacobbe's hand slipped under his arm.

'Are you in pain?' Giacobbe asked.

'No,' Farkas said. 'I'd like to sit down.'

Giacobbe leaned him against the wall, then bent down and lifted a blanket out of somewhere. Farkas blinked and saw that they were by the opening. 'There,' Giacobbe said. Farkas was afraid the wet warmth would suddenly burst open and spurt forward if he bent down. Giacobbe helped him to slide down, with his back touching the wall. For one second there was a slashing pain, but it went again. He sat in the corner, propped up by the angle of the walls. Giacobbe was fussing with the blanket, wrapping him up.

'Give me a cigarette,' Farkas said.

Giacobbe stuck a cigarette in his mouth and held a match for him. Then he sat down in the opening and Farkas saw a machine-gun in front of him.

'Can you see the water from there?' Giacobbe asked.

'Yes,' Farkas said.

Slowly the warmth was spreading. He felt comfortable and warm and grateful, for the nausea had gone and his feet were warm, too, and his collar did not irritate him any longer. Huddling up in the corner, a great quietness came over him as he watched Giacobbe crouching by the machine-gun, silent and intent. He felt as if he had taken a dose of morphine: the pain of being alive was gone, his skin felt as if wrapped in tender cotton wool by a motherly hand, like nestling in a big soft circle of space with no edges, where he could stretch in all directions and yet meet no hardness. The warmth around his stomach radiated throughout his body, filling him with lightness, and soon the world, this dark, nightly world, stood around him as behind a filter, or tears. Yes, his breath was clearing; like moving clouds it felt inside his head, moving

clouds that revealed a clear and certain background, a
busy, moving, colourful background. He tried to move
his fingers, but he could not.

*Now it is no more no more this sour sickness in head
and stomach no more sweaty hands I cant move my fingers any more — sometime ago I still could but now I
cant let me see —*

*My feet theyre warm now very warm and I cant feel the
hard wet cold soles any more — Giacobbe put this blanket
around me Giacobbe who shot me therefore this is the end
as they say it who says it — now it is no use thinking of
them in inverted commas whoever they are —*

*Now quickly I must see if there is anything to do if
there is anything I have forgotten let me see — Tony Tony
Tony is buried Tony is buried up in the village beneath
the hills with lots of Italians poor Tony quite by herself
even now by herself with no friend and protector I really
did not love her not really love her it was pity that senti-
ment I always hated because women always abuse it always but Tony did not Tony was genuine Tony deserved
it I could have taken her to Geneva lived with her in villa
by the lake let her grow confident and happy happy no
use thinking vaguely what is happy*

*Was I happy when was I happy I could count occasions
five times ten times — running down to lake which lake
must have been lake Balaton yes of course lake Balaton
father was there mother still alive big white villa where
we lived cook came with us cooked in back room on open
stove and Daniel and I would go there before lunch big
redfaced cook flushed because of heat we asked her to give
us pancakes she made lovely pancakes with apricotjam*

*eating pancakes in courtyard and then sleeping after lunch
in big room I shared with Daniel lying naked on bed sleeping
till five and next door father read newspaper but fell
asleep and we found him asleep with newspaper covering
his face against flies*

*What else what else what was the name let me see the
name of that girl I was happy with her what was her name
I know yes I know that name oh yes Elsa something Slo-
vak name she had Elsa something real bitch she was but
young men fall for real bitches tall blonde chorus girl
Elsa — one night we walked by Danube she made me
jealous with whom I cant remember oh yes Radeczki the
journalist strong dark boy very good poet died in Galicia
last war she made me jealous but then told me she didnt
care for Radeczki and we sat on lower steps by river and
I kissed her it rained soft spring rain it fell on my face
while I kissed Elsa whatshername — her mouth like the
rain*

Very dark now

*What else quickly what else what else — first play first
play wrote it in Vienna oh yes I know near Rotenturm
Strasse in attic father sent money to study at university
wrote play instead father arrived one day angry scene
showed him play he didnt like it I had to return home but
gave play to old Balogh — the night he sent messenger
little messenger knocked at door mother let him in little
messenger brought little message from old Balogh he liked
my play next morning went to see him I wore new suit
new dovegrey suit — remember standing in front of mirror in our hall looking at mirror at new dovegrey suit my
hair was parted in middle wore monocle already had*

*walkingstick and gardenia in my buttonhole took cab to
go to Balogh big old Balogh kissed me took me to Café
Newyork to introduce me to critics — here he said here is
new genius of our stage oh no use counting*

No use counting

*Not many moments not many moments — some long
cold journey one day in Germany some long journey arriving and hot meal at Adlon and who was Viennese
singer so pink so silly so violent who came to my room
unexpectedly not many unexpected moments always knew
what would happen always knew could always calculate
often I prepared my little happinesses prepared them carefully like plot of play everything prepared best possible
scenery Swiss lakes South France Tyrol Tuscany best
scenery and best food and proper temperature of both
champagne and women carefully done carefully prepared
let me see let me see —*

No use counting

*No use counting past no use what else have I forgotten
what else to do quickly not much time getting dark please
quickly what else — paid my bill no didnt pay my bill who
the hell cares what about money well money in America
how much I cant say perhaps twohundredthousand it will
go to Daniel and Anna hope there will be no trouble
havent made will havent made will but Daniel next of
kin Daniel and Anna what will they say if they hear one
morning tomorrow morning newspaper will come headlines or will it not be headlines newspaper will say Stefan
Farkas killed — Daniel will read it Anna will read it who
will write obituary probably Rubin that rat always disliked me always quoted Ibsen Shaw ONeill to prove he*

*didnt like me he will write long column my name in
black frame there will be speeches maybe a street named
after me which street which street please sir which street
would I like — little street on Gellért Hill full of blossom
in May who lived there who lived there — once I walked
there very long ago with whom oh yes Maria little Maria
lovely dark eyes we sat on bench I read poems to her the
last time I wrote poems was when Maria walked with me
in that street*

What is this

*In that street — did I love Maria did I love Gizella and
others let me see could I have lived without them of
course I could but did I love anybody did I love Maria
No Gizella No others No Tony No — did I love Anna
Anna dustyfaced Anna we talked little she was Daniels
fiancée when she slept with me she must have loved me
better than Daniel she could not have done it unless she
loved me better yet she married Daniel — good for Daniel
they fit together I would have hurt her she was too frail
frail little heart she had she blushed often she wouldnt
have been happy with me I would have been rude to her
Daniel was never rude she married Daniel though she
knew he was going to be paralyzed she knew I was successful — always better dressed than Daniel always more
successful no newspaper wrote about him he lived in
stupid old flat translating oh well poor Daniel — oh no
one cant dismiss him all the time I try to dismiss him as
someone who doesnt matter he does he does he does —
wherever I went whatever I wrote I did it for him to show
him —*

It can be admitted no shame in it I did it for him I

*wanted Daniel to see to see I wanted him to see my name
in big white letters over Josefstaedter Theater and Opera
Comique and Shaftesbury Avenue — wanted Daniel to see
the reviews always sent him some reviews with cynical
note but I wanted him to know — thats how it is one
writes for one man only not for audience or money not for
strangers not for critics*

   For one only

   *I know he didnt like my stuff oh yes I know it doesnt
matter oh yes it does it made me angry why did I write
that silly religious drama who was talking about it the
other day oh yes the Abbot such awful fiasco it was — why
did I write it of course because of Daniel to show him I
could write such plays to show him to show him he wrote
short note saying how impressed he was I know he wasnt
he probably knew all the time all the time that what I
did was for him he knew but would not speak about it he
wanted me to say it he wanted me to admit Daniel my
dear Daniel this I wrote for you — I never did say so but
he expected it but I never told him and never will —
Daniel sitting in the armchair now Giacobbe sitting by
the gun — would they like one another they would they
would understand one another better than I did any of
them — what would Daniel have done tonight he would
have fought he couldnt have fought he is crippled he cant
run as I have tonight he couldnt have gone to see Leonardo and Abbot and couldnt have helped Tony — did I
help Tony no I didnt I should have the first night instead of playing about playing with words playacting making her miserable teasing her persuading her that it wasnt
worth while persuading her as I did Leonardo — poor*

Tony I should have been good to her right away she needed me perhaps I needed her and we could have gone to Geneva and been happy but I played about — Daniel would just have looked at her with those eyes and she would have felt he really meant to help her he wouldnt have played with words he couldnt have he cant speak he is crippled he cant speak only look

The little Brussels boy

What else what else please quickly very dark now Giacobbe quickly how warm it seems sunny day how warm never been so warm like hot bath quickly Giacobbe anything else to do — no bills need be paid no suitcases packed no tickets taken for train nothing any more no more haircuts and shaving and taking pills in the morning no more doctors and dentists and tailors and agents no more producers first nights I am free tonight free this week nothing to do no appointments no taxes and cheques no taxis and shoehorns and lifts and cufflinks no restaurants and lights nothing — I can leave discreetly French way ssht just sneak out quietly as did once when Daniel sat sucking mothers breast or is there anything else

Quickly Giacobbe oh yes oh certainly writingpad writingpad never wrote that play wanted it badly to show Daniel that I could write about myself if I wanted oh yes certainly I almost forgot writingpad mustnt forget as soon as this little darkness temporary darkness mere passing darkness goes as soon as sunny day stays sunny as soon as possible must go back must go back must finish to show Daniel what was play about what was it about quickly Giacobbe

What was it about